THE PERFECT DREAM

With a tired smile and a slow wink, Hannah bid the moon and the stars goodnight, departed the window seat and made her way to her bed. She doffed her slippers and her robe and slipped between the sheets.

As she blew out the lamp on her bedside table, she wondered how it would feel to slip between the sheets and into the arms of the gentleman she loved, and she thought she could imagine it. She made the attempt to do so, and as sleep overcame her, she floated into a dream where Ian Michael Denham, Marquis of Kearney and Mallory, lay beside her, his arms snugly around her as he whispered words of love into her ear. She kissed him passionately, thoroughly, soundly.

And then—and then—he took her breath away.

<u>BOOK YOUR PLACE ON OUR WEBSITE</u> <u>AND MAKE THE</u> <u>READING CONNECTION!</u>

We've created a customized website just for our very special readers, where you can get the inside scoop on everything that's going on with Zebra, Pinnacle and Kensington books.

When you come online, you'll have the exciting opportunity to:

- View covers of upcoming books
- Read sample chapters
- Learn about our future publishing schedule (listed by publication month *and author*)
- Find out when your favorite authors will be visiting a city near you
- Search for and order backlist books from our online catalog
- Check out author bios and background information
- Send e-mail to your favorite authors
- Meet the Kensington staff online
- Join us in weekly chats with authors, readers and other guests
- Get writing guidelines
- AND MUCH MORE!

**Visit our website at
http://www.kensingtonbooks.com**

JUST PERFECT

Judith A. Lansdowne

ZEBRA BOOKS
Kensington Publishing Corp.
http://www.kensingtonbooks.com

One

The Marquis of Kearney and Mallory turned in the saddle to scrutinize the harsh landscape behind him. His green eyes narrowed as he attempted to peer through the diminishing twilight, to distinguish some movement amongst the bracken and the heather. He could hear the damnable beasts well enough, but he could not see them at all. Ought to be able to see one of them at least, he thought. Ought to be able to catch a glimpse of fur, a glint of eyes, something. "Where the devil am I?" he muttered, abandoning his search and facing forward once again. "Martin never mentioned a moor along the way, but if this is not a moor I'm on, then I've lost my mind entirely."

He thought back over the directions Gazenby had sent him. A copy of them was stuffed safely away in his coat pocket, but he saw no sense in actually taking the directions out and attempting to read them. Not enough light remained for that and he didn't treasure the idea of pausing at this precise moment to climb down from Simon's back and light a bit of a fire, not with the dogs so close on his heels. No, his memory of the directions would have to suffice.

Although, trusting to my memory is what brought me to this unlikely place, he thought. What an arrogant fool

I am. Always so sure of myself. Always so damnably independent. I ought to have remained with the coach or followed in its wake as Lakerby and Jack begged me to do. But did I? No. I sent them on ahead, just so that I might dawdle about a bit and ride down any interesting path that presented itself. Jupiter! At the very least I ought to have studied Martin's directions more thoroughly before I departed the inn at East Hill Downs. But no. I must trust to my infallible memory. Infallible, ha! I have missed a turning somewhere—lost the main road somehow. But how and when the deuce did I do that?

The baying of the pack grew louder and more intimidating. They had not yet whipped themselves into a frenzy and probably would not until they were upon their prey, but the likelihood of that happening soon made Mallory gulp, because he was beyond anything certain that he and his horse *were* the prey.

It's decidedly bone-chilling, the sound of them advancing like that, Mallory thought, keeping a firm hand on the reins, holding the horse beneath him to a walk. Much more bone-chilling when you're ahead of the pack than when you're behind it. "By gawd, Simon!" he exclaimed. "Now I know how a fox feels. If we get out of this alive, I will never hunt again. I vow it."

Mallory's horse shivered and he gave the big gray's neck what he hoped would be a calming pat. "No, we'll not run yet, Simon," he murmured. "Likely you'd step in a hole, break a leg and send me flying over your head. Then those beasts would be upon us in the blink of an eye. Besides, old boy, it never does the foxes much good to run, does it? No. We have the upper hand yet, Simon. They are hungry, but leery of us. Right now, they are being sly, holding back, wondering why we don't skitter away from them and dash for our lives as the rest of the animals do. Not accustomed to bravery in the face of their approach, they are not. I dare say we shall be able to intimidate them into keeping a prudent distance for a while longer. Hopefully for long enough to find our way off this blasted moor and back to whatever civilization can be found hereabout."

The thought that his pursuers might be wolves occurred to Mallory abruptly. Did wolves prowl the Marches in this day and age? He thought not, but he was uncertain. Still, the idea of a wolf pack circling around him—speaking to each other, directing each other cautiously toward the kill—sent a shiver through him equal to the one that had set Simon's withers to quivering.

"Well, and that's utterly stupid," Mallory whispered to himself. "What difference does it make if Simon and I become a meal for a wolfpack or for a pack of wild dogs? Not a one. Eaten we'll be either way. But we'll not go down without a fight, Simon," he said more loudly, his hand going to the rapier at his side. "We'll give as good as we get. There will be a plethora of canine bodies at our feet before we leave this earth. I promise you that." At that very moment, as if at the sound of his voice, the baying ceased and a silence enveloped the moor—a silence that proved more unnerving to Mallory than all the cacophony that had gone before it.

"I cannot think what happened to him. He is generally the most punctual gentleman." Martin Gazenby gazed worriedly from his in-laws' drawing room window. The sun had set long ago. The last of the twilight threatened to depart, and still his cousin had not arrived at Tofar House.

"Punctual?" Anne, her arm supportively linked with Gazenby's, smiled up at him. "What has punctual to do with anything, Martin? He cannot be expected to arrive at a precise hour, you know. It is not as though Lord Mallory lives just up the lane. He is coming all the way from Yorkshire."

"Just so," Gazenby agreed. "But his traveling coach, his coachman, his valet, and his trunk all arrived well before dinner, Anne, so why not Mal? Something has happened to him. Somewhere between East Hill Downs and Tofar House my cousin has had an accident or something of the sort. I ought to be out there searching for him right this moment."

"I agree," offered Squire Tofar, rubbing nervously at the back of his neck. "And does your cousin not arrive in another quarter hour, Gazenby, you and the grooms and I will mount a search for the gentleman."

"You gave him the proper directions, did you not, Martin?" queried Mrs. Tofar, looking up from her embroidery hoop, a worried frown on her countenance.

"Of course he gave the man the proper directions, Emily," sighed the squire. "The gentleman's coach and coachman, his valet and trunk, all arrived without incident."

"And Mallory has a separate copy of my directions in his coat pocket," Gazenby added. "His valet assured me of it. If Mal did get lost, he merely had to take the copy out and look at it."

"What else might have detained him?" Anne asked. "Think, Martin. You know him well. If he cannot be lost and there has been no accident—"

"Well, he has been known to dawdle along from time to time," mused Gazenby. "Likes to gaze at the scenery, explore an odd path here and there. Still, four hours is a considerably long dawdle."

"Perhaps he came upon something of interest and lost track of the time, Martin," Anne offered. "You did tell me that your cousin sometimes loses himself in his thoughts and imaginings when he finds himself in a particularly interesting place."

"Did I? I did not intend to say that, precisely."

"What did you intend to say, precisely?" the squire queried.

"Well, Mal's difficult to explain, sir," Gazenby replied, turning his back on the drawing room windows to meet his father-in-law's gaze, Anne turning with him. "It is not that he loses himself in thought or imaginings—not exactly. What he does is—Mal—He *feels* things."

"Feels things?" Squire Tofar's eyes widened considerably.

"Gentlemen do feel things, Papa," Anne replied noting the considerable skepticism in her father's voice. "You men may all pretend that you possess no sentiments whatsoever, but we women know that you do. Though how Lord Mallory's possession of sentiments can have put him so far behind his coach is most perplexing. Do you mean to say, Martin, that perhaps your cousin saw something that had an exceptional effect upon his sensibilities—a particular glade or tree or plant, perhaps—that caused him to pause and sob over a long lost love?"

"No," Gazenby replied, with distaste. "Mal would never do such a thing as that. Even if he did have a long lost love, which he does not, he would shoot himself before allowing such a morbidity of emotion to overwhelm him."

"Oh."

"I did not mean that Mal feels things like—like—ordinary people feel things, Annie."

"Well, of course he does not," Mrs. Tofar said with a sniff. "Lord Mallory is a marquis, after all."

"It has nothing to do with his being a marquis," protested a harried Gazenby. "It has to do with his being his mother's son. It is something passed down to him from his ancestors. Mal feels things that other people cannot feel. Like—like—" Gazenby, at a loss for words, stuttered to a stop.

"Like ghosts?" queried Mrs. Tofar artlessly. One hand then fluttered to her lips as if to deny that the word "ghosts" had come from between them. "I do beg your pardon, Martin. I did not intend to say that," she apologized at once. "I cannot think why that particular word popped into my mind. Of course your cousin does not feel ghosts. What a nonsensical thing that would be for a marquis to do."

"He does *not* feel ghosts, does he, Martin?" Anne asked, giving her husband's arm a bit of a shake. "Martin?"

"No, of course not. No such thing as ghosts. You must not think Mal to be anything at all like your Mr. Harvey Langton from Barren Wycche who sees ghosts every time he turns around. Doesn't believe in ghosts, Mal does not."

"Well, thank goodness for that," Anne replied. "I cannot think it would sit well with Will to marry Hannah off to a gentleman who believes in ghosts."

"Won't sit well with Berinwick to marry his sister off to a gentleman who *feels* things either," the squire offered, crossing one knee over the other, resting his elbows on the arms of his chair and forming a steeple of his fingers. He gazed solemnly up over that steeple at his son-in-law. "Best think again about what you're proposing to do, Gazenby. Don't allow Anne and Emily to cajole you into taking part in this little matchmaking scheme of theirs, I say. Tell Mallory straight out to focus all of his attention on Snoop and none of it on Lady Hannah. Warn him as soon as he arrives. I don't know the gentleman, mind, but even so, I should not like to awaken one morning to find a marquis lying dead on my drawing room floor with my son-in-law all stiff-limbed and still beside him."

"Papa!"

"What?" asked Squire Tofar with an innocence that quite bewildered his daughter.

"You are being dreadful."

"Am I? How so, my dear?"

"You are implying that Will would kill both Martin and Lord Mallory should Lord Mallory take it into his head to court Hannah—and do it simply because Lord Mallory may prove to be a bit unusual."

"Oh. Well. I did not intend to imply that, Annie."

"Of course, you did not."

"No, I intended to state it as a fact. Berinwick will run Mallory through for being both odd and audacious enough to court Lady Hannah in spite of it, and then he'll make garters of Gazenby's guts for bringing Mallory to Lady Hannah's attention in the first place."

Mallory kept a tight grip on Simon's reins with his left hand as he clasped the hilt of his rapier in his right. The prolonged silence had served to set the marquis's teeth on edge and had caused him to bring the big gray to a halt and step down from the saddle. He had thought, at first, to free the horse and send it dashing for safety.

But such sudden movement as Simon galloping off into the brush might well bring the pack down on m'horse, he thought, now, in agitation. They'll be on Simon before he gets twenty yards. Likely forget about me in charging after him. Can't let that happen. No right to offer up Simon's life in defense of my own. I'm the fool who brought all this down our heads. I'm the simpleton who got us lost. Why should I be left standing, unassaulted, with an opportunity to escape? No, I'll not allow Simon to play decoy for me at the cost of the old fellow's life. Make what use I can of this blade in defense of us both, I will. And Simon will fight. He'll slash and bite and toss any number of dogs to their deaths does he see that I stand and fight beside him. He's not some despicable poltroon, not my Simon. He won't cringe and shiver and do nothing until the time comes for us both to lie down and die.

Mallory noticed that his hand shook a bit as he held the rapier and he scoffed at himself. "Dogs," he muttered. "Nothing but dogs. We aren't frightened of dogs, are we Simon? Certainly not." But then Mallory gulped and that ruined his speech completely in his own ears. It would be insane not to be afraid of a pack of wild dogs, he acknowledged to himself, especially when they fall abruptly silent as they have done now. No telling where they are or what's on their minds. Perhaps they have us surrounded and are merely biding their time, organizing themselves for the attack as wolves do. Or perhaps they are waiting for complete darkness.

Mallory was not fond of the dark. Not complete darkness. Not the sort of darkness that had swallowed him up when he was a lad in Yorkshire. But it will not grow as dark as all that, he told himself silently. Be a quarter moon at least and a sky filled with stars to lend some light.

"Why the devil don't the blasted hounds come?" he muttered as his palms began to sweat.

And then a dog bayed, and another, and another, and just to Mallory's right there was a great swishing sound and the skittering of hooves against rock. Mallory and Simon both recoiled, startled, as a hart sprang from the ragged cover of heather and bracken, leapt into and out of their sight in an instant and thundered off across the moorland, the ground trembling beneath it. Only then, in the last flickering of the twilight, did the pack show itself—long, lean bodies airborne in pursuit of the deer. Five, ten, fifteen of them leaping, soaring through the night like savage four-footed hawks unleashed.

"Jupiter! Saved by a hart!" Mallory sighed in relief. He returned his rapier to his side, stepped up into the saddle, gave the shivering Simon an encouraging pat and turned the horse back in the direction from which they had come—toward the North Star clearly visible in the crushed velvet of the night sky. "If we've missed a turn, we will go back and find it, Simon," he said. "I'm not for going any farther along this route, are you?"

The horse whinnied and stepped out at a trot, back across the portion of moorland it had already traversed, obviously relieved that the stench of the pack diminished with every step it took.

When, at last, Mallory felt they were safe, he brought his horse to a halt, stepped down, and with Simon's reins riding loosely over his shoulder, gathered together bits of heather and twigs and bracken. Fishing his flints from his waistcoat pocket, he set the brush alight. It was a small fire to be sure, but large enough for his purposes. He took Gazenby's directions from his coat pocket and squinted at them. "What the devil?" he mumbled as Simon, close behind him, lowered his head and began to munch nervously on the top of Mallory's tall hat. "We did exactly as we ought, Simon. But there's no mention of a moor to be crossed. Not one. There's something wrong with Martin's directions. Oh, great heavens," he murmured, sliding his hat farther back on his head, thus offering more of it to Simon's teeth. "You don't think my coach is lost on this blasted moor as well, do you? No, no, of course not. Jack would not take the coach across a moor without I was with him. Lakerby would have had palpitations of the heart at the mere suggestion. And they would have arrived here in full daylight and realized that it was moorland that stretched out before them. They'd not mistake it for anything else. Wait for me to catch them up, that's what they would have done. Then why didn't I catch them up? Is it possible that their copy of Martin's directions is different from mine? Is something miscopied on this paper? Something altered? Damnation, but I wish I had not sent Jack and Lakerby on without me!"

It occurred to Mallory that he might not be able to

find his way off the moor until morning, but he pushed that thought aside. The moon was bright and stars filled the sky and not a hint of mist hovered about. It was not nearly as dark or as threatening as the moor that surrounded Brambles. Undoubtedly he could make his way to safety tonight. Surely, did he merely retrace the path he had taken, he would discover a road, a turning, something he had overlooked that would set him aright and safe again on his way to Tofar House.

"And when I get there, I will wring Martin's neck," he said, rising, tugging his hat from Simon's clutches and scuffing dirt over the fire with his once-gleaming riding boots. "Set us out to be dinner for a pack of wild dogs, will he? He'll answer for it, Simon, I promise you. Though why he would make such a mistake—No, Martin would not. Whoever made this copy for me misread something Martin wrote and nothing more."

Mallory smiled as he climbed back into the saddle. "Nothing more," he chuckled, patting the horse's heavily muscled neck. "Nothing more than a moor. Tell Martin we don't require any more moor when we find him, that we will. You don't think playing with words is at all humorous, do you, Simon? But it is rather. We don't require any more moor anymore."

The big horse snorted.

"Then again, perhaps it's not all that humorous, Simon," Mallory replied, grinning. "Perhaps not."

"I did see a fire, Davey Lancaster," Lady Hannah declared stubbornly, gazing out across Little Mynd moor from the top of the tiny ridge above it. The road to Blackcastle skittered softly across this outcropping just before it dipped downward through the midst of Grydwynn Wood into the high valley below.

"Miasma," the groom replied.

"No, a fire, Davey."

"Naught but a bit of a flicker," the groom insisted. "We be very late, my lady. This be no time to go chasing after bits of effluvia setting itself alight on the moor. His grace will comb my hair with a milking stool do I not get you home soon."

"His grace will not do any such thing. And you know perfectly well that he will not, too. He will likely not so much as notice that the sun has gone down and the moon risen."

"Not notice? *Our* duke?"

"Well, he may notice, but he'll not hold you responsible. I'll see to that."

"Already he'll be up pacing the ramparts. Blackcastle will be ablaze with flambeaux—he and the castle awaiting your return with equal apprehension and anticipation," declared the groom.

"My, but you've grown poetic in your old age," Hannah observed with a smile. "Whoever would have guessed such words could spring from your lips, Davey Lancaster?"

"It comes from reading books," Lancaster replied, proudly. "The Reverend Mr. Dempsey has got all of us reading books now. And I ain't all that old, m'lady. I be merely five years older than I were five years ago. In the prime of m'life, I be."

"Indeed? And I am nothing more than a lass, eh?"

"Aye. A mere lass."

Hannah laughed. It was a low, comfortable laugh like fingers rippling over pianoforte keys in C major. "That's not at all how they see me in London," she said. "In London, a lady of twenty-three is never a mere lass."

"Bah! London!"

"Just so. Bah! London! I was never intended for London Society, nor they for me, I expect. Which has nothing at all to do with the fire I saw, Davey. Someone lit that fire. Someone is on Little Mynd moor and they ought not to be there—not now with the twilight gone. I heard the dogs baying earlier."

"They don't be baying now, my lady."

"A bit of good luck for whoever struck that fire. And I intend to offer whoever it is another bit of luck if they will have it." So saying, Lady Hannah removed her riding gloves, placed two fingers in her mouth and sent a shrill whistle out into the night. She repeated it a second time and a third. Then she waited quietly, attempting to see anything at all moving across the moor below her, but the most she could see were shadows among shadows. And then a whistle, equally as shrill as her own, rose up toward her. "I told you so, Davey!" she said. "That was a fire on the moor and someone lit it. Call down, do. Your voice will carry a good deal better than mine."

"Ahoy! Do ye be requiring assistance?" Lancaster shouted.

"Ahoy?" Hannah queried with a tilt of her head. "Wherever did you learn such a word as that?"

"It be what sailors say when they be hailing each other on the high seas. I read it in a book, I did."

"Oh. And you think some sailors have washed ashore on Little Mynd moor, do you?"

Lancaster grinned. "More likely some gentlemen come to bid on the squire's Snoop have got themselves lost, my lady. They be everywhere in Barren Wycche, the fancy London gentlemen. The-Three Legged Inn be overflowing with 'em."

The clock on the Tofars' drawing room mantel chimed the quarter hour.

"That does it," murmured the squire, rising just as Gazenby leaned down to place a soft kiss on Anne's cheek.

"Be careful, Martin," Anne whispered. "And look after Papa."

"Indeed, I will, m'dear." Gazenby turned on his heel and strolled from the drawing room a step behind his father-in-law. "You don't think Mallory has missed us and gone on toward Blackcastle, sir?" Gazenby queried as he caught up with the squire in the corridor and strode along beside him.

"Could have done," Tofar replied. "Though how he might come to be on Widowen Lane instead of on the high road, I cannot guess. Still, stranger things have happened, Gazenby. Norton!" the squire called as he caught a glimpse of his butler crossing toward the servants' staircase. "Norton, send out to the stables and have horses saddled for Gazenby, myself and four of the grooms. We're off to search for our missing guest."

"Indeed, sir," Norton replied. "At once, sir."

"We'll change into riding gear," Tofar murmured as they reached the main staircase and he began to climb toward the second floor. "Not fit for mucking about, these togs are not."

"True," Gazenby agreed. "But we must hurry, sir. I cannot help but think Mal's in some peril. I have been feeling most uneasy about him for the past hour and more."

"Don't tell me that you *feel* things too, Gazenby."

"Yes. I do, a bit."

"I said *don't* tell me. Don't understand it. Sounds odd as an egg in a clothespress. If I didn't know you as well as I do, I should say it takes a namby-pamby sort of a fellow to go about *feeling* things—a male milliner, perhaps, or a dancing master. Mind my words, Gazenby. Whatever you do once we find this cousin of yours, do not mention that he feels things to Berinwick. No, and warn Mallory not to do it either. If your cousin is as fine a fellow as you say, and brave to boot, then I rather think Lady Hannah ought to have her chance at him. But she will not, you know, should Berinwick take it into his head that the man is some kind of a fribble."

* * *

"Look up," Lancaster called. "We be up here on this outcrop what people think to be a ridge."

Mallory, who had barely been able to believe his ears when the whistles had shrilled through the night and then Lancaster's voice had rumbled out above him like the voice of God, did as he was told and stood for a moment, amazed that he had not noticed until now the formation of sandstone that pouted out above him. Very near the edge of it, a small torch winked into being.

Whoever it is, it's not Gazenby or one of his in-laws, Mallory thought, staring upward. They would have set out realizing that light would be needed. They would have carried lanterns with them.

"Who are you?" Mallory shouted. "And how the devil did I get here? I don't recall descending any hills."

"Little Mynd moor does not be down," Lancaster replied loudly. "Atop a plateau it be. And this road we be on runs along the edge of it here afore it descends again. Did ye come from East Hill Downs?"

"Indeed."

"That'll be it then," Lancaster replied. "Took the wrong road at the fork. Ye can see our light, eh?"

"Yes."

"Then look to your left and when you see it again, ride toward it."

With that, Lancaster and Lady Hannah, quickly fashioned torch in hand, rode off and left Mallory alone once again. He did as he had been told and gazed to his left. He saw nothing but shadows—some darker than others, some moving, some not. Simon shifted uneasily beneath him. A wind rose and whispered through the bracken behind them and through what sounded like conifers ahead. And then the flicker of light appeared once more. It was to his left, just as the voice had said it would be, and closer. Mallory steered his mount toward it. Far off across the moor, the dogs began to bay again. The sound sent a cold chill racing up Mallory's spine.

"You've come far enough," Lancaster called to the man. "Stop right there and look to your left again. We be traipsing through Grydwynn Wood, we be, and our path will take us from your sight for a bit."

In a matter of minutes the light reappeared and Mallory rode toward it once more. This time the torch advanced steadily in his direction. "Lady Hannah," ordered the groom, whose voice had now become sheer music to Mallory's ears, "wait where ye be now. Don't be going no farther onto the moor. Let the fellow ride to you."

The torch ceased to advance and held steady.

Lady Hannah? Mallory mused. It's a lady holding that torch? Well, God bless her. And then he could see a figure on horseback and a second coming to a halt just beside the first.

"You are not injured?" asked a soft, low voice as Mallory drew near. "Say if you are and Davey and I will come to you and bring you the rest of the way into the wood."

"No, we're fine," Mallory replied. "Simon and I both, though we were nigh to being eaten by a pack of wild dogs not long ago."

"Aye, the hounds of Little Mynd moor. Savage, they be," replied the voice that had led him to safety.

"And sad," added the lady. "My brother wishes to drain the moor and set his plows to it, but he'll not have the dogs shot—not if they can be tamed and saved. We have been attempting to lure the pack to the edge of the moor for a year now, but they will come only so far and no farther. And since Will will neither kill the hounds nor place his workmen in danger, we go on as we have always done. If only one or two of them would place their trust in us, the entire pack might be saved, you know."

"I will place *my* trust in you," Mallory replied as he drew

Simon to a halt before her and gazed into eyes as dark as the night sky and sprinkled with brilliant stars all their own—stars that struck a golden light. "I intend to place my trust in you for the rest of my life, Lady Hannah. It was Lady Hannah he called you?"

"Aye, and trust her in everything you ought," Davey Lancaster noted. "Who be ye?"

"Mallory, I'm called. I am bound for an establishment called Tofar House near the village of Barren Wycche."

"Oh! You will be Mr. Gazenby's cousin!" Hannah exclaimed. "You've come to have a look at Snoop and the other horses and perhaps bid on some of them."

"You know Martin Gazenby, Lady Hannah?"

"I certainly do. Come with us, Lord Mallory. Davey and I will be pleased to escort you safely to Tofar House."

"He be a lordship?" Lancaster queried in a semi-whisper.

"He is a marquis," Hannah replied quietly. "Davey Lancaster, you know very well that Mr. Gazenby and Anne have come to visit with the squire and Mrs. Tofar. And you know that Mr. Gazenby's cousin has been invited to put up at the squire's as well during the auction. Everyone in Barren Wycche knows of it."

"Just so. I be remembering now," Lancaster admitted with a nod. "Well, I expect his grace will not rain blows down upon my head for being late if we tell him we took time to rescue Mr. Gazenby's marquis."

"His grace has never rained blows down upon your head in his life," Hannah protested with a chuckle as she turned her horse back toward the path through Grydwynn Wood.

"Your father is a duke?" Mallory asked, ticking off in his mind the dukes he knew who had daughters of a certain age.

"My brother," Hannah said, her chin lifting proudly, "is Berinwick."

"Oh," Mallory replied.

She waited for him to say more, for even if the man had never met her brother, she knew from Anne and Martin that rumors of Will's often audacious behavior had reached as far as the wilds of Yorkshire years ago.

He said nothing further on the subject, however. He merely smiled a smile that was most disconcerting and bowed to her from his saddle. "It is a distinct pleasure to make your acquaintance, Lady Hannah. I thought I was a goner, you know. Thought I should end up nothing but a scrap of skin and a bit of gnawed bone before this night ended."

The little group of searchers from Tofar House were just straggling back, lanterns winking against the night, when Mallory and his rescuers reached the squire's drive. "See there, they have been searching for you," Hannah pointed out as the single lanterns merged into one large light beyond the house at the first of the squire's stables. "Hail them, Davey," she ordered. "No, no, let me," she rescinded the order at once. "Ahoy!" she called. "Martin Gazenby, are you there?"

"Lady Hannah?" came an answering call.

"Indeed, it is I. I have a gentleman here who belongs to you, I think."

"Thank gawd," Gazenby murmured to no one in particular. "Mal did miss the house and go on to Blackcastle." Together Gazenby and the squire remounted and urged their animals across the green and into the drive. Within two twitches of a cat's tail they reached Lady Hannah, Mallory, and Lancaster. "Mal! Where the deuce have you been?" Gazenby exclaimed. "What the devil happened to you? We went as far as the second fork to East Hill Downs to see if you were lying dead somewhere beside the road and could find neither hide nor hair of you."

"Merely because I was nowhere near the proper road," Mallory replied. "I was on the moor being hunted by a pack of savage dogs. Sad, savage dogs, I think Lady Hannah said."

"On the moor?" Gazenby stared at his cousin aghast. "On Little Mynd moor? And at this hour? How could you possibly have ridden onto the moor? What did you do?"

"I followed your directions, Martin. That's what I did."

"Never. I never sent you anywhere near the moor. I made certain to point out—to make it excessively clear, Mal—that you must avoid taking any turnoff to the west once you departed East Hill Downs."

"Did you? How very odd," Mallory replied. "The directions I read stated explicitly that I was to bear right at the first fork in the road—which was west, since I was coming from the north, you know."

With no greater illumination than a single lantern, the moon and the starlight, Mallory could see Gazenby's face grow pale at his words.

"And the dogs were h-hunting?" Gazenby stuttered. "You—you might well be dead now."

"Yes, but I'm not, Martin. Thanks to Lady Hannah and Mr. Lancaster, here, I am not only safe, but safely at the establishment at which I intended to arrive in the first place. I give you my thanks once again, your ladyship, Lancaster. You have been more than kind."

"Welcome, ye be," Lancaster replied. "And very late we be," he added with a significant glance at Hannah.

"Just so, Davey," Hannah agreed. "We really must be going, Martin, Squire. My brother expected us home hours ago. It has been a pleasure to make your acquaintance, Lord Mallory. Do give my best to Anne, will you not, Martin?"

"Indeed, I will," Gazenby replied. "And I thank you, Lady Hannah. I truly do."

"You need not." Hannah smiled as she turned her

horse's head in the direction of home. "We would have helped him off the moor even if he had not proved to belong to you, Mr. Gazenby," she called over her shoulder. And with that, she galloped back down the drive, her groom beside her and three admiring gentlemen staring at her back.

"Most amazing young woman," Tofar murmured, turning his horse toward the stables.

"Is she?" Mallory asked.

"Indeed," Tofar replied. "Wasted on all those fops and fribbles in London. Right not to take her back again this year, Berinwick is. She'd have rescued you with or without Davey Lancaster beside her. Aye. And she'd have rescued you had the pack been upon you as surely as she did when it was not."

"Your father-in-law is fond of his neighbor, eh, Martin?" Mallory observed.

"And so am I," Gazenby replied. "And so is all of Blackcastle and Barren Wycche. Well, you'll discover that. But I did never tell you to bear right after East Hill Downs, Mal. I swear I did not. Your coach arrived without incident. They never once swerved off course and they were following the same directions I mailed to you, were they not?"

The Duke of Berinwick was not pacing the ramparts as Lancaster had predicted. He was, however, pacing back and forth before the steps at the head of the turnaround and muttering under his breath. And though all of Blackcastle was not ablaze with flambeaux, the drive was alight with them all the way from the gatehouse to the great double doors of the front entrance.

"Where the devil have you been?" Berinwick exclaimed as his sister and her groom rode up and drew their horses to a halt before him. "Lancaster, you were to have Lady Hannah safely home before nightfall. Need I point out to you that night fell an hour ago? And do not tell me that one of the horses picked up a stone or some-such, because I am not in the mood to hear any faery tales at the moment."

"No, no trouble with the horses, your grace," Lancaster replied at once, stepping down from the saddle.

"What's the excuse then?" Berinwick asked, swinging Hannah to the ground and placing a protective arm around her.

"The excuse is that Mama and Richard and I talked for so long after dinner that it was well into twilight before Davey and I could depart," Hannah said. "It was none of it Lancaster's fault, Will, I assure you. What could Davey do? Come stomping into the rectory parlor and interrupt our conversation? Of course he could not. And then on the way home we were forced to cease our forward progress in order to rescue a gentleman who was lost on the moor."

"Lost on the moor? What the deuce were you and Lancaster doing on the moor?"

"*We* were not on the moor, Will. The gentleman was. *We* were on the road, just at the ridge, when I saw the man's light. Well, it was not a light, precisely. He had set fire to some brush—to reread the directions his cousin had given him, he said—to see where he had gone wrong, you know."

"Cousin? Do you mean to say it was Gazenby's cousin?"

"Just so."

"And the dogs did not eat him?"

"Certainly not. Nor would they have dared to eat me with Davey Lancaster beside me. You know that's true."

"Well, then I'll not have you drawn and quartered tonight, Lancaster," Berinwick said. "See to the horses, eh? I'll look after this particular filly myself."

"I wish you will not refer to me as a filly, William,"

Hannah protested as they climbed the front steps of Blackcastle together. "I do not find it complimentary in the least to be compared to a horse."

"What ought I to say then?"

"Can you not just refer to me as your sister?"

"Yes, but that's proved to be disastrous in the past."

"How so?"

"Your first Season in London I referred to you as my sister as often as possible and that turned more men to puddings than I care to count. Frightful thing to see. Stripped their spines clean away, one after the other, and left nothing but a mass of quivering jelly upon which to gaze."

Hannah giggled.

"You would find it amusing, but it was not. Not for me. I truly wished to see you as happy as all the other young ladies in London, Hannah. And I promised Mother that I would do everything I could to find you a proper husband, too. But I could not find you one. And lord knows, I could not marry you off to a mass of trembling intestines."

"You did, however, find the perfect husband for Anne."

"Yes, but only by assuring Gazenby that Anne was neither my sister nor my ward. I cannot tell you how many times in Gazenby's presence I mentioned that Miss Anne Tofar was merely a neighbor of ours. Speaking of Gazenby, how could he possibly have given his cousin the wrong directions to Tofar House? How many times has he come down from Yorkshire himself? He could not possibly mistake the way. Unless he directed his cousin out onto Little Mynd moor on purpose, Hannah," Berinwick added as he escorted his sister through the great double doors and up the main staircase. "He is not next in line for the title, is he? Gazenby?"

"Will!"

"Yes, cruel of me to suggest it. He is not next in line?"

"Martin is not in the line at all. They are cousins on the distaff side. Their mothers are sisters."

"And the cousin, do you think he resembles Gazenby? I have seen Mallory in London, but I do not recall any resemblance to Annie's Martin."

"What possible difference would it make if Lord Mallory and Mr. Gazenby did resemble one another?" Hannah asked.

"Only that Gazenby might be able to pass himself off as Mallory should the fellow disappear down a dog's gullet—if they looked enough alike."

"William Thorne! Of all things! How is it that such devious thoughts always seem to worm their way into your brain?"

"I cannot say. I'm blessed, I expect. You do not think they resemble one another, eh, Hannah?"

"Of course not. Lord Mallory is a good deal taller than Martin, for one thing."

"Gazenby might wear higher heels on his boots."

Hannah giggled. "Lord Mallory has dark brown curls while Martin's hair is as bright and golden as the sun."

"Yes, but there are ways to color one's hair, Hannah."

"You are utterly impossible, Will! Oh, I know! Lord Mallory has the most cunning nose, and Martin's is short and to the point. Martin would have no hope of remaking his nose to resemble Lord Mallory's."

"There is putty of some sort. Actors use it all the time. A cunning nose? What's a cunning nose?" Berinwick queried, a grin teasing at his lips as they reached the first floor landing and he paused to stare down at her.

"Why a nose that appears to be straight, narrow, and quite aristocratic when one looks at it straight on, but sidles a bit to the left and then back to the right again in profile."

"Broke it."

"Indeed, though you cannot tell at first glance."

"Lucky he still has any nose at all, wandering around on Little Mynd moor once the sun has set. Did you like him, Hannah?"

"Lord Mallory? I expect so. He seemed nice enough. And courageous as well. I confessed to him that you were my brother and he did not turn pale and begin to quake at the very mention of your name."

"Ha!"

"May I keep you company for a bit, Will? Must I change out of my riding clothes if I do?"

"Not as far as I'm concerned, m'dear. I am not opposed to the smell of horse in the parlor. Should you like to play a game or two of macao?"

"I should love to, but I cannot afford to lose any of my pin money. I am saving up for the most delicious bonnet for Mama."

"We'll play for wishes then."

"Done," Hannah agreed, turning to walk beside him down the long corridor. "It was a jest, was it not, Will, about Martin Gazenby sending his cousin out onto the moor on purpose."

"Yes. A jest. Can't see any reason for him to do so if he's not in the line, can you?"

"No. Besides, Martin is a good and gentle man. He would never do such a thing even if he were the very next in line."

"Just so. A good and gentle man. I hadn't thought of Gazenby. Perhaps I ought to ask *his* advice on the matter."

"On what matter, Will?"

"Just a bit of a problem that has come up of late. I thought to ask Dempsey, because he is a good man, if not particularly gentle, but I don't want Mother to learn of it. Not until I decide what's to be done. And you know Dempsey. Unless I force him to give me his word on it, Mother will know everything before the cat can swish its tail."

Two

"Some of the finest horses in all of England reside on this little farm," Tofar said with a proud smile. "You'll see in the morning, my lord, what a fine lot they are. And then, of course, there's Snoop."

"Yes, Snoop," Gazenby agreed enthusiastically while poking his semi-sleeping cousin subtly in the ribs with an elbow as he sat down on the sofa beside that weary gentleman. "Drink your tea, before it goes sloshing over the side," Gazenby hissed. "You'll be pleased you came, Mal," he added in a voice loud enough for the others to hear. "Do you leave Tofar stables with Snoop in tow, Cousin, you will be the happiest man in the world, will you not?"

"I shall be quite pleased, Martin. That's true. Though I rather think, of late, that you are the happiest gentleman in all the world, now that you have your Anne beside you forever."

"What a lovely thing for you to say, my lord," Anne said, her cheeks turning a most attractive pink.

"Merely an observation of fact," Mallory replied, urging himself to keep his eyes open and drink his tea. "But I must admit that I *will* be exceedingly happy should I be the one to acquire Squire Tofar's Snoop. I have always wished to have a descendant of The Byerly Turk in my stables. He's a fine horse, Martin says. Excellent composition, fleet of foot, friendly."

"Friendly?" Squire Tofar's left eyebrow rose significantly. "Gazenby told you that Snoop is friendly, my lord?"

"Indeed. He is, is he not?"

"Mal has little patience with highly-strung horses," Gazenby said hurriedly with a meaningful glance at Tofar.

"No patience whatsoever," Mallory agreed. "I expect I'm a bit eccentric in that. I care not what a horse's bloodlines may be if he is exceedingly temperamental, Tofar. I have actually had two opportunities before this to bid on beasts descended from the Turk, but I decided against them. Bite you as soon as look at you, each of them. Attempt to kick the stuffing out of a fellow for the least little thing. I've no use for a horse like that, no matter its bloodlines."

"Well, but Snoop is a bit temperamental," Tofar said with a thoroughly amazed gaze fastened on Gazenby. "He is not always the friendliest of animals. As a matter of fact, Lord Mallory—"

"As a matter of fact," Gazenby interrupted, "my father-in-law cannot believe, with all the gentlemen who have been milling about, studying him, that Snoop hasn't eaten at least one of them. Must make a yearling nervous to have throngs of gentlemen watching him day after day, don't you think, Mal?"

"Just so. Are you rescinding your statement, Martin, about his being friendly?" Mallory queried.

"Not at all. Merely saying that he may shy away from some of the gentlemen, or appear a bit recalcitrant because of all the attention he has been attracting of late. But he'll not shy away from you, Mal," Gazenby added with great confidence. "I am certain of it."

"Are you?" Mallory queried, his green eyes weary, his eyelids beginning to droop.

"Yes. Come straight to you and take an apple from your hand, he will. No doubt in my mind. He cannot help but realize how much you long to have him and how you'll treat him like a king. He will smell it on you, I should think."

Mallory smiled and attempted to stifle a yawn. "We'll see," he managed. "Tomorrow, eh?"

"It is half past eleven and you are exhausted, Lord Mallory," Anne observed from the chair she had taken beside her mother once tea had been poured. "You ought to finish your tea and your tart and take yourself off to bed, I think."

"Anne! Telling a marquis when to go up to bed! Of all things!" Mrs. Tofar exclaimed.

"Mama, his lordship is going to fall asleep right there on the sofa if he continues to attempt to be polite," Anne responded. "You have been polite enough, Lord Mallory," she added with an impish grin. "My mama and papa will not be offended do you seek your bedchamber, nor will Martin and I. You have had a most unnerving experience and likely have exhausted all of your energy in the surviving of it. And besides, Papa is generally in bed and asleep by ten o'clock."

"I am a bit weary," Mallory confessed.

"Of course you are," Gazenby agreed.

"But not so weary that I have not noticed what has been going forward in this room."

"What?" Gazenby asked. "I cannot think what you mean."

"Everyone but you, Martin, is entirely too formal—even Anne. We are cousins, now, my dear Anne," Mallory said with a soft smile. "We have been cousins officially for two entire years. You must call me Mal as Martin does. And you, Mrs. Tofar, may call me Mal as well, if you wish to do so. This marriage between my cousin and your daughter has made us members of the same family, after all. And I will not be `my lorded' by you either, Tofar. Just plain Mallory will do, I assure you."

Such condescension was not lost on Mrs. Tofar. Her

hand flew to her cheek and her lips parted with a little sigh. "How kind of you," she murmured.

"No, no, not kind. It is merely that we are family now and formality among family members does not sit right with me. I believe that I *will* go up to my chamber, if you don't mind, Mrs. Tofar," he added, finishing his cherry tart in one bite and setting his tea aside.

"Emily. You must call me Emily," Mrs. Tofar gasped on a small breath, her cheeks flushing with pleasure at the thought of her Christian name on the lips of a marquis.

"I thank you for the honor, Emily," Mallory replied. "We will speak further about your Snoop in the morning, eh, Tofar? I am looking forward to making his acquaintance."

"Will your cousin truly refuse to bid on Snoop if he discovers him to be difficult, Martin?" Anne asked, as Gazenby snuggled down beside her in the bed and placed his arm cozily around her. "Because Snoop *is* difficult. You know that he is. I cannot believe that you told Mal that Snoop is friendly. Tomorrow he will walk down to the stable, where, if he is very lucky, Snoop will merely ignore him and not take his hand off at the wrist. And then, Mal will stand and watch the animal nip at the grooms and chase the stableboys about, attempting to trample them into dust. He will know very well that you lied to him, Martin. And he will say 'Thank you very much, but no thank you,' return to the house, tell his man to pack up his trunk, and take himself back to Yorkshire. And Hannah will not have one opportunity with him, Martin. Not one."

"Never happen," Gazenby replied.

"But, Martin, he will have no reason to remain until the auction because he will not wish to bid on Snoop at all. And he will be angry with you for lying to him, so he won't wish to remain on your account, either. In order to keep him here, we will be forced to tell him that it was all a devious plan to lure him to Shropshire so he would come to know Hannah. And you know what will happen if we tell him that. He will be off to Yorkshire faster than a fox with a pack of hounds on his heels."

"Do you know," Gazenby replied, propping himself up on one elbow and gazing down at her with the most bemused expression, "that you are the greatest worrier in the history of all civilization?"

"I am not, Martin. It is merely sensible to conclude that your cousin will depart on the instant."

"Only if you don't know the secret," Gazenby informed her, kissing her eyebrows and then her nose.

"Martin, do stop! What secret?" Anne demanded pushing herself up to a sitting position so that the two of them were nose to nose. "Why are you grinning at me, so? What have you done?"

"I put Liddy in Mal's bedchamber."

"You *what?*" A smile teased the corners of Anne's mouth upward and betrayed the dimples in her cheeks to Gazenby's delighted eyes. "Oh, Martin, how devious of you!"

"Yes, I know."

"Will it work?"

"I can't think why not. Snoop is excessively fond of that cat, Annie. He wants her with him day and night. Wherever Liddy goes—if he can manage to do so— Snoop will follow. They are the very best of friends. So I thought, did Liddy sleep with Mal, he would smell of her, you know, and does her scent remain on him, Snoop will be utterly bemused. He'll prove the friendliest horse Mal has ever met. At least, I think he will."

"And then Mal will truly wish to bid on him," Anne finished excitedly. "Oh, Martin, you're a perfect genius. And Snoop is a fine horse. Once he and Mal come to know each other properly, I am certain they will get on together. Snoop is skittish, merely, and—"

"—he bites and kicks and slashes at people with his hooves," Gazenby finished for her. "I wouldn't have him if someone gave him to me as a gift. But Mal has wanted a colt from the Turk's bloodline forever and I think that if he and Snoop meet with Mal smelling of Liddy, it will give Mal the opportunity to win the animal over. He has a gift with horses, Mal does. I would not think to trick him into this, else. But once he begins to speak with Snoop and stroke the beast's nose and such, I've little doubt that a rapport will arise between them. Of course, he must outbid everyone else in the end or he will not have the animal, but at least establishing a rapport with Snoop will give Mal reason to remain here until the auction. And the longer Mal remains, the more opportunities he will have to spend time with Hannah. And the more time he spends with Hannah, the more he must come to love her."

"You are very certain of that," Anne observed, giving one of Gazenby's curls a tug. "That Mal *must* come to love Hannah."

"Yes. Aren't you?"

"I hope it will prove to be the case, Martin. I cannot think of anyone else truly suited to be Hannah's husband. Of all the gentlemen we met in London, there was not one among them worthy of her."

"And there's not a woman I have met worthy of Mal, either, so they must be intended for each other. He is the best of men, Mal. He saved my life once when we were lads. Did I ever tell you that? And he saw to it that the estate at Centrewell came to me as it ought, despite my elder brother's protest that it was part of the entail and not mother's to give to me at all. And you and I, Annie, would never have met had Mallory not taken it into his head to send me off to London for a Season. Gave me the loan of his townhouse and his horses and carriages, he did. Wrote letters of introduction for me to any number of people.

Why, I might not have been invited anywhere, a country bumpkin and a commoner to boot, had Mal not made the effort to see that I was. I owe him a chance at Snoop and Lady Hannah and more. I owe him everything."

"Apparently, you do," Anne observed with a giggle.

"Indeed. And he did never once say that I ought to look higher for a wife, Annie, when I first took you to Brambles to make his acquaintance. Did I tell you that? He said that you were lovely and that I was the luckiest man alive that you had consented to marry me."

"Did he? How very sweet of him. It is not every marquis who would welcome the daughter of a squire into his family without the least complaint. We do owe him a great deal," Anne agreed.

"And just to be certain that Snoop does welcome him properly, I will tell you what else I plan to do, Annie. I do not intend to leave Mal's forced association with Liddy to chance. I plan to sneak into Mal's room this very night and rub Liddy all over his clothes so that no matter which coat and shirt and breeches he chooses to wear tomorrow, her scent will be on them."

"And her fur," Anne pointed out.

"Lakerby will remove the fur. He's a deucedly good valet, Lakerby. He will take note of it when he sets out Mal's things in the morning and remove every bit of it. And Mal will stroll down to the stables carrying the scent of Snoop's chosen stablemate without realizing a thing."

"Lakerby, there's a cat on my bed," Mallory observed with a tired sigh.

"Yes, my lord."

"Get it off, will you? I'm exhausted and I should very much like to lie down and go to sleep without a cat for a sleeping partner."

"I cannot get the creature off the bed, my lord."

"Well, that's absurd. What do you mean, you cannot? It's a cat. Merely shoo the thing off onto the floor."

"I have attempted to shoo it off the bed time and time again, my lord. It will not move. It glares at me and growls."

Mallory grinned in spite of himself. "It growls, Lakerby?"

"Indeed. And it glares at me in the most barbaric manner."

"Good lord, what a night," Mallory sighed. "First savage dogs, now a barbaric cat. What is this place that it proves to be wilder even than Yorkshire? Martin ought to have warned me of it, I think, such a place as this. Cat, scat!" Mallory demanded, approaching his bed, his nightshirt billowing out around him. "Off my bed, out of my chamber, right this minute, sir!"

"It's not a sir, m'lord," offered the valet quietly. "It's a lady cat."

"A lady cat? How do you know?"

"Mr. Norton said as much. An elderly lady cat, he said. A very elderly lady cat. The Tofars' butler, Mr. Norton is. He knows her well, he does. Mr. Norton came while you were sipping tea in the drawing room with the family, my lord, and attempted to remove the animal."

"And he did not succeed."

"No, my lord. It bit him."

"Oh, for Jupiter's sake! Give me my coat, Lakerby. You are going to be forced to clean it, regardless, after my ride on the moor. Give it here and I'll throw it over the cat, scoop the baggage up, and toss the entire package out into the corridor."

Lakerby, his brown eyes filled with reluctance, took Mallory's coat from the chair near the door and delivered it into his master's hands. Then the valet took five giant steps backward, crossed his arms across his chest, shook his head, and set about nibbling at his lower lip.

Mallory approached the bed, threw the coat over the cat, reached down and scooped the entire bundle up into his arms. "Dang!" he shouted as one of the four paws inside the coat came free and claws raked across his hand. As he attempted to reentangle that paw in the cloth, another paw came free. "Open the door, Lakerby," Mallory ordered. "Hurry, man."

Like a mad juggler, alternately cursing and readjusting the constantly erupting bundle, Mallory made his way out into the corridor, pitched the squirming coat three feet beyond his bedchamber door and spun quickly back inside. On the instant, Lakerby closed the door.

"There. Now what was difficult about that?" Mallory queried, taking another step into the room and nearly falling on his nose as the tail of his voluminous night shirt, caught between door and jamb, brought him to an abrupt and unexpected halt.

"Oh, dear! Oh, dear!" Lakerby exclaimed in a soft, worried voice, reaching quickly for the door knob.

"Do not open it far, Lakerby," Mallory warned, attempting to avoid expressing his exasperation in word or tone. "Simply open it wide enough to set me free. Don't want the beast to sneak back in, do we?"

"No, my lord. Never, my lord. Wretched animal!"

Beyond the door, the cat scrambled out of Mallory's coat, set its hindquarters firmly upon the corridor carpeting and yowled in outrage.

"I daresay Mallory has discovered Liddy and tossed her out," Gazenby observed, drawing Anne back down beside him and kissing her cheek. "I hope she doesn't run far."

"I will step out into the corridor and fetch her, shall I?" Anne queried. "That way you will not need to go searching about for her once Cousin Mal has fallen asleep. She will come with me without the least complaint, you know. How you ever managed to carry her in from the stables without her making a great hubbub, Martin, I cannot guess."

"I stuffed her in a sack, is what I did," Gazenby confessed. "Scratched me for it, too. See?"

"Oh, my poor Martin," Anne teased. "Let me kiss it and make it better."

"You certainly may," Gazenby grinned, offering her his hand. "And you may kiss various other parts of me, too, if you wish, because she was a regular demon to get out of that sack, let me tell you. I've scratches everywhere. What?" he asked as Anne paused in the midst of tenderly healing his cat wounds.

"I was just thinking what a particularly appropriate learning experience Liddy will prove to be for Lord Mallory."

"A learning experience?"

"Yes, Martin. Only think how much that cat is like Will."

"Berinwick? You're comparing Berinwick to that danged cat?"

"She is not a danged cat. She is a perfectly lovely cat who suffered most undeservedly in her youth and has grown a bit recalcitrant because of it."

"I see," Gazenby laughed. "Just like the duke."

"Precisely."

"I doubt Berinwick would like to hear himself compared to a cat," Gazenby observed.

"He would not care in the least, not if the cat is Liddy. He saved her and her kittens from the fire right along with me and he has allowed himself to grow fond of her because of it. He brings her presents when he comes to visit Papa. Did you know?"

"Berinwick brings a cat presents?"

"Simple things, merely. A bit of cooked pheasant. Toys made of pheasant feathers. Once he brought her a tiny ball and taught her to fetch it."

"Berinwick? The Berinwick I know?"

"No, not the Berinwick you know, Martin. The Berinwick *I* know and the Berinwick I have loved since I was a child. You do not really know him at all, dear one."

"You loved him?"

"Yes. I always did. I was determined to marry him, too, when I grew up."

Gazenby pushed himself upright in the bed and stared down into Anne's laughing eyes. "You were determined to marry the Duke of Berinwick? Then what, may I inquire, am I doing here beside you, madam?"

"I cannot imagine," smiled Anne, reaching up to tug at his blond curls which peeked temptingly out from beneath his night cap. "Perhaps you bewitched me with your handsome face and your overwhelming charm."

"My handsome face?"

"Yes, Mr. Gazenby."

"My overwhelming charm?"

"Indeed, Mr. Gazenby."

"Dear heavens, you've run mad, m'dear."

"Have I? No, I think not," Anne replied softly, ceasing to fiddle with his curls and placing her hands on his cheeks instead, drawing him down until their lips met. "Liddy can wait," she whispered as their lips parted. "Bewitch me all over again, Martin Gazenby. Do. Take me away with you to that splendid place that only you can share with me. I should like to soar up into the clouds and taste the lightning. Oh, yes. I should like that of all things, my love."

"You are not pretending that I am Berinwick, are you?" Gazenby queried, smoothing his fingers along her cheek.

"No, my dear one. I am pretending nothing. I am delighting in the reality that you, Mr. Martin Gazenby, in spite of your noble lineage, had the temerity to choose me, a mere squire's daughter, to be your wife."

"Well, in that case, m'dear," Gazenby said huskily, removing his night cap and tossing it across the chamber. "Collecting Liddy from the corridor can wait for hours and hours as far as I'm concerned."

Mallory watched his valet safely from the room. Apparently the cat, having abandoned its yowling, had also abandoned its claim on Mallory's bedchamber. It did not attempt to sneak back in as Lakerby exited. In fact, it was nowhere to be seen. With a sigh of relief, Mallory bid Lakerby good night, closed the door, and took himself to bed. It was a wonderfully comfortable bed.

Most likely why the dratted cat wanted it, Mal thought, a smile spreading across his face as he pulled the counterpane up over his weary body. Who would have thought a mere squire would own such a comfortable bed as this?

"Must cease thinking of Tofar as a mere squire," Mallory mumbled, enjoying the cool linen of the pillowcase as it touched his cheek. "The gentleman is Martin's father-in-law. Cannot go about with my nose in the air lording it over them. Part of the family now, the Tofars are. I have said as much to them."

Always been fond of Martin, Mallory thought as he closed his eyes. Still am. Like him more than I like my own brothers and sisters. It is not his fault he married beneath him. My fault, that. It was I sent him to London with no one of any experience to keep him from making foolish mistakes. Jupiter, send a man to London one time in his life and home he comes with a squire's daughter! Martin might have looked much higher for a wife than Miss Anne Tofar. With his distinguished ancestry, his estate at Centrewell and his fortune, even an earl's daughter would not have been above his touch. But no, the moonstruck calf must fall heels over head in love with a nobody. Catched and delivered, he was, before anyone could reach him. Not the least quiver of common sense involved in it.

Though I liked Anne from the very moment I met her, he reminded himself. And she loves Martin as surely as Martin loves her. That's a good thing. An extremely good thing. So good, in fact, that I find I do not care if she is a squire's daughter or the daughter of a befuddled drunkard. I wonder who Lady Hannah loves? His eyes popped open wide. "Now what the devil put that thought into my head?" he whispered, watching dark shadows chase even darker shadows across his bed-chamber ceiling in the glow from the dimmed lamp on his night table.

With a mental shrug he closed his eyes once more and set himself to achieve sleep. He was bone-weary from the long ride and his experience on the moor and he had al-most fallen asleep right in the midst of tea in the Tofars' drawing room. If Martin had not poked him in the ribs with that sharp elbow of his, he would have fallen asleep with the tea cup in his hand. Why then was his brain sud-denly abuzz with nonsense that kept him awake?

"She did have the most amazing eyes, Lady Hannah," he murmured. "In the torchlight, they were utterly dev-astating."

It was a quarter to twelve when Hannah lay down her winning hand for Berinwick to see. "I win," she declared. "And I wish to know what secret you are keeping from Mama, Will. I wish to know it now."

"No."

"Unfair! You said we would play for wishes, William. I won this hand, and that's my wish."

"Well, you can't wish for things like that. You know very well we've never done any such thing. You may wish for me to fetch you tea or buy you some doo-dad, but—"

"It's something dreadful, then," Hannah interrupted, her brown eyes saved from black only by the golden sparks that sizzled within them. "You have done something horrid, haven't you? And you cannot think how to escape the consequences, and you do not wish Mama to know."

"I have not done anything horrid. Not of late, I have not," Berinwick replied calmly. "I have been most circumspect in all things."

"Oh, Will, I am your devoted sister. Why can you not confide in me? Surely I can be of more assistance to you than Martin Gazenby whom you barely know at all."

"You won't tell Mother?"

"Certainly not. Not unless you change your mind and allow me to do so. I have never carried tales to Mama about you, Will. You know that I have not."

"No, you never have. And yet most of the tales about me, Mama hears all the same."

"Gossip. Tea and scandal. You know how it is. But she does not believe a quarter of what people say."

"Thank gawd for small favors."

"You want to tell me the secret, Will. You know you do."

Berinwick nodded, sending his dark curls bouncing a bit. In the light of the lamps the scars that straggled out from beneath the black patch he wore where his right eye once was seemed to tremble. But the midnight blue of his remaining eye stared thoughtfully at Hannah for a considerably long time. "No, I think not," he said at last. "I'm not going to tell you. Not until I decide what to do about it. Then you will know and not before. So if that's the price of your winning, then you'll have to take my voucher for it and collect sometime in the future."

"Will!"

"It has nothing to do with you, Hannah. Not at the moment at least. All depends upon my decision. Will we play another hand, or will you go up to bed?"

"We'll play another hand, William, and I will win again. And just to put you in your place, when I win, I will wish for something extremely expensive and utterly useless."

Berinwick gathered the cards together and began to shuffle them. "What is your opinion of this Mallory fellow?" he asked.

"I told you, Will."

"You told me what he looked like. I want to know what sort of person you think him to be. Were you there when he met Tofar? Was Mallory uppity or condescending or kind when they met?"

"He was weary and thankful to have reached Tofar House at last. I did not notice anything particularly uppity about him. He seemed, simply, a gentleman."

"Yes, well, there are gentlemen and then there are gentlemen," Berinwick offered, dealing the hand.

It was well past midnight when Veronica Dempsey in nightdress and slippers walked out to stand before the front door of the rectory of St. Milburga's of the Wood. "What did you hear, Richard?" she asked as she took her husband's hand into her own and gazed into the night, listening.

"A scream, I think. It was quite far off. Still, it made the hairs on the back of my neck stand up, I can tell you that."

"And I heard nothing."

"You were lost in your reading."

"I hear nothing now either, Richard."

"No. Perhaps I imagined it."

"Or perhaps it was one of Harvey Langton's ghosts," Veronica said, smiling up at him.

Dempsey chuckled and drew her into his arms. He rested his chin on the top of her head. In the nine years since their marriage, age had chiseled a number of lines upon Veronica's face and streaked her hair more fully with silver. It had added more roundness to her figure and a faint trembling to her husky voice. But her wide brown eyes still glowed, still warmed his heart as they had always done. He could not forget, even for a moment, how lucky he was to have her with him. He did not wish to forget that, not ever.

"Ought not to make a jest of Langton," he said, leaning down and tickling her ear with his breath as he spoke. "He is not the only one hereabout who believes in ghosts."

"No, but he is the only one who admits to it, Richard," she replied, delighting in the feel of his arms around her as she always did. "The rest of us strive to laugh at poor old Harvey merely to ease our own uncertainty on the subject."

"Are you uncertain, Vernie? About the existence of ghosts?"

"Yes. I never was until I married Julian and became the Duchess of Berinwick and took up residence at Blackcastle. But there is something about the Marches, Richard—about living on the Marches for years and years—that plays with one's mind."

"And yet your son scoffs at the very idea of ghosts."

"That is William's way. I have learned his ways at last, you know. I have finally come to see through all of his facades and peer over all the walls that he has erected around his heart. He ridicules everything that might bring him harm. And thus, he ridicules the very idea of ghosts. He intimidates everyone he thinks may prove threatening to him, too."

"That's true enough. You do not think that he sees any man who would marry Hannah as a threat, eh? I mean to say, you don't think he intimidated her suitors these past Seasons and sent them running for cover to keep her unmarried?"

"He did not send you running for cover, Richard, when you wished to marry me."

"No, but then I am exceptionally odd and that made him like me, I think. Plus, I did find him entertaining from the first. And we did all share that amazing adventure when I arrived here. By the end of it, your son actually wanted me to marry you."

"He wants someone to marry Hannah as well. He has said as much to me many times."

"Good. Because I think it likely that with all the gentlemen come to bid on Tofar's Snoop—"

"Are there many gentlemen, Richard?"

"Scads of them. So many that they are falling out of the windows at the Three-Legged Inn. The streets of Barren Wycche are littered with them. And I think it likely that there might be one gentleman or two or perhaps three who have come not merely to bid on the horse but to pay their respects to Hannah as well. There! That's the sound I heard!" he said abruptly as a veritable shriek split the night and then was cut off abruptly. "Well, no, it is not exactly the sound. This is even more startling than the last one was."

Veronica shuddered and drew his arms more tightly around her. "It comes from the direction of the Widow Thistledown's cottage, Richard."

"Yes, just what I was thinking myself."

"There is no one remains at the Widow Thistledown's. Perhaps it is her ghost shrieking for the return of her children. Perhaps she has risen from the grave to discover that Charlie and Millie have gone to abide with her brother in Herefordshire and that Meg has been lost to us all in the dark, dank streets of London for years now, and Mrs. Thistledown cannot bear the injustice of it."

The sound came again, equally as shrill and was cut off in the middle again as though slashed with a blade.

"That's it," Dempsey declared, taking his arms from around his wife. He grasped her shoulders and turned her to face him. "It is not the Widow Thistledown's ghost, Vernie," he declared. "You do not for a moment believe that. Someone is near the cottage—or in it.

Someone in serious trouble." Dempsey released her and took a step away, then another.

"I am going with you," Veronica declared.

"Going with me?"

"To the stables. That is the direction in which your feet are taking you, is it not? And when you get there, you are going to saddle Norville and ride to the Widow Thistledown's."

"Yes."

"I am going with you. It will take me no longer to don my riding clothes than it will take you to don yours. You cannot go in your nightshirt, Richard. You forgot you were wearing it, did you not? Come inside and change. Hurry."

Mallory had tumbled into sleep at last. Thoughts of Lady Hannah and Snoop and the dogs of Little Mynd moor had run together in his mind, had tangled into images that proved indecipherable and then had ceased to buzz about his brain at all. Slumber lay heavily on his limbs and shadows danced across his ceiling with no one to watch them. But Mallory was a light sleeper and the slight click of the door knob turning urged him back into wakefulness.

What the devil? he wondered, peering cautiously through barely opened eyes, feigning sleep while his senses heightened to cope with what might very well be a dangerous situation. Cannot be Lakerby, he thought. Cannot be morning already. No, much too dark for morning, and Lakerby is never quiet when he enters. Slippered foot-steps met his ears and another click. A slight squeaking. A decidedly female giggle. A decidedly female giggle? What the deuce? Mallory sat straight up in the bed and turned up his lamp. "Halt!" he demanded, unable to see to whom he spoke as his eyes took a moment to adjust.

"Uh-oh," murmured a familiar voice.

"Caught in the act," announced another.

"Martin? Anne?" Mallory asked, astounded. "What the deuce are you doing sneaking about in my bedchamber? Have you got the wrong room?"

"Mmmeowwww," replied another familiar voice and Mallory's attention was immediately drawn away from the sheepish faces of the two figures in nightdress to a small brown and black striped head with yellow eyes as large as saucers peering over at him from the safety of Anne's arms.

Mallory's lips parted at the sight of the cat, then closed again without once emitting a sound.

"Lie back down again, Mal, and pretend that we are not here, will you? We've only just begun," Gazenby said.

"The devil I will. You've only just begun what?"

"Oh, nothing much," Anne replied. "Martin merely wished to, ah, inspect your armoire."

"Inspect my . . . ?"

"Yes. Precisely," Gazenby agreed hurriedly. "Wished to see if you had remembered to—to bring—ah—your bottle green riding coat and—ah—the shirt your mother gave you all those years ago. You know. The one with the lace collar and cuffs."

Mallory could not believe his ears. "You've gone mad," he murmured, studying his cousin with considerable amazement. "And you've driven your wife mad with you."

"No, no, not at all," Gazenby protested.

"No? Look at yourself, Martin. You are standing in my bedchamber in robe and slippers peeking into my armoire, and your wife is beside you doing the same—with a cat in her arms, of all things. Do not set that cat down, if you please. I had enough trouble removing it from this chamber earlier."

"I have no intention of turning Liddy loose," Anne replied, shifting the elderly feline from her arms into

Gazenby's. "And Martin is not searching for your bottle green riding coat or your shirt either," she added, stepping from the open armoire to the side of Mallory's bed, her hands clasped innocently before her. "I cannot think why he said that."

"Because he's lost his mind and so have you," Mallory replied, turning to meet her eyes. "Odd. You don't look mad."

"I'm not," Anne giggled. "Oh, but you should see your face, Cousin Mal. You are so utterly bewildered."

"You'd be flustered as well, to awaken to two people and a cat sneaking into your bedchamber."

"Yes, indeed. But we were not sneaking precisely. We merely wished not to wake you from your rest, my lord."

"Don't call me my lord now. Not when you are standing before me in your robe and slippers, Anne."

"I beg your pardon. It is simply that you look so very much more like a lord than a cousin at this moment. My, such a serious frown. All those lines gathering on your brow. And all for nothing, because we have not come to murder you in your bed, you know. We have simply come to see if—if—Liddy's kittens are hidden away in here somewhere."

"Liddy's kittens? That cat has kittens? Lakerby said it was an elderly cat."

"Not as elderly as all that," Anne replied.

"Oh."

"Not in the armoire," Gazenby announced. "Let me check the clothespress, eh? Don't want Liddy setting up a racket outside your door the rest of the night, do you, Mal?"

"No, of course not. Don't want to keep her from her kittens either," Mallory replied, turning his bewildered gaze on Gazenby.

"Although, we are not positive that the kittens are here," Anne said, bringing Mallory's gaze back to her. "Some-

times Liddy forgets where she put them and thinks they
are one place when they are actually in another."

"She forgets where she puts her kittens?"

"Well, she *is* elderly."

"Not here," Gazenby declared, closing the clothespress noisily. "We shall be forced to look elsewhere,
Annie. Perhaps we ought simply to close Liddy in our
room for the rest of the night and finish our search in
the morning."

"A splendid idea," Anne agreed with a bright smile.
"We do beg your pardon for disturbing you, Cousin Mal.
Do say that you forgive us."

"Yes. Certainly."

"Goodnight then. We will bother you no longer."
Anne swept across the room to Martin's side, took Liddy
into her arms and with another smile and a nod, exited
the chamber.

"Sorry to have bothered you, Mal," Gazenby murmured, stopping with his hand on the door knob.
"Women, you know."

"Just so," Mallory replied.

"Sleep late in the morning, eh? Breakfast is most informal and always to be had," Gazenby added and then
stepped out into the corridor, closing the door behind
him. "Kittens! Of all the bouncers I have ever heard," he
declared as he and Anne wandered back down the hallway
to their own room.

"Did you rub her against everything while I held his
attention?"

"Indeed. She thought it a game, I expect. She didn't
protest a bit. Snoop will be thoroughly charmed with
Mal tomorrow."

Clomping flat-footed over the parquet of the Great
Hall with lamp in hand, his hair mussed, the tail of his

nightshirt half in and half out of the waistband of his
hastily donned breeches, Gaines hurried to answer the
pounding on the front doors of Blackcastle. He set the
lamp on the hunt table and fiddled anxiously with the
door lock. "One moment," he called. "One moment.
This blasted lock will not—Ah, there we are. Your grace!"
he exclaimed as he opened the left-hand door. "Mr.
Dempsey! What is it? What has happened? The rectory is
not afire? The church has not fallen to the ground?"

"No, nothing to do with the rectory or the church,
Gaines," Veronica said as she and the Reverend Mr.
Dempsey stepped into the Great Hall. "Is the duke abed?
Well, but it does not matter if he is. You must rouse him,
Gaines, because Mr. Dempsey and I must speak to him
at once."

"Yes, your grace. He has just now gone up and will not
yet be asleep. Will you wait in the gold saloon? I shall fetch
him as quickly as I can. A light, a light," he added, twisting
about one way and then the other. Finding nothing but
the one lamp he had carried with him, the butler took
hold of it and faced Veronica with a sheepish smile. "A
change of plans, I fear. I shall lead you up to the gold saloon, set the lamps alight there, and then fetch his grace."

Veronica nodded.

"And once you have fetched him to us, Gaines,"
Dempsey said, following the butler and Veronica up the
main staircase to the first floor, "you had best wake one
of the footmen and send him down to the stables with
word to have his grace's horse saddled and waiting at the
front door."

"Wh-what has his grace done?" the butler queried be-
fore he could stop himself. "No, no, I beg your pardon.
I did not intend to say that. He can have done nothing.
He has been here in Blackcastle the entire day."

"Just so. His grace does not require the horse to escape from anyone, Gaines," Dempsey assured the butler.

"His mother and I require him to ride off with us, is all. We require his assistance, and as soon as possible."

"Indeed, Mr. Dempsey," Gaines said in undisguised relief. "It is merely that one never knows with our duke."

"Ask Tom Hasty to be prepared to ride out as well, will you, Gaines?" Veronica said as they reached the top of the staircase and turned in to one of the long corridors and then into the gold saloon where Gaines hastily set a number of lamps alight and then rushed off to fetch Berinwick.

It was a good ten minutes before the duke, attempting to shrug into his coat and tug on his riding gloves at one and the same time, strode into the room. "What is it, Mother, Dempsey?" he asked. "The rectory has not caught fire?"

"Why do people keep asking that?" Dempsey muttered. "No, the rectory has not caught fire nor has the church fallen down."

"There has been a young woman murdered, William," Veronica said. "At the Widow Thistledown's cottage. And though I have not seen her in almost nine years now, I think . . ."

"What?" Berinwick interrupted, not believing he had heard his mother aright. "What happened?"

"A young woman is dead, Berinwick," the Reverend Mr. Dempsey said. "Murdered. Your mother and I believe it to be Meg Thistledown."

"It must be Meg," Veronica declared. "She has aged greatly, but she was wearing the little trinket that Hannah presented to her when first the lot of you went off to London. Pinned to her dress, it was."

"Well, and I could not leave your mother at the cottage with the body, not alone," Dempsey said. "There was no way to know, after all, if the madman who killed the girl was still around. Nor could I remain with the body and send your mother here to fetch you. Could not take the risk that whoever did the thing might attack her along the way."

"Tom Hasty must ride to Barren Wycche and make Constable Lewis aware of what has happened," Veronica declared. "And you must come with us, William. Oh, but I cannot think how such a thing could happen. There has been nothing so vile occurred on Blackcastle lands in almost a decade. When did she come home? Why did no one know of it? What was she doing at the cottage in the middle of the night with no one to protect her?"

"Perhaps she expected her mother and Charlie and Millie to reside there still," Berinwick replied, leading the way from the room, hurrying toward the staircase. "Are you certain she's dead, Dempsey? What made you go riding out to the Widow Thistledown's cottage in the first place at such an hour?"

"We heard a cry . . ." Dempsey began as the three of them clattered down the stairs.

"Two cries actually," inserted Veronica. "No, no, three. Richard heard three. One that I did not hear and then perhaps three or four minutes afterward we both heard two more."

"We could not ignore them," Dempsey continued. "They seemed to come from the direction of the cottage, so we took our lanterns and rode that way. We found nothing along the road but—well, you will see what we found, Berinwick, soon enough."

Three

Hannah pushed the low-crowned hat of deep red velvet farther back on her head allowing a jumble of short, dark curls to cascade across her brow. From the turnabout before Tofar House, she surveyed the gentlemen gathered around the first of the squire's paddocks which lay just to the east of her and down a small hill. Tall, short, lean, heavy, young, old—a veritable potpourri of English males lounged along the paddock fence or stood conversing in a stableyard crowded with saddle horses, curricles, and drags.

"I expect they are all waiting for a glimpse of Snoop," she murmured. "What a multitude of gentlemen, Davey."

"Aye," her groom replied. "The Three-Legged Inn could not find rooms for them all. Some be staying with Mrs. Blesser. Rented out rooms, she did, and Mrs. Dearing did likewise."

"And they all wish to bid on Snoop?"

"I expect there be one or two what have come just for the society and a number who be wishing to bid on the other horses, but aye, most of them be hoping to outbid everyone and go home with the squire's Snoop in tow."

"Whoever would have thought it? But then, he will make a fine race horse one day, will he not?"

"Exceptional. Descended from the Byerly Turk, he be, through the elegant Herod. By the noble Attica out of Tofar's Folly. And Tofar's Folly be—"

"Yes, I know, a descendent of the great Flying Childers. But Snoop is thoroughly unproven, as yet. A yearling not yet accustomed to saddle and bridle. I did not imagine that so many gentlemen would be interested in him until he had proven himself at The Oaks or Newmarket or Doncaster."

"It be his breeding, my lady. Put notice of the auction in all the London papers, the squire did. Made certain Snoop's pedigree was printed. And this be the result of it."

"And the auction is not until next Thursday. What can so many gentlemen do, Davey, in such a tiny village as Barren Wycche, with so much time until the day of the auction comes?"

"Eat, drink, lounge about the shops and the Fallen Dog, and attempt to race the sheep in the village square," Lancaster replied blandly.

"Race the sheep?"

"So says Mr. McGowen," Lancaster nodded. "Funniest thing he's ever seen, he says—gentlemen attempting to keep their seats on the sheep's backs, long gentlemen legs sticking out to keep feet from dragging the ground, gentlemen arms akimbo, attempting to urge the poor animals in the correct direction."

That put a smile on Lady Hannah's face—a smile Lancaster was pleased to see as he helped her from the saddle. After the news of earlier this morning, he had doubted she would smile again for the rest of the day.

"Do you go down to the paddock to wait while I speak with Mrs. Gazenby, Davey?"

"Yes, m'lady." Spying Norton already holding open the front door for his young mistress, Lancaster nodded to the butler. "Mr. Norton be waiting on you, my lady. Go and speak to Miss Anne—I mean, Mrs. Gazenby. She will wish to know about our Meggy." And with a comforting smile, he turned and led his mount and hers toward the paddock.

* * *

Mallory entered the morning room in search of his breakfast to discover Anne and Lady Hannah standing together before the windows speaking in hushed voices. Both lovely young brows were creased by frowns. Not wishing to interrupt what he could easily observe must be a serious conversation, he turned on his heel to exit the room.

"Oh! Cousin Mal! No, don't go!" Anne called to his back.

Mallory turned around again and smiled a tentative smile. "Are you certain? You and Lady Hannah appear to be deeply involved in a matter of some importance."

"Yes, a very sad and disturbing matter, but it is not a private one," Anne replied. "At least, it will not be once word spreads through Barren Wycche."

"And word will spread," said Hannah. "Constable Lewis will see that everyone in the vicinity knows of it by this evening. Good morning, my lord," she added. "I do hope you are feeling better for a sound night's sleep in a comfortable bed."

"I am in much better form this morning, my lady. Thank you," Mallory replied, wondering how she knew that his bed had been comfortable and then thinking himself perfectly silly to wonder such a thing at all. "This matter that concerns you, is it something in which I may be of assistance?" he queried.

"Not unless you happen to be intimately acquainted with some beast in human clothing and can give us his name and direction," Hannah replied. "A young woman has been murdered—a young woman known to both Anne and myself. She was my abigail and accompanied us to London for our first Season." Both Hannah and Anne crossed to the serving table, helped themselves to tea and toast and sat down beside each other at the dining table. "She disappeared three weeks after we arrived there," Hannah sighed, lifting the tea cup to her lips.

"Do help yourself to whatever you desire, Cousin Mal," Anne urged, nodding toward the prepared dishes on the table. "And if there is anything you wish that is not present, do speak up and I will send to the kitchen for it."

Mallory took a plate and explored the contents of the silver serving dishes. "I cannot think that anything at all is missing, Cousin Anne. There is enough here to satisfy an army. The young woman disappeared in London?" he asked as he settled into a chair opposite them. "How did she disappear? Why did she disappear? Did she run away?"

"No one knows." Hannah smoothed a wrinkle from the tablecloth before her, caressing the fine Irish linen with strokes so innocently sensuous that the action sent shivers racing up and down Mallory's spine. "One evening Meg was helping Anne and I to dress for the Fontaynes' ball and the next morning, she was gone. My brother searched everywhere for her. He even drew Meg's portrait and had it printed on a poster offering a reward to anyone who would step forward with information. He had the grooms and footmen pass the posters out all over London, but no one ever did come to say that they had seen her.

"And you are not to think that anything untoward took place between my brother and Meg, Lord Mallory," she added, startling Mallory no end because that was the precise thought that had just entered his mind. "William was fond of Meg because she was the eldest daughter of our father's coachman and was born and lived on Blackcastle land her entire life—until we took her to London. Her father died with our father in a tragic—accident—and Will always felt responsible for her and her family."

Mallory noted the pause Hannah had taken before enunciating the word *accident* and immediately suspected that, whatever had happened to her father and his coachman, there had been nothing accidental about it. He studied her for a moment, considerably intrigued. She was tall for a woman and held herself proudly with shoulders back and chin up. Her deep brown eyes glowed with an inner light as they met his own directly, and her dark curls framed her pretty face like soft feathers and fluttered when she took her gaze from his with a tiny shake of her head.

"You do not wish to be bothered with this, my lord," she said quietly. "You have come on holiday to see Snoop and bid on him. Martin is already down at the paddock, I think, awaiting your arrival there."

"That is precisely where Martin is," Anne agreed. "But only because he has not yet heard the news. He would be here offering his assistance, else, Hannah. You know he would."

"Yes, but of what assistance can he be? Martin knows no one of such evil propensities as those required to murder an innocent young woman."

"One need not personally know a villain to discover a villain's name," Mallory offered.

"Perhaps not," Hannah agreed, "but I will not spoil Martin's visit by involving him in such nasty business. Nor will I spoil your holiday, Lord Mallory. My brother and Constable Lewis will see that whoever did this deed is brought to justice. I merely wished to tell Anne that, after all this time, Meg has been found—but found too late. Too late."

There was such honest sadness in Hannah's voice that it touched Mallory's heart. It was beyond his experience that any lady of rank should care as dearly as it appeared Lady Hannah had for a servant girl—be the girl born and raised in the service of the lady's family or not. He vowed to himself then and there that he would keep his eyes and ears open. There was no telling but that one or another of the gentlemen gathered to view the squire's horses might know something of the young woman's death.

"I expect I had best go down to the paddock, eh?" he murmured, rising. "Martin will think that I have changed my mind about the yearling, else. Should you like to accompany me, Cousin Anne, Lady Hannah?"

"Yes," Anne replied, causing Hannah's finely drawn eyebrows to rise slightly. "It will cheer us both, Hannah, to watch Snoop frisk about the paddock for a bit, don't you think?"

"Of all the things to say. When have I ever been cheered by a horse frisking about a paddock?" Hannah asked as she and Anne stood together a bit apart from the gentlemen gathered along the paddock fence.

"Oh, such a short memory," Anne teased. "I believe the last time was the day that my father brought Hannah's Darling to make her bows before Will. You laughed that day. I remember it well."

"Yes, but that was different, Annie. I had not just learned that a young woman of whom I was fond had been strangled. And I had just purchased Darling for Will and could not help but laugh to see the two of them appraising each other."

"And now, despite Meg's death, you will laugh again, because Snoop and Lord Mallory are just about to take stock of each other. See, Martin is just accompanying Mal into the paddock."

"Yes, but there will be nothing to smile at, Annie. Snoop will not approach Lord Mallory, or frisk about hoping to attract his attention. He will simply ignore the man. He ignores everyone. Or, he will charge at Lord Mallory like an enraged bull and attempt to take a bite out of him. I have known Snoop from his birth. He is not a pleasant animal."

"Not in general, no. He is generally a rascal and a scamp. But you know he's a prize, Hannah."

"A prize sought after by an amazing number of gentlemen, too," Hannah agreed. "I have not seen such a plethora of gentlemen gathered in one place since we sneaked into Tattersall's in our second Season."

"Sssssh!" Anne giggled.

"Oh, they will none of them hear us. Even your Papa's attention is totally absorbed by the yearling now. Well, for goodness' sake! Annie, look. Snoop is not ignoring Lord Mallory at all. Nor is he charging at him. Anne, Snoop is walking directly up to Lord Mallory."

"Is he?"

"Yes. And by Jove, if that scoundrel is not taking an apple right from Lord Mallory's hand! I cannot believe it! I never thought to see the day that Snoop would approach a perfect stranger in such an amiable manner. There must be something very special about the gentleman to put Snoop into such good humor with him on the instant."

"Martin and I think Cousin Mal is very special," Anne said quietly. "And look at Papa, Hannah. Papa's eyebrows have flown clear up to touch his hair. Now that must make you laugh if nothing else can."

Berinwick roamed the corridors of Blackcastle muttering under his breath, restless, unable to settle himself to review with Gaines the household accounts or to discuss the latest agricultural innovations and how they might be put to use with Hopkins, the farm manager. Nor could he set himself to any of the other responsibilities that faced him this particular day. No. Because he could not drive from his mind the worn, pale, lifeless face that had met his eyes early this morning at the Widow Thistledown's cottage. The more the vision of

Meg, murdered, tumbled about in his mind, the more his anger gnawed at him.

"And she looked so—so—shabby," he muttered, his hands fisting at his sides. "I was correct all this time. Some villain lured her away that night in London, took advantage of her and has been taking advantage of her ever since. The damnable fiend has been wearing her down, wearing her out. Do I get my hands around the dastard's neck, I will squeeze the breath out of him, just as he did to Meg, and I will laugh all the while I am doing it, too." It must be one of the men who has come to Barren Wycche to bid at Tofar's auction, he thought, stomping into his study and taking a rapier down from where a pair of them were mounted on the wall behind his desk. How would she come to be here unless one of the men brought her with him?

Unless Meg found the courage at last to run away from whoever held her captive, Berinwick thought. Could she have run away from some man in London and made her way to Barren Wycche and the cottage hoping to find sanctuary there with her family?

"And all the time poor Meg had not the least idea that her mother had died and Charlie and Millie had gone to live in Herefordshire," he sighed. "But she might have come here to Blackcastle, once she discovered that the cottage was empty. She *ought* to have come here to Black-castle. She *would* have come here to Blackcastle," he exclaimed angrily, "if she had been free to do so!"

Berinwick bent the tip of the rapier tentatively, testing the blade, feeling it spring to life in his hand. "Be too kind of me merely to strangle the villain," he murmured thoughtfully. "First I'll run him through. Then I'll carve Meg's name into his chest, then I'll strangle him."

"And tales of your actions will fly near and far on the wings of the mail coach horses. And twisted by the winds of their own progress, the tales will somehow come to name you the villain of the piece and your reputation will grow even more despicable than it be today," Tom Hasty observed as he entered the room. "You wished a word with me, your grace?"

"Not now," Berinwick replied with the cock of an arrogant eyebrow. "Of all the cheeky things to say. I doubt I'll wish for a word with you ever again in my life, Hasty. Ought to dismiss you on the spot."

"If you'll be permitting me an observation, your grace," the groom replied, "rubbish! As if you'd ever send me off from Blackcastle! Tell me this, eh? Should you be requiring someone to hold this fiend down while you go carving Meggy's name into him, who would you be calling upon?"

"You, Tom," Berinwick admitted with a slight smile.

"Just so. And pleased I'd be to do it, too."

"Then we will. We'll carve the fellow up together, Tom. At the moment though, I merely need you to ride to the squire's for me. I require a word with Mr. Gazenby and it would be better if we spoke here, he and I."

"Aye, your grace," Hasty nodded. "I be off at once."

Hannah did actually laugh at the sight of the squire's eyebrows rising up to meet his hair. Then she allowed her gaze to return to Lord Mallory and discovered that gentleman to be gently stroking the yearling's nose.

"He is a handsome gentleman, Martin's cousin, don't you think?" Anne asked, following Hannah's gaze. "I thought him most impressive when first we met. All those dark curls and those broad shoulders and he has the kindest smile."

"Has he?"

"Indeed, when he is not weary from chasing about on moorlands or worried by news of a possible murderer in our midst, he smiles a good deal and it is very kind."

"In our midst? Do you think Meg's murderer may be one of the gentlemen standing here, Annie?" Hannah asked, thoughtfully.

"Yes. You suspect it as well, do you not?"

"It seems logical. One of the gentlemen who has come to bid on Snoop, if he did not realize that Meg was born and raised here, might well have brought her with him. But what happened then? It appears that she attempted to escape from him and run to the cottage hoping to find her mama and Millie and Charlie. And if that is what happened, why would the man strangle her there? Once he learned it was her home, why kill her anywhere near Barren Wycche and Blackcastle? He must have realized that everyone would know who she was. Why not take her back to London at once and perform the horrendous deed somewhere along the way or in some hovel in Seven Dials where surely no one of any standing would recognize Meg or care in the least that she was dead?"

"I haven't the vaguest idea. Perhaps the man is a simpleton or a lunatic. Well, he must be one or the other to kill Meg Thistledown on Berinwick land. There cannot be a rational person in all of England who would purposely taunt Will in such a way—and expect to remain alive."

"I am going to be forced to do something to find this villain. I can see that plainly," Mallory said, softly.

Hannah had not so much as seen him depart the paddock, much less come up beside her, and the soft, low tone of his voice most unexpectedly near her ear made her jump.

"Oh! Lord Mallory!"

"Startled you, did I? Well, you were intent on your conversation with Cousin Anne. Speaking about the murder, were you not? It sounded so to me."

"Yes. But it is none of it your concern, my lord. My brother will see that the dastard is found and punished."

"Will he?"

"Yes." Hannah could not think why the nearness of Lord Mallory made her nervous, but decidedly, it did. She stepped away from him and began to walk back toward the house. Anne hurried after her and when she caught Hannah up, took hold of her arm and strolled beside her.

"That was a bit impolite of you, I must say," Anne scolded softly. "To turn and walk away from Lord Mallory without so much as a `by your leave' Of all things, Hannah!"

"Is he following us?"

Anne glanced over her shoulder. "Indeed. He and Martin both."

"Then perhaps I ought simply to signal to Lancaster to bring the horses up."

"No, Hannah. Why?"

"I cannot say precisely. I took no note of it last evening, but this morning—He makes me uneasy, your Lord Mallory."

"But he has done nothing at all untoward, Hannah."

"No, not at all. It is merely—Well, to be honest, I cannot think what it is. He did not go out again, last evening, Annie?"

"Mal? Well, of course not."

"You are certain?"

"Actually, I am as certain as anyone can be. He was already in his bed asleep when I entered his bedchamber. Oh! I ought not to have said that."

Hannah paused in midstride and studied Anne's suddenly flaming cheeks. "Anne Marie Tofar! Do you mean to tell me that you were in that gentleman's bedchamber last evening?"

"Y-yes," Anne replied on a breath of a chuckle. "Do not glare at me as though I am some fallen woman, Hannah. Martin was with me. It was all of it Martin's idea in the first place."

"What? What was Martin's idea? Tell me."

"No, not at this very moment. They are right behind us now," Anne replied in a whisper, urging Hannah to walk forward once again. "I cannot take the chance that Cousin Mal will overhear us. He has excellent ears, I think. Goodness, who is that? Hannah? Is that not Tom Hasty? And coming at a terrifying pace."

"Tom?" Hannah queried as the groom reined his mount to an abrupt halt and descended from the saddle all in one graceful movement before her. "What is it? Nothing has happened to Will?"

"No, no, nothing whatever, my lady. He merely wishes to speak with Mr. Gazenby and has sent me to attend the gentleman to Blackcastle."

"Me?" Gazenby asked, he and Mallory now abreast of the young women and Hasty.

"Aye, Mr. Gazenby. His grace would have a word with you, if you please. At your convenience, he said."

"Oh, my gawd," murmured Gazenby.

"What? What's wrong, Martin?" Mallory queried.

"At my convenience," Gazenby reiterated. "Berinwick wishes to have a word with me *at my convenience*. Have you any idea what that means, Mal?"

"I should think it means whenever you find yourself free to ride over to Blackcastle and speak with him, Martin," Anne said, a smile teasing at her lips.

"No, no, not the actual words, Annie. Berinwick's being polite to me. What can that portend? He is never polite to anyone. Why me? Why choose to be polite to me? He never has been before, not even when I was courting you, my dear. Oh, he attempted to keep his tongue somewhat in check. He did not call me a male milliner or anything of that sort, and he did assure me over and over again that you and he were not related, but he was never, never, polite."

Hannah sought Tom Hasty's eyes, read the laughter in

them, and chuckled. "Tom, confess, before Mr. Gazenby has palpitations of the heart."

"What? Confess what?" asked Gazenby, nervously.

"His grace did not say 'at your convenience,' Mr. Gazenby. I fibbed about that," Hasty said, "seeing as you were occupied and all. His grace merely sent me to fetch you to him and didn't say anything at all polite."

Mallory, who had noted the sudden stiffening of Martin's shoulders as the groom first relayed the duke's message, now watched them relax again. Mallory's eyes, alight with silent laughter met Hannah's. "Will you go at once, Martin?" he queried of his cousin. "You need not put off the duke on my behalf. I hope you know that. I am perfectly capable of entertaining myself until you return."

"Yes, yes, of course you are, Mal. Shouldn't think otherwise. I'll go and have a horse saddled and join you in a moment, Hasty."

"And Davey and I will return with you as well, I think, Tom," Hannah said. "Will you tell Lancaster to bring my horse up please, Mr. Gazenby, when you are ready?"

"No, don't go, Hannah," Anne said, holding tightly to her friend's arm. "Remain just a bit longer."

Gazenby, who had taken two steps toward the stable, halted and took one step back, waiting for Hannah to decide. He read a plea in his wife's eyes and cleared his throat. "There is something of importance Annie wishes to discuss with you, I believe," he said, unable to think of any other excuse to hold Lady Hannah at Tofar House.

"Just so," Anne agreed. "Something of importance."

Hannah looked from one to the other of them. "Very well," she replied at last. "Then I will not accompany you back to Blackcastle, Martin."

Gazenby nodded and began his trek toward the stable once again with Mallory falling into step at his side.

"Well, if the ladies have something of importance to discuss, I am not going to impose my company upon them," Mallory said. "I shall just have Simon saddled and ride about for a bit. Enjoy the landscape. Discover that stream you are always going on about whenever you return from a visit here."

"Don't get lost again, eh, Mal?" Gazenby grinned.

"Not a chance of it. I won't have your directions to guide me this time, Martin. That alone ought to keep me safe, eh?"

Anne hesitated. To cover her indecision, she poured the tea that had only just arrived and passed Hannah a cup with a determinedly steady hand. "Do have a gingersnap, Hannah," she urged, her mind sorting through all the possibilities open to her, choosing one, discarding it, choosing another. "Mrs. Grayson made them just this morning and they are wonderful."

Hannah, seated beside her friend on the flowered settee in the Tofars' front parlor, took a gingersnap from the tray, bit into it and smiled. "Delicious," she said. "Almost as delicious as watching the play of thoughts across your face, Annie. You did not actually have anything of importance to discuss with me, did you? That was a tremendous bouncer on Martin's part just to keep me from accompanying him to Blackcastle."

"No, no, it was not a bouncer. Not precisely. I am merely wondering how to approach the subject without—You said, at the paddock, that Lord Mallory made you uneasy."

"Yes. What has that to do with anything at all?"

"A great deal, because I—Martin and I both—we were hoping to convince you to spend a good deal of time with Mal while he is here."

"You were what?"

"Hoping you would take the time to help us entertain Martin's cousin."

"Annie! You have not taken it into your head to attempt to make a match between Martin's cousin and myself? I cannot believe it of you. I could believe it of your mama, mind, but not you."

"No, no, it is nothing to d-do with a match," Anne said hurriedly, surreptitiously crossing her fingers to ward off any evil that might flow from such a large fib as that.

"Good. Because I am weary of all the primping and posing and playacting that goes with attempting to make a match of it with some fellow, Annie. I have come to conclude that I am not the sort of woman a man wishes to marry. And I am not going to pretend to be someone I am not—not for your Lord Mallory or for any other gentleman."

"Of course not. I would not expect it of you. It is just that Martin's cousin has been—has been—most melancholy of late. And we—Martin and I—we thought that perhaps here, in Shropshire, he might discover happiness again."

"He is melancholy? He came here to discover happiness again? I thought he came to bid on Snoop?"

"Yes, well, that is why Mal thinks he has come, too. But we did hope that time away from the wilds of Yorkshire, in such a beautiful place as this, would—would—soothe his heart at last and bring a touch of joy to his soul."

Her teacup paused partway to her lips, Hannah stared in awe at her dearest friend. "Annie," she said, her eyes wide with wonder, "do you know that you sound precisely like the narrator of a romance novel?"

"I do?" Anne giggled nervously. "Well, but I cannot help that. The truth is that it grows very cold and lonely in Yorkshire when the winter sets in, Hannah. And even when one has no cause to be unhappy—even at Centrewell with Martin beside me—I have felt the fingers of melancholy reaching out to stroke my mind. But coming home to Shropshire in the spring always chases the sadness away and I—Martin and I—hoped it might have the same effect on Mal. You, Hannah, are a great part of what always cheers me about this place. And I hoped—I hoped—that you would help to cheer Mal as well."

"Oh." Hannah leaned forward and set her teacup on the tray. Then she sat back and took one of Anne's hands into her own. "I did never realize, Annie, that you might grow lonely in Yorkshire. I always picture you as madly in love and oblivious to everything around you when you are at home with Martin. And then, I imagine you out and about in society having a wonderful time of it on Martin's arm."

"So it is, most of the year," Anne agreed with a nod. "But Yorkshire can be such a fierce place in the winter, Hannah. It makes one yearn for the company of one's family and friends. And Mal lives so far from all of us that it is near impossible for us to visit him at Brambles, and so he has no defense against the melancholy. He has suffered a tremendous tragedy, besides," Anne added on a whim, hoping to draw forth all of Hannah's considerable sympathy and bestow it on the gentleman.

"What sort of tragedy?"

"I—I—cannot say. It is a very private matter and he would—he would not wish for me to speak of it."

"Oh. Well." Hannah released her hold of Anne's hands and leaned back thoughtfully against the settee.

"You know what it is like to have a gentleman who has suffered a great tragedy in the family, Hannah. You know how one wishes to be of aid to him. You have Will, after all. And William has you and your mother and Richard," she added with a distinct flair for the romantical. "Mal has no one. His mother and brothers and sisters are more trial to his soul than balm."

"Very well," Hannah sighed, considering the brother she knew so well and wishing that she could do more to make him happy than she already did. "I will do what I can, Annie, to make your Lord Mallory's visit here as pleasant as possible for him. Everything short of primping and posing and playacting, that is. You may depend upon it."

"A child?" Gazenby asked, attempting to loosen his neckcloth with one finger, his eyes fastened in astonishment on Berinwick. "What on earth will you do with it?"

"That's just the thing, Gazenby," Berinwick replied, slouching down into one of the new chairs that Hannah had purchased for the smallest drawing room, dangling his left leg over the arm of the chair which was carved to represent a crocodile's head, stretching his right leg out before him, folding his arms across his chest and leaning his head against the high chair back. "That's just the thing. What will I do with it? Raise it as I would raise my own child? But how would I raise a child of my own? And what would people say if I brought a child to Blackcastle? Then again, if I don't bring the child to Blackcastle, where do I send it?"

"Where do you send it? You have it already, your grace?"

"Yes. No. That is, I expect the boy must have arrived in London a week or so ago, but I have not seen him as yet. He's to abide with my solicitor until I decide what's to be done. I know it seems an insignificant problem, Gazenby, next to a murder, but it preys on my mind and—"

"Next to a *what*?" Gazenby gasped, leaning forward in his chair, clasping his hands between his knees.

"A murder. Meg Thistledown was murdered. Hannah rode to Tofar House to tell Anne about it. Did neither of them mention it to you?"

"No. Who—When—Meg who?"

"She was Hannah's abigail," Berinwick said without once taking note of the bewildered expression on Gazenby's face. "She disappeared in London during

Hannah's first Season there. You had not yet set foot in London then, I think."

"She was murdered in London?"

"No—she was murdered in a little cottage near Hatter's field sometime last evening—or early this morning, I expect I should say. Near midnight, it was."

"By gawd, Berinwick, a young woman murdered in our very midst and you did not think it appropriate to inform the squire and me of it?"

"I didn't think of you at all, actually, Gazenby. And I was certain the squire would hear of it when Hannah spoke to Anne."

"Annie might be in danger! Lady Hannah as well! Every woman in the vicinity!"

"Perhaps, or perhaps not. We've no idea who murdered Meg or why. Constable Lewis is looking into it. I trusted that the squire would look to the safety of his household once Hannah informed Anne and Anne informed him of what happened."

"*I* am the one will look to Annie's safety," Gazenby announced, rising from his chair and beginning to pace the room. "She is my *wife* now, Berinwick. It is *my* duty to keep her safe!"

"Yes, yes, true," Berinwick acknowledged with a negligent wave of one hand. "Do with Anne what you will, then. Take her back to Yorkshire on the instant if you fear to have her remain in the neighborhood with a killer roaming about."

"Well, I can't do that."

"You can't?" Berinwick stared at the man, amazed. "But you are her husband, Gazenby. She must do whatever you say."

"Oh? Well, I wish you would inform Anne of that. No. She won't go back to Centrewell yet, murderer in our midst or not. We arrived only last week and—"

"And what?"

"And there are—things—she has promised herself that she will do while she is here."

"Things? What kind of things does she wish to do that would prove more important that protecting her own life?" Berinwick asked with considerable suspicion.

"Merely—things."

Berinwick glared through his lone eye at the pacing Gazenby with such intensity that Gazenby ceased to pace at once and returned to his chair. "I promised I would not tell you what she intends to do, Berinwick. I gave Anne my word and I mean to keep it, regardless of how you threaten me."

"Did I threaten you? I do not recall—"

"I am not in the least intimidated by you, Berinwick," Gazenby proclaimed, his voice rising to a squeak near the end of the sentence.

"Are you not?" Berinwick queried softly, all thoughts of murderers and "things" slipping from his mind at Gazenby's effrontery. "What if I were to rise from this chair," he asked, matching his actions to his words. "What if I were to walk over here to this sideboard, open a particular drawer—this drawer right here—and take from it one of my dueling pistols—this one, I think— and aim the deuced thing directly between your eyes like so? Are you intimidated by me now, Gazenby?"

"I—I—"

"Of course he is. What sane man would not be intimidated under such circumstances?" asked a voice from the drawing room doorway. "Go on—Gazenby, did he call you?—admit that you're intimidated so he'll put his little popper away and cease making a villain of himself. I should detest to run him through on behalf of a fellow I don't even know. Yes, and I should hate to be forced to do it before the wretch has so much as welcomed me to Blackcastle, too."

"Elliot? Josiah Elliot? Is it truly you?" Berinwick lowered the pistol, placed it back into the drawer and took a step toward the officer in the blue dolman-sleeved jacket and white breeches of the Twelfth Light Dragoons who leaned nonchalantly against the door frame, a wide smile on his face.

"Of course it's me, you peabrain. Whom did you expect, the Prince of Wales?" asked Elliot, straightening and stepping forward, taking Berinwick's proffered hand into both of his own and giving it a tremendous shake. "I thought I would never find the place, it's been so long. Hasn't changed, though. Still the same hodge-podge of stones and history that it always was. I forbade Gaines to announce me. Told him I could find you on my own. Damnation, if it didn't take me ten minutes at least to do that, too. Got lost in that blessed corridor that runs back and forth between the two towers and the west wing."

"What the deuce are you doing here?" Berinwick queried, freeing his hand from the trooper's grasp. "You never wrote you were coming. Why aren't you off fighting somewhere? This is Gazenby," he added. "Married Anne Tofar."

"Indeed." Elliot replied, grinning at Gazenby, who had risen promptly upon the soldier's entrance and now seemed to follow the conversation in a daze. "What's wrong with the man, Berinwick? What did you do to him?"

"Nothing. I merely pointed a pistol at his head."

"Come, Gazenby, has this son of a demented demon never pointed a pistol at your head before?"

"N-no."

"He has pointed one at mine four times at the very least. Would not have fired it, you know. Doesn't like blood, Berinwick does not. Not all over his own carpet. So, invite me to sit, Berinwick. Pour Gazenby and me a glass of brandy. Be hospitable."

"I don't pour brandy at this hour of the day."

"Send for some ale then. Nothing wrong with ale. I've had a long ride, you wretch, and I'm thirsty."

Mallory, having discovered that he was truly not in the mood to ride about the country alone this particular morning, cut his excursion short and returned to the squire's stables within a quarter hour of having left them. Giving Simon into the care of one of the grooms, he stood alone at the side of one of the outbuildings, staring over at the paddock. His arms crossed, his shoulders resting against the worn boards, he watched Snoop thoroughly ignore a number of gentlemen just then sizing the horse up from the opposite side of the paddock fence.

"There be any number of horses here better than that one," said a voice from just around the corner of the building. "Were it me, I'd think twice before spending my blunt on such an evil-tempered animal as Snoop."

"Would ye?" asked a second voice.

"Indeed. Spend my money on Little Lass, I would. Or Dreamy Daisy, p'rhaps."

"But neither of them is in the least auspicious, Jem. Ordinary horses from ordinary bloodlines."

"Ha! Nothing ordinary about Little Lass. From the same sire and mare as Hannah's Darling, she be."

"Yes, but Hannah's Darling is not a race horse, Jem."

"P'rhaps not. But did she race, did your duke allow her to step up and run in competition, Davey, she would show Snoop and all them other high-blooded animals her tail, she would."

"Hannah's Darling?" Mallory asked, striding around the corner of the outbuilding and encountering the two grooms who were sitting on the ground in the shade.

Both men gained their feet at once.

"I'm sorry. I did not intend to disrupt your conversation, but I could not help overhearing. There is a horse called Hannah's Darling who is faster than Snoop?"

"Faster than any horse I ever see'd race," Jem Stokes declared proudly. "Thought she would never make a race horse, the squire did, on account of her being caught in the fire shortly after she were foaled. Thought the smoke did damage to her lungs. But it didn't."

"It did," Davey Lancaster disagreed. "But that was near nine years ago and Overfield, Trewellyn, Hasty and I nursed her through it. You cannot tell now how she struggled early on."

"Hannah's Darling," Mallory murmured. "I expect this paragon of a horse who shares her antecedents with Little Lass belongs to Lady Hannah then?"

"Not at all," said Lancaster with a lift of his chin. "Belongs to the Duke of Berinwick, she does. A present she were to his grace from Lady Hannah."

Mallory nodded to them both and wandered off toward the house, his hands clasped behind his back, his boots kicking up dust as he passed through the stableyard. He wondered if Martin had returned from Berinwick's residence yet. He wondered why the grooms had seemed equally accepting of the fact that Snoop was skittish when the horse had appeared most calm and even-tempered to him. And he wondered why, at the name Hannah's Darling on the grooms' lips, visions of Lady Hannah, torch held high, her dark eyes sparkling, had suddenly appeared in his mind and taken his breath away.

Well, but she is a lovely young woman, he told himself in silence as he continued on toward the house. Stunning, actually, with that high brow, those sweetly rounded cheeks, that proud chin, and those incredible eyes. As devastating as a summer storm, those eyes. It's a wonder she is not married. She has been to London for a Season or two, I believe Martin said, and yet no gentleman was interested enough in her to propose a union between them. Or perhaps it was Lady Hannah who did not find any of the gentlemen interesting? Not that it matters to me, Mallory assured himself with a shake of his head. I am certainly not looking for a wife. Though if I were. . . .

"But I am not," he whispered as he approached the house. "I have come here to bid on and win a particular horse, nothing more. I will not be distracted from that purpose by a young woman with a lovely face or by some unknown filly named Little Lass or by a mare called Hannah's Darling, no matter how intriguing they all seem to me at this particular moment."

"Talking to yourself, Mal? Never known you to do that. Must be the glorious day and the romance of the Marches, eh?"

Mallory looked up at once. Standing nonchalantly before him, whip in both hands, left hip cocked, beaver hat tilted at a rakish angle over his brow, stood a gentleman with hair the color of summer wheat and eyes the color of turquoise. "Silverdale?" Mallory asked, amazed. "Where the devil did you come from?"

"From London, of course. What better excuse to depart the city and visit the Marches than an auction at the Tofar stables? Number of winners bred in these particular stables, you know. May bid on a horse or two myself. It's the one called Snoop in which your interest lies, eh, Mal? Who knows but that I may bid on that horse in particular."

"You? Bid with what?"

"Really, Mallory. What business is that of yours? But my luck has been in of late and my pockets are well-lined. I assure you of it. And if I do not outbid you for the yearling, it matters not, because I *will* outbid you for the filly."

"What filly? What the deuce are you speaking of, Sly? I haven't come to bid on any filly."

"No? Well, that's excellent news, although I find it difficult to believe. Most difficult to believe after having spoken with Harry. He gave me to understand that Gazenby lured you here just so you would meet and fall in love with the Duke of Berinwick's sister. Bit of matchmaking, you know."

"What?"

"It does seem difficult to believe, now that I give it some consideration. Gazenby? A matchmaker? And to lure you all this way when you might just as easily have met Lady Hannah during any of the past four Seasons in London? But then the things that Harry gets into his head always seem frightfully confusing to me. I never did understand him, even when we were lads."

"When the devil did you speak with Harry?" Mallory asked, his face puckering into a frown. "And how does he come to know of my visit here? He is with the Nineteenth in India. I wrote to him that I intended to come here to Shropshire to bid on a horse, but I doubt the letter will have reached him as yet. I sent it merely a week ago."

Silverdale grinned. "Yes. Well. I've no idea how Harry learned of your visit to Shropshire, but I know for a fact that he's not in India."

"The Nineteenth was in India with Wellesley last I heard."

"Either the Nineteenth has returned to England or Harry is no longer with the Nineteenth," Silverdale laughed, "because I bumped into him in the Two Sevens in St. James's Street no more than a fortnight ago. He seemed most upset about the likelihood of your finding a wife, Mal. Wished to know all I could tell him about Lady Hannah Thorne. Wished to know if I thought you might be attracted to her."

"Of all things!" Mallory exclaimed. "If Harry were here now I'd bloody his nose. What business is it of his if I'm attracted to Lady Hannah?"

"None. Which is precisely what I told him. Told him to stick his nose in someone else's business and keep it out of mine. And Lady Hannah *is* my business. I warn you of it, Mal. Never did like Harry. Not all that fond of you, either, when it comes right down to it. But I dislike Harry a great deal more than I dislike you."

"I have never liked you much either, Sly," Mallory replied, stuffing his hands into his breeches pockets. "And yet, I like you more than Harry. Gives us something in common, does it not?"

"Yes. And as long as that's all we have in common, and you do not suddenly become all calf-eyed over Berinwick's sister, we shall stumble along very well together just as we have always done. You don't intend to, do you?"

"Intend to what?"

"Get all calf-eyed over Lady Hannah."

"By Jove, Sly, if you and Harry do not realize by now that I have no intention of growing calf-eyed over any woman, then you are both stupider than two partridges in a pie! And besides, I barely know the young woman."

"Good," Silverdale declared. "Be assured, Mallory, that I shall do all in my power to keep you from knowing her, too."

Four

"Hannah, there you are!" Berinwick exclaimed as his sister swept into the Great Hall, her boot heels clicking across the parquet, her red velvet riding dress whispering around her. "I could not imagine what kept you away so long. I thought to be forced to ride to the Tofars to fetch you home myself."

"Did you?" Hannah replied curtly.

"Indeed," Berinwick said, taking long strides in order to meet her very near the front of the hall. "There is someone here who wishes to visit with you for a bit."

"Someone to visit with me? Well, it had best not be a man," Hannah declared, stripping her riding gloves from her hands with short, impatient movements. "I vow, Will, I have had my fill of gentlemen for one day. You will not believe who has traveled all the way from London to Barren Wycche on the pretense of wishing to bid on Snoop."

"Who?" Berinwick asked, taking her riding gloves from her as she began to unpin her hat.

"Lord Silverdale, that's who. He says he has come to bid on Snoop but not once did he go to look at the beast or any other of the squire's horses, for that matter."

"No?"

"No, he remained beside me outside the Tofars' front entrance until Lancaster arrived with my horse and then, when Lord Mallory would help me to mount, Lord

Silverdale stepped right in before him and lifted me up into the saddle himself. And then he declared that he would escort me home to Blackcastle," she said, tossing her hat to Berinwick to hold along with her gloves as though he were the butler and not the Duke of Berinwick at all. "To protect me, he said. Well, I told him that I required no man's protection, not even Davey Lancaster's, though I am always proud to have Davey beside me when I ride. And I said that did Lord Silverdale wish to escort me thither, he ought to have escorted me hither first. And since he had not—Why are you staring at me so, and with such a look on your face, Will? I am not speaking in tongues."

"I'm astounded, Hannah. I have never heard so many words tumble out from between your lips all at one time."

"No? Well, it is frustration that makes me gabble on. It has been a particularly frustrating morning, Will. And it is highly likely that the afternoon and evening will not be any better because I have invited the Tofars and Anne and Martin and Lord Mallory to dine with us. I did not intend to do so when I departed this morning, but Anne—Anne is so concerned about Lord Mallory—and I promised that I would help her entertain him and all of sudden, there I was, inviting the lot of them to join us for dinner. Yes, and then I invited Lord Silverdale as well, for I could not neglect him when he stood right there, those eyes of his absolutely begging for an invitation. I vow, a gentleman has no right to have such beautiful and expressive eyes as Lord Silverdale has."

"You have still not forgiven Silverdale for declaring his love for you last Season, eh?"

"I do not hold that against him, Will, though I did not believe that he loved me then and I do not believe it to this day. What I hold against him is that he—he—Well, he knows perfectly well why I am angry with him," she said, refusing to tell her brother the tale of Silverdale's offense just as she had refused to tell him when it had occurred. "At any rate, now I must set all Cook's plans aside and we must devise a new menu that can provide for so many people in so short a time. And Gaines must see covers laid for eight in the west dining room. It is an even number, thank goodness. Uneven numbers are so unlucky at dinner parties. Though it is not to be a party precisely—"

"Uh-oh," Berinwick murmured as she paused for breath.

"Uh-oh? Why do you say that, Will?"

"Because I am about to tell you that you are going to have an unlucky number at your dinner table."

"You are not thinking to run off somewhere and abandon me when I have guests coming? Will, you cannot."

"No. I merely feel a pressing need to point out to you that there will be nine covers required in the west dining room rather than eight."

"Nine covers? No, Will. You miscount. There will be the Tofars, the Gazenbys, Lord Mallory, Lord Silverdale, you and me."

"And that odd looking fellow who is chuckling at you from beside father's collection of Roman antiquities," Berinwick added, directing her attention to the officer who stood watching them from the shadows deep in the middle of the Great Hall. "Somehow that particular nodcock tricked me into inviting him to reside here at Blackcastle for a day or two before he continues on to some ridiculously named place in Yorkshire, so I'm afraid we will be forced to feed him as well."

Hannah peered into the shadows to where the collection of Roman antiquities stood encased in glass and guarded by two shining but empty suits of armor.

"I'll not come down to dinner. I'll eat in my room now that I know I will make you uneven," the gentleman said, stepping out of the shadows into a patch of sunlight.

"Lieutenant Elliot? Josiah? It *is* you!" Hannah exclaimed, running to him as though she were a girl of ten and not a young woman of twenty-three. He caught her up in his arms and twirled her around in a circle when she reached him, and when he set her feet back on the floor, he kissed the very tip of her nose.

"Berinwick, are you quite certain that this young woman is Lady Hannah?" he asked over Hannah's shoulder, his hands still firmly on her waist. "The last time I lifted her, she weighed no more than a wet feather."

"The last time you lifted me, Josiah Elliot, I was merely thirteen years old," Hannah declared.

"Yes, and not near as heavy as you are now," Elliot replied with the most engaging smile.

Hannah stamped her foot in protest.

Berinwick guffawed.

Over her shoulder, Hannah gave her brother the most quelling look. Then, she smiled pleasantly up at Elliot. "I expect I *have* altered a dab since last you decided to cease playing at war and pay us a visit, Josiah Elliot. You, on the other hand, have not changed at all. You are *still* a mere lieutenant."

"A hit!" Elliot laughed. "A direct hit! As crisp and clean as any your brother ever inflicted on me. Oh, but I have missed you, little one! Indeed I have!"

The moment the coach left the lane and turned past the circular gatehouse into the Blackcastle drive, a flurry of intense emotions battered at Mallory, causing him to stumble over his words in mid-sentence.

Gazenby took note of it at once and peered around Anne to where Mallory sat on her other side. "Is something wrong, Mal?" he asked.

"No, no, nothing," Mallory assured him. "I was merely distracted for a moment by—by—"

"By the sight of Blackcastle unfolding before your

eyes," Mrs. Tofar said with a proud smile. "We are most accustomed to the sight, of course," she added. "But I knew that you would be impressed, Cousin Mallory."

"Indeed," Mallory agreed, gazing from the coach window at the silent vision of Blackcastle as it took shape before him in the twilight. Four towers cornered a magnificent, yet eclectic, collection of rock and stone that clung to the land like a stubborn toad, refusing to be displaced. "How old is Blackcastle, Mrs. Tofar?"

"No, no, you must call me Cousin Emily, remember?"

"Just so, Cousin Emily," Mallory conceded with a smile.

"The Thornes built the first of the towers and the Great Hall in the ninth century, we believe," Mrs. Tofar replied. "We don't know for certain. Our ancestors did not arrive, you see, until well after the Norman Invasion."

"Celts, the earliest Thornes were," the squire added in explanation. "Came, found the land desirable, settled on it and held it against all odds. Fierce lot, the Thornes."

Fierce, yes, Mallory thought, nodding in reply to Tofar's statement. He could distill from the chaos of emotions that continued to assault him, a great fierceness.

"Well, Hannah is not," Anne proclaimed as the coach pulled up before the great double doors.

"Not what?" Gazenby queried.

"Fierce," Anne replied with a speaking look directed at her husband and her mama and papa as well. "Hannah is the dearest, kindest, sweetest young woman in all the world."

"Of course! Of course she is!" Mrs. Tofar piped up at once. "I do not know a sweeter, more refined young lady than Lady Hannah Thorne, unless it be my own daughter."

"Just so," Gazenby agreed in an instant. "Once you come to know Lady Hannah better, you will wonder that she is a Thorne at all, Mal."

"Lady Hannah is strong and brave for a woman and she is as decisive in her thinking as Berinwick," offered the squire, hesitantly, hoping to take some part in the matchmaking. But he was at a loss for what to say next, his mind chasing after an acceptable statement as frantically as a starving fox would chase after a clucking chicken. "Berinwick, I expect, must strike you as fierce, Mallory. And he is. He is. But he's a good man to his friends. Saved my Annie's life he did, the year our old house burned to the ground. Went right in after Annie and carried her out. Lady Hannah would have done the same had she been—had she been—a gentleman."

"Of all things!" Mrs. Tofar declared, punching her husband in the arm with a fist enclosed in a white linen glove. "Had Lady Hannah been a gentleman, indeed! We are all decidedly blessed that Lady Hannah is not a gentleman!"

Having succeeded in quelling the first onslaught of feelings that had assaulted him, Mallory discovered himself facing another onslaught as Berinwick's butler welcomed them into the residence and led them through the maze of corridors and staircases to the west drawing room.

It's like being in the midst of a war, Mallory thought as he attempted to subdue this new attack on his sensibilities. Difficult enough to deal with the plethora of emotions that haunt Brambles, but this place is extraordinary. I should like to linger here for a time and discover the origins of these sensations. Undoubtedly some of them come from the early rivalries and uprisings and battles. I am in the Marches, after all. But others of them feel much more recent. Not that that should surprise me. This pile of stones is Berinwick's main residence, after all, and Berinwick is—

Mallory's thoughts were interrupted as Gaines ushered the party into the west drawing room and Lady

Hannah stepped forward. She welcomed everyone, then took Mallory's arm and, smiling pleasantly up at him, led him across the room toward the spot where Berinwick stood, his shoulders propped nonchalantly against the edge of a marble mantelpiece, his hands in his pockets.

"Allow me to introduce you to my brother, Lord Mallory," she said as she walked beside him. Her light touch on his sleeve sent a most unexpected tingling up Mallory's arm as high as his shoulder but he attempted to ignore it and smiled as graciously back at her as he could.

What the devil is it about this woman? Mallory wondered, coming to a halt before the duke. What does she do that sends parts and pieces of my body to tingling?

"We need no introduction, Lady Hannah, your brother and I," he said. He offered the duke his hand. "We are already somewhat known to each other."

"In a manner of speaking, we are," Berinwick agreed, taking the proffered hand and shaking it once only.

"You are?" Hannah asked. "But Lord Mallory, you said nothing of having met William when I told you that he was my brother."

"No. I ought to have done, I expect, but I was so relieved that evening to see you there before me—you were such a welcome sight—that all thoughts of Berinwick seemed most inconsequential."

Hannah grinned, causing two tempting dimples to appear, one in each smooth-skinned cheek.

"What?" Mallory asked, his heart stirring at the sight of those dimples. "What have I said to give you such a gleeful look, Lady Hannah? Is it because I was such a coward as to welcome a young lady's assistance rather than be eaten by dogs?"

"I expect the bravest man in all of England would have welcomed a milkmaid's assistance in similar circumstances," Hannah chuckled. "No, it is not that at all. It is merely that I have never heard Will described as inconsequential before. You must come to visit often while you remain with the Tofars, my lord. You will keep Will's head from outgrowing his hat." The dimples remained as Mallory hoped they would. "Will," she continued, "how could you allow me to rattle on and on about Lord Mallory when you were already acquainted with him?"

"Did I? Allow you to rattle on and on?"

"Yes. In fact, you made me describe him down to his very cunning nose."

"My cunning nose?" Mallory grinned.

"Merely cunning because it appears to be straight when in reality it does have a bit of a twist to it," Berinwick explained. "We met in London, Hannah, Mallory and I."

"In Lords," Mallory replied. "A most unfortunate meeting, to say the truth."

"Was it?" asked Berinwick. "How odd you should say so. I would name it several things, but never unfortunate."

"His grace had just finished an extraordinary speech against the uniting of Great Britain and Ireland—a union almost everyone favored and which has since come to be," Mallory explained. "And yet, no one stood up to speak against him. Everyone just sat there in shocked silence. Actually, I think they were all flabbergasted that he had spoken as he had and could not think of a word to say." With a decided upward tilt of his chin, Mallory placed a hand defiantly over Hannah's hand where it rested on his sleeve and met Berinwick's single glaring eye with two emerald eyes that sparkled with silent laughter.

Berinwick cocked a warning eyebrow at him but Mallory did nothing more than immediately shift his gaze to smile down at Hannah. "The silence alone was most remarkable," he explained, his eyes gazing into hers, enjoying the sparkle of humor he discovered there.

"Can you imagine it? The entire House of Lords brought to speechlessness? And just as your brother was making the most splendid exit, he stumbled and crashed to the floor."

"Mallory tripped me," Berinwick declared.

"Not on purpose, Berinwick. I attempted to explain to you that it was an accident. He did not believe me then," Mallory said, giving her hand a pat. "And I think that he does not believe me now, Lady Hannah."

"What did he do?" Hannah queried. "What happened? Oh, Will, you did not challenge Lord Mallory to a duel or anything of the sort? Please say that you did not."

Around them the drawing room had grown quiet and all the faces present but one had taken on a somber aspect.

There goes a perfectly fine match out the window, Gazenby thought with a sigh. Mal ain't likely to marry a girl whose brother has called him out.

I told Emily, thought Squire Tofar. I told her there was likely not a nobleman in England into whom Berinwick had not put the fear of God at one time or another. But she would have it that Gazenby's cousin lived so far off that he had likely never set eyes on our duke.

Oh please, please, don't let Will have challenged him to a duel, Anne prayed, her hands clasped tightly together. How will Hannah and Cousin Mal ever make a match of it if Mal has already been forced to meet William on some foggy heath?

"Of course his grace never challenged Cousin Mallory to a duel," observed Mrs. Tofar loudly. "Cousin Mallory is still alive."

"Quite so, Cousin Emily," Mallory replied. "I simply begged his grace's pardon, helped him to his feet, and he punched me soundly in the nose to show his gratitude for my assistance."

"Broke it," drawled Berinwick. "Blood gushed everywhere. Frightfully messy."

"What's a little blood?" Mallory grinned. "Did not keep me from landing you the devil of a facer, Berinwick."

"You came near to break my jaw with that punch," Berinwick acknowledged.

"Merely came near to it, did I? Should you like to see me try it again?" Mallory asked in a most affable manner.

"*I* should like to see you try it again," Lieutenant Elliot piped up from where he stood, heretofore unnoticed, before the drawing room windows. "I missed it the first time."

That set Berinwick to laughing and Mallory as well, and by the time Lord Silverdale arrived, resplendent in a blue velvet coat and buff-colored breeches, his blond curls in studied disarray and his turquoise eyes agleam, the conversation had turned to other matters entirely.

They went in to dinner thoroughly satisfied with each other's company, the ladies smiling, the gentlemen in good humor. The informal atmosphere of the hastily arranged entertainment carried through to the dinner table itself, where Lieutenant Elliot took the seat on Berinwick's right hand and Silverdale the seat on his left while Mallory discovered himself tucked neatly away between Anne and Lady Hannah. The squire and Mrs. Tofar beamed at the arrangement and Gazenby, at Anne's other side, beamed back at them. Perhaps, he thought, this matchmaking business is not going to prove as difficult as I imagined. Mal looks perfectly comfortable beside Lady Hannah.

The only dinner guest who looked the least bit uncomfortable was Silverdale, his glance drawn to the foot of the table each time Hannah's voice reached his ears, each time Mallory or Anne caused Hannah to chuckle, each time the motion of Hannah's head or hand seized his attention.

"In love with her, are you, Silverdale?" Elliot queried, cutting off his conversation with Berinwick in midsentence and addressing the gentleman whose constant inattention to his own end of the table was proving most distracting.

"I beg your pardon?" Silverdale replied, startled at being addressed at all.

"Elliot asked if you are in love with Hannah," Berinwick repeated. "Are you?"

"I fail to see that it is any of—"

"My business?" asked Berinwick with a slightly raised eyebrow.

"Lieutenant Elliot's business," Silverdale replied. "Of course it is your business, Berinwick. I mean—If I was—If I thought she would have me—If I were to wish permission to—"

"Definitely in love with her," Elliot commented. "Poor fellow cannot so much as complete a sentence. Go back to mooning over her then, Silverdale. Berinwick and I will attempt to carry on without you."

"We will?" queried Berinwick.

"Of course, we will. Not fair to distract him with conversation as long as Lady Hannah is within his sight. Especially not when she is seated beside a marquis who happens, I expect, to be unattached. Is he?"

"Unattached?" Berinwick queried. "Yes. It's a plot, Elliot. What you see from this vantage point are Annie and Mrs. Tofar in the midst of matchmaking. Gazenby's in on it as well, I think. Or at least he knows all about it and has not forbidden the attempt. And the squire is doing his best not to disrupt the plan. Tofar is always to be counted upon not to disrupt his wife's attempts at matchmaking if he can possibly avoid it."

"And you?"

"I am attempting not to quash their entire plan by breaking Mallory's nose for him again. Speaking of plans, Elliot, are you home to stay?"

"No. Shouldn't think so. Things are heating up again with France. Declare himself emperor sooner or later, Napoleon will and then, if he holds true to character, he'll attempt to extend his power across the entire continent. Bound to be a considerable lot of blood spilled soon. Some of it mine."

"Never," Berinwick frowned.

"From your lips to God's ear, Will. But I've come through numerous battles unscathed—well, in general unscathed—and I rather think my luck may be running out. So I took the time I was given to come home and see m'brother. He's got himself a wife at last, Nathaniel has, and a son. I'm an uncle. Never expected to be an uncle. It's a bit of a joy, actually. You'll discover it when Lady Hannah marries."

"If she marries."

"She will. Such a treasure cannot be intended to remain unmarried forever. She'll find the right fellow. At any rate, having spent a fortnight plaguing Nathaniel and his wife, I'm on my way to Yorkshire to visit Lily and her vicar." Elliot laughed. "We've something in common now, Berinwick. Your mother has married a rector and my stepsister has married a vicar. Who would have thought it?"

"Not I, I assure you."

Hannah looked to the head of the table at the sound of Elliot's laughter and noting the smile playing about her brother's lips, she smiled widely as well.

"You are very fond of your brother," Mallory observed, setting aside his fork and centering his attention fully on Hannah. "Cousin Anne is fond of him as well, I think. You're both smiling because he's being adequately entertained."

"Because he is being adequately entertained and because his lips are twitching. Josiah will have him laughing outright soon."

"A duke and a dragoon. Who would have guessed?"

"Oh, Josie is much more than a dragoon. He is a good friend. He and Will were schoolmates. As I recall the story, Josiah and his brother Nathaniel took on five other boys in Will's defense once. Sent them off tattered and torn and crying, too."

"I would not have thought your brother ever required defending from anyone."

"Well, he did. He lost his eye when he was three years old and was sent away to school when he was six to face a world filled with boys who thought him freakish and treated him so. They plagued him ceaselessly, but Will survived and has conquered them all in the end."

The tone of her voice set Mallory's heart to pounding. It was filled with such love and pride and there was not a tinge of pity to be heard. He could not help but imagine how it must feel to be so loved and admired by someone like Lady Hannah Thorne. "He's a lucky gentleman, your brother," Mallory murmured. "A very lucky gentleman, to have a sister like you."

"Do you think so, Lord Mallory?" Hannah replied. "How odd. Because I think I am the lucky one, to have a brother like Will."

The cloth was off the table, the ladies had withdrawn and the gentlemen were deep in conversation over their port when the first tremor rippled through Mallory. The crystal wine glass began to shiver in his hand. He set it down at once. From beneath hooded lids he peered at the gentlemen around him. None of them, apparently, had taken note. Thank goodness for that, he thought. Think I'm a veritable lunatic do they see me trembling without the least reason. What the devil made me do that? He studied his right hand, now flat on the table. It trembled still, though barely so. He attempted to ignore it and directed his attention to Squire Tofar who was just then speaking of the murdered girl—the girl of whom Lady Hannah had spoken earlier that morning.

"She was a good little thing before she went off to London," the squire said. "Not the brightest candle in the chandelier and frightened of her own shadow, I daresay, but a good girl, Meg was, nonetheless."

"How old was she?" Silverdale queried, his turquoise eyes fastened on the port in his glass as he turned the crystal in a circular motion. "I mean to say, when you took the girl to London, Berinwick, how old was she?"

"I don't know for certain," Berinwick replied, his hand tightening around his own glass. "I don't keep track of the age of the maids who work in my establishments, Silverdale. Young, is all I know. Perhaps younger than Hannah and Annie. Sixteen, seventeen, I should think. Why?"

"Well, you know how it is, Berinwick. A young girl—the City—She'd not be the first servant girl to run off in hope of an adventure with an excessively happy ending. Like to think of themselves as creatures in a faery tale, young serving girls do."

"They do?" Squire Tofar fixed his attention entirely upon Silverdale. "How is that?"

"Oh, you know," Silverdale murmured. "See themselves as poor little maids who will one day meet a lord and the fellow will fall in love with them despite their antecedents. This Meg most likely met a fellow and expected him to marry her. Expected to live in a castle and be rich and happy forever after."

"Shouldn't think Meg would do that," Tofar replied. "Not Meg Thistledown. Frightened of a loud sneeze, Meggy. Not in the least prone to adventure. Something frightened her into running off from you in London, Berinwick. That's what I think. And something else frightened her into running back home again."

"Perhaps you frightened her, Berinwick," Silverdale suggested, peering through lowered lids at the duke. "Lord knows you've frightened a goodly number of stalwart young gentlemen."

"Have I?"

"Yes, indeed. I know some of them personally. Quicken, for instance. Now there's a gentleman was heels over head in love with your sister, until he discovered she *was* your sister."

"I have never so much as set eyes upon a Quicken."

"No, but your reputation reached his ears. It was the first Season that you took Lady Hannah to town. Rumors were floating everywhere that you had killed an innkeeper along the road. Shot him dead where he stood, I believe they said, because he had had the audacity to suggest that you keep your hands off his serving girl. She was his daughter, as I recall, the serving girl."

"Rubbish," Berinwick replied.

"Yes, of course," Silverdale said with a most pacifying look, "but Quicken could not have known it. And there are endless numbers of Quickens out there, unable to tell gossip from gospel. All I'm saying, Berinwick, is that perhaps this young woman heard one or two of the rumors and, being the timid little thing that Squire Tofar has named her, she ran off in fear of you."

"Pshaw," Squire Tofar commented on an exhaled breath. "She were born and raised on Blackcastle land, Meg Thistledown."

"And?" Silverdale queried.

"And the gel would not have believed any such rumors of our duke. We none of us do, you know," Tofar said with a frown. "Oh, the people hereabouts have been known to start a rumor or two about our duke, but 'tis only fools take them seriously. And Meg Thistledown was never a fool."

"No, she was not," Berinwick agreed. "She was not the brightest lamp in the parlor, but she was not without a wick and a glimmer either. What is it, Mallory?" he added. "You don't like my port? Or my conversation?"

"What? No, no, nothing wrong with the port."

"Doesn't drink much," Silverdale commented. "Never known Mal to down more than a glass or two. Doesn't talk much either unless he knows what he is talking about."

"The two of you are good friends, eh?" Lieutenant Elliot asked.

"Relatives, actually," replied Silverdale.

"Only by marriage," Mallory was moved to protest. "Not a drop of blood shared between us. Silverdale's mother married my uncle after Silverdale's father passed on."

"Died in a frightful accident, my father," Silverdale added with a sigh. "Gryphon fell on the old fellow and squashed him."

"A gryphon?" Elliot asked.

"A stone gryphon that had sat above the door of the Silverdale residence in Deerly Pond for years and years," Mallory explained. "Most unusual thing. Just decided to jump down from the roof one day and flatten the poor old gentleman."

"When you look at it in a certain way, it was the best thing that ever happened to m'mother and me," Silverdale said, downing what remained of his port in one gulp. "After a respectable time, mother married the man of her dreams and I got both m'father's title and Mallory for a cousin."

"And was it the best thing that ever happened to you, Mallory?" Berinwick asked, his single eye fixed on the marquis, urging the man to raise his own gaze and meet it. "Gaining Silverdale for a cousin, I mean."

"Not particularly," Mallory replied, doing exactly as Berinwick wished, meeting the duke's gaze straight on. "I do think we have fiddled about long enough, Berinwick. We ought to go and join the ladies, don't you think?"

Berinwick nodded. "Why not, Mallory? Why not?"

Mallory thought to approach Lady Hannah immediately after the gentlemen entered the drawing room and engage her in conversation about this pile of stones that was Blackcastle. The tremor that had afflicted him after dinner had departed, but a decided uneasiness remained like a voice whispering inside his skull that was not a voice at all and could never actually be heard or understood. There was something about Blackcastle that was disrupting his general good nature and though he would never admit as much to Lady Hannah, it was likely she would hold a clue to whatever it was. She would be pleased to speak with him about the history of her home. Most young ladies were proud of their families and their ancestors and many took great pleasure in telling all the tales they knew. Lady Hannah, he suspected, would be one of them. But before Mallory could cross the carpeting to the chair in which Lady Hannah sat, Silverdale slipped in ahead of him, going so far as to settle himself on the footstool at Lady Hannah's feet. Mallory altered his direction on the instant and went to sit beside Mrs. Tofar.

"You will not think me forward, I hope," Silverdale murmured, his eyes clearly begging for Hannah's understanding. "I would not have settled precisely here, but I could see that Mallory was bound in this direction and I thought it best to thwart him in his objective."

"Why?" Hannah asked without the least hint of a smile.

"Well, because he was your partner all through dinner

and I have not had the opportunity all evening to speak with you privately. Besides, once you come to know him, he's a dull fellow, Mallory. He will put you directly to sleep with his droning on about one thing or another. I am amazed you did not nod off in the midst of the main course. I have known him for years and there is not an adventurous bone in Mallory's body. He is all horses, horses, horses, Mal is. That's why he's here, is it not? To bid on Squire Tofar's Snip?"

"The beast's name is Snoop."

"Snoop. Yes. I beg your pardon. But that is why he has come down from Brambles—to bid on the horse?"

"Yes."

"Just so. And if he did find something else to speak of at dinner—aside from horses—that means he has likely exhausted his supply of conversation. Had I not slipped in here ahead of him, he would be regaling you with tales of one animal or another until you could no longer bear it and fell asleep."

"And what do you intend to speak of to keep me awake, Lord Silverdale?"

"You," Silverdale replied at once. "And me. I should like the opportunity to speak with you about all that has occurred between us, Lady Hannah. I should like to apologize once again, with all my heart. It is why I came to Barren Wycche and hoped so heartily for an invitation to Blackcastle. You did never speak to me of Blackcastle but once, you know, and you were quite angry at the time. It took me a good while after that to gather my wits and my courage about me and come to this place. You told me that evening that did I ever show my face at Blackcastle, you would be pleased to blacken both my eyes, break my nose, and abandon me on the moor for the dogs to chew upon."

"Yes, well, I had had my fill of you."

"But you have relented," Silverdale said, looking up at

her like a hopeful puppy. "You have relented, have you not? You did invite me to join this dinner party."

"Only because of the woeful look in your eyes as you stood before me outside Tofar House. For no other reason. I have forgiven you your indiscretion, but I am not about to be courted by you again."

"Unfair," Silverdale protested, his hands reaching out to take hold of hers. "I love you, my dearest Lady Hannah. I have loved you from the day we first met. I admit that I made a dreadful mistake. I ought not to have done what I did, but I shall not do it again. Give me one more opportunity to win your heart. Please do. I beg it of you."

"Lord Silverdale is disturbing Lady Hannah no end," Mrs. Tofar said quietly to Mallory.

"He is?"

"Indeed. Only look at her."

"I am. She is allowing Silverdale to hold her hands, Cousin Emily. I cannot think she would do that did she find the fellow disturbing."

"She is simply determined not to make a scene over his forwardness," Mrs. Tofar declared. "What he holds are hands that have turned themselves into fists and he will be very lucky if our Hannah does not give way to her natural inclinations and plant him a punch right on his nose. Oh!" cried Mrs. Tofar, suddenly waving her hand before her lips as if it were a fan and she could whisk her words away with the breeze it produced. "Oh, my goodness! Did I say that aloud? About Lady Hannah planting Lord Silverdale a punch on the nose?"

"Indeed," Mallory replied, his eyes alight with sudden laughter. "She would be giving way to her natural inclinations, you said, should she do so. Learned the art of it from her brother, I should think. Put a decided bend in my nose, Berinwick did. No, no, don't attempt any further explanation, Cousin Emily. I rather like the idea of a young lady who knows how to flatten a fellow's nose. It's a bit terrifying, of course, but intriguing, too. Perhaps you're correct. Perhaps I ought to go over there and interrupt their conversation. It would be the polite thing—to go to her rescue—if she really does wish Silverdale to go away. She will not plant me a facer for going to her aid, eh?"

"Never."

"Well, then, if you will excuse me," Mallory said, a smile curving his lips upward as he rose from the chair beside Mrs. Tofar and stepped across the room in Hannah's direction. Of all things, he thought. A young lady whose natural inclinations are to punch a man for holding her hands. Well, and I knew she was extraordinary when she and her groom came riding to my rescue on the moor. But what the devil am I going to say to free her from Sly's advances? I have never attempted to do such a thing in my life.

"Mal is off and running at last," Gazenby whispered in Anne's ear. "Your mama has said something to him to make him bestir himself, and thank goodness for it. I thought we should be forced to spend the rest of the evening watching that wretch Silverdale work his magic."

"What magic?" Anne asked, setting a strand of hair that had wriggled free of its pins back behind her ear.

"Have you never noticed? Sly possesses a certain magic with the ladies," Gazenby replied. "It has to do with his eyes and the way he uses them to speak silent thoughts. All the ladies find it thrilling the way he does that."

"They do? All of the ladies?"

"Well, all of the ladies I ever saw him approach."

"You were merely one Season in London, Martin, and Lord Silverdale has been on the town for years. Certainly, though you were not present, there must have been one or two ladies who could not be cajoled into a preference for him simply by the beauty and expression of his eyes."

"I hope there is at least one," Gazenby murmured, "because Mal and Hannah looked to get along famously at dinner. I should never have thought of a match between them had you not suggested it, Annie. I should never have imagined a match between Mal and any woman."

"Why not?" Anne asked, astonished. "Certainly Cousin Mal must marry someone."

"Must he? He has never thought he must. There is his brother Harry, you know, and his brother James, as well, to see that the title is passed on."

"Marriage is not only about providing an heir, Martin."

"Yes, I have learned that, my dear. But Mal has been raised to think it is. He has been told from the cradle that it is his duty to provide an heir and a spare. And he has never had any intention of providing either. Says he has two brothers can provide those. Fond of horses, Mal is. Not fond of women. Thinks them weak, silly, useless things."

"He is quite out there," Anne replied with a glare.

"He is. He is. And he admits that you are not weak, silly or useless. But he says that you are an exception to the rule. Possibly the only exception. You have met his mother, Annie, and his sisters. What would you think of women in general were you constantly surrounded by such as they?"

"I would think women weak, silly, useless things," Anne replied with a sigh. "But Lady Hannah is not at all like those ladies, Martin. You know she is not."

"Well, I believe she is not. I take your word for it, because you have known her ever so much longer than I. And I wish Mal to find a young lady to love, just as I love you. There is nothing better in the entire world, Annie, than to love a woman with all your heart—a woman who loves you back in the same fashion. Though how Mal is ever going to fall in love with Hannah if Silverdale intends to monopolize her all the while Mal is here, I cannot think."

"Lord Silverdale will not monopolize her. You and I and Mama and Papa will see that he does not."

"Did you take note of it?" Lieutenant Elliot asked, watching as Mallory came to a stop beside Hannah's chair and stood looking down at the girl, his hands stuffed into his breeches pockets.

"No," Berinwick replied. "I was intent on my conversation with Tofar and Silverdale. Are you certain?"

"Hand began to shake as if he had the palsy," Elliot declared with a curt nod. "Had to set his glass aside and flatten his hand against the table, and even then it trembled."

"And it began when Tofar and I began to discuss Meg's murder?"

"Just then. As if the mere mention of it touched something inside of him."

"Perhaps it did, Elliot. Perhaps he knew a young girl once who was wickedly murdered."

"Or perhaps he knew Meg and did her in."

"No."

"How can you be so certain, Berinwick?"

"Because he never set foot outside of Tofar House once Hannah took him there. Anne told Hannah she was certain of that."

"Then perhaps he proposed Meg's end to one of his minions and sat quietly at Tofar's while his wishes were carried out."

"And perhaps Meg fell in love with you, Elliot, and followed you from battlefield to battlefield until you tired of her. You brought her back to England with you and did her in yourself. You did not appear upon my doorstep until this morning, you know. Said you rode the entire night. Perhaps you lied about that." Berinwick's single midnight eye bored into Elliot's two blue ones. Then the duke lowered his head and ran his hand through his hair, unleashing a riot of dark curls. "I ought not have said that, Josiah," he muttered. "I have known you since school days, you and your brother both. You have always been honorable gentlemen, even to me."

"You mean to say that we did never make a jest of you, Nathaniel and I, that we stood by you when it came to spilling a drop or two of blood from some bully's nose, whether we agreed that you were a regular cyclops or not."

"Just so."

"Well, but that's no reason to refuse to suspect me of the girl's murder now, Will. I'm grown, you know. Soldiering has changed me a great deal. And I have no one to say where I was when the thing happened."

"No one?"

"Not unless you discover some fashion in which to speak with my horse, no," Elliot replied with a stubborn gleam in his eyes. "You ought to think about that."

"I don't wish to think about it."

"But you will."

"Hannah loves you. I dare not think about it."

"And perhaps Hannah will come to love someone else as well," Elliot pointed out, nodding his head toward the chair in which Hannah sat. She was gazing up just then at Mallory, her eyes alight, her lips quivering with laughter as Silverdale, still seated on the footstool at her feet, bowed his head and shook it slowly from side to side. "Mallory has said something to make her like him just now and Silverdale cannot believe it. Do you see?"

"Yes. What I don't see is the object of this lesson with which you seem determined to present me."

"It's merely that evil may disguise itself as innocence, my lad. It's merely that men—and women, too—may be taken in by, and develop a fondness for, the most disreputable people do those people present themselves in an acceptable fashion. It's a lesson I should not have to teach you. You know from experience, old fellow, that what a man presents on the outside is not always what lives in his heart. I learned that particular lesson first from you."

"Then I ought to suspect you and Mallory both, and every gentleman who has come to Barren Wycche for Tofar's auction, and Gazenby and Tofar himself."

"Until you find reason not to do so. But let me point out one more thing to you, Berinwick. Neither I, nor Gazenby, nor Tofar began to tremble when the discussion of the girl's murder began after dinner. Only one gentleman did that. Mallory."

Five

Hannah could not help but laugh as she sat on the window seat with her legs curled beneath her and gazed out into the darkness. By courtesy of the slice of moon and a multitude of stars, shadows flitted here and there across the lawn. Some hid behind the sheep. Others dodged into and out of the maze—a maze formed of holly bushes, hawthorne, and wild roses— that one of her many-greated grandmothers had planted centuries ago. And still other shadows hovered in midair above the crumbling rock wall that formed the western boundary of the park, dividing it from the wild, unplanted field beyond.

"Of all the things to say," Hannah murmured when her laughter faded. "That my eyes put him in mind of his favorite horse. Of his horse! Now there's the way to a lady's heart! Still, that particular comparison did serve to make Lord Silverdale speechless for which I was truly grateful. And perhaps Lord Mallory has no intention of discovering a way into my heart. Why should he, after all? He is a handsome man and wealthy and a marquis to boot. He might ask any young lady to be his bride, and be certain of being accepted."

No, he was not searching for a way into my heart, Hannah decided, remembering the laughter in his emerald eyes even before he had compared her eyes to his horse's. He merely thought to come and rescue me from

Lord Silverdale's unwanted attentions. Though how he knew that I had no desire to be the object of Lord Silverdale's artifices, I cannot think. Perhaps it was Mrs. Tofar sent Lord Mallory to me. Yes, it must have been. She must have noticed that Lord Silverdale took hold of my hands and thought it most forward of the man. It *was* most forward of him. Silverdale is such a presumptuous twit. He fancies himself irresistible to all women with his uniquely perfect eyes, and his perfect face, and his perfect hair, and his perfectly formed body. I've no doubt he expected me to swoon and plead for him to take me back again when he took my hands into his own. He is most fortunate that I did not bloody his perfect nose for him.

At least Lord Mallory is not perfect, Hannah thought, leaning back amongst the multitude of pillows strewn about the window seat. His eyes are as green as the holly in winter, but they are not uniquely green and they do not latch onto one and suggest things without one word passing his lips. No, and Lord Mallory's face is not perfect either. His brow is rather nice when all those dark curls, some of them lighter than others, some gleaming with red and gold, come tumbling down over it, but his chin is much too strong and stubborn. I did like how lean and soft his cheeks seemed in the lamplight, but his nose quite distracts one from his cheeks with that little turn it takes.

It might do Lord Silverdale a world of good to have his nose broken—or bloodied at the very least. And oh, how I should like to be the woman to do it. I ought to have done it months ago, and would have, too, if we had been here at Blackcastle at the time and not in Town. I cannot think why London is so very dampening to my spirit. I cannot be the only lady who has ever harbored the desire to punch some fellow in the nose. No, I am certain that I am not. "Though I am possibly the only Lady of

Quality likely to lose my patience and actually do it," she
sighed. "And I would have done tonight. One more un-
spoken word from Lord Silverdale's eyes and I would have
pulled my hands free from his and bent his nose smack
around on itself. How lucky he was that Lord Mallory
came to his rescue."

Mallory was pacing the width of his bedchamber. His
nightcap, pushed back on the very crown of his head,
seemed likely to go tumbling to the floor at any moment. His nightshirt billowed out around his bare
ankles. His soft leather slippers, made to his own design
by the most fashionable cobbler in York, slap-slapped
across the floor, muffled by the carpet, but still audible.
His hands clasped behind his back, his thoughts directed
inward, he was unaware of all around him—which was
most likely why he smacked his knee against the clothespress. "Damnation!" he hissed, hoping the noise had
awakened no one. He rubbed at the knee, then hobbled
over to the bed and climbed up to sit on the edge of it.
His feet dangled above the floor. His slippers dangled
from the tips of his toes.

"She does not find Silverdale at all appealing," he muttered. "Not her. She is intelligent and funny and quite
rational for a woman. And if once she did allow Sly to
court her as he claims she did, it was merely a whim on
her part. She sees right through him, recognizes all his
posturing and posing for precisely what they are. There
is no reason to worry about Lady Hannah falling into
such traps as Silverdale knows how to set. So why can I
not cease thinking about the lady?"

But he knew perfectly well why—because despite his
determination never to fall heels over head in love with
any woman, never to end up a veritable calf-eyed nodcock as most of his friends had done—as Gazenby had

done—there was nevertheless the oddest sensation wriggling about in the region of his heart. A sensation that hinted at the possibility that not only was he capable of falling in love, but had already done so.

Mallory frowned. He nibbled at his lower lip. He kicked his feet into the air and sent his slippers flying across the room. Then he fell back on the bed and in the glow of the lamplight, stared up at the little cherubs cavorting about on his bedchamber ceiling, and sighed.

There is something most extraordinary about Lady Hannah Thorne, he thought as one of the cherubs inexplicably assumed Hannah's face. Disconcerted, he attempted to blink the cherub back into its own face, but the tiny angel would not be altered. "Well, I'll be deviled," Mallory muttered. "Lady Hannah is everywhere I look tonight." And even if I don't wish to be, I am pleased that she is, too, he thought. Her eyes are like the evening skies threaded with stars, and her hair like tethered feathers in a high wind. And her voice low and husky like secrets whispered in a cupboard. How can I not be pleased to see her everywhere? I feel as though I have known her all my life, as though I have never been without the sight of her in my mind. Her smile takes my breath away.

"All these things I might have said to her and more," he sighed. "And what did I say? That her eyes put me in mind of my favorite horse, that's what I said." She must think me a lunatic or a dunce or both! he decided with a groan. And yet, she laughed when I said it. She was not in the least offended, regardless of the despairing look Silverdale sent me and all the tut-tutting he did to convince her that she ought to take offense. And in the end, we did manage to have a sterling conversation, she and I. It was almost as interesting as speaking to another fellow. No wonder Silverdale declares he is serious about this particular lady and determined to have her. If all pretty women were as composed and rational and humorous as Lady Hannah, I should be inclined to consider marrying one of them myself.

"Of course, I am not going to do that," Mallory informed the cherub with Lady Hannah's face aloud and instantly. "I am not the marrying type. Not me. I have had enough women tangled about my feet, acting and speaking in totally irrational ways from morning till night, to keep me from ever stepping into the parson's mousetrap. I have learned the lesson Father unwittingly taught me and learned it well. I will never say 'I do.' Never. Not to any woman. Because I don't. I definitely do not."

But I am going to seek out Lady Hannah's company while I'm here, he thought, tugging the coverlet and the top sheet out from under him and then pulling them back over him. I shall make a point of it—as often as I can. I'll be damned if I am going to give Sly an open field with her. He will plague the woman to death with his flirting. It's my duty to extricate Lady Hannah from Sly's company as often as I can. It's the noble thing to do—and the honorable thing as well. I will make it a point to take up as much of her time as I can so she need not deal with Silverdale overmuch. And besides, there has been a woman murdered right on Blackcastle land. Some man must be present always to protect Lady Hannah just in case this murderer is some madman who thinks to strike again and does not care what woman he kills.

It did occur to Mallory that Lady Hannah's brother was quite capable of protecting her, but he shunted that thought aside because everyone he knew thought Berinwick, himself, a madman—fierce and violent—and so, of course, not at all to be depended upon to act rationally or in Lady Hannah's best interests. *Why, Berinwick might well have murdered that poor Meg girl himself.* The disturbing thought entered Mallory's mind so abruptly that it took him a full minute to digest it. Berinwick? A murderer? No, he told himself silently. Everything I know about that particular gentleman is fraught with rumor and innuendo, stories of duels and murders have tagged along behind Berinwick for years and years now, but not a one of them has ever proved true. Not one. He is not all that he appears to be, the Duke of Berinwick. But until I am certain just what he is, I shall look to Lady Hannah's safety myself. Thus having decided his future course, Mallory closed his eyes and sought sleep.

Shortly after five-thirty the following morning, the Reverend Mr. Dempsey, in buckskin breeches and white linen shirt, combing his gold and silver hair hurriedly with his fingers, opened the rectory door. "Langton?" he asked at the sight of the harried looking elderly man on his doorstep. "Langton? What the devil's wrong? I know you're an early riser, but the sun is barely up. You've no business to be—Good heavens! Mrs. Langton has not fallen ill, has she? The girls are not—?"

"No, no, m'family be well as ever Mr. Dempsey. Eulie be coming later to fix breakfast like she always does. I left her the dogcart to drive, I did, and rode old Roddy here."

"I see. Well, come in then, Harvey, and tell me what brings you pounding on my door at this hour," Dempsey said, stepping aside and urging his self-appointed deacon into the tiny vestibule. "It must be something of great import for you to knock me up before the sun has actually risen."

"It is. It is," Langton replied, following Dempsey into the front parlor and taking a seat in one of the two wing chairs before the cold hearth.

Dempsey lowered himself into its mate. "You won't

mind if I pull my boots on while we speak, eh, Langton?" he queried, tugging one scuffed riding boot out from beneath the chair. "Cannot remember how they got here—my boots, I mean—under this blessed chair. But I'm pleased I've found them. Floors are still cold in the mornings, you know."

"Let me help," Langton replied, beginning to stand again.

"No. No. Sit down, Harvey. I have been donning my own boots since I was four. Of course, they were a sight cleaner when I was four. I have not got around to putting a polish on these as yet this week. Tell me what brings you."

"I have come to tell you to ride straight to Blackcastle, Mr. Dempsey. Right this minute."

"Something has happened to Berinwick?" Dempsey guessed, standing to stamp his foot down into one boot, then bending to tug the other out from its hiding place. He seated himself and began, hurriedly, to pull on the second boot. "Or has something happened to Hannah? Great heavens, not Hannah! Is it one of the grooms? Tom Hasty? What's happened, Langton? Part your lips and spit it out, man. And why have you word of it before I do? I am miles nearer Blackcastle than you are and I am Berinwick's stepfather as well. He ought to have sent word directly here."

"The word did not come from Blackcastle," Langton replied. "The word come from the Fallen Dog."

"From the pub? Langton, of all things! You came riding out here at this hour of the morning because of some gossip you heard at the pub?"

"It do not be gossip, Mr. Dempsey. It be real. It were my son-in-law, Giles Pervis, himself, and Angser the woodcutter with him, who told me. They seed the fellow step off the mail coach and order the room what was saved up for him themselves. An' they heard it, too, right from the fellow's own mouth when he come into the Dog last evening."

"Saw what? Heard what?" Dempsey queried, no longer as anxious as he had been because the villagers of Barren Wycche were notorious for making up stories about their duke and through the years he had learned to take most of what they reported about Berinwick with a dose of skepticism. The rumors, however, had always provided him with a good deal of entertainment just as they provided the villagers with what had always seemed a jolly pastime.

"Come on the mailcoach, he did, Mr. Dempsey. A tall, thin sort of fellow all dressed in black like a parson. Well, like some parsons," Langton said, exempting the Reverend Mr. Dempsey, his sky blue coat and his buckskin breeches from the dress of the preachers who had dispensed a multitude of sermons in the village square for the twenty years before Mr. Dempsey's arrival. "Leading it into the inn, he were, when Giles saw him. Wondered at it, Giles did. But then he thought the fellow had come, like the others, to bid at Squire Tofar's auction and had just brought it along with him. No accounting for what people will do, you know. Especially men who be horse-mad. But then the fellow come into the Fallen Dog and got to drinking, and it turned out he did not come to bid at Squire Tofar's auction at all. No, he did not."

"What did he come to do?"

"Come to deliver it into our duke's hands, he did. Told Giles as he was bound for Blackcastle first thing this morning, which is why I come riding out here so early-like."

"And what is it, Langton?"

"What be what?"

"The *it* that the fellow brought with him and is planning on delivering to Blackcastle."

"Why, it be a child. Didn't I say as much?"

"A child?" Dempsey's eyebrows soared upward. "What on earth are you saying? Begin again."

"I be saying that some bloke be bound and determined to deliver a child into our duke's hands. And he be bound and determined to do it first thing this morning, too."

"But what child, Harvey? Whose child?"

"I expect I don't know that for certain, Mr. Dempsey. I expect, I don't. But Giles, he did say that it had dark curls and dark eyes, just like our duke, and the gentleman what kept it in his care were certain that Blackcastle were where it belonged."

Dempsey stared at Langton as though the man had just announced the commencement of Armageddon.

Dempsey rode as if every wild dog on Little Mynd moor were giving him chase. At the end of the Blackcastle drive, he leaped from Norville's back, took the front steps as quickly as a gentleman of his years might be expected to take them if he were in a veritable panic, and sounded the door knocker over and over without the least pause until Harold Belowes pulled open one of the double doors and stood staring at the parson in amazement.

"Quickly, Belowes. I must speak to Berinwick at once."

The footman wiped the amazement from his face and nodded. "Yes, sir, Mr. Dempsey. Come in, sir. His grace has not yet arisen. I shall tell Mr. Nordstrom that you require his grace's presence as soon as possible. You be welcome to wait in the morning room."

"Berinwick's still abed?"

"Yes, sir. It be merely a quarter past six o'clock in the morning, Mr. Dempsey. Even the sun be just barely risen."

"Just so. I forgot. But I'll not wait in the morning room, Belowes. And do not bother Berinwick's valet. I will go to his grace's bedchamber and wake him myself."

Belowes' face took on an ashen aspect. "Wake him yourself, Mr. Dempsey?"

"Indeed. Lead the way, Harold."

"But—but Mr. Dempsey—"

"I realize he's likely to throw a lamp at my head," Dempsey assured the flustered footman. "It doesn't matter if he does. I must speak to him at once and not in Nordstrom's presence or anyone else's for that matter."

Harold Belowes had been in service at Blackcastle for more than thirty years. He had risen from fireboy to the position of first footman in that time. He had served this Berinwick and this Berinwick's father. He had been present when first the Reverend Mr. Dempsey had come tramping across Blackcastle land in search of his old hound, Theophilus. Had, in fact, introduced the Reverend Mr. Dempsey to her grace, the Duchess of Berinwick, on Thrwick Hill. He had seen murder and mayhem in his time at Blackcastle. He had plotted plots and thwarted plots and plotted other plots. His heart was and always had been loyal and true to the Thornes of Barren Wycche and he was as proud and protective of them as any man could be. But at that precise moment, he was truly hesitant to lead the Reverend Mr. Dempsey through the regular rabbit warren of Blackcastle corridors and staircases to the master bedchamber. His feet did move, however, and his legs carried him, with Mr. Dempsey on his heels, in that general direction.

"He has not done anything untoward, our duke?" Belowes asked over his shoulder.

"I don't know," Dempsey replied. "I think so, but perhaps I'm wrong, Harold."

"You bean't about to shoot him or anything, eh, Mr. Dempsey?"

"Shoot him? No. You know I would never shoot him. Great heavens, I'm a man of God, a peacemaker."

"You would have shot that Mr. Hurley person."

"No, I would not. I am not good with pistols. I am much better with my fists. Besides that was nearly ten years ago. I am a good deal older now and less prone to act before I think. And I am his grace's stepfather, for goodness sake. What on earth makes you think I would ever do Berinwick the least harm?"

"The look on your face, Mr. Dempsey. You be looking like a gentleman at his wit's end. And, you be wishing to see our duke alone, before he is even awake."

"No, no, it's not because of anything he's done, Belowes. Well, it might be because of something that he's done, but that's neither here nor there. I've come to warn him of something and to see what aid I can give him in the matter."

"Oh," Belowes replied, leading Dempsey up a short staircase, around a corner and up a steeper staircase. "That's different then." Belowes led Dempsey down a short corridor to a door at the very end of it and knocked for him. He knocked again. He was about to knock a third time when Dempsey prevented him by taking hold of his wrist.

"Never mind, Belowes. I doubt you'll raise him if he was up late last evening. I'll just go in and shake him awake myself."

"He will punch you in the jaw," Belowes declared with authority. "Even Mr. Nordstrom knows better than to shake our duke awake."

"Well, how does Nordstrom raise him, then?"

"He don't," Belowes replied. "He did once, but he never did again. Waits until he is summoned, now, Mr. Nordstrom does."

Hannah wrapped her robe around her, hurried into her slippers and rushed out into the corridor. She paused just outside her bedchamber door for a moment, listening. A great thump and a groan met her ears. It came, she was certain, from the direction of her brother's bedchamber. A man's voice took the name of the Lord in vain, she thought, though she could not quite make out the words. She stepped back into her room, seized one of the heavy silver candlesticks from off her dressing table, and hurried back into the corridor again. The dim light of morning entered hesitantly through the narrow window at the end of the hallway and lit her way as she rushed toward the short staircase that led down to Will's chambers. Surely, she thought as her slippers whispered along the carpeting, surely, even though it sounds as though someone has come into this house and is presently attacking my brother in his bed-chamber, it cannot be so. Will is having a bad dream merely. A loud bad dream. But she clung tightly to the candlestick just in case she was mistaken.

Berinwick's door stood open. She could see that much from the opposite end of the corridor where she paused. Well, whoever is in there, she thought with mounting dread that some villain had managed to gain entry to Blackcastle, discovered her brother's whereabouts and attacked him, whoever it is, he cannot have departed as quickly as this. No, and he must depart as he came, through this very corridor. And I did not catch one sight of him, so he is still in William's chamber.

With slow, steady, quiet steps, Hannah made her way toward her brother's room. Pressing herself against the wall, the candlestick held high above her head, she peered around the door jamb. And there stood a tall, broad-shouldered man, his back to her, his gold and sil-ver hair in disarray, his hand raised. And just beyond him, Will, still in his nightshirt, attempting to rise from the floor. Hannah slipped into the room and came silently up behind the villain, the candlestick ready to de-scend on the man's head with significant force.

"Hannah, no! Do not!" Berinwick shouted as he caught a glimpse of her.

"Hannah?" the Reverend Mr. Dempsey said, lowering the hand he had just raised to his aching jaw and turning at once. "What the devil!" he shouted, dodging aside just as the heavy candlestick skimmed past his ear. "Hannah, what are you doing? It is I, Richard."

"I—I—began to swing before Will called out and I could not stop," Hannah replied in a voice that ended with a bit of a squeak. "Oh, Richard! I am so sorry. It did not hit you?"

"If it had, he'd be flat on the floor. Dead, likely," Berinwick muttered.

"I—I heard a thump—and a groan—and someone muttering," Hannah explained apologetically.

"I was the thump," Berinwick grumbled. "He was the groan and the muttering. Stupid thing to do, Dempsey, shake me when I was fast asleep. Lucky that all you got was a knock on the jaw."

The Reverend Mr. Dempsey smiled.

"I wouldn't smile if I were you," Berinwick muttered. "Not unless you want a bruise on the other side of your jaw to match the one that's rising now."

"William hit you?" Hannah asked with a touch of indignation on Dempsey's behalf as she set the candlestick aside. "Will, of all things! Are you all right, Richard? No, you are not. You have lost your wits. You are standing there smiling at me like a lunatic. Come and sit on this chair. I will fetch you a glass of water, shall I?"

Dempsey nodded. "At least the candlestick missed me," he murmured and then he chuckled.

"Will, you have knocked him silly," Hannah observed with just a hint of accusation as she filled a glass with water from the pitcher on her brother's nightstand.

"He has done no such thing," Dempsey protested. "By

gawd, I'm not so old that I cannot take a bit of a punch without losing my wits."

"But you are grinning in the oddest fashion," Hannah pointed out as he took the glass of water from her. "You were smiling before, in the midst of rubbing at your jaw and then you chuckled, too."

"Yes, but merely because of what happened."

"Yes, precisely," Hannah said. "Because Will punched you and knocked you silly."

"No," replied Dempsey, taking a sip of water. "Because your brother swung at me from his bed so hard that even his fist landing on my jaw could not keep him from propelling himself onto the floor. It was one of the funniest things I have ever seen."

"You're an odd duck, Dempsey, do you know that?" Berinwick declared, attempting to look composed and authoritative as he rose from the floor in his disheveled nightshirt with his feet bare and his curls in wild disarray. "You're an odd duck and always have been. The simplest things delight you. Well, I expect I am awake now. What is it that you want?"

"Do you never take that blasted patch off? Not even when you sleep?" Dempsey queried, rubbing his hand against the back of his neck, attempting to look stern in order to cover an unexpected wave of sympathy at the sight of Berinwick looking like a beleaguered schoolboy.

"You came here to discover if I sleep with or without my eyepatch?"

"No. Another reason entirely. But I cannot help asking, now that I see it."

"I learned not to take it off, not even at night, when I went away to school. I grew tired of awakening with groups of boys peering at me as if I were some freakish whim of nature. What do you want, Dempsey? Spit it out."

"I came to warn you," Dempsey replied, taking a large

sip of water and rolling it around in his mouth before he swallowed it.

"Warn me? Of what?"

Dempsey glanced hesitantly at Hannah, then back at Berinwick, then back at Hannah.

"Do not think for a moment that I am leaving now," Hannah declared. "If Will is in such terrible trouble that you must come with the dawn to warn him of it, Richard, then, by Jupiter, I will know what kind of trouble he's in. I will not be shunted aside like some puling, ineffective infant when you both know that I will likely be called upon to stand beside William, whatever he's done. And I will, too—stand beside him, I mean."

"It's not some terrible trouble, Hannah," Dempsey murmured, and finished the water. He carried the empty glass back to the nightstand and set it down carefully. "It is merely that what I have to say to Berinwick is a rather private matter."

Hannah folded her arms across her chest and stared at both of them. "Just how private can it be?"

"Very private, I believe. Langton came riding to the rectory this morning, Berinwick, to inform me that a gentleman arrived in the village last evening. A tall, thin gentleman, come on the mail coach with a—with a peculiar sort of package for you."

Berinwick's eyebrows rose considerably.

"A tall, thin gentleman dressed all in black," Dempsey stated. "Looked like a parson, Langton said. And the fellow intends to deliver this—this—package—first thing this morning, or so he said. Langton thought you ought to know of it before the man arrives. I agreed with him. Am I making the least bit of sense to you, Berinwick?"

"Drat! Drat and blast!" Berinwick grumbled.

"Then you know—you were expecting—"

"No, I was *not* expecting him. I told him to keep the—

the—package—in London until I had decided what to do."

"What to do about what?" asked Hannah. "You may as well tell me as fiddle about with delivery this and package that. If the gentleman is arriving this morning, I will know the whole of it soon, will I not?"

"Yes, but it's not my place to say," Dempsey declared. "It is a private matter concerning your brother."

"It's a child," Berinwick sputtered. "The gentleman's name is Shuttlefield and he's delivering me a child, Hannah."

"A child? Oh, Will! Is it—is it—yours?"

"No, it ain't mine! Jupiter! Of all the things to say!"

"Thank goodness. I thought it was his, too," Dempsey admitted with a relieved smile at Hannah. "I believe Harvey Langton had the same thought."

"You did not tell my mother, Dempsey?"

"No. Still in bed, your mother is."

"Good, because I have got to decide what to do about this and I do not wish to involve Mama in the decision-making. Or you, Hannah," Berinwick stated with a decided glare.

"Oh! This is the secret! The secret you would not tell me. The secret you intended to discuss with Martin Gazenby."

"Precisely, though Gazenby was not the least help. Don't bring it to Blackcastle is all he said. And that bit of advice is useless, totally useless, because it will arrive at Blackcastle this morning whether I wish it to come or not."

"If this Shuttlefield hires a carriage at the inn, we can always waylay it, abduct him and the child, and carry them off to another part of the country," Dempsey suggested facetiously.

"Won't matter. If one man in Barren Wycche heard that Shuttlefield was bringing a child here, then everyone in the village knows by now. Rumors will already be flying as thick as a flock of sparrows caught up in a whirlwind. Drat! They'll all be thinking it's mine just as you did, won't they?"

"I expect so," Dempsey replied. "Well, Berinwick, it's a logical assumption."

Silverdale sat at the Fallen Dog, his breakfast only half eaten, pondering what to do about Lady Hannah Thorne. His elbows on the table, his chin resting on his fists, he stared at the gentlemen eating their own breakfasts at the table across from him without actually seeing them at all. I almost had her, he thought bitterly. I almost had her last Season and then I had to lure her into Willoughby's little garden and—and—What the devil was wrong with me? Where was my mind to treat her like some little parlor maid? She says she has forgiven me, but she has not. I shall be forced to work twice as hard as before to win her now. She'll not place her trust in my tender words and gentle gazes ever again. I shall have to prove by my actions that I love her and that I am worthy of her love. And how the deuce am I going to do that out here in the hinterlands where the greatest social occasion of the Season is Squire Tofar's horse auction?

"Silverdale?"

"Huh? What? Oh, Cumberton."

"You were so deep in thought, I hesitated to address you," observed the pudgy young gentleman standing beside Silverdale's table. "You are here to bid on Tofar's Snoop, eh?"

"No, no, could not care less about that blasted horse. Have perfectly good horses of my own. Sit down, Cumberton. Join me. I've contemplated quite enough for this morning."

"Just so." Mr. Cumberton smiled, betraying a dimple in one chubby cheek as he took a chair across from Silverdale. "M'brother says too much thought will ruin a gentleman's reputation. Says a gentleman can think himself into the most outrageous schemes if he wastes too much time at it. Best to go about acting as one naturally does. Unless one is a dastard, of course. Fellow is forced to be thoughtful and wily if he's a confirmed villain."

"No one would ever mistake you for a villain, Cumberton," Silverdale observed with a slight smile.

"And thank goodness for that," Cumberton agreed with a nod as he accepted his own breakfast from one of the new serving girls the owner of the Fallen Dog had hired when he'd realized what an enormous mass of London gentlemen was about to descend upon him. "I shouldn't like to be suspected of villainy. Not here. Not now. There's a woman has been murdered, you know."

"Yes, so I've heard."

"A woman once under Berinwick's protection. Heaven forbid that that ruthless glare of his should fall upon *me* for the doing of the crime. Were I the villain I should be nonplussed at the very thought of Berinwick seeking vengeance."

"You'd be quaking in your boots, eh, Cumberton?"

Cumberton nodded. "And it's difficult to run in your boots while you're quaking in them."

Silverdale laughed. "True," he agreed.

"It's the oddest thing, Silverdale."

"What is?"

"That Berinwick is such a devil and yet someone has made him guardian to a lad."

Silverdale's eyebrows shot upward with considerable energy. "Berinwick? Guardian to a boy? Whose boy?"

"Don't know. Asked, but the gentleman wouldn't say. Name of Shuttlefield, the gentleman. Berinwick's solicitor, he says he is. Met him at the inn when he arrived last evening. Odd, don't you think, someone entrusting a lad's care and fortune to a demon like Berinwick?"

"Unless Berinwick is not the boy's guardian at all," Silverdale murmured, myriad possibilities rising to his mind.

"Well, he must be. Why else carry the lad all the way from London to Shropshire? Can't think a lad would choose on his own to come to such a place as Barren Wycche. I certainly wouldn't."

"What does he look like, Cumberton?"

"Thin, handsome sort of fellow, well onto six feet tall, I should think."

"The lad?"

"No, the solicitor."

"I meant what does the lad look like."

"Oh. Well, I did not get an excessively good look at him. Did not stare, you know. Not the thing. Dark curls, he had and dark eyes. Looked mostly like a tiny colt, all legs and arms and ears and nose."

"Were his curls as dark as Berinwick's, Cumberton?"

"I should think so. Nearly as dark at any rate. Why?"

"Nothing. Nothing. Merely a thought leaped into my mind. You do not think, Cumberton, that the boy might actually belong to Berinwick?"

"Belong to Berinwick?"

"Be his son, Cumberton."

"His son? Never. Why Berinwick ain't married and ain't ever likely to be. Women cringe when they see him. M'sisters did. Cringed and hurried away when he came to speak with m'father that time. Ugly, they said he was and rude into the bargain."

"Yes, but men can have sons even though they aren't married, Cumberton," Silverdale replied with a sense of frustration. "A woman doesn't have to marry a gentleman—or even like him to—"

"Pshaw! Never happen!"

"Why not?"

"Because there is not a woman in all the world desperate enough to sell herself to an ogre like Berinwick."

Delaford Shuttlefield tied the reins of the carriage horse around a hemlock at the side of the lane, then walked back to study the right wheel of the gig. No doubt about it, the thing was lopsided. If he remembered anything at all about carriages, a lopsided wheel could prove disastrous.

"That's if I remember anything at all about carriages," he muttered, walking around the gig to look at the other wheel. "I'm correct, this one is perfectly upright. There is something wrong with the other."

"The wheel is falling off. That's what's wrong with it," announced a voice from the gig's flat board seat.

"Well, then, I shall be forced to put it back on," Shuttlefield responded, walking back around the gig and studying the offending wheel again.

"I'll help," offered the voice.

"I would appreciate it, George," Shuttlefield responded. "But the thing of it is, I don't know how to put it back on properly. If we merely straighten it up and drive on, it will likely just go all crookedy again."

"There are things that hold it in place."

"Are there? And what do these things look like?"

"I don't know."

"No, and neither do I, George. Neither do I." Shuttlefield tugged at his earlobe as if hoping to pump some knowledge up into his brain by the doing of it, but nothing at all resulted of the effort. "I'm London born and bred," he muttered. "In London, a fellow orders up a carriage and it takes him where he's bound, and that's the end of it."

"Have you never traveled into the country before, Mr. Shuttlefield?" asked the small boy from the box.

"No, never. I ought not to have done so now, either, but I must deliver you to Berinwick. I promised him to look after you for a time, but I cannot look after you any longer, George. Not with all the hubbub over Mr. Cambridge Wittendell's will, I cannot. That wretched dispute takes all of my time and all of my wits at the moment. I am in Chancery from morning till night."

"Yes, you are," agreed the lad.

"Just so. And there is no one else with whom to leave you, George. And I cannot take it upon myself to send you off to school, you know. I'm not your guardian."

"Lord Berinwick is."

"For goodness sake, George, don't call him Lord Berinwick. He's a duke. You must call him your grace."

"Are you certain?"

"Yes," mumbled Shuttlefield, ceasing to tug on his earlobe and removing his hat to scratch the top of his head instead. "I am positive. Dukes are graces."

The lad giggled.

"It's not at all humorous, George. It's simply a fact."

"Sounds queer as Bob's hatband," the boy replied. "A grown man wishing to be addressed as your grace."

"Nothing to do with wishing for it. Just what's done," sighed Shuttlefield, ceasing to scratch his head and placing his hat solidly back on it at a most conservative angle. "Climb down, George. Safest thing to do is walk the rest of the way, I think. It cannot be far now. We have already passed St. Milburga's church. Merely a matter of a mile or two farther according to the innkeeper's directions. We can walk a mile or two, can we not?"

"I don't know," the boy responded, his voice shrinking. "It's a long way, a mile or two."

"If you grow tired, we'll stop and rest a bit. Come, George. You're a game one. Let's have a go at it, eh? Or better yet, I'll unhitch this beast and put you aboard and lead him to Blackcastle. That's the ticket!"

And thus it was that Mallory, out for an early morning ride and prone as he was to follow odd little trails through woodlands and investigate rutted tracks long overgrown with weeds, discovered a solicitor trudging up the lane leading a carriage horse with a lad astride. Doffing his hat, Mallory introduced himself. "Accident?" he asked, when Shuttlefield responded with good will.

"Not actually. Preparing to have one, we were. Gig was about to lose a wheel. Thought it best to abandon the thing and travel the rest of the way on foot," Shuttlefield explained.

"Where are you bound?" asked Mallory.

"Blackcastle. This is the road to Blackcastle, is it not?"

"Yes, indeed," Mallory acknowledged. "Though, if you'll pardon my saying so, you don't look as though you will make it quite that far."

"Mr. Shuttlefield is very weary," offered the child, who had remained quite silent at Mallory's approach. "We rode on one mail coach or another for two days and two nights. And then we got up with the sun to drive the gig out here."

"Did you really?"

"Uh-huh. We've come all the way from London. And we cannot rest until we reach his grace, because Mr. Shuttlefield must return to London as soon as can be or everyone involved in Mr. Wittendell's will will be dead before it is all straightened out. And that will not do at all."

"I see," smiled Mallory. "You are known to Berinwick, eh, Shuttlefield?"

"I am, in fact, his solicitor," Shuttlefield replied, taking a handkerchief from his pocket to dab at the perspiration that had begun to bead on his handsome brow.

"Deucedly odd that Berinwick did not send his own carriage to meet you then."

"He is not expecting us," the lad replied from atop the carriage horse. "We're to be a surprise."

"Is that so?"

Mallory wondered precisely what kind of surprise the solicitor and the boy would prove to be. The more he considered it, the more he doubted that the Duke of Berinwick would leap for joy at the sight of them. And yet, perhaps he was mistaken. "Can you ride without a saddle, Shuttlefield?" he asked abruptly.

"What? The carriage horse do you mean? I should think I could ride a carriage horse without difficulty but—"

"I'll take the boy up before me, then, and you climb aboard that beast. Reach Blackcastle a good deal more speedily that way, and save you what energy you have left."

Now why did I say that? Mallory wondered as he swept the child from the carriage horse's back onto Simon's. It's none of my business to be delivering Berinwick's solicitor and this waif to Blackcastle. None of my business at all. Would have done better to keep my nose out of it and let them reach Blackcastle on their own. He'll likely not thank me for it, not Berinwick. "But perhaps Lady Hannah will," whispered a voice at the back of Mallory's mind. That voice, those words and the rush of warm expectation that spread through him at the very thought of Lady Hannah—grateful to him—startled Mallory no end.

Six

The Reverend Mr. Dempsey, with explicit instructions not to mention the child to Berinwick's mother, had long since ridden back to his rectory and Lieutenant Elliot, who had taken great delight in the feel of a real mattress beneath him and soft pillows upon which to rest his head, had finished an enormous breakfast and was just departing on the next stage of his trek to Yorkshire when the little party composed of Mallory, Shuttlefield, and George appeared in the Blackcastle drive. Hannah stood in the turnabout waving goodbye to the dragoon and Berinwick stood beside her, his hands in his pockets, a smile on his lips. His smile faded as he caught sight of the two horses approaching and their riders. "The devil's in it, now," he muttered.

"What does that mean?" Hannah queried, and then she, too, noticed the two horses and their three riders. As Elliot came even with the little group, he nodded to the boy up before Mallory and, amused by the manner in which the child's jaw dropped at the sight of him in his uniform on his massive warhorse, he slowed the beast, saluted the boy, and set the powerful horse through a number of intriguing paces. Then he grinned at the lad, and urged the horse to rear once and set off down the drive at an amazing pace.

"Jupiter," George murmured, turning to look up at Mallory. "He's a soldier, isn't he?"

"A dragoon," Mallory replied with a nod. "One of His Majesty's finest."

"I should think so," the boy agreed. "Jupiter!"

"His name is Lieutenant Elliot. He and the Duke of Berinwick were schoolmates when they were about your age."

"Truly? Is the duke a dragoon, too?"

"No, I'm afraid not. His grace has too many responsibilities at Blackcastle to run off and join the cavalry. But he's a bruising rider, I've heard, and has a stable filled with fine horses. Perhaps he will let you ride one or two of them if you ask politely."

"I don't know how to ride a horse. Not truly," George sighed, turning forward again. "Papa was going to teach me, but he died, you know."

"No. I did not know," Mallory replied. "I am sorry to hear it, George. That is the Duke of Berinwick, the gentleman standing beside the lady."

"Him?" George replied in a squeak of a voice. "Mr. Shuttlefield said he was a duke, but he didn't once say that he was a pirate, too!"

Mallory chuckled. It had never occurred to him to think of Berinwick's patch as piratical. But I might have done, he thought, studying Berinwick critically. Had I first seen him through much younger eyes, I might well have thought him just back from wreaking havoc on the seven seas.

"Good morning," Mallory said as he drew his horse to a standstill. "I beg your pardon for arriving unannounced at this hour of the morning, but I was out for a ride and discovered this young man and your Mr. Shuttlefield in some distress beside the road, Berinwick. About to lose a wheel, their gig was. Thought I'd give them my escort to Blackcastle."

"How very kind of you, Lord Mallory," Hannah smiled as Mallory dismounted and lifted the boy down. Behind them, Shuttlefield slid from the carriage horse's back, his face a study in worry as he advanced on the duke.

"I am sorry, your grace," Shuttlefield said. "Very sorry. I kept him with me as long as I could, but there is such a hubbub over Wittendell's will and I am in Chancery from morn till night. And if I am not present when I must be present, there is no telling but that the family will lose all and—"

"Give me one reason, Shuttlefield," Berinwick interrupted in a quiet voice, "why I should not separate your head from the rest of your body."

"I—I— There is no one to take charge of the lad. Not in London. And you did not say whether I might send him to one of the public schools or not. Besides it is so very late in the quarter and the boy is so young that it's not likely any of the schools will take him. And you closed up Berinwick House, you know. There is only Carson remains there. He certainly cannot look to a child."

"I told you to keep him with you until I had decided upon a plan," Berinwick persisted with a scowl.

"Yes, but there was no opposition to Wittendell's will, then, and I—"

"Never mind, Shuttlefield. Never mind. Your name is Warren, lad. What's the rest of it? I knew once, but I have since forgotten it."

"G-George Ethan Warren, sir. I m-mean, your grace," the boy replied, somewhat taken aback by the manner in which Berinwick scowled down at him.

"George. After your father, eh? I ought to have remembered that. I am Berinwick and this is Lady Hannah. Mallory has doubtless already made himself known to you. Not such a dullard as to climb up on a horse before a gentleman whose name you do not know, are you?"

"Yes, sir. I m-mean, your grace. I m-mean, no, your grace. I am not a dullard and I do know Lord Mallory's name."

"Just so. Good for you. Gaines!" Berinwick bellowed then, loud enough to make the stones of Blackcastle shudder. "Gaines! I want you!"

"Is he always so loud?" George asked of Lady Hannah in a tiny whisper as she bent down to the little boy whose hands had gone immediately to cover his ears.

"No, George, not always," Hannah replied. "Sometimes he is moderately quiet and sometimes he is loud, like this. But sometimes," she added with a wink at Mallory, "his grace actually shouts. You can hear him all the way to the village when he actually shouts."

"For shame, Lady Hannah," Mallory grinned.

"Well, it does seem as if he can be heard all the way to the village when he shouts," Hannah replied. "Especially when you are the unlucky person at whom he happens to be shouting."

"Gaines!" Berinwick bellowed again just as that worthy came rushing through one of the double doors.

"Yes, your grace. Here, your grace. At your service, your grace." Gaines recited what had become for him a ritual litany as he descended the front steps to Berinwick's side.

"Have we a bedchamber at the ready, Gaines?"

"A bedchamber, your grace?"

"Yes, Gaines. A bedchamber. Elliot has departed and a new guest has arrived. Wait. Perhaps two new guests. Will you spend the day and the night with us, Shuttlefield?"

The solicitor shook his head. "No, your grace. I f-fear I c-cannot. I must start back for London on the next mail coach. It leaves at two o'clock from the inn."

A hint of laughter rose to Berinwick's eye and glittered playfully there. "At two? You have time, then, to partake of breakfast, Shuttlefield. Come inside with me."

"I c-cannot, your grace. I must return the carriage horse to the inn and explain to the innkeeper that his gig is languishing along the lane with a radically tilted wheel and—"

"Gaines!" Berinwick interrupted the young solicitor enthusiastically. "One bedchamber only. The kings' chamber, I think. Set a few of the maids to preparing it and then send to the stables for Tom Hasty. Tom will see that the gig and the horse are returned to the inn, Shuttlefield. And I'll drive you back to Barren Wycche in my own curricle in time to catch the mail, eh? That way, you will have sufficient time to join me at the breakfast table."

"I—I—You are most kind, your grace."

"Indeed, I am. Exceeding kind. Come in with me, Shuttlefield. Come. I am ravenous. And you, George Ethan Warren, are you hungry?"

"Say yes," whispered Hannah in the boy's ear.

"Yes," replied George.

"Good! Come along, then. Hannah, you will accompany Lord Mallory back to the squire's, will you not?"

"I have no idea," Hannah replied as her brother urged Shuttlefield and George toward the great double doors.

"Yes, you will," Berinwick replied. "And ride Hannah's Darling for me, when you do. She needs an airing. And take one of the grooms with you. I'll not have you riding about alone. Not today, I will not."

"I wasn't bound for the squire's, actually," Mallory said as he gave Hannah a leg up into the saddle just outside the Blackcastle stable while a number of grooms looked on.

"No? Where were you bound, Lord Mallory?"

"Nowhere in particular," Mallory replied, the light of her smile, like sunshine, beaming down upon him from above and warming him through. "He's a forceful gentleman, your brother."

"Is he? I had not noticed," Hannah replied with a husky laugh that thrilled along Mallory's nerves to his very core, causing him to falter in his first attempt to set his boot in his own stirrup.

"So forceful," Mallory said, finding the stirrup at last and swinging up onto Simon's back, "that I feel compelled to ride back to Squire Tofar's in spite of my original intent."

"No, do not alter your plans because of Will, or because of me," Hannah replied. "You are hoping to explore more of the Marches on your own, are you not? Then you must do so. I will simply take Darling out for a gallop and bring her back. It will never cross Will's mind that I did not accompany you."

"Do not take Darling for a mere gallop," Mallory protested. "I should enjoy your company. Ride with me. Help me to explore. We will go up one lane and down another, eh? You will be my own personal guide and tell me some of the history of the place. Are there many paths through the wood? There must be. Ride them with me. Does it have a name, this wood that wanders hither and thither through the countryside? Or is it not one wood, but many?"

"Grydwynn Wood, it's called," Hanah replied, dismissing Lancaster with a shake of her head as the groom prepared to mount and accompany her. "I shall not require you, Davey. Lord Mallory will see to my well-being. You will, will you not?" she added, turning Darling toward the drive.

"Indeed, Lady Hannah. Lay down my life for you, should it prove necessary."

"Let us hope it does not, my lord. It has been here for centuries, Grydwynn Wood, and threatened for centuries to eat all of us up, too."

"To eat you up?"

"Oh, yes. Every year we must cut the wood back and

release the fields and the lawns from Grydwynn's grasp or we would all disappear from sight in a decade or so. When the Thornes first came here, there were no fields at all, simply the wood, the hills and the moor."

"And from where did the Thornes come?"

"Wales."

"Ah, beneath your brother's Anglo-Saxon veneer beats the independent heart of a Welshman, eh?"

"Indeed."

"And your heart?"

"Is independent as well," Hannah said as they passed the gatehouse at the bottom of the drive and turned into the lane. "Before we explore the lesser ridden paths, Lord Mallory, there is one place in particular that I should like to visit."

"Merely name it," Mallory smiled.

"The Widow Thistledown's cottage."

Mallory cocked an eyebrow at her. "A charity call?"

"No. There is no one lives there now. But it is the place where Meg's body was discovered."

"And you wish to go there?" Mallory stared at her in disbelief.

"Certainly. Why should I not?"

"Well, because—because young ladies are generally squeamish about such things and—they squeal at the sight of a fish on a hook, all the ladies I know. Did anyone ever suggest to them that they ought to visit a cottage in which a murder had recently been committed, they'd faint dead away on the spot."

"I expect none of the ladies you know are Thornes, then," Hannah observed with a twinkle in her eyes. "I wish to see whatever there is to see there, Lord Mallory. Perhaps I will notice something that Mama and Richard overlooked when they found Meg. Perhaps there is something that will give us a clue to the villain's identity."

"It was your mother who discovered the girl?"

"My mother and my stepfather. You have not as yet met either of them. But you will on Sunday."

"I will?"

"If you plan to attend Sunday services at St. Milburga's of the Wood, you must. You cannot avoid them. My stepfather is the rector there."

Mallory felt amazement ripple through him. "Your mama married a plain parson?"

"Richard is more than a plain parson, I assure you. He is—an exceptional gentleman in many ways."

"Yes, but—I beg your pardon—but it is difficult to grasp the idea. The dowager Duchess of Berinwick is a parson's wife?"

"A very happy parson's wife. There is no shame in it, I think, for a widowed lady of rank to marry beneath her. Not when she marries for love."

"Love," Mallory repeated, tasting the word on his tongue.

"You do not believe in love, Lord Mallory?"

"Did I say that? No, I did not. Certainly I believe in love. What a fool I should be if I did not. I experienced it myself once, at the age of nine."

"What came of it?"

"I lost my collection of painted buttons."

Hannah laughed so hard that tears sprang to her eyes and she was forced to bring Darling to a halt to wipe them away.

"I beg your pardon," Mallory said, pretending a pout as he halted beside her. "It is not a laughing matter. It was an enormous tragedy. I was quite fond of my painted buttons and Ellie Summers charmed me out of every last one of them before she departed."

Silverdale carefully let it slip, as he departed the Fallen Dog, as he waited for his horse to be saddled in the stableyard of the inn, and as he rode with a group of gentlemen bound for Squire Tofar's, that a boy the image of Berinwick had arrived in the village last evening. A boy seven or eight years of age. "Was it not seven or eight years ago that Berinwick was searching all of London for a missing servant girl?" he asked quietly of the gentlemen after a bit. "I hear they have found that particular wench at last. A day or two ago, I believe. Dead, she was, in a cottage on Berinwick's land. I wonder," he said after a quarter mile or so. "I cannot help but wonder at the coincidence of it."

"What the devil are you babbling on about, Silverdale?" growled the elderly Baron Wycove. "Spit it out, man."

"No, it is nothing," Silverdale replied. "It is merely curious that the girl should disappear, a boy resembling Berinwick be born and raised and then the wench reappear—dead."

No one replied. Not one of the gentlemen cared to reply, for it was a murky, yet undeniable accusation against a man they all feared and they did none of them wish to acknowledge that there might be something of truth in it. They did none of them wish to face Berinwick with such an accusation, not even in their own minds. And yet, their very silence told Silverdale that they understood perfectly what he had intimated and a small smile turned the corners of his lips slightly upward. Satisfied, he parted ways with the group. Exclaiming that he had quite forgotten that he must stop and pay a call on an elderly gentleman who was a friend of his mother's, he turned his horse around and started back toward Barren Wycche.

They'll discuss it sooner or later, he thought with satisfaction. The possibility that the boy is Berinwick's son is already buzzing around the village, so it is not as though I concocted the story from whole cloth. I have merely added the part about the dead girl. Sooner or later Hannah will come to hear the rumors. Hopefully, very soon. She'll stand beside Berinwick, of course. And then I will

stand beside him myself. That is bound to impress her. She
will see me in a different light then. I doubt that any gentleman of her acquaintance ever stood up to speak in her
brother's defense. But I will speak for him everywhere, at
every opportunity. She must find some love for me in her
heart when I do that.

Bringing his horse to a halt, Silverdale tugged his
watch from its pocket and flipped it open. The morning
was flying by. It was nearly eleven o'clock. He hesitated,
wondering if he ought to ride out to Blackcastle and,
under pretense of outrage, carry the rumor to Lady
Hannah himself. He did, in fact, decide to do just that
and was just clicking his watch case shut to place it back
into his pocket when he discovered his loss.

"What the devil?" he muttered under his breath.
"Where the deuce did my lion go? I had it yesterday, did I
not?" Silverdale sat in the saddle pondering. The golden
crocodile with emerald eyes swung nonchalantly to and
fro on his watch chain. The crystal peacock spread its gem-
adorned tail feathers as jauntily as ever. But the silver lion
with its ruby eye had definitely escaped the long gold
tether and had gone wandering off on its own. And try as
he might, Silverdale could not remember when he had actually taken note of the lion's presence last. "Blast it," he
muttered. "Is it in my room at the inn, perhaps? Yes, it
must be. There or at Blackcastle. Perhaps I lost the thing
at Blackcastle last evening? Or earlier in the afternoon at
Squire Tofar's? Why can I not remember the last time I
saw the thing?"

Because I have not actually looked at my watch in
days, he thought, his stomach beginning to churn slowly.
I have simply placed it in my pocket and not looked at
it or my fobs at all.

"It will be at the inn," he declared in the most confident voice he could muster, bucking himself up. "I will

find it lying behind my brush and comb on the chest of drawers or some such. I cannot have lost it."

With a cold sheen of perspiration rising abruptly across his brow and his stomach churning forcefully, Silverdale abandoned all thought of carrying the rumor about Berinwick to Lady Hannah, turned his horse back toward Barren Wycche, and spurred the animal into a run.

"Cease quaking in your boots, Shuttlefield," Berinwick said from the head of the table in the breakfast room, his elbows resting on the Irish linen cloth, his chin resting on his fists as he watched the boy at the foot of the table finish off a second rasher of bacon, a third coddled egg, and a piece of toast with jam. The lad then washed it down with his second glass of milk. "I'm loath to admit it, Shuttlefield, but I know that saddling you with the boy was a tremendous imposition."

"You—you do, your grace?" asked Shuttlefield, seated at Berinwick's right.

"Yes. Though what good are solicitors if they cannot be imposed upon from time to time, I should like to know?"

Mr. Shuttlefield's lips parted to reply, but they came together again instantly. He had no reply. Oh, he should like to have set before Berinwick a long list of all the highly involved and skilled tasks that he and his associates had performed for the duke over the past eight years, but truth be told, he couldn't think of one thing they had done that Berinwick would not have been able to do for himself had he deigned to travel to London at the time the incidents arose.

"At least drink your tea, Shuttlefield, and have an apple tart or something before we start for the village. Llewellyn will bring my curricle around in a quarter hour or so. We shall reach Barren Wycche in plenty of time. He's very small."

"Llewellyn?"

"No, the boy, Shuttlefield."

"Oh, yes. Small."

"Not so loud, Shuttlefield. He'll hear you. How old is he?"

"Eight, your grace."

"Eight? What's wrong with him? He's not an elf, is he?"

"No, your grace," Shuttlefield gasped. "Not at all. He is merely—"

"He is all arms and legs. He has barely any body at all. And his face—his face is all nose. And those ears—"

"These ears are hearing every word you say, your grace," announced George Ethan Warren from the foot of the table with considerable outrage for one so young. *"Every* word."

"Oh? I do beg your pardon then, Master Warren. I thought you could not possibly hear what I said over the echo of your own chewing in those enormous ears of yours," Berinwick replied just as the boy took a large gulp of milk.

George Ethan Warren snorted with laughter and milk sprayed from his nose into the air, the sunlight highlighting the glorious white droplets as they scattered everywhere. He coughed and more milk dribbled down his chin.

Shuttlefield paled at the spectacle.

George's eyes met Berinwick's stoic gaze as the youngest of the Blackcastle footmen, who had taken up a position at the dining board, hurried forward to mop up George and the tablecloth as well.

"Like a frothy white waterfall," Berinwick observed in such an imperturable tone that George could not help but giggle. "Jack, as long as you are bound for the kitchen with that sodden napkin, fetch Master Warren another glass of milk, eh? He has not yet addressed the apple tarts. I shouldn't like to have him neglect a tart or two simply because he has nothing with which to wash them down."

"Yes, your grace," the footman replied and departed at once with the milk-soggy napkin and George's glass tight in his hand.

"You are awfully keen on urging people to eat the apple tarts, your grace," George observed once the footman had disappeared from sight. "What's wrong with them?"

"Master Warren!" Shuttlefield hissed.

"Brash for an elf, aren't you?" Berinwick said with a decided glare.

"I am not an elf," protested George. "I am small because I'm sickly. I have always been sickly."

"Balderdash! No boy who eats two rashers of bacon, three coddled eggs, toast and jam, and finishes it off with apple tarts and a third glass of milk is sickly," Berinwick declared.

It was precisely at that point that the youngest of the footmen set the third glass of milk and a plate with two apple tarts perched temptingly upon it before the lad. George, with a look of extreme suspicion, took up one of the tarts and nibbled at it. Then he took a small bite. Then he took a rather large bite. "I say, there's nothing at all wrong with these, Mr. Shuttlefield," he observed happily, and followed the last bite with a large swallow of milk.

"He has been sickly," Shuttlefield whispered to Berinwick. "His father wrote you a letter concerning the lad and what must be done if he should fall ill."

"He did?"

"Yes, your grace. I have it with me."

"Well, give it to me then. Darn fool, Warren, to make me guardian of his only son. Can't think what drove him to it. We were never actually friends, Warren and I."

"Papa chose you because you are rich, intelligent, noble, courageous, and to be depended upon in any situation," George announced from around the second apple tart. "He said you were just the man to see to my upbringing should he die like Mama. And he did. Die," the boy added more softly, "like Mama."

"I know he did, George," Berinwick responded quietly. "And I was sorry to hear it, too. He grew to be an excellent gentleman, your father, even if he was a wretched plague to me all through our schooldays."

"He was? Papa? A wretched plague?"

"I should think so. Called me a pirate and a Cyclops and charged other boys two pennies apiece to sneak in and see me asleep without my patch."

"My papa did?"

"Indeed. But he ceased to be a plague once I grew old enough and strong enough to beat the stuffing out of him."

Mallory lifted Hannah down from the saddle. His hands lingered a moment around her waist before he called them to order and stuffed them soundly away into his breeches' pockets. A light breeze caressed the embarrassed warmth of his cheek as he turned to look about him. "What a charming place," he said, and then his broad shoulders hunched and rose toward his ears for a moment.

"What is it?" Hannah asked, taking his arm.

"What is what?"

"Something happened to you just now. Are you ill, my lord?"

"No. Never."

"But you moved your shoulders in the most awkward way, Lord Mallory. If you are not ill, perhaps your shoulders reacted so at the prospect of the touch of something hideous?"

"My shoulders, Lady Hannah, have not moved in any way other than they ought. Your imagination, merely."

"I think not. Is it my touch you were anticipating and hoping to avoid? There, I shall set you free," she declared, taking her hand from his arm. "You need not lend me the least support. I am perfectly capable, you know, of walking on my own. I do not require a gentleman's arm to cling to."

"Of course you don't," Mallory agreed, considering the look she bestowed upon him with some surprise. He had thought from her words that she was offended, but her slightly raised right eyebrow and the set of her jaw implied more suspicion than offence. "I merely—I felt something peculiar, Lady Hannah. Nothing more. Do you know what it is when someone says that they felt a goose walk over their grave?" he asked in a rush, hoping to allay whatever suspicion had taken hold of her.

Hannah stared at him. Then her eyes lit with the tiny stars that so intrigued him, and her lips turned upward in a broad smile. "Of all things, Lord Mallory. As if a goose could possibly walk over one's grave before one is even in it."

"Well, but apparently it can happen, and it does make one feel something. At least people say that it does. It gives one an unexpected shivering sensation."

"Is that so?" Hannah replied. "And what happens, Lord Mallory, when a gander walks over one's grave? Or a gosling? Or, heaven forbid, a stork?"

"Don't know," Mallory chuckled, taking one of her hands and drawing it through his arm. "Only know about the goose. This is a beautiful little cottage. Was that a flower garden I noticed at the front as we came up the drive?"

"Yes. One of the Blackcastle gardeners comes every few weeks to look after it and this kitchen garden as well. And there is a little pool that must be cleaned of leaves and replenished from time to time so that the hedgehogs do not grow thirsty and leave the place."

"A pool for the hedgehogs?"

"Indeed. There is a regular village of hedgehog nests hereabout. Will brought the first of the darlings here years ago and Charlie and Millie were accustomed to—"

"Your brother? Brought a hedgehog to this lovely spot? Sends people from Blackcastle to care for the gardens and clean a pool of water for the little beasts?"

"I ought not have told you that," Hannah replied. "It will do William's reputation no end of harm if it gets out. You will not say a word to anyone, will you, Lord Mallory? About the hedgehogs, I mean."

"Me? Tell people that beneath the granite exterior of the Demon of the House of Lords lies a heart that bleeds for the welfare of hedgehogs? I should think not. Think I had lost my senses, the lot of them. Send me off to Bedlam directly."

She smiled again and Mallory discovered himself highly cognizant of it. Odd, he thought as he strolled with her past the kitchen garden, up the step, and onto the tiny porch. I cannot remember ever being so aware of a woman's smile. Women either do or they do not smile at me, but I seldom take any note of it at all. Mostly they do smile, I expect, now that I think about it. Especially they do when they are on the hunt for a title to marry. But Lady Hannah is not on the hunt, he told himself as he opened the door for her and she released his arm to step inside. I can tell that much. She is honest and open and has not shown the least tendency to bat her eyelashes in my direction. "Oh, m'gawd!" he murmured as he followed her into the cottage.

"What? What is it, my lord?"

Mallory did not reply and Hannah turned back to find that his face had turned the color of ashes, his lovely green eyes hid themselves beneath lowered lids and his hands were placed tightly over his ears.

Hannah thought at first that he was, despite his

protestation in the yard, ill. Gently she placed one arm around his waist, thinking to lead him through the kitchen, down the short hallway, and into the front parlor where he might lie down for a bit on the sofa. She urged him slowly forward. One step. Another; another; until they reached the entrance into the tiny corridor. His hands continued to press against his ears and he was breathing heavily now, as though he could not gulp enough air to keep himself alive. Hannah could see the sheen of perspiration glistening above his upper lip.

"It is only a few more steps to the parlor. You can lie down there until you are feeling more the thing," she told him gently.

If we can make it to the parlor, she thought. If he does not faint. I cannot possibly carry him if he faints.

"Did you hear me, Lord Mallory?" she asked as he came to a sudden halt. When he did not answer, she reached up and took his right hand from his right ear. "There is a place to lie down in the parlor," she enunciated with great care.

"No," Mallory said in a gruff whisper as he freed his hand from her grasp and peered at her from eyes barely open. "Not this way. I cannot go farther this way. Back. Back outside."

"Outside?" Hannah could not but wonder at such a suggestion. It seemed perfectly silly to take him out of the cottage when he might be made comfortable in but a few more strides inside the cottage. She moved from beside him to stand directly before the man and placed both her hands on his waist. "Just a little farther," she said, attempting to tug him toward the parlor. "I promise. A step or two more and you will lie down and feel more the thing in a matter of moments."

Mallory, whose right hand had not returned to his right ear but had gone to her shoulder as she faced him, now took his hand from his other ear as well and before

Hannah could imagine what he intended, he swept her up into his strong arms, turned about on his heel and carried her swiftly back the way they had come. In a matter of moments they were out the kitchen door, past the kitchen garden, down to the little fence where they had tied the horses. There, Mallory set Hannah's feet firmly on the ground, took a deep breath and turned away from her, as if to hide his face. Hannah, confused and worried at one and the same time, reached out and placed her hand on his shoulder, tugging him back, urging him to face her again.

"Do look at me, Lord Mallory," she pleaded.

"In a moment. I—I—"

"You wish to compose yourself. I understand."

"I am so sorry," Mallory said, turning to gaze down at her at last. "You did not hear any of it, did you?"

"Hear what, my lord?"

"The sobbing. The screams."

Hannah's hands went to touch his cheeks, then moved tenderly upward and smoothed his unruly curls back from his face which was still pale but no longer the color of ashes. He accepted her silent attempt to comfort him gratefully, at last taking hold of her hands and for a moment burying his face in them. Then he kissed the palms of her riding gloves and without the least thought, pulled her into his arms and hugged her mightily, taking comfort from the firm solidity of her very being.

Not the least offended by what must seem in any other gentleman a brash forwardness, understanding that he needed her at this moment, required the feel of her in his arms, Hannah put her arms around his neck and hugged him back. Together, they stood unmoving for the longest time, and then Mallory set her away from himself and stared down at her, his eyes wide and clear again. His lips parted as if to speak to her but then closed tight without a single word having passed between them.

"Tell me," Hannah said, taking his hands in hers.

"You must already think me a fool," Mallory managed. "I cannot bear to have you think me a lunatic as well."

"You forget, my lord, that I am the Duke of Berinwick's sister," Hannah replied with a hint of a smile. "If I do not think Will a lunatic, what could you possibly do or say that would make me think you one?"

"Th-there are things I f-feel," stammered Mallory, embarrassed. "I h-have always felt them. Th-things that are not—not—"

"Real?"

"No. That is to say, I believe that they are real, but no one else actually—Well, Martin does, sometimes. Martin feels them. But not often. Not as often as I. Generally," he continued, freeing his hands from hers and stuffing them into his breeches' pockets. "Generally, it is merely a hint of some strong emotion that I feel. On ancient battlegrounds, for instance, there lingers a distinct grief and savagery and something of triumph. But in that cottage, there was such violence and fear and. . . . And then the cries, and pleadings, and screams came. You did not hear them? Not at all?"

"I heard nothing," Hannah replied, stunned by the thought that anything she could not feel or hear could be felt and heard by the gentleman standing directly beside her. "Was it a woman you heard sobbing and screaming?"

"Yes. You think I imagined it, do you not? Because you told me that this is the place where the servant girl's body was discovered."

"I have not said that you imagined it."

"No, that's true, but it would be a logical assumption. I wonder myself if it was not all my imagination, because I do not feel or hear anything at the moment. There was a—a feeling of threat when first we arrived, but I do not feel it now, or feel anything else, for that matter."

Which is an out and out lie, Mallory thought, gazing down into Hannah's wonderfully caring eyes. I feel as though I am surrounded by a cloak of compassion and strength that shields me from everything. I feel the breath of springtime on my cheek and wings fluttering in my heart. Good gawd, I haven't felt like this in twenty years! Not since Ellie, when I was nine. I am besotted with this girl!

"Will you remain here until I return?" Hannah asked, reaching up to touch his cheek. "Will you be all right alone? I should like to go inside now that I am here and search for some clue to the villain's identity."

"Cannot Berinwick do it?"

"Oh, yes. And he intends to come and have a look around for himself. But I must look as well, because perhaps I will notice something that Will does not and vice versa."

"Then I am going back inside with you."

"No, how can you?" Hannah asked.

"I can. I will. I can close the feelings and the sobbing and the screams away—lock them in some distant chamber of my mind—if they do not take me by surprise as they just did. I learned how to do so long ago. I had to learn or else be constantly battered by sensations that do not belong to me at all. Trust in me," Mallory urged, offering Hannah his arm. "I will not make you ashamed of me again."

Together they walked back to the cottage and entered. "I was not ashamed of you, Lord Mallory," Hannah said as they paused just inside the kitchen door. "I feared for you and wished to give you aid, but shame did never enter into it." She touched the fingertips of her soft gloves lightly against his cheek, then took hold of his arm and together they crossed the kitchen, traversed the short corridor and entered the cottage parlor.

* * *

Silverdale searched his room at the inn from top to bottom. He opened every door, tugged out every drawer. He went so far as to lie down and peer beneath the chest of drawers and the bed and the clothespress. He opened his portmanteau and ran his fingers through its emptiness, then turned it upside down and shook it violently. His blond curls limp with sweat, he covered every inch of the chamber floor on his hands and knees, but his silver lion was nowhere to be found. Sinking down into a corner of the room and wrapping his arms around his knees as he used to do when he was a boy, Silverdale allowed himself a brief moment of despair. And then, with considerable fortitude, he sucked in a great gulp of air and attempted to calm himself.

Perhaps one of the chambermaids found it and gave it into the innkeeper's hands, he thought. Yes, that's possible. Or perhaps it fell from my chain in the corridor and some gentleman picked it up and is even now asking around to discover its owner. I will go down and speak to the innkeeper at once. That's what I'll do. I will say that I've lost a watch fob of great sentimental value and will pay a reward of—of—twenty pounds—to have it returned to me. If it isn't here and the innkeeper does not have it and no one is wandering about seeking its owner, then I will ride to the squire's and have a look about. Yes, and I will keep a sharp eye on the roads, too. I may discover it glistening in the sunlight along one of the lanes. And if no one at the squire's has seen the thing, I will go on to Blackcastle and inquire there.

"Why can I not remember if I wore it to Berinwick's last evening or if I did not?" he pouted, rising to his feet and brushing at the knees of his breeches. "Surely, I did. Surely, I would have noticed that it was missing when I dressed for dinner last evening, and I did not notice a thing."

Likely it's at Blackcastle then, he decided with a certain finality. Yes, it must be. I need not mention it to the innkeeper or offer a reward for it or bother the squire at all. I will simply go straight to Blackcastle. Likely it's even now lying atop Berinwick's mantel, waiting for me to claim it.

Silverdale stepped over to the looking glass to see if he could possibly step outside in the coat and breeches he wore or if he would be forced to change his clothes. Certainly he had to do something with his hair and don a clean neckcloth. He looked a veritable madman. "I cannot possibly ride straight to Blackcastle and allow Lady Hannah to see me in such a state as this," he murmured, doffing his neckcloth and using it as a towel to wipe the perspiration from his face, his neck, and his curls.

"So, will this chamber do?" Berinwick asked, observing the astounded look on George's face. "If it is unacceptable, you and Gaines must wander about until you discover one that will satisfy you. He will not appreciate that, Gaines will not, because he's growing old and his legs are not as springy as they once were. It's an enormous old pile of stones, Blackcastle. Man can walk for miles and miles through it and never see the same chamber twice— at least, it seems that way."

"Our entire house in London would fit into this one room," George said in awe.

"Surely not."

"It's enormous. It has six windows!"

"Which are not for climbing out of," Berinwick replied with a raised eyebrow. "It is a considerably long way to the ground."

"Why is it so big? Are all the bedchambers as big as this?"

Berinwick, his hands in his pockets, rested his shoulders

against the door jamb and cocked a knee as he watched Master Warren wander around the room with one finger extended, cautiously touching one piece of ancient furniture after the other, feeling the draperies, pressing lightly on the old four poster bed. "No, none of the other bedchambers are as large as this," he replied at last, when the boy's attention once again centered on him. "Not even mine. I merely thought you would enjoy having a bit of space. Boys do, do they not?"

"May I run about in here if I like?"

"You may run, stamp, jump, fly, if you like. There is nothing below this particular chamber but the Great Hall, so whatever you do, you will disturb no one, and no one from below is likely to disturb you. Will you have it then? Or must I set the staff to opening up one of the smaller rooms?"

"I should be honored to have it," George replied quietly. "Did King George truly sleep here? You did call it the King's chamber when you ordered it prepared, but I thought you were merely jesting."

"As far as I know our present king never did sleep at Blackcastle," Berinwick said. "His Queen and the Princesses came to visit a few times, but they all slept in the south wing, I believe. I was not here. I was away at school. I was almost always away at school. But other kings have used this particular chamber and one or two gentlemen who thought that they ought to be king or who thought that they ought to choose who would be king. They have taken advantage of it as well."

"Who?" asked George, wide-eyed.

"Let me think a moment. Well, as for kings, there was Edward the Third, Richard the Second, and Henry the Fourth. And Charles the Second, though there was some debate as to whether he was a king or not at the time he stopped by. William the Third spent a week or two. And the last actual king to come calling was our present King

George's father. There may have been others sprinkled about, but I've yet to find records of them. And as for gentlemen who thought they ought to have been king or at the very least designate who the next king would be— I have always found them the most interesting ones. There was Piers Gaveston, Owain Glyndwr, Henry Stuart, Richard Neville. Dukes or earls most of them. Interesting house guests to have about, I should think."

"I should think so, too," breathed George. "And they all slept right here in this chamber?"

"Yes, indeed. In this very chamber. What is it, George Ethan Warren? You are looking sad of a sudden."

"B-because I have just thought," the boy replied. "I expect I ought not to have this chamber after all."

"No? And why is that? I thought you approved of it."

"B-because I'm a commoner. I shall never be so much as a baron even."

"You never know," said Berinwick with a shake of his head.

"You don't?"

"Absolutely not. Why a man might find favor with a king and gather up titles one after another. You might do that. Then, when I am an old man, I will boast that *you* slept here. In fact, I believe I will boast about you even if you collect no titles at all, George."

"Why?"

"Because you're a bright lad. I can tell that already. And whatever you grow up to be, if you will do your very best at it, I expect I will be as proud of having had your company here as if you had turned out to be a king. There is a good deal of honor in being the best man that you can be. And I must always boast about having given refuge to an honorable man."

"Mr. Shuttlefield is the very best solicitor that he can be, I think, and you don't even like Mr. Shuttlefield," George accused, suspiciously. "Much less do you boast of having had him here. You are just trying to make me feel better about being a commoner, aren't you? You are feeling sorry for me because I'm an orphan, too."

"Never. You'll learn soon, George, that I am not in the least renowned for my pity or sentimentality. I wish you were not an orphan for your sake, but as to being a commoner—nothing in that to feel either good or bad about. As to Shuttlefield—I am appallingly envious of Shuttlefield and envy, you know, colors a man's perception and his responses. I do not perceive Shuttlefield as being the best solicitor that he can be, because he is so appallingly handsome. Whenever I see him, I feel like a veritable troll, and so I dislike to think well of him at all."

"Is that the truth?"

"Um-hmmm. I'm rich and powerful. Shuttlefield is handsome as a Greek god. So I wave my money and my title in front of him and wield my power over him to convince myself that a comely face does not make him a better man than I am."

"My mama used to say that I am handsome," declared George. "Perhaps you will take me into dislike because of it."

"Not a chance," drawled Berinwick, straightening up and strolling across to where the boy was swinging back and forth with his arms wound around one of the bed posts. "And we've had as much discussion on the subject as I can stand for the moment. Time to drive Shuttlefield back to the village. Will you ride up behind me on the perch?"

"Indeed!" George exclaimed. "That would be the most excellent thing!"

"There's not a chance in Hades that I'm going to come to dislike you because you are handsome," Berinwick said as he placed a hand on the boy's shoulder and escorted him from the kings' chamber.

"Why not?"

"Because, despite your mother's assessment, you look like an elf, George. And if I may be honest with you, it makes me feel a good deal less like a troll to have an elf flitting about my main residence. I imagined all sorts of ways that I might feel did I keep you here, George, but never once did I imagine that."

Seven

Hannah, on hands and knees, peered under the old sofa for the third time in the hope of finding something that would give Will and Constable Lewis some clue as to how Meg had got home at last to the little cottage, only to die there.

"I cannot think where else to look or what to look for," she sighed from midway beneath the high old sofa, her riding dress hitched up almost to her knees to allow her room to crawl about. "We have searched everywhere."

"Just so," Mallory acknowledged, taking great pleasure in the sight of well-turned ankles and curvacious calves flirtatiously encased in pink tights. "Time to give it up and admit defeat, I think, Lady Hannah. You did say your brother intended to come here himself. Perhaps he will have better luck than we have had."

"Or perhaps there is no luck to be had at all," Hannah replied, backing out from beneath the sofa. She gave her hand to Mallory, allowing him to help her gain her feet. "You do not think that perhaps we ought to search the upstairs again?"

"No. I think we ought to leave this place now."

"Oh! Where is my mind? Are the screams—are they coming back, my lord?"

"No. It is merely that we have been here a considerable time, Lady Hannah, and I am not at all certain how much longer I can keep the sobbing and the screams at bay."

"Just so. We will depart at once." So saying, Hannah took his arm and together they strode hastily from the cottage. "Should you like to take a closer look at the flower garden?" she asked when they were what she thought must be a safe distance from the little house and very near the horses. "It is a lovely place, the flower garden, and I cannot think but that it may calm you, Lord Mallory. No, no, I do not intend to say calm, precisely, but perhaps it will drive the haunts from your mind."

Mallory stared at her, unspeaking.

"I expect I do not intend to say haunts, precisely, either," Hannah said with a confused frown. "I expect that I mean to say that—that—"

"That the flower garden is likely far enough from the cottage that I won't be bothered by the sobbing and screaming and such," Mallory offered.

"Yes! And as far as I know, no battles or duels or anything of the sort have ever been fought in the Widow Thistledown's flower garden, so you will not be forced to contend with any strong emotions that are not your own, you see."

"I do see," Mallory smiled. "You are fond of flowers?"

"Oh, yes. Isn't everyone?"

"No."

"You do not care for flowers, Lord Mallory?"

"I would not say that precisely," Mallory replied, assisting her into the saddle. "That is to say, they are pleasant enough to look at. Not awkward looking like carrots or potatoes or peas."

"But?" Hannah asked with a smile. Honestly, this gentleman from Yorkshire, discoursing on this particular subject, sounded exactly like Will.

"But?" Mallory asked, swinging up into the saddle. "Oh! You mean what is it that I do *not* like about them. Well, there's nothing, actually. They don't offend me in any way. It is merely that I cannot think that I would take an extra step one way or another merely to look at flowers. Nor have I ever had any desire to sit amongst them or stroll through them. Nor would I be likely to expend an enormous amount of time and energy attempting to grow them—in glass houses, you know, like some people do. I cannot think that I would actually go out and purchase any, either—not to stick in my buttonhole or set about the house, I mean. I might purchase a flower or two for my hostess at some entertainment or something like that."

"But you do not actually dislike them," Hannah said with a beguiling grin.

"Not when they just happen to pop up in front of me."

Hannah turned Darling's head toward the Widow Thistledown's front garden. "Come with me, then," she said. "We shall simply ride along the edge of the garden and I promise that these particular flowers will demand nothing of you. They will simply be there and I should like to see them. You may close your eyes if you wish."

"It is a rather pretty little place," Mallory admitted as they rode along beside the late Widow Thistledown's favorite place in all the world. "Is that a stone bench?"

"Yes, indeed, Lord Mallory."

"And there is a statue of some sort."

"Of Cupid, I believe. And those very tall, leafy things are called trees," Hannah pointed out facetiously, causing Mallory to chuckle. "And that, my lord, with the wings and the spindly little legs—that is called a sparrow."

"A sparrow, eh? How kind of you to inform me of it." Mallory laughed.

"Well," grinned Hannah, "I did think that you would like to know."

"He is the oddest gentleman I have ever met," Hannah declared as she wandered into Berinwick's study to discover him with his riding boots planted atop the huge mahogany desk, his chair leaning back, balanced quite steadily on two legs and his arms across his chest. "He is even odder than you are, Will."

"Who is?"

"Lord Mallory."

"Oh? Odder than I am? I shall be forced to adopt a greater degree of eccentricity, then, eh?"

"No," Hannah said with a hand raised in protest. "It is not a contest, Will. You are sufficiently eccentric in your own right, I assure you."

"But Mallory is more eccentric. How?"

"He—he—he *feels* things that other people do not. Yes, and he hears things, too."

"I hear things," Berinwick offered.

"You do? Things that no one else can hear, not even someone standing right beside you?"

"Well, no. But I hear things that I am not intended to hear. We have just returned from Barren Wycche, for instance, George Ethan Warren and I, where I heard that our Meg did not disappear in London all those years ago. That I, in fact, took the girl as my mistress, sent her away when she began to breed, and when she returned here to force me to acknowledge my own illegitimate son and provide for him, I killed her—or at the very least, I had her killed. They cannot decide on that particular point, the gossips."

"Will!" Hannah's lips rounded in disbelief and then straightened in anger. "How dare they! After all you have done for the people of Barren Wycche, how dare they say such things about you!"

"As to that, they say any number of things about me whenever they are bored and long for adventure. You know very well that they do. And I don't mind, truly. My reputation for fierceness swells each time they begin to invent an adventure for me, and the more fierce I seem, the less fierce I actually need to be."

"Even so, Will, to lay Meg's death at your feet! I do believe I shall make a trip into Barren Wycche myself this very afternoon."

Berinwick shook his head slowly from side to side. "I do not require my sister to rise to my defense," he said quietly. "And besides, the villagers did not invent this particular adventure on my behalf. They do not actually believe a word of the nonsense. In fact, none of them are repeating it except in anger that someone conceived of the idea in the first place. It's the gentlemen who have come from London to bid at Tofar's auction who are batting this particular shuttlecock about. Mallory did not say anything at all to you about it?"

"Not a word."

"Likely it has not yet reached his ears. But it will. I wonder if he will believe it? Do you like the fellow, Hannah? You have got to know him better now."

"What? Yes, I expect I like Lord Mallory well enough. But that is not of the least importance. Will, you cannot possibly ignore such a rumor as this one. You must do something to quash it at once."

"What?"

"Find the gentlemen who are passing it along and—"

"Challenge them to meet me on Little Mynd moor at dawn? Run them through? Shoot them between the eyes?"

"Bury them in the ground up to their necks and then let everyone throw stones at them," suggested a little voice from across the room.

"Oh!" Hannah gasped, startled at the unexpectedness of someone else's presence.

"Forgot about the elf, did you, m'girl?" asked Berinwick.

"No, I simply did not see him when I entered and so— I do not see him now, Will. Where is he?"

"Pop up, Elf," Berinwick ordered.

"Uh-uh. You said if you were to see my face one more time, you would carve it off."

"Well, now I retract that particular statement. I was merely aggravated by the rumors that you and I are—related. Pop up."

Hannah, following Berinwick's gaze, smiled as George Ethan Warren's shining little face appeared over the back of a wing chair that sat before the study window, facing outward, providing a view of the park, the sheep, and a bit of the maze.

"Hello," he said, kneeling on the chair, resting his arms on its back and smiling at Hannah. In his hands he held a book bound in green leather, one finger holding his place between the pages.

"That was a purely disgusting suggestion about burying the fellows up to their necks, Elf," Berinwick observed with considerable enthusiasm.

"Yes. I knew you'd like it. Some Indians in America used to do that to their enemies. I read it in a book."

"You ought not believe everything you read in books. I doubt anyone, even the Indians in America, ever did such a thing as that," Berinwick replied thoughtfully. "Though I must admit that it's an intriguing idea."

"William!"

"He knows I'm jesting, Hannah. He's a bright lad, the elf is. He's not some delicate little miniature of a man milliner. He doesn't shrink away and cry his eyes out at the least bit of intimidation or rudeness, not George Ethan Warren."

"Thank goodness for that," Hannah replied. "He'd never have a moment without tears in this house, else."

"What does that mean?"

"She means that you are always intimidating and rude," George provided.

"I am not. I am often perfectly polite, even friendly."

"You are?" asked George.

"Often?" asked Hannah, with a broad smile.

"All right. Now and then I am polite and friendly. When

I am forced to be. And apparently, I am going to be forced to be soon. Gazenby was here while you were gone, Hannah. Gazenby and Anne both. They came to ask a favor of me and I said I would."

"Said you would what?" Hannah queried suspiciously.

"Hold a ball here at Blackcastle. This coming Saturday."

"A ball?" Hannah could not believe her ears. "At Blackcastle? This Saturday? William, you don't know the first thing about holding a ball. And why Annie and Martin should wish you to—on such short notice—without so much as—"

"It's not to be a formal thing, Hannah, just a bit of entertainment for the gentlemen who have come to bid at the auction. That and an opportunity for some of the young women hereabout to have a bit of fun and put their dancing lessons to use without traveling all the way to Ludlow to do it."

"But there must be invitations delivered and time for families to respond and the ballroom must be opened and cleaned and decorated and—"

"Anne and Martin will see to the invitations and acceptances and all that rubbish," Berinwick assured her. "Gave me their word that they would. And Gaines has already set the staff to preparing the ballroom. And the elf and I are going to see to the decorating of the place."

"You and George?"

"Yes," George agreed enthusiastically. "We are going to sit down and draw up plans and everything."

"So you see, there is nothing for you to worry about at all, Hannah. Everything will be attended to quite competently, I assure you."

"Music," Hannah said. "If there is to be a ball, there must be music and—"

"We've enough musicians in our midst to hold a ball, Hannah. I've already advised Belowes and Hasty that they will be spending this evening at the Fallen Dog recruiting musicians for us. There's Pervis and his fiddle, and the youngest Miss Compton with her harp, and—well, there are any number of musicians in our midst. And if it comes to it, I will play the pianoforte for the thing myself."

"You can play the pianoforte?" George asked in wonder.

"Yes. Quite well, too, if I do say so myself."

"I cannot believe it," Hannah said, sinking down into the chair made from deer antlers that stood before Berinwick's desk, her hand going to her head, her eyes fastened on her brother.

"What can you not believe?"

"That you are going to invite the very gentlemen who have slandered you and accused you of murder to an evening's entertainment at Blackcastle."

"You think they will not come?"

"Of course they will come, Will. If merely to glare at you and speak ill of you behind your back."

"Yes, well, they will not do either for very long, because I intend to put an end to those nasty rumors that Elf and I are related the moment I have the lot of them gathered in one room, don't I, Elf?"

"I should think so," George replied. "His grace is going to walk about and speak to everyone and assure them that I am merely his ward and not his son. He promised me to do it. Not that I should be ashamed to be his son," George added thoughtfully. "It is just that I am not, you know. I am a Warren, and proud to be a Warren."

Mallory walked along the path connecting Tofar's stables, one to the other. The farthest of them held stalls with divided doors that opened to the outside, so that the occupants might gaze at the scenery. One of those privileged stalls belonged to Tofar's Snoop. Mallory, peering into one after the other, at last located the animal at the far end where Snoop was just then quietly munching hay, his rear to the outside world. Mallory noticed almost at once that a cat reclined in the corner of the horse's stall, stretching luxuriously, its claws extended, its mouth wide in what appeared to be a most satisfying yawn. The feline looked suspiciously familiar. Mallory paused, frowned, leaned his arms on the closed bottom half of the stall door and whispered, "Liddy? Is that you?"

The cat's ears perked up at once and she glanced in his direction. Snoop's ears turned a bit and he abandoned his munching to gaze at Mallory through suspicious brown eyes. Then the cat stood, ambled toward Mallory and leaped to the top of the door. She sniffed at his coat sleeve, purred and rubbed gently against his arm.

"It is you, is it not?" Mallory murmured. "Why the devil was Gazenby looking for kittens in my bedchamber when it's obvious you're a stable cat and your kittens would more likely be here in the stables somewhere? If you even have kittens," he added with a tilt of his head and the cock of an eyebrow. "Don't look to me as though you've been nursing any kittens."

"Mmmmrrrrr," the cat replied softly.

It was precisely there in the conversation that the yearling approached and carefully poked the cat with its nose. The cat reached up with retracted claws and patted that nose of deep brown velvet congenially.

"Now, I begin to understand," Mallory murmured. "You are stablemates, the two of you, and Martin hoped to make me appealing to one by causing the other's scent to be upon me."

The yearling burred and Mallory stroked its nose. "If that's the case, then it's likely that you are a stubborn, ill-tempered sort of a horse just as so many contend. Are you, Snoop? Stubborn and ill-tempered? And Martin has gone to devious means to make you appear otherwise?

I never would have guessed Martin capable of such ma-
nipulation. No, or Anne either. For some reason,
however, they seem determined that I should bid on
you, young fellow. But why should it matter to Anne and
Martin if I purchase you or not? Surely Anne's father is
not in dire need of money. He has a thriving business
here, and there are any number of gentlemen will pay a
good price not only for a yearling with your breeding,
but for a goodly number of your mates. Unless Martin
merely wishes me to be happy and believes that my having a descendent of the Byerly Turk will make me so. Yes,
I should think that's the thing. I have not been a particularly jolly sort of fellow of late, and I could not possibly
confide in Martin that my lack of letters from Harry is
the true reason for it. Not fond of Harry, Martin's not.
Will simply tell me that I'm blessed not to hear from
him. But the lad's been in India, Snoop, old boy, and
there's fighting going on there even now."

The horse shook itself and nuzzled Mallory's shoulder. Liddy hopped down from the top of the door and
began to twine herself around Mallory's legs. Mallory
bent to stroke the cat then straightened and reached
into his coat pocket to see if he had a bit of something
there to give the yearling. He found nothing. The horse
nuzzled him again.

"I do apologize, Snoop," he said, "but apparently I am
all out of treats and I am out of sorts as well or I'd run
and fetch you something. But I don't wish to go anywhere near people at the moment, not until I have
settled things in my mind. I have disgraced myself, you
see, right in front of Lady Hannah.

"She is quite an extraordinary person, Lady Hannah,"
he said in a most tender tone, addressing Liddy now, as
the cat leaped back to the top of the stall door. "She remained with me even after I played the fool and dashed
out of that cottage as though the devil himself were at my

heels. Ran off like a poltroon, I did, from screaming and crying that I knew were not real. And, even after I shamed myself completely by confessing to what I had felt and what I had heard, she did not decline to have anything further to do with me, but allowed me to accompany her on her search. And she made me laugh, too. I would have laid odds that no one could have made me laugh after such a shameful display of pure cowardice on my part, but she did."

Hannah welcomed Silverdale with a slight nod, accepted the bouquet of wild flowers he offered her and sent the flowers with Gaines off to the kitchen to be arranged in a vase while the butler ordered up tea. "You will have tea, will you not, Lord Silverdale?" she asked politely.

"Yes. Thank you."

"I did not expect you."

"No."

"Will you sit?"

Silverdale nodded, waited for Hannah to seat herself on the chintz-covered love seat in the blue saloon, then sat on the very edge of the chair facing her. His back was very stiff and straight, his hair was brushed to a golden sheen, his neckcloth was spotless and his blood-red morning coat was fashionable and tailored to perfection. "You were used to call me Christopher once," he stated in a voice barely above a whisper.

"Yes, but that was before—"

"I know. I merely thought—I miss it, you know, the easy familiarity that once existed between us. I thought that, perhaps, did I come here and apologize with all my heart, we might begin anew. That is all I intended to do after dinner last evening, apologize. But Mallory interrupted and—"

"There is no need for an apology, Lord Silverdale," Hannah interrupted, folding her hands in her lap. "I have forgiven you. I said as much when I saw you at Squire Tofar's."

"Yes, but you did not mean it."

"I did. Life is much too short to be forever holding things against people. It disturbs the person who is unforgiving more than it does the person who requires forgiveness, I think. Besides, I am not some girl of seventeen without an ounce of town bronze. I know very well how men are—how they can be. I did not just fall off the farm wagon last Season."

"No. It was your fifth Season in London. I was very aware of that because it took me four entire Seasons to work up the nerve to approach you."

"It never did."

"It did, indeed."

"Because of Will?"

"Not at all. Because I—Because I could not consider myself worthy of the liaison I wished to propose between us. I knew from the moment I saw you that I wished to marry you, but I was not then, nor am I now, a wealthy man and I feared that you and Berinwick both would think me nothing more than a fortune hunter."

Hannah's hands unfolded. She began to smooth the soft emerald silk of her skirt in short, agitated strokes. "Christopher Mentor," she declared, "of all things! As if I would have turned you away simply because you possessed no grand estate or could not boast of a fortune invested in the funds!"

"But I did not know you then as I know you now," Silverdale replied. "I was foolish beyond belief to have waited so long to approach you. And more foolish still, to have courted you so properly, to have discovered for myself what an admirable woman you truly are, and then, for no reason whatsoever but my own fears, attempt to compromise you."

"You were more than foolish that night," Hannah declared, her cheeks coloring even now at the remembrance of it. "You were bold and brazen and without conscience."

"And desperate," Silverdale murmured. "Desperate to have you and petrified that Berinwick would not allow it."

"Desperate or not, you had no right to touch me as you did, to say what you said, to attempt to abduct me."

"I did not attempt to abduct you."

"You did," Hannah persisted. "Why, you had your coach ready and waiting. You would have tossed me over the garden wall if I had not punched you in the stomach."

"And kicked me in the knee. And hit me over the head with your reticule. And yet, here I am before you again. More battered than I have ever been and just as desperate to have you, but grown a good deal more sensible in the year of my life that has passed without you. I have learned my lesson and learned it well, my Lady Hannah. You say you forgive me. Why, then, will you not allow me just one more opportunity to win your heart?"

Hannah gave immediate thanks as Gaines entered with the tea tray, closely followed by her brother who took up a stand directly behind her, nonchalantly resting his shoulders against the fireplace mantel.

"Do pour, Hannah," he said to her back as the butler departed. "I am in great need of a cup of tea and a gingersnap or two. Not expecting you, Silverdale. Is this a social call or is there something I can do for you?"

"As a matter of fact," Silverdale replied, "there is something. I seem to have lost a trinket of mine last evening. A watch fob, actually. Silver. You have not by any chance seen it, Berinwick? Perhaps one of your staff discovered it this morning? I would not ordinarily bother about such a little thing, but this one is actually of considerable value to me."

"Not had a glimpse of a loose fob. Are you quite certain you lost the thing here, Silverdale?" Berinwick replied. "Gaines has not mentioned anyone finding such a thing, but we'll ask him, eh, before you depart? Hannah, you do not recall—I do beg your pardon—Silverdale will have asked you already, eh?"

"Actually, he did not," Hannah replied as Berinwick stepped forward to take the cup of tea she had poured for him. "We spoke of losses, but the subject of that particular loss did not arise. I am sorry to hear one of your fobs has gone wandering, Lord Silverdale. You used to like cream and one sugar in your tea, if I remember correctly. Does that remain your preference?"

"Indeed. My preferences seldom alter," Silverdale responded with such a meaningful look in his extraordinary eyes that Hannah could certainly not mistake the *double entendre* of his words.

"The London gentlemen are saying that Berinwick hid the girl away, got her with child and murdered her when she came to him demanding that he acknowledge the boy," Gazenby said as, hurrying from another of the outbuildings, he fell into step with his cousin Mallory on the way to the house. "They were all talking about it when they came to look over the horses again. You missed the lot of them. Several new gentlemen in the group—men with pockets likely as deep as your own."

"And what did you say to them, Martin? About Berinwick?"

"That they were heartily mistaken, of course. Crackpot idea, that Berinwick would do such a thing."

"Yes. Met the lad. He's Berinwick's ward, bestowed upon him by a gentleman named George Ethan Warren. Child bears the same name himself. Old enough to know who his mother and father were, he is. Father and mother are both dead now. Slow down, Martin. My legs are not all that springy at the moment."

"Why? How far did you ride? You look exhausted."

"Merely to Blackcastle, then on to the Widow Thistledown's cottage, back to Blackcastle to escort Lady Hannah home and then here. It's not the ride exhausted me. Something happened, Martin, at that cottage."

"You felt something," Gazenby declared knowingly.

"More than that. I felt something and I heard something. A young woman sobbing and screaming. I thought for a moment I should go mad from the sound of it."

"And Lady Hannah was there? I had no idea you intended to ask Lady Hannah to ride with you when you set off this morning. Was it she who wished to stop at the cottage?"

"Just so. She wished to look for clues to the murderer's identity, but we found nothing."

"But you heard cries and felt—?"

"Evil. Something hideous and evil in the air. Perhaps a remnant of the crime itself, eh? I should like to go back there, Martin. Without Lady Hannah. With you."

"To see if I feel or hear anything?"

"Precisely. Say you'll give it a try, Martin."

Gazenby nodded. "I cannot think that I will feel anything, though, Mal. It's been a goodly long time since I felt anything. I am not as talented in that direction as you are."

"Talented? You think it a talent?"

"Yes. And a most interesting one. But we cannot go anymore today. We've been ordered off on a quest, you and I, as soon as you have had a bit of rest and a bite of nuncheon. Perhaps tomorrow morning we can visit the cottage. You will not say anything to Annie though, about my *feeling* things."

Mallory smiled. "Haven't told her as yet? Well, and I don't blame you. It's a considerable lot for people to swallow. Especially a wife. And yet, Lady Hannah believed me at once when I explained to her what had happened— why I exited the place so abruptly. I felt two feet high, Martin. Truly, I did. But she did not for a moment think to make a jest of me, nor did she accuse me of telling a regular whopper of a lie."

"What did she do?" Gazenby asked with considerable interest.

"None of your business, Cuz. You mentioned a quest. What sort of quest?"

"We are being sent to purchase a hound."

"A hound? Are there not enough hounds for everyone dashing about on that moor? The squire wishes to purchase another one?"

"Well, it's not the squire exactly. I mean to say, as I understand it, a goodly number of people have gotten together and raised a sum of monies among them for this particular hound. It's to be a present."

"For whom?"

"The Reverend Mr. Dempsey. Had a hound once, Annie says, but it died a few years back of old age. People hereabouts are wishing to buy him another."

"Best ask if he desires another," Mallory observed, stepping into the Tofars' morning room through the French doors.

"Can't. It's to remain a secret until they present him with it at the church on Sunday," Gazenby replied, following his cousin inside.

"Another secret? This whole blasted house is filled with secrets, Martin."

"It is? Why do you say that?"

Mallory narrowed his gaze and focused it directly on his cousin. "Because I can feel them. All around me."

* * *

The Reverend Mr. Dempsey sat in the parlor of the rectory at St. Milburga's of the Wood staring at the cold hearth and pondering.

"Are you having a difficult time of it, Richard?" asked his wife with considerable compassion as she set aside her knitting. "It's not to be wondered at, you know, for you barely knew Meg."

"What? Oh! No, Vernie, it is not what I will say at Meg's funeral tomorrow that plagues me."

"What is it, then? Richard?"

"It's a secret. Though I cannot understand why it is to be a secret because you are going to find out about it anyway. There is no possible way that you will not learn of it sooner or later. And yet, I did promise Berinwick not to tell you and—"

"William made you promise not to tell me something?" Veronica's dark eyes flashed and then began to smoulder in the most unnerving fashion.

Dempsey wiggled uneasily in his chair watching them. "I wish you will not look at me in just that way, Vernie. My mind always turns to mush whenever you do. I mean to say, that particular look is making me want to scramble over there and kiss you until we are both senseless."

"This particular look is intended to intimidate you, Richard Dempsey."

"Yes, I know. But it never does. It makes me ache to love you more than humanly possible."

"Well, don't."

"Don't?"

"No. Not at the moment. Tell me, instead, what William has requested that you not tell me."

"I cannot do that. I gave the boy my word."

"Devil it!"

"Precisely. But you know what we might do?"

"What?"

"Step into the kitchen and share a cup of tea with Mrs.

Langton. She cannot be terribly busy at this hour of the day, do you think?"

Veronica smiled. "She's baking bread. You know perfectly well that she is baking bread because the smell of it is all over the house."

"And has filtered down to the stable by now. Which means that Harvey will be making his way to the kitchen in a moment or two. Langton was not there when I gave Berinwick my word not to tell you what has happened. He is as free to speak of it as any man in England. Eulie is just as free, I expect."

"Do you mean to tell me that Mr. and Mrs. Langton know this particular secret when I do not?"

"Just so."

"Well then, I do long for a bit of bread and butter and a cup of tea," Veronica declared, rising. "Come, Mr. Dempsey. Let us join our cook and our man of all work in the kitchen."

With her gown, as green as spring peas, whispering around her ankles, Veronica crossed the room and tugged a grinning Richard to his feet. She put her arm through his and urged him toward the corridor that led to the kitchen. "Cease grinning like a madman," she scolded. "Eulie and Harvey will think—Never mind. I don't care to imagine what the Langtons will think."

"I do," Dempsey replied with a chuckle. "They will *not* think we have just come from the parlor. That's for certain."

"Richard!"

"Well, your eyes are practically on fire, Vernie. And I can feel my face all crinkled up with the most extraordinary glee. Do you know, I am beginning to feel the most urgent need to sweep you up into my arms—to carry you up the staircase and not into the kitchen at all."

"Richard Dempsey, don't you dare!"

* * *

The afternoon wavered on the edge of evening as the broad-shouldered young gentleman with hair the color of Yorkshire soil and a face like an angel departed the room he had rented in Mrs. Dearing's house, smiled on Mrs. Dearing herself as he passed her in the corridor, and exited the establishment. He was on his way to the Fallen Dog to share an early dinner with friends, or so he told the widow as he bid her farewell. And Mrs. Dearing, a lady who had attained the age of seventy years without once having doubted the truthfulness of anyone with whom she was in good humor, did not doubt that he was.

Long, confident strides carried the young man toward the Three-Legged Inn and, in but a few minutes, he was standing in the inn's stableyard while one of the hostlers rushed to saddle his horse for him. It was a grievous fact, thoroughly bemoaned by the inn's owner, that at times like these, when Barren Wycche fairly bubbled with gentlemen of Quality, that his establishment had more space for horses and carriages than it did for guests.

The young man, his high-crowned hat pushed back on his head so that a jumble of dark curls fell becomingly out from beneath its brim to tumble over his brow, stood leaning against a hitching post, waiting. Even with one leg cocked at the knee and his hands in his breeches' pockets, he exuded an air of elegance and privilege that set the lowliest stableboy to staring.

"Jupiter, who's that?" Danny asked as he peered from out the stable door at the gentleman.

"Ain't none of your business," Donald Hoak replied, ruffling Danny's hair as he led the gentleman's horse past the boy and out into the yard. "Back to work, Danny, m'lad. There's stalls yet to be mucked out." Hoak led the sassy bit of blood and bone up before its owner and for his promptness, the gentleman took his hands from his pockets and tossed Hoak a coin.

"Thank you, lordship," Hoak said at once. "It be much appreciated."

The gentleman nodded, swung up into the saddle and rode off down the main street at a most respectable trot. Once beyond sight of the village, he chose the lane that traveled in a roundabout way past a number of small farms, a goodly bit of Grydwynn Wood, and at last to the graveyard of St. Milburga's. He paused there for a moment to gaze across the low iron fence at a newly opened grave beneath a willow sapling. He pursed his lips, pushed his hat farther back on his head, and then began to whistle a tune—an old, old tune about a young woman who lost her life for the love of a highwayman. This he cut off in the middle and with a shake of his head, gave his horse the office to proceed.

He rode soberly and quietly past the church, taking note of the rectory as he did so, then turned his horse's head into an adjoining lane and spurred the beast into a gallop. The sun was even then beginning to set, the sky exploding, dividing into streamers of pink and orange and yellow as he looked up at it. "Red sun at setting, more girls for petting," he murmured, and laughed. As he approached the place called Hatter's field and the little cottage across from it, he brought his horse to a halt and sat for the longest time, staring at nothing. Then he reached into his waistcoat pocket—a waistcoat of the finest silk with blue and green stripes—and took from it a silver lion with a ruby eye. His fist closed around this trinket as he gazed about him with a stoic sigh, checking before himself and behind himself and to both sides. Then he urged his mount up the cottage drive, dismounted and tied the animal to a post. Long, confident strides carried him to the front door where he knocked loudly. When no one answered, he began to whistle again, lifted the latch and stepped inside.

Gazenby was laughing aloud.

"I do not believe it's all that humorous, Martin," Mallory protested, struggling to keep the puppy from leaping out of his hands and off the saddle as Simon walked slowly along the lane.

"That's merely because you are not seeing what I'm seeing," Gazenby replied. "Do you want me to take him again?"

"No. I am quite as capable of carrying this demon as you are, I should think. And as I recall, you were not doing all that well at it, either. Wait! I have it!" Mallory exclaimed abruptly. And so saying, he drew his horse to a halt, unbuttoned his coat, stuffed the puppy inside and buttoned it again.

Gazenby laughed louder to see the tiny brown and black face with its liquid eyes peer out over the top button. Long ears flopped against Mallory's lapels as Mallory urged Simon into a walk once more.

"I vow, it is the ugliest hound I have ever seen," Mallory observed. "Are the people who sent us off to purchase this thing fond of the parson or not? Because, if I were to guess from the look of the dog, I should guess that they despised the man."

"And you would be greatly mistaken, Mal. They love him dearly. And it is not ugly. Not for a blooded hound. For a blooded hound, it's appealing."

"What did you say? It's what?"

"Appealing."

"Oh. I thought for a moment you said it was—Never mind. I'd know if it was. I'd feel it."

"Lady Hannah will fall in love with it on sight."

"I thought it was to be for the parson."

"Yes, but he's her stepfather, after all. She will be over at the rectory playing with that hound day after day for hours at a time."

"Do you think so?"

"Um-hmmm. Perhaps we ought to have purchased two hounds."

"One for Lady Hannah?"

"No," grinned Gazenby, "one for you, you twit."

"Kindly do not refer to me as a twit, Martin, or I shall be forced to bloody your nose for you. I am not now nor have I ever been a twit. Why should I have purchased a hound for myself?"

"So that Lady Hannah would be over at the Tofars' day after day for hours and hours to play with you and your puppy."

"Gazenby!"

"Don't deny it. You like the lady."

"I don't deny it, but I am not interested in playing with the lady. That is to say—"

"Yes?"

"I have told you before, Martin. Many times. I am not interested in unattached young females because all they desire is to become attached—to me. Cease wiggling about, you blasted hound!" Mallory exclaimed, looking down at the beast. Long ears flopped back. A black nose sniffed upward. A pink tongue reached quickly out and licked his chin three times before he could blink once. Mallory chuckled.

"Now, I understand," Gazenby drawled. "The manner in which you detest that puppy is quite the same manner in which you do not care for Lady Hannah. You are heels over head for the girl, Mal. And don't spout off to me again about how you are never going to be caught in parson's mousetrap, never going to stand up in the church and say 'I do,' because I'll wager this minute that you will walk straight into the mousetrap *and* stand up in the church and say I do—if Lady Hannah allows you to do either, that is. She might not."

"She will not," Mallory said, adjusting the puppy's rump with one hand to keep it from wiggling out the bottom of his coat. "Why would she? She already knows that I'm odd and she's a duke's sister besides."

"What has that to do with anything?"

"Well, it means that she has no reason to marry me, Martin. She doesn't require my title. And Berinwick is rich as Croesus, so she doesn't require my money either. She—" Mallory ceased to speak on the instant. His eyes widened in seeming disbelief. Simon's reins dropped from his hand and before Gazenby could imagine what was happening, his cousin slumped forward in the saddle, setting the puppy to howling beneath him as Mallory's confused horse stumbled to a standstill.

"Mal? Mallory? What the devil is wrong with you?" Gazenby queried, halting his own horse directly beside his cousin's. It was only when he reached out to touch Mallory's shoulder that he noticed the blood already streaming down the back of Mallory's neck and beginning to soak into the gleaming white of the marquis's neckcloth. At once Gazenby, keeping his cousin in the saddle through the sheer force of his grip on Mallory's arm, looked hastily around for a sign of movement, a glimpse of someone in the woods or on the road behind them. To his left he heard the rustle of underbrush and, glancing quickly in that direction, he saw a flash of color and then nothing. As the puppy whimpered and the two horses, skittish at being so close to each other, moved uneasily, Gazenby continued to hold Mallory upright with one hand while fumbling at the buttons of his cousin's coat with the other. He got them undone, seized the puppy before it fell and lowered it as carefully as he could onto the road. Then, with quick, confident movements, he transferred himself from his own mount onto Simon and, his arms cradling Mallory, took Simon's reins in his own hands. There was considerable blood now, staining Mallory's neckcloth and soaking down into the collar of his burgundy morning coat. Fearing for his cousin's life, Gazenby urged Simon forward as fast as the horse could manage with two men on his back. His own mount followed and then outdistanced Simon, heading straight and true for the squire's stables where it knew full well a measure of oats and hay awaited it. The puppy scampered along behind Simon until it was so far outdistanced that it lost sight of the horse. Whereupon, thoroughly confused by such treatment and utterly alone for the first time in its life, it plunked itself down in the middle of the road and howled the most heartbreakingly despondent howl to which any hound—blooded or unblooded—had ever given voice.

Eight

"It is nothing but a knock in the head," Mallory said, hoping to sweep the worry from Lady Hannah's eyes. She hovered on the threshold to his bedchamber, uncertain as to whether she ought to enter or not, but the Reverend Mr. Dempsey waved her in and her mother nodded from her place at the washstand where she was just rinsing the last of the blood from the piece of linen she had used to finish cleaning Mallory's wound.

"Do not fib to my daughter, Lord Mallory," the duchess said in her most authoritative voice. "Hannah cannot abide to be comforted by lies."

"He is not lying to her, Vernie," Dempsey declared. "I grant you it was a sizeable knock in the head and was accomplished with a sharp bit of shale, and it did send Mallory off into the land of nod, and Squire Tofar into enough of a panic to send for me, but a knock in the head is precisely what it was. Now that the bleeding is staunched and the wound is cleaned and bandaged, I have no doubt that the lad will live. Shouldn't think you require a surgeon at all, Mallory. Mr. Timmons's apothecarian wizardry should set you up in excellent shape. One of the squire's grooms has already gone to fetch whatever concoction Mr. Timmons might think best."

"Apothecarian wizardry?" Mallory smiled an exhausted smile. "What the deuce kind of a parson are you?"

"He is the kind who will not complain if you say what

the devil instead of what the deuce," Hannah replied from the foot of the bed. "You are fond of words, are you, Lord Mallory?"

"Extremely fond of playing about with them from time to time," Mallory admitted. "I like apothecarian wizardry."

"You'll like it even more when Timmons makes use of his and comes up with a concoction to ease the pain for you," grinned Dempsey. "Extremely talented man, Timmons."

"Just so," Hannah agreed as she took the chair at the head of the bed that her stepfather offered her. "The time I sprained my ankle, Mr. Timmons sent me off into the most amusing world—a world where my ankle did not hurt at all but the queerest creatures cavorted about in Grydwynn Wood. I hope he sends you a concoction that contains dreams quite as wonderful. Why would anyone throw a rock at your head, Lord Mallory? What did you do?"

"It's highly unlikely that the rock was merely thrown," the duchess offered, tossing the water from the bowl out Mallory's window. "If it came from the distance Mr. Gazenby described and hit with such force that it knocked Lord Mallory senseless on the instant, I should imagine the man used a sling to heave it."

"Martin saw the fellow?" Mallory asked. "He never said—"

"Yes, he did, but you were quite incapable of making any sense of his words at the time," Veronica replied. "You merely smiled up at him and agreed that a tart would be tasty."

"I did?"

"Indeed. I thought Richard would laugh himself into the grave at the look on poor Martin's face when you said that. But that is neither here nor there, Lord Mallory. Hannah's question is most apropos. What did you do to make some fellow hit you with a rock?"

"Nothing that I know of, your grace—I mean, Mrs. Dempsey. I have never been to Shropshire before, much less Barren Wycche. How I could have angered anyone enough in the short time that I've been here, that he would think to use a rock and a sling against me, I cannot guess. Unless it was someone who feared he could not outbid me for Tofar's Snoop," he said thoughtfully.

"Preposterous," Hannah declared. "Only a madman would harm another human being to prevent him from bidding on a horse."

"There does appear to be a madman running about," Veronica reminded her daughter. "Your brother and Mr. Gazenby have gone back down the lane to have a look around. Martin did see a flash of color and hear someone running away through the wood, you know. He could not give chase, of course, because Lord Mallory required his full attention at that particular moment. But everyone is eager to discover who the fellow might have been. You will remain here for a bit, will you not, Hannah? Anne and the Tofars are off looking about the stables and the paddocks and such for lurking strangers, and I have a word or two to say to your stepfather, alone. But I do not like to leave this young gentleman with no one beside him."

Hannah nodded and then smiled as her mother, with formidable determination, took Dempsey's arm in both hands and swept him from the room.

"She is quite a woman, your mother," Mallory observed.

"She is, indeed. If you knew all that she has suffered and overcome in her life, you would be overwhelmed with admiration for her. Who hit you with the rock?"

"I told you. I have no idea. But it very well might be someone who wishes to eliminate me from the bidding next Thursday. You are mistaken about that. There are

Take A Trip Into A Timeless World of Passion and Adventure with Kensington Choice Historical Romances!
—Absolutely FREE!

Enjoy the passion and adventure of another time with Kensington Choice Historical Romances. They are the finest novels of their kind, written by today's best-selling romance authors. Each Kensington Choice Historical Romance transports you to distant lands in a bygone age. Experience the adventure and share the delight as proud men and spirited women discover the wonder and passion of true love.

4 BOOKS WORTH UP TO $24.96— *Absolutely* FREE!

Get 4 FREE Books!

We created our convenient Home Subscription Service so you'll be sure to have the hottest new romances delivered each month right to your doorstep—usually before they are available in book stores. Just to show you how convenient the Zebra Home Subscription Service is, we would like to send you 4 FREE Kensington Choice Historical Romances. The books are worth up to $24.96, but you only pay $1.99 for shipping and handling. There's no obligation to buy additional books—ever!

Save Up To 30% With Home Delivery!

Accept your FREE books and each month we'll deliver 4 brand new titles as soon as they are published. They'll be yours to examine FREE for 10 days. Then if you decide to keep the books, you'll pay the preferred subscriber's price (up to 30% off the cover price!), plus shipping and handling. Remember, you are under no obligation to buy any of these books at any time! If you are not delighted with them, simply return them and owe nothing. But if you enjoy Kensington Choice Historical Romances as much as we think you will, pay the special preferred subscriber rate and save over $8.00 off the cover price!

We have 4 FREE BOOKS for you as your introduction to
KENSINGTON CHOICE!
To get your FREE BOOKS, worth up to $24.96, mail the card below or call TOLL-FREE 1-800-770-1963.
Visit our website at www.kensingtonbooks.com.

Get 4 FREE Kensington Choice Historical Romances!

❤ **YES!** Please send me my 4 FREE KENSINGTON CHOICE HISTORICAL ROMANCES (without obligation to purchase other books). I only pay $1.99 for shipping and handling. Unless you hear from me after I receive my 4 FREE BOOKS, you may send me 4 new novels—as soon as they are published—to preview each month FREE for 10 days. If I am not satisfied, I may return them and owe nothing. Otherwise, I will pay the money-saving preferred subscriber's price (over $8.00 off the cover price), plus shipping and handling. I may return any shipment within 10 days and owe nothing, and I may cancel any time I wish. In any case the 4 FREE books will be mine to keep.

Name _____

Address _____ Apt. _____

City _____ State _____ Zip _____

Telephone (_____) _____

Signature _____

(If under 18, parent or guardian must sign)

Offer limited to one per household and not to current subscribers. Terms, offer and prices subject to change. Orders subject to acceptance by Kensington Choice Book Club.
Offer Valid in the U.S. only.

KN113A

men who would not only injure but kill other men over the possession of a particular horse."

"Lord Silverdale?" Hannah asked.

"Sly? Why would you think such a thing about Sly? No. Silverdale hasn't much interest in horses—except to bet on races from time to time. And even if he were interested in purchasing Snoop, he likely could not afford it. He'd have to kill all of the bidders to bring the price down to his level. No, Sly's interest lies in—in—another direction."

"In me, you mean."

"I beg your pardon for bringing it up, but yes. He seems determined to have you."

"He was so determined to have me last Season in London that he attempted to compromise me and then when he could not, he thought to force me into his carriage so that he could carry me off into Scotland to be married over the anvil."

"He did what?" Mallory bellowed.

"Hush, Lord Mallory. You haven't the energy to bellow. You will make yourself more ill than you are."

"I am not ill. I am simply knocked in the head."

"Same thing," Hannah replied.

"It is not. It is not the same thing at all. That's like saying that dying at home in one's bed and being torn apart by the wild dogs on Little Mynd moor are the same thing. There is more than an ounce of difference between the two, let me tell you. I will have Sly's head in my hands before the night is out for treating you in such a manner. Does Berinwick know? No, how could he? Silverdale would be dead and in his grave by now if your brother knew."

"Lord Silverdale and I, and now you, are the only people who know of it. And why I told you, I cannot think," Hannah replied, rubbing at the crease in her forehead just above her nose which appeared as she frowned. "There is something about you—"

"What?"

"I don't know. Just something. You will not say a word to Lord Silverdale or to Will about what happened last Season. I have said all that must be said and done all that must be done. Lord Silverdale could not walk without a limp for days after he attempted to compromise me. He will never attempt such a thing again, I promise you. I am not some young lady who faints dead away at the least adversity."

"No, I'm certain you are not," Mallory agreed, his eyes sparkling despite the ache in his head. "Why, you did not so much as blink twice at the adversity of being left alone with a gentleman in his bedchamber, and the gentleman in his bed, too."

The frown departed Hannah's face on the instant and she giggled. It was a thoroughly seductive sound to Mallory's ears, that giggle, and he felt his heart stutter a bit.

"It is not a trap, eh?" he asked with a wide smile.

"A trap?"

"You know. You and I alone in a bedchamber. Discovered by your father. Well, in this case, your stepfather. Forced into marriage with each other. That kind of trap."

"Do people truly do that?" Hannah asked on a ripple of laughter.

"Oh, yes. Not everyday, ordinary people, mind you. But mothers and daughters who are desperate beyond belief for a title or a fortune. I have been hunted many a time, but thus far, I have managed to avoid all the traps. And apparently, you have managed to do likewise."

"You are the strangest gentleman," Hannah replied, her eyes aglow with laughter. "Do you mean to say that you believe gentlemen set traps for ladies? Why should they? They cannot gain much from the doing of it."

"Fortune? Power?"

"There are so few women with any power of their own that I cannot think it bears consideration," Hannah replied thoughtfully. "I had not truly thought of fortune, though. I expect an heiress like Olivia Thigby might have a trap or two set for her, though she has never confided as much in me."

"You have both fortune and power."

"Me?"

"I have been inside Blackcastle. It must be obvious to everyone that your brother's coffers are overflowing. And as to power—you have considerable power over Berinwick and his actions, I think."

"Balderdash! I haven't the least power over Will and I have no fortune but what William chooses to give me. If he does not approve of the gentleman I marry, I expect he will give me nothing. So what would be the purpose of entrapping me? None at all, unless the man wishes merely to intimate to others that he is related to Berinwick. And what gentleman with any sense would wish for that?"

"Your brother would do anything you required of him, did he think you in serious need of his services. Yes, and he would give all his fortune to see you happy," Mallory declared. "He would give all freely did a gentleman you loved require it of him. And he would give just as freely to see you released from the power of a gentleman you did not love."

"What makes you think that?"

"I saw the love and pride in Berinwick's eye at dinner and later in the drawing room each time he looked to see what you were doing, who you were with, if you were happy. He is not as fierce as he makes himself out to be, I think. He hides behind a mask. He has constructed a wall around himself, too. But one need merely peer behind the mask or scale that wall and gaze over the top of

it to see the true Berinwick. Of course, I did not come to
this particular realization for all the time that I knew him
in London—not until last evening when I saw him in his
own establishment, with you, did I realize that the utterly
mad, bad demon that is Berinwick—the stuff of London
legend—is actually a kind, decent man. Very kind, I
think. Quite decent."

Hannah did not reply. She stared at Mallory in silence
for the longest time. Then she stood up, bent over the
bed, and kissed Mallory soundly on the lips.

"What was that for?" Mallory asked breathlessly when
she had finished.

"A gift. For lifting Will's mask, for seeing beyond
Will's wall. You would be amazed, sir, how many people cannot climb as high or see as clearly as you have
just done."

"Whoever it was, Gazenby, he was on horseback,"
Berinwick announced, one knee on the ground as he
studied the undergrowth beneath a sycamore about ten
yards into the wood from the lane where Gazenby and
Mallory had been riding. "Here's where he tethered his
animal. Likely rode in along this deer path from the direction of Hatter's field. Whether he rode out again the
same way is going to be deucedly difficult to discover. If
I remember correctly there are five or six separate paths
that lead into this one farther back into the wood and
the light is dwindling. Likely we won't be able to distinguish his horse's tracks from the deer tracks deeper into
the trees."

"Just so. It will be considerably darker farther in,"
Gazenby agreed, offering Berinwick his horse's reins immediately the duke rose from the ground. The horse was
an enormous black without blaze or stocking and with
a fiery gaze that made Gazenby most uneasy. He had no

intention of holding to the animal any longer than proved necessary.

Regular demon of a horse, he thought as Berinwick reached up to pat the beast's nose. Like to trample you to dust as soon as look at you, I should think, just like his master. He might have ridden Hannah's Darling. I should not mind traveling beside Darling, but this brute—

"What the devil is it about your cousin that makes people want to kill him, Gazenby?" Berinwick asked, rudely interrupting Gazenby's silent soliloquy. "I mean to say, what the deuce has the fellow done? And to whom? First someone alters his directions to the squire's so that he will lose himself on the moor and become a meal for the dogs, and now someone heaves a rock at his head—fired from a sling most likely, if one considers the distance it traveled and the force with which it hit."

"You think someone altered the directions I provided for Mal on purpose?" Gazenby asked, astounded.

"Certainly. Don't you?"

"I—No—That is, it never occurred to me that anyone would. *Why* would they?"

"That's what I'm asking you," Berinwick replied as he draped his horse's reins over his shoulder and began to walk out of the wood, Gazenby and his mount following just behind them.

"I—I haven't the vaguest idea," Gazenby stuttered. "I assumed the mistake in the directions was nothing more than the copymaker misreading my handwriting or misinterpreting something I had written."

"Who made the copy?"

"I don't know. Someone at Brambles. Mal's secretary, I should think."

"He has a secretary?"

"Of course he has a secretary," Gazenby replied defensively. "Very important gentleman, Mal is. Scads of business to attend to, any number of political speeches to write, breeds some of the finest race horses in England, too. That takes a bit of dedication and worry, let me tell you. And he has his mother and sisters and brothers to look after. A gentleman like Mallory requires a secretary."

"Well, la-de-da and I beg your mother's pardon," grumbled Berinwick as they reached a wide space in the path and Gazenby came up beside him.

"I beg your pardon? I do not think that I heard you correctly," Gazenby said, hoping it was true because he thought he had heard the duke say `la-de-da and I beg your mother's pardon.'"

"I expect a duke is just as important as a marquis, isn't he Gazenby?" Berinwick replied.

"I expect a duke is more important."

"Just so. I have as much as Mallory to attend to, I assure you. But do I have a secretary?"

"No?"

"No, I have not. Does he have any wards, your cousin?"

"Wards? No, no wards."

"Well, at least there's that separates us, then. The only people I have to assist me, Gazenby, are a fledgling farm manager and a solicitor with a face like a Greek god and the liver of a chicken. I expect Mallory has those, too— a farm manager and a solicitor, I mean—not a face like a Greek god and the liver of a chicken."

"Indeed. And he has a full staff at Brambles and in London."

"Well, at least I have a full staff at Blackcastle, though my London house goes on with merely a caretaker when I am not in residence. By gawd, Gazenby, if my sister and your cousin should fall in love and decide to marry, I shall be forced to go out and hire a secretary and a full staff for the London house just to keep up with my brother-in-law."

"You—you are thinking in terms of a union between Lady Hannah and Mal?" Gazenby asked, amazed.

"That *is* the reason you and Anne invited him here, is it not—to match the fellow up with Hannah?"

"I—We—How did you know?"

"You forget, Gazenby. Your mother-in-law has been a neighbor of mine for years. She is the busiest body in all of Barren Wycche when it comes to matchmaking. How could Anne not emulate her mother in such things, especially when it is Hannah who is without a husband?"

"You have not hinted as much to Lady Hannah? That we invited Mal here because—"

"Of course not. I am not a fool, Gazenby. I want my sister to be married—to a gentleman she finds completely desirable. It's possible she may discover that Mallory is just the man for her. Why would I lay ruin to the possibility of that by exposing Annie's scheme? He seems a likely enough match."

"He is. Mal and she would be just perfect together."

"Yes, well, that's for them to decide, isn't it? But I assure you, I am not about to spoil Hannah's opportunity with Mallory by suggesting that you and Anne lured him here precisely for her benefit. She would send him and you and Anne running for cover on the instant if I did that."

Gazenby nodded. "We know."

"Certainly, Annie knows. Shhh. Listen."

There was a rustling in the underbrush. A twig snapped; a rabbit dashed out and across the path brushing the toes of Berinwick's boots. Behind it came a miniature bay and a whine and, nose to the ground, ears dragging, a tiny brown and black hound. It pounced onto the path, tumbled over Berinwick's boots and rolled off into the wood on the other side.

"Oh, my lord, I forgot!" Gazenby exclaimed, slapping

a hand to his forehead. "Grab the beast, Berinwick. Can you get him?"

Berinwick took three strides off the path, bent down and scooped the animal up into his arms. Startled, the puppy stared up at him with fear-filled eyes for a moment. Then, recognizing a creature much resembling those who had abandoned him but a short while before, he began to wriggle with joy. He yelped. He panted. He scrambled up Berinwick's shoulder and licked madly at the duke's ear.

"He's a present for Mr. Dempsey," Gazenby explained. "That's the reason Mal and I were out riding. We went to purchase that little beast from Clare Simmons with the monies collected by the congregation of St. Milburga's. Simmons breeds the best blooded hounds in the shire, Tofar says. And they wanted an excellent hound, the congregation, to thank Dempsey for all he's done putting the church back together. And for being the sort of parson he is. And because Theophilus died. I did not know Theophilus personally, but Annie says he was the most extraordinary hound."

"Oh, he was," Berinwick replied, supporting the puppy's rump with one hand while attempting to rescue his own ear from sharp little puppy teeth with the other. "Extraordinary hound. Used to sit before the pulpit during Dempsey's sermons and yawn and burp and sometimes roll on his back and stick all four feet up in the air. Kept us all happy with his master's preaching, Theo did."

"Did he drink homebrewed at the Fallen Dog?" Gazenby asked, sounding like a child who was hoping for a tale he had heard to prove true. "Tofar claims he did. Would lie down beneath Mr. Dempsey's table and drink homebrewed from a dish, the squire says."

Berinwick chuckled. "Don't believe that, eh, Gazenby? Well, it's true. Theo much enjoyed trips to the Fallen

Dog and a bit of ale. Not something from the squire's imagination. It's a tradition in Barren Wycche, actually. If you have a favorite hound, you bring it with you to the Fallen Dog. It needn't drink the ale, but you bring it with you, nonetheless. If you don't, the other fellows will think you're uppity."

"Do you—Did you ever—"

"I never had a favorite hound. Never had any hound, actually. Hush, you little twit," Berinwick added as the puppy began to whine and attempted to burrow into his armpit. "You're hungry, I expect. Thought you were abandoned, eh? Thought you must catch that hare and eat it? Well, never mind. You'll be safe and fed to bursting soon enough. We had best be off, Gazenby. We'll not discover anything here tonight. We'll ride back to the squire's and look in on Mallory. Then I'll escort Hannah home and send Constable Lewis word of what happened."

"We cannot," Gazenby said.

"We cannot what?"

"Ride back to the squire's with this puppy. Dempsey is there. At least, he was when we left. My name will be cursed for eternity at the Church of St. Milburga's of the Wood if Dempsey learns of this puppy before Sunday. And Annie will cease to speak to me for a day at the very least do I ruin the surprise. I cannot take such a risk."

The Reverend Mr. Dempsey stood at the very end of the corridor in which Mallory's bedchamber lay, his broad shoulders leaning against the wall, his hands in his pockets. Beside him, Veronica leaned against the wall in much the same manner, her hands clasped behind her back. They stared straight ahead of them at the opposite end of the corridor where the staircase descended to the first floor.

"So, what is this thing about which you must speak to me in private, Vernie?"

"What? Oh, there's nothing, my dear. I merely wished to give Hannah time alone with the gentleman."

"In his bedchamber? Veronica, has all sense of propriety flown out your ear?" Dempsey asked with the merest hint of laughter in his quiet voice.

"Yes, indeed. It flew out of my left ear years ago when I came to know you again."

"Oh, no. Do not go blaming me for it. I have always been a high stickler. I still am."

"Oh, what a bouncer!" Veronica laughed. "For a gentleman who spent time alone with me at every opportunity and allowed me to kiss him whenever I wished without the least protest, you would do best not to mention *your* sense of propriety, Mr. Dempsey. And do not let go that guffaw. Swallow it at once. I do not want them to hear that we are waiting out here."

Dempsey, grinning madly, attempted to gulp back the burst of laughter just then springing up in him and came near to choking on it. But he did his very best to choke quietly.

"Emily and Anne invited Mallory here in the hope that he would make a match of it with Hannah, you know," Veronica said.

"Did they? They did not say as much to me."

"Well, of course they did not. They did not say as much to me either, Richard, but it's true all the same. You know what an incorrigible matchmaker Emily Tofar is, and Anne is so frightfully happy with Gazenby and so fond of Hannah, that she cannot but wish for Hannah to be married and have such joy for herself, so she was most easily drawn into Emily's plot."

"Mere conjecture on your part, m'dear," Dempsey replied.

"Perhaps, but conjecture based upon experience. Do you like him, Richard? This Mallory?"

"I know little of him."

"You liked William from the first."

"It was in my best interest to like Berinwick from the first because I loved his mother. No, no, nullify that. I did like Berinwick for his own sake before I ever knew he was your son. There was something about him. He proved to be excessively entertaining in a rather belligerent way. There is something about Mallory, as well, I think."

"There is? Is it the same something?"

"Not quite, but very close. He is not near the dissembler that Berinwick is and I doubt not that Mallory's reputation is as pure as the driven snow, but I think he'll prove just as entertaining do I get to know him better. Will that do?"

"Yes," Veronica said with a thoughtful smile. "For now. Do you think, Richard, that he is correct about why someone aimed a rock at his head? About wishing to eliminate him from the bidding on Snoop, I mean? It was a very dangerous thing to do. He might well have been killed. Are there gentlemen who would go so far as that to own a horse?"

"To own that particular horse, perhaps, though I wouldn't have him did Tofar offer me ten pounds to take him home with me."

"You would not?"

"No. I am much too old to think of training such an obstinate, bad tempered animal. I have never once seen him behave properly for anyone."

"And yet, he strolled straight up to Mallory with the most amiable demeanor the first time the man went to view him and took an apple from Mallory's hand. Hannah told me so. She could not believe it."

"Took the apple and left him his hand?" Dempsey quipped. "Horse must need spectacles."

"Be serious, Richard. If Hannah should develop—feelings—for this particular gentleman, then we must do something to keep him safe. I will not have her falling in love with a man only to lose him to some murderer."

"Yes, well, I expect we ought to do something to keep him alive even if Hannah does not choose to fall in love with him. Invited guest of the Tofars, you know. Only polite to keep him from getting himself killed. Wish me to discover what's going on, do you?"

"Yes."

"I'll put it on my list, m'dear, immediately following: Discover who murdered Meg and why."

"Oh!" Veronica exclaimed, pulling away from the wall, one hand going to her lips as she turned and stared up at him. "Richard! What if it is the same person? What if the fiend who murdered our Meg is the same man who attacked Lord Mallory?"

"Then I shall not be forced to make two separate investigations," Dempsey said, straightening away from the wall and taking her into his arms. He leaned down, then, and put the rest of their time as hall guardians to good use by kissing the woman until she was certain she would burn to death from the fire that flamed within her.

George Ethan Warren's eyes came near to popping from his head as he spied the puppy in Berinwick's arms. "Is it for me?" he asked excitedly as the duke dismounted before the paddock fence and handed his reins over to Llwellyn.

"Is what for you, Elf?"

"That puppy. I have never had a puppy, you know. Never in my entire life. Mama was not fond of hounds."

"Oh. Well, I'm afraid that I'm not terribly fond of hounds myself. Not that I hold them in disdain, mind you, but—No, I lie. I was fond of one hound. It did not belong to me, however. Here. Take this little beastie, Elf. We shall be forced to carry him up to the house and feed him, I expect, now that I've been appointed his guardian."

"You're a puppy's guardian?" George asked, giggling.

"The guardian of two puppies."

"I am not a puppy."

"That, my dear Elf, is merely your opinion."

They strolled together from the edge of the paddock, across the stableyard, toward the kitchen entrance to Blackcastle, Berinwick taking wide, bold strides while George scurried along beside him like a terrier beside a mastiff. They were forced to pause a moment or two at the midway point when the puppy began to lick George's face and ears and neck to such an extent that it sent the boy into spasms of laughter, but then Berinwick ordered them both to assume *some* decorum and they were off again.

"Remember that he's not to be yours, Elf," Berinwick said just before they reached the kitchen door. "We are merely looking after him until Sunday. He's to be a present for the rector of our church."

"Oh."

"You will not mind looking after him, will you? Even if he's not to be your own? I expect he will need someone with whom to play, someone to take him for walks and such between now and then. I can get one of the grooms to look after him if you don't wish to do it."

George shook his head vehemently. "I shall be pleased to do it. It's a he, eh? Not a she?"

"Definitely not a she," Berinwick replied with the merest hint of a smile.

"What's his name?"

"Name? He hasn't got a name. I expect Dempsey will name the beast once he's presented with it. Mrs. Grant, we require food for a dog," Berinwick declared, pushing

open the kitchen door and hustling George and the
puppy inside.

"Food for a dog?" queried the cook. "When you departed you was desiring food for a boy, your grace.
Goodness, will you look at that!" the woman exclaimed
as she turned away from the ovens. "One of Clare Simmons's puppies it be."

"Just so," Berinwick nodded. "It's the present for the
Reverend Mr. Dempsey to which you and I and everyone
in the shire, I think, contributed. I expect Simmons will
be able to send Bart to Scotland to study medicine
now—the price we paid for *this* beastie. A number of
mishaps have placed us in charge of the animal for the
duration, Mrs. Grant, and it's hungry. I expect hounds
are like everything else that's small and wiggly," he
added with a pointed glare at George, "always hungry."

"Aye," laughed the cook, good-naturedly. "Boys and
hounds, your grace. One and the same when it comes to
eating. Is Lady Hannah not with you?"

"No. Gazenby will escort her home, or one of Tofar's
grooms will. I could not return for her, you know, because the rector was there, at the Tofars and—"

"Oh, you dared not let him see the hound," agreed
Mrs. Grant at once. "That would spoil the pudding to be
sure."

At the hour of seven, Silverdale made his way out of
the Three-Legged Inn, around the street corner and
into the Fallen Dog. His step was not as energetic as it
might have been, and his face was a study in desolation.
He sat down at a table close before the hearth, ordered
up a pint of homebrewed and a bit of rabbit stew and
with his chin resting on his fists, stared at the tiny flames
just beginning to sputter into life among the logs.

It's not fair, he thought dismally. I could make her

happy. I know I could make her happy. It's true enough
that I've gambled away a considerable fortune in my
time and that a goodly sum of money would not go amiss
if Berinwick were to bestow it on us with the wedding set-
tlements. But it is not as though the only thing I see
when Lady Hannah is near to me is the vast extent of her
brother's holdings or the monies he has invested in the
funds, or even the collections of antiquities that fill
Blackcastle from top to bottom, one end to the other. I
see her as well. I do. And I see the true beauty of her,
too, not merely her comely face and her trim figure.
She's funny. She's smart. She's a pure delight to be with
and to speak to. Except when she's angry. She's a regular termagant when she's angry. I've learned that lesson
well enough and I will never do anything to make her
angry with me again.

But damnation, how her eyes burn when she takes a
fellow on! She is more exciting and alluring and seductive when she's attempting to maim a chap than all the
women I have ever courted when they are attempting to
seduce a fellow. There is not another woman in the
world like Lady Hannah Thorne. Not one. And I have
lost her. Through my own stupidity, I have driven her
away. She will not have me, she says. Not ever. All because I attempted to compromise her in that blasted
garden and when she would not surrender to my passion, I thought to abduct her. Glory, what an arrogant
fool I was! Arrogant and audacious and without a
thought in my head about the consequences of what I
was determined to do. And now the only woman I will
ever truly love has set me aside like a barrel of spoiled
pork. Oh, she speaks to me, but that is merely to be polite. I can see clearly that she does not wish to speak to
me—not ever again.

And now I have lost the silver lion as well, he mourned
in silence. I have managed to keep it safe and with me

ever since m'father's death. It is all I have left of him, actually. The only thing that reminds me constantly of him. And it might well sell for ten thousand pounds or more, as old as it is. Certainly if the jewelers would not pay up for it, some collector would. Why the devil was it not at Blackcastle or at Tofar's or in my room at the inn? Where could it have gone?

Not that it matters, he thought with a sigh. I only thought to sell it to prove to Berinwick that I could support his sister in as decent a manner as any man. But it wouldn't have been enough, really, ten thousand. Berinwick would think ten thousand nothing but pocket change most likely. Still, it would be something. If Hannah would change her mind and give me another opportunity to court her, and I could convince her to accept my proposal, it would be something.

"What the deuce has thrown you into a morass of despair?" asked a familiar voice at Silverdale's shoulder. "You look as though you have swallowed a canary whole and it is on its way back up in the same condition."

Silverdale smiled despite himself. "Sit down, Cumberton. Join me for dinner."

"Don't mind if I do. You ain't found it yet, eh? Your little watch fob? The one you was asking about at Tofar's stables?"

"No. No one has seen the thing. Disappeared completely. With my luck, it fell off somewhere along Widowen Lane and rolled down a rabbit hole."

"I seriously doubt that," Cumberton replied soberly. "Rabbit holes are generally far from the roads and they're generally covered over with grass as well. Difficult for a fob to roll down one. But it must be somewhere, Silverdale. Watch fobs do not simply grow legs and stroll away, you know. I'll tell you what. I will look high and low for it tomorrow. Scout about the town. Speak to this person and that. Perhaps it fell off in one of the shops—have you been in any of the shops? Perhaps no one noticed it today, but tomorrow they will."

"Perhaps," Silverdale agreed, not at all depending upon it, but not wishing to offend Cumberton by refusing to accept his offer of aid. "I did go into one or two of the shops. I went to look at the most splendid cane with an ivory top, and a buggy whip, and the most intriguing snuff box. It's odd, don't you think, Cumberton?"

"What's odd?"

"That such items should be for sale in a tiny village like Barren Wycche. What would a farmer do with an ivory-topped cane, or a woodcutter with a silver snuff box? A buggy whip might be sold to anyone, I expect. But that particular whip had gold circlets woven into the handle."

"Ah, but you forget," Cumberton replied, noting the pint of homebrewed and the rabbit stew that the serving girl set before Silverdale and pausing to order up the same for himself. "You forget, Silverdale, that there are a goodly number of noble and genteel families sprinkled throughout the Marches. Don't doubt that any number of them come into Barren Wycche for an outing from time to time and are pleased as punch to be able to purchase such things here without traveling to Ludlow or London. We're going to have the opportunity to meet them, I hear."

"Meet whom?"

"The nobility and gentry of the Marches, old chap."

Silverdale stared at his friend as if the pudgy young Cumberton had just popped open his head and sprinkled his brains across the table in hope of finding some beans among them.

"No, truly, Silverdale. There's to be a ball, Saturday evening at Blackcastle. Gazenby said as much to me this very afternoon. And we're all to be invited—every gentleman who has come up from London for the auction. It's to be a rather informal thing. Spur of the moment and all that. And it does not matter if we have not brought our dancing togs with us because even hunting jackets and riding boots will be allowed on the ballroom floor, Gazenby said—because we could not be expected, after all, to know there would be a ball."

For the first time since he had departed Blackcastle that afternoon, Silverdale's hopes rose. *A ball? At Blackcastle? And all the gentlemen who have come up from London are to be invited? That means I shall be invited. I shall have another opportunity. One last opportunity to gain Lady Hannah's hand in marriage.*

Hannah settled herself cozily among the pillows on the windowseat in her bedchamber and gazed out at the park and the maze. Dew-annointed grass sparkled like crystal. A soft breeze touched the holly, the rose and the hawthorne bushes and set them to rippling like a dark tide. Sheep glowed like ghosts as they moved along paths of moonlight. Undoubtedly the elves will come out to play soon, Hannah thought with a smile. It is a night fashioned just for them. "Oh, how I should like Lord Mallory to see this," she whispered. "What would he see, I wonder, sitting here staring from my window?"

They had spoken together for a goodly long time at the Tofars. Until Mr. Timmons's magic potion had arrived on the winged feet of Jem Taylor and Richard had shooed her from the bedchamber so that Mallory might take the stuff and get some sleep. But it had been long enough, that quiet conversation, to lead Hannah to suppose that in the Marquis of Kearney and Mallory she had discovered a gentleman unlike any other. A gentleman confident enough in his own logic and reason to allow himself to accept that the world was filled with unknown wonders; that everything could not be seen, touched, tasted, smelled or heard by everyone, all the time.

He is a gentleman unafraid to engage in flights of fancy, she thought. And one likely to acknowledge that ghostly knights and princesses, legendary kings and queens, shimmering faeries and energetic elves might just rule the land whenever the moon rises high in the sky and we of the everyday world are soundly asleep in our beds.

I could come to love this man, she thought with surprise. Why, I believe that I already do love him in some ways. I can see without the least doubt that although he is a gentleman carved from the harsh and rugged landscape of Yorkshire, he is nevertheless a perfect gentleman for life in the Marches and the world beyond the world that lingers always around Barren Wycche.

And then she smiled more broadly. "Elves," she said. "William is going to call that boy Elf for the rest of the lad's life if George does not protest soon." But she had seen already that George delighted in the appellation and would not protest and she was thankful that he would not, for it was one of the few times in his life that Berinwick had chosen to use an endearing term for anyone of his acquaintance. And it *was* an endearment—Elf—no matter what anyone else might think of it.

"I wonder if Lord Mallory would understand it to be so?" she murmured. "Would he understand that Will offers George a portion of his heart by calling him Elf, or would he think it an insult to the boy? Lord Silverdale would think it an amusing indignity and Mr. Gazenby would find it to be exceedingly rude."

And then Hannah prayed what she thought must be a silly little prayer as she sat gazing out at the night. A prayer so silly and insignificant that certainly not even the smallest of the angels would bother to bring it to God's attention—because God had so many more important prayers to answer, so many more important events with which to deal and everyone knew it. The short peace between Britain and France had ended. Napoleon was growing more and more powerful and would likely declare himself Emperor of France soon. Fine English soldiers like Josiah were even now dying and preparing themselves to die on foreign soil in the defense of their country. And in England itself, evil still flourished. One need only think of poor Meg to realize that. But Hannah prayed the prayer regardless. "Dearest Father in Heaven," she prayed, "please let Lord Mallory be just the sort of gentleman who would choose to call a lonely, orphaned little boy Elf, because I could love him with all my heart if he were."

Mallory drifted through drug-induced dreams like a voyager on a ship of phosphorous in a sea of murky, undulating mist. There were so many dreams. Strange, awkward dreams, with no beginnings and no ends. Some of them he found utterly alluring—warm and cozy and filigreed with silver—and he longed to reach them and remain within them. Others were chill, nightmarish, shrouded in black and when he sailed into them, he wished nothing more but to escape at once. And he did escape, because none of them lasted. Light or dark, cozy or chill, not one of them took hold of him. One after another he sailed through dreams, over dreams, around dreams without the least hope of discovering some solid shore upon which to land. From time to time he thought he could peer through the mists that surrounded him, but when he attempted to do so, the mists achieved a greater density and closed him off from all visions. It was in the midst of one of these bouts of blindness—the dark emptiness of it more fearsome even than the nightmarish dreams themselves—that Mallory heard her voice. "Ahoy," she called. "Lord Mallory, is it you? Come to me. I await you here." In dulcet tones, she summoned him.

With enviable patience she attempted to guide him from out his blindness, through his hubble-bubble world of things remembered, things imagined, things that might have been and things that still might be, to the safe harbor of her warm embrace. Her laughter sailed to him on the breeze. The stars in her eyes ignited and held a steady flame to light his way. "Here," she called through the mayhem that was his drug-altered mind. "Here, **Mal**. I am waiting for you. Come to me, my love."

"Hannah," he murmured, as he tossed about on his bed, tangling the sheets around himself, struggling against their confinement to reach out and seize the comfort she offered him so freely. "I'm coming, Hannah. Wait for me."

Nine

It was a quiet, solemn group of citizens who gathered in the cemetery of St. Milburga's of the Wood the following morning as the church bell tolled for Meg Thistledown. Black scarves, black gloves, black armbands and hatbands ruled the day. And though some of the women had chosen to wear white, thus recognizing Meg's age and unmarried state, most had chosen black bombazine or crepe because they did none of them know, after all, whether Meg had married during the years of her absence or not. But whichever color the women wore, their men stood stolidly beside them in their best Sunday clothes—whatever color those Sunday clothes happened to be—their respect for life, even the life of a young servant girl, apparent in the straightness of their backs and the somberness of their faces.

The Reverend Mr. Dempsey closed his prayer book, took a lump of dirt into his hand and dropped it atop the wooden coffin in the open grave. "I do not know what happened, Meg," he said as the lump puffed into grains of soil against the pine. "I don't know why you disappeared or where you have been or what you did in all the time that you have been gone from us, but you did not deserve to have your life so cruelly taken from you. May God grant you peace now, and may He grant to those of us who love you the opportunity to give you justice as well."

"May you rest in peace, Meg," Veronica added, contributing a handful of soil herself. Hannah, dry-eyed and angry, followed her mother, and Anne, sobbing, followed Hannah.

Only then did the Duke of Berinwick, his hat in hand and a black armband circling his upper arm, stoop to pick up a clod of earth. He held it up before him, crushed it in a wrathful fist and sprinkled the pulverized remains over the coffin. "I will find the villain who did this, Meg," he murmured. "I will see the fellow dead. I promised Charlie and Millie that I would and now I promise you as well. Your murder will not go unavenged."

One after another the congregation of St. Milburga's of the Wood, together with representatives of all the families of the neighborhood who were not members of the Church of England, passed by the grave. All tossed pieces of the good earth atop the coffin. All whispered final goodbyes or prayed or wept. Had the little servant girl been a princess, she could not have had a more moving, more well-attended funeral. When it ended, the people of Barren Wycche gathered together on the cobbles outside the old church and agreed that despite the absence of Meg's immediate family, it had proved a perfectly elegant farewell.

But it was not Meg's *final* farewell. Berinwick and Dempsey and Constable Lewis all agreed to that. The final farewell, the farewell Meg Thistledown deserved to have, would be the sight of the man who had murdered her swinging from a gibbet in Barren Wycche's public square. It was the thought of that final farewell that sent Dempsey and Berinwick off together to Thistledown cottage that afternoon.

Dempsey sighed as he dismounted and tied his horse to the hitching post. "Your mother and I came out here the following day, Berinwick, to clear away the broken lamp and mop the lamp oil from the floorboards, and look about for any sign of who might have done this thing. But we are neither of us as young as we once were and our eyes—"

"—are growing less dependable by the day," finished Berinwick for him. "I know. And you've left your spectacles at the rectory again, haven't you? It might help you to see, Dempsey, if you carried them with you from time to time. Still, Hannah came as well and she found nothing."

"Hannah came? Here? Alone?"

"No, came with that Mallory fellow. Said the strangest thing, Hannah did. Said Mallory heard Meg sob and scream."

If the Reverend Mr. Dempsey had been a terrier, Berinwick might have seen Dempsey's ears perk up directly he said the words. But since Dempsey wasn't a terrier, the duke merely imagined that the rector's ears perked and smiled secretly at the vision.

"Utterly impossible, I should think," Berinwick added. "Vivid imagination, Mallory has. But Hannah has developed a fondness for the gentleman nonetheless, and I thought it best not to mention—"

"He *heard* Meg scream?" Dempsey interrupted. "That night? The night it happened?"

"No. Yesterday when he and Hannah came to search the place. Wasn't anywhere near here the night it happened. He was in his bed at the squire's. I made certain to check on that. And one cannot hear anything that happens at the cottage from as far off as the squire's. Not even the fire bells will sound loud enough to reach from one place to the other."

"And yet Mallory could hear it happening from as far off as a day afterward?"

"I know it sounds ridiculous, Dempsey, but Hannah believed him and who am I to say it can't be so? 'There are more things in heaven and hell, Horatio'," he misquoted with a shrug of his shoulders as he opened the cottage door. "I don't hear anything," he added, standing stock still in the front parlor.

"It's a gift. You don't have it," Dempsey observed.

"Hearing things that aren't there is a gift?" Berinwick asked with a cock of his haughty eyebrow. "And to think I always believed it a sort of madness. He feels things too, this Mallory. Lingering emotions, Hannah says. I never thought emotions lingered anywhere—not once the people experiencing them were dead. But Mallory claims they do."

"It *is* a gift," Dempsey insisted, taking a stand in the middle of the parlor, his fists planted firmly on his hips as he looked around him. "It's much like second sight, Berinwick. You ought to know about these things. You're a Celt. Celtic history is filled with mystical happenings and people with extraordinary abilities."

"Just so. And I think I must have the gift as well, Dempsey, because I'm hearing something right now."

"What? Sobbing? Crying?"

"Horses coming up the drive. Take a look out the window, will you?"

"Speak of the devil," murmured Dempsey as he reached the window and tugged the curtains aside.

"Mallory?"

"Just so. He ought not be out riding with that aching head of his. It's much too soon. Of all the peabrained things to—"

And that was when the Reverend Mr. Dempsey noticed it for the first time—clinging to the net curtains just behind the winter draperies.

"Is Hannah with him?" Berinwick queried, stripping off his riding gloves and tossing them to the floor, then tugging off the sofa cushion and stuffing his hands down the small space where the back of the piece of furniture connected with the base.

"Hannah? No. Gazenby. Gazenby is with him," murmured Dempsey, stripping off his own gloves and reaching out to disentangle the tiny object which dangled at waist height from the curtain threads. He held his breath as it came loose and fell into the palm of his hand. It glittered in the sunlight and he stared at the thing with utter disbelief. Then he closed his fist tightly around it, hiding it from sight, just as Mallory and Gazenby entered through the front door.

"Gaines, I wish to see the child," Veronica declared, confronting the Blackcastle butler at the great double doors with both hands on her hips. "Do not protest that there is no child, even if his grace has ordered you to do so, because word has reached me at the rectory that there most definitely is."

"Yes, your grace. No, your grace. Yes, your grace," the flustered butler responded. For most of his years, until she had married Mr. Dempsey and moved to the rectory, this glorious woman had been his employer. Poor Gaines had adored the Duchess of Berinwick for most of his adult life—utterly adored her—since first she had come to Blackcastle as its new mistress. He adored her to this day, and his loyalty to her son could be shaken only by his loyalty to her. "They are in the park, your grace," he said. "The boy and Lady Hannah both. I should be pleased to escort you there."

"Oh, heavens, no, Gaines. Up and down all those stairs and through all those drafty old corridors at our ages? I think not. But I should greatly enjoy your company if you would care to stroll with me around the outside of the house. It has been a goodly long time, Gaines, since we have had a conversation together, you and I. What is the boy's name?" she queried as the butler, beaming, stepped out into the sunlight and closed the doors behind him.

"George, your grace. George Ethan Warren," he replied, offering his arm to support Veronica down the front steps, lest she trip and fall.

Veronica smiled graciously and continued to cling to his arm as they reached the drive. Gaines, without one thought of calling for a groom to perform such a lowly task, unwound the reins of her grace's horse from the brass flambeau holder to which she had tied them and with the horse trailing behind them, escorted her toward the west wing of Blackcastle.

"Is he a nice boy, Gaines?" she asked, well aware of the pleasure twinkling in the butler's eyes because she deigned to hold a conversation with him.

"An extremely nice boy," Gaines replied. "He is eight years old. Almost nine, he tells me. And a bright lad, too. His grace has given him the kings' chamber."

"What a grand idea, to put a young lad there. He may run and jump as much as he likes and disturb no one."

"Just so, your grace. And Master George wishes his grace to teach him to fence. If his grace complies, the kings' chamber will be just the place for it."

"Will his grace agree, do you think, Gaines? To teach the boy to fence?"

"Well, George has not asked him as yet, but, yes, I cannot think but his grace will agree to it. He is a master of the art, you know, and will like to have someone to practice with and he is already quite fond of the boy."

"I am pleased to hear it."

John Workman, the youngest of the Blackcastle grooms had just stepped from the stable when he noticed her grace on Gaines's arm and her grace's horse trailing along behind them. He dashed in their direction at once and took the reins from the butler.

"Good afternoon, John," Veronica greeted the young man. "I have not seen you in weeks. Have you decided against church? And decided against learning to read as well?"

"Oh, no, your grace. I have been busy is all. I am coming to church this very Sunday and I be planning to attend lessons that afternoon, too. Mr. Hasty has seen to it that I'll be free."

"Good for you and good for Tom Hasty too! Mr. Dempsey will be so pleased to see you again."

"Yes, your grace."

"It's a wonderful thing that you and Mr. Dempsey are doing," Gaines said as the young man led the horse off toward the stable.

"And something I ought to have done years ago, Gaines. But I did not think of it, you see. It was Mr. Dempsey proposed it."

"Indeed. He's a splendid sort of fellow, Mr. Dempsey. Everyone thinks so."

"Everyone?" Veronica laughed softly. "Surely, Gaines, you exaggerate."

"Oh, no, your grace. Some of us were a bit leery about him at first, to be sure, but your Mr. Dempsey has proved himself time and again. He's a bit odd for a parson, but he's to be depended upon no matter what, your grace."

"That's true," Veronica nodded. "There is no one can say that Mr. Dempsey is not to be depended upon. Why, he would not so much as tell me that his grace had taken on a ward, Gaines, because he gave William his word that he would not. If I had not heard the tale from Eulie and Harvey Langton, I should not have known about the child's presence here until his grace chose to speak to me of it himself."

Gaines, as savvy a butler as ever was born, gleaned from this bit of conversation that the Duke of Berinwick had chosen to keep George's presence a secret from his mother and that her grace wished Gaines to settle the duke's ruffled feathers immediately upon his grace dis-

covering that she did know. She had just given Gaines
the words by which to accomplish this task and he would
see that they were readily repeated to his grace the instant they were required—before the duke tore off in
search of Mr. Dempsey's head.

Veronica brought Gaines to a halt on the edge of the
park, her eyes filling with love as she saw Hannah,
dressed in a pair of buckskin breeches—quite like her
brother's, but obviously tailored for the young woman—
a white linen shirt beneath a black velvet jacket, and
gleaming riding boots. Foil in hand, Hannah faced a
thin little boy with dark curls who held a foil of his own.
"Thank you, Gaines. I shall go on by myself from here,"
she said, removing her hand from the butler's arm, and
bestowing a brilliant smile upon him. "I shall see you at
the church on Sunday, shall I not?"

"I would not miss it for the world, your grace," Gaines
replied. With a gracious bow and a knowing smile, he departed the way he had come.

Veronica stood very still, enjoying the sight of her
daughter, *en garde,* dressed in the most inappropriate
and yet charming clothing. The little boy, chewing at
his lip, was attempting to set his feet in the appropriate position but was greatly hampered by a long-eared
puppy who was just then playfully attacking the lad's
ankles.

"Cease and desist, puppy," the child ordered, bending
down and patting the hound's head.

Veronica strolled farther into the park. "You will not
teach a hound to cease and desist by patting his head
when he does not, young man," she said.

"Mama!" Hannah stuck her foil into the ground and
hurried across the grass, enveloping the dowager duchess
in a hug as soon as she reached her. "You never said you
were coming. George," she called, turning back to the
boy. "George, come and make my mama's acquaintance.

Will said I was not to say a word to you about George, Mama. He was adamant about it, so I did not."

"Yes, I know. He bound Richard to secrecy as well," Veronica replied. "Thank goodness for Eulie and Harvey Langton. Why would William not tell me that he has taken charge of a child? Did he tell you that?"

"Because he wishes to decide what to do with George without your influence," Hannah replied truthfully. "I cannot think why that may be. You always have the best ideas. Mama," she said, placing her hands on the lad's shoulders as he stopped before the duchess, "may I present Master George Ethan Warren. This is my mother, George, the Duchess of Berinwick."

George bowed from the waist. "How do you do, ma'am—"

"Your grace," Hannah whispered in his ear.

"Your grace," George repeated at once. "It is a pleasure to make your acquaintance, I'm sure. Is everyone in your family a grace but you, Lady Hannah?" he asked turning to look up into Hannah's laughing eyes.

"No," Veronica replied before her daughter could do so. "Hannah's stepfather is not a grace at all. He is a plain mister. And to tell you the truth, Master Warren, I prefer to be called just plain Mrs. Dempsey sometimes."

"I prefer to be called Elf," George responded at once.

"Elf?"

"It's what William calls him, Mama."

"Because I am little and have enormous ears," George added proudly, his chest swelling just a bit. "His grace says I am the closest thing to an elf he has ever seen in all his life. I know it sounds rude, but he does not intend it to be so. He thinks I don't know the truth of it, but I do. He calls me Elf because he likes me."

"How splendid," Veronica declared with a wide smile, noting, now that the child stood directly before her, that despite his dark curls and dark eyes, there was truly no resemblance between the lad and Berinwick. Thank goodness for that, she thought. He cannot possibly be a by-blow of Will's. "What is your puppy's name, Master Warren?" she asked.

"He has no name as yet, your grace. He must wait until Sunday to have a name, his grace says."

"Until Sunday?" Veronica's eyebrows lifted as she glanced questioningly at her daughter. "Why is that? His grace does not imagine that our Mr. Dempsey will christen a hound?"

Hannah and George both giggled, which was precisely what Veronica intended them to do.

"Hannah told me that you heard Meg's screams when you came here with her, Mallory," Berinwick said without preamble as Mallory and Gazenby offered to help search the cottage one last time. "Did you? Or was it merely a ruse to gain my sister's attention—and compassion?"

"She had no business to tell you that," Mallory replied with a scowl.

"No? Why not? Did you swear her to secrecy?"

"No, but—"

"Then I fail to see your point."

"He is embarrassed for you to know of it, Berinwick," Dempsey said, surreptitiously stuffing the hand that held the trinket into his pocket and loosing the thoroughly worrisome thing there. "Anyone would realize that."

"Embarrassed?" Berinwick stared questioningly at Dempsey.

"You will forgive Berinwick," the parson continued, directing his attention to Mallory. "He long ago wiped the word embarrassment from his vocabulary and any sense of embarrassment from his heart and mind. A matter of survival, I believe, for a boy with one eye who spent his life in public school from the age of six."

"Balderdash!" Berinwick protested. "I merely fail to see what there is in hearing the screams of a dead woman to be embarrassed about. Did I hear them, I would find it most disconcerting, but embarrassment would not enter into it. Did you hear them or not, Mallory?"

Mallory nodded.

"Do you hear them now?"

"No."

"Could you, if you wished to do so?"

"I expect so," Mallory responded, slipping his hands into his breeches pockets and cocking a knee. "Why?"

"Because if you can hear her screams, Mallory, perhaps you can make out a word or two of what she says as well. A name, perhaps. Something to give us a clue to her murderer's identity."

"You ought not ask him to allow himself to hear her again, Berinwick," Gazenby said, standing supportively beside his cousin. "You don't realize what it's like, something like that. It's a fearsome thing."

"Life is a fearsome thing," Berinwick observed without so much as a blink. "Are we not to go on living it because it is, Gazenby? He was born with a special gift, your cousin. Or so Dempsey calls it—a gift. Why have it if not to use it for someone's good? He is not about to use it for evil, is he?"

"Never," Gazenby protested.

"No, I thought not. He's a favorite of yours, after all. And if Annie and Hannah are to be believed, you are the most honorable of gentlemen."

"And so is Mal, honorable and courageous and—"

"Martin," Mallory interrupted, "before my cheeks burn with all this praise—do you *feel* anything? Anything at all? It's why I begged you to come with me, to see if you did—to see if your feelings match with mine. Do not be embarrassed to say the truth, Martin. Apparently, we are in the company of gentlemen who will not make a public jest of you for doing something they cannot. At least, Mr. Dempsey will not."

"Nor will Berinwick," Dempsey declared with a glare at his stepson. "Word of your gift will not escape his lips, Gazenby. He will not so much as whisper of it to another human being."

"You can do the same things as Mallory, Gazenby, and no one knows?" Berinwick asked. "Not even Annie?"

"Only Mal. And I have never heard anything. I doubt I will. I only feel—feelings. Do not look at me so, Berinwick. If you went about feeling things that weren't there, would you tell your wife of it?"

"We'll never know, will we?" Berinwick replied. "There's not a woman in the world desperate enough to marry the likes of me. Nevertheless, I will not spill the beans, Gazenby. Not even to Annie. You have my word on it."

Martin Gazenby nodded. He wiped his hand nervously across his brow and took a deep breath. Then he grasped the back of a chintz-covered chair with both hands and closed his eyes. For two minutes that seemed liked twenty, he allowed a particular barrier in his mind—a barrier he had worked enormously hard to construct bit by bit since first he found he could do so, to tumble down. "I f-feel terror," he said after a moment, "thick as drying mud. And an appalling chasm of emptiness, despair. And evil, like a cold hand on the back of my neck. And something—something I cannot put a name to, Mal. Something familiar."

"Is your entire family odd, Mallory?" queried Berinwick.

"Is yours?" Mallory tossed back at him.

"No. Only myself and Dempsey here. But Dempsey is not a blood relative," Berinwick replied with such earnestness that Mallory was taken aback by the sincerity of it. "I have some ancestors who were notably odd, but they're dead, you know, so they don't actually count. And there is not a one of us, living or dead, who could claim to—do what Gazenby has just done. I expect it *is* a gift, if the two of you are not hoaxing us."

"Just put the cushion back on the sofa, Berinwick," Mallory commanded, "and I will attempt to hear the screams again. But I should like to sit down while I do so. I've been knocked in the head, you know, and there's no telling but letting down my guard will give me a vile headache or make me dizzy or some such thing. Hate to get dizzy and fall on the floor at your feet. Most demeaning."

Berinwick cocked an eyebrow, but then gave a short nod and replaced the sofa cushion. "Your throne, Mallory," he said with a teasing bow. "What the devil are you doing now?" he asked as Mallory sat down.

"I'm covering my ears. The sobbing and the screams were awfully loud last time."

"So?"

"So, what?"

"So, what good does it do to cover your ears, Mallory?" Berinwick expanded his thought. "I mean to say, if no one else can hear them, they must come from inside your head, no? I should think that covering your ears would only make them louder."

"Because my head is empty and they'll echo around in there?" Mallory asked with a hint of a smile.

Berinwick laughed. "I did not say that. Dempsey, you stand witness to it should word of the accusation reach Hannah. Not once did that particular observation cross my lips."

"But it crossed your mind," Mallory pointed out. "And I expect Lady Hannah knows you well enough to realize that, too."

* * *

"Who is that?" Veronica asked. She had stooped down to pet the puppy and now stood straight, her gaze fastened on the wood beyond the tumbling wall that marked the far edge of the park.

Hannah turned at once to follow her mother's gaze. "Someone who did not expect to see us here. He has dodged back beneath the trees," she observed. "I did not glimpse enough of him, Mama, to so much as guess who he might be. Merely a flick of his coattail and a beam of sunlight glancing off his buttons. Perhaps we ought to take the puppy for a stroll, eh?"

"Yes, I think so," the duchess agreed. "George, run to the stable and tell the grooms that Lady Hannah and I require one of them at the rear of the park."

"But I want to go with you," George protested. "Suppose it is a highwayman. You will require my protection."

"Then run very fast, George, and run back here again. Come, little one," Veronica added, taking the scarlet sash from her riding dress and tying one end of it around the puppy's neck. "You come with us. George does not require you prancing about his feet to make him trip and fall. We will pretend that we are simply taking this little beast for a stroll, Hannah, and stroll directly toward the place where our visitor seems to have disappeared. Now run to the stable, George. Quickly."

"It is likely one of the gentlemen from London, Mama, who has got himself lost wandering through the wood," Hannah offered as the two set off toward the spot where the figure of the gentleman had disappeared.

"If he is lost, why did he not come out and ask us to put him back on the correct path?"

"Perhaps he was going to do so, and then he noticed a woman in breeches and ran away with his hands over his eyes," Hannah replied as she paused a moment to take up the foil she had left thrust into the ground.

"Which does beg the question, Hannah. Where on earth did you come by such garments as those?"

"Will came by them for me. He went to his London tailor and had the man make up the coat and breeches and shirt from my measurements. I do not believe that he mentioned that they were for his sister."

"Oh, for heaven's sake," Veronica sighed. "You dressed like that in London? I knew I should have gone with you. I knew William was not to be trusted to stand chaperone to you and Anne. He hasn't the least sense of propriety."

"Yes, he does, Mama. He did not permit me or Anne to dress in breeches for any of the entertainments."

"He bought Anne such clothes as well?"

"Um-hmmm. But Mrs. Tofar does not know, Mama, so you will not tell her."

"No. I wouldn't think of it."

"We only wore them once in London at any rate. To sneak into Tattersall's to look at the horses up for auction there. And to look at the gentlemen, as well. Gentlemen are entirely different creatures when women are not present, Mama."

"Are they?" Veronica asked with a knowing smile. "Come, little one," she commanded as the puppy, having grown tired of bouncing around their heels, sat down at the end of his lead and refused to move. The duchess tugged. The puppy moved forward an inch and sat down again. The duchess tugged once more. The puppy tugged back and rolled over in the grass, tangling the makeshift lead around him. "At this rate, the man will be all the way to Barren Wycche before we reach the trees," Veronica sighed.

Hannah walked back and scooped the hound up into her arms. "Never mind, Mama. If he is at the edge of the wood watching us, he will never swallow the lie that we are simply out walking this little beast anyway. We may as well give up all pretense and simply look like we are searching him out. "Ahoy!" she shouted, then, as they strolled forward once more. "You in the wood! What is it you require?"

"Ahoy?"

"Davey Lancaster read it in a book. It's your fault, Mama, or Richard's, that I heard the word and have adopted it."

"Richard's," the duchess said at once.

They had just reached the edge of the wood when George came running up behind them, followed closely by Davey Lancaster. "A man in the wood?" Lancaster asked, somewhat breathless. "Where?"

"Somewhere close by, Davey," Hannah replied, the puppy struggling to be free of her arms. "His coattail seemed to be eaten right up by the willow when he moved away. Yes, see, someone has been here for the grass beneath the tree is badly trampled. Here, George, hold on to this scamp," she added, setting the puppy down and handing the boy the lead as she stooped to study the ground beneath the tree.

"Aye, someone has been here recently," Lancaster agreed, squatting beside her. "Not one bit of the grass has risen back up as yet. It does seem queer that some fellow should stand about here with people present in the park and yet not hail anyone. There. The mark of a boot heel to be sure."

"Where?" asked George eagerly.

"There, George," the duchess said, directing the boy's gaze toward the imprint in the grass.

No sooner did she do so than George fell to hands and knees and crawled under the willow tree, the puppy following eagerly. "Come, puppy, smell this," George ordered the little hound, picking it up and aiming its tiny black nose at the boot print.

"He does belong here, that boy," Lancaster whispered to Hannah. "Ready to leap into any adventure he seems.

He be too young, that hound, to follow a single scent through the wood, Master George," added Lancaster, loud enough for the lad to hear. "Hounds must be taught to keep to one scent and not be distracted by others. There be plenty of others in the wood, all beguiling to a bit of a pup like that. He'll not hold to one unless you teach him."

"But perhaps he'll hold to it long enough," George replied. "Perhaps the man is not far away."

"We will allow George and the little hound to make the attempt, David," Veronica declared, taking a small, silver pistol from the pocket of her riding dress.

"Mama!" Hannah exclaimed at the sight of it as George's eyes grew wide with astonishment.

"You do not for one moment think that your stepfather would approve of my riding the lanes alone without I promised him to arm myself, Hannah? Not when he knows there is at least one villain about and quite likely two? There is nothing to stare at, young Master George," she added. "You are old enough to learn that women are neither simpletons nor puling infants. We can learn to shoot guns just as competently as gentlemen."

"And use swords, too," George acknowledged, his eyes still wide with wonder. "Lady Hannah can fence."

"Yes, dear, I know. She pestered her brother until he taught her. Onward, I think, David. Have you a weapon by you?"

Lancaster nodded and pulled a long, wide knife from inside his boot.

"Well?" Berinwick said at last, his knee cocked, his shoulders leaning against the mantelpiece and his hands in his pockets as he stood staring down at Mallory.

"Sssshhh, Berinwick. Give him time," Dempsey said.

"No, it's all right, Dempsey. I don't hear anything," said Mallory. "Not a scream. Not so much as a whisper."

"But you did before. Why not now?" Berinwick asked.

"I don't know. I expect that they've faded away. I only ever heard sound once before—years ago—words they were. And nothing at all since—until yesterday. I could not think, when it happened, why I heard anything at all here. But, perhaps, it was because I arrived so soon after the beastly thing occurred. They're gone now."

"But you do feel something, Mal?" Gazenby asked.

"Just what you said, terror, despair, evil, and something—familiar. What the devil is that, Martin?"

"Don't know."

"Whatever it is, it doesn't help us one bit," muttered Berinwick. "We have discovered nothing new."

"Perhaps you did not, but Martin and I did," Mallory protested.

"What? What did you discover?"

"That sound, perhaps even speech, may be present for a bit and then disappear. Sounds diminish, Berinwick, but emotions, apparently, linger for centuries."

"I meant, we discovered nothing about what happened here that Dempsey and I did not already know," Berinwick grumbled. "Get off the sofa, Mallory. I haven't finished searching it yet."

"Mallory, Gazenby, come outside with me and we'll give Berinwick a free hand to peer in and under things to his heart's content, eh?" the Reverend Mr. Dempsey suggested, picking up his gloves in one hand and crossing to the door. "Who knows but with three of us searching, we might find something in the garden or near the chicken house, or possibly even in the drive."

The cousins agreed and, wishing Berinwick good luck in his hunt, followed Dempsey out the front door and around to the side of the cottage where the parson halted, stuffed his hand into his pocket and retrieved the trinket he had hidden there. Keeping it covered in his fisted hand, he studied Mallory and Gazenby for a moment, causing two pairs of eyebrows to rise in question.

"I did find something in there," Dempsey said at last. "Something I obviously overlooked the last time I was here. It was tangled in the curtains and—I do not wish to show it to Berinwick," he confessed with a shake of his head. "Not now. Not until I can find some explanation for it."

"What is it?" Mallory asked.

Dempsey held his fisted hand out before them, opened it. The trinket on his palm glittered in the sunlight.

"By gawd!" Gazenby exclaimed. Mallory poked him in the ribs with an elbow on the instant and Gazenby pressed his lips together to keep from uttering another sound.

"Don't plague the man, Mallory," Dempsey said. "I have said 'by gawd' and worse in my life, parson or not. It happens, you know. To almost everyone. Even women, when they are startled, will sometimes say it."

"Just so," Mallory nodded. "You will forgive Gazenby, then. May I have a closer look at it?" he queried, taking the trinket into his own hands. "Why do you not wish to show it to Berinwick, Dempsey? Is there something special about it?"

"I'm not certain. I have not had the opportunity to study it closely as yet. But it is much like another trinket I found once. I showed that one to Berinwick and came near to getting run through with a rapier on the spot. That particular one, centuries ago, belonged to the Poles of Wyke."

"Who?"

"You likely have never heard of them. Except for some tenuous connections on the distaff side, they all died out long ago. But there may be one or two of those relatives left. And they would carry the silver lion as a matter of pride. A gentleman who called himself Mr. Dight assumed the living at St. Milburga's of the Wood almost thirty years ago pretending to be its new rector. He was not. He was a man steeped in hatred of the Thornes and envy of all they possessed. He had murdered the true Mr. Dight and his plan was to murder Berinwick's mother and father and the boy, loot Blackcastle and burn it to the ground."

"Obviously, he did not succeed," Mallory observed.

"No. Berinwick's father killed the false parson and all but one of the gentleman's accomplices. This Dight claimed a tenuous relationship to the Poles and he carried one of their silver lions. Then, a mere nine years ago, Berinwick's father *was* murdered, and his mother and sister were attacked by the son of this false Mr. Dight. A man named Hurley, though he did not use that name at the time. He did not carry a silver lion, but he knew well the significance of it."

"What happened to this lion, Dempsey, if the son did not have it?"

"It's as I said. I discovered it and gave it into Berinwick's hands."

"Then this cannot possibly be the same one."

"No, but supposedly there are five of them, exactly alike. Berinwick has three and this looks remarkably like it might have been a fourth before it was altered—if it was altered. I cannot tell without my spectacles."

Mallory held the silver lion with the ruby eye up between forefinger and thumb and stared at it with considerable concentration, turning it first one way and then another, upside down, right side up. "Well, I'll be damned," he murmured at last.

"What?" asked Gazenby.

"This little trinket *has* been altered. Apparently it has been severed from a larger piece."

"Are you certain?" Dempsey asked.

"It's a watch fob now, Dempsey," Mallory said.

"Yes, I know that. Some jeweler added a circlet to hold it to a chain. That's what came loose and then got caught up in the curtain threads. But how can you be sure that it was severed from a larger piece? Is there a mark?"

"Two marks."

"Where on the lion are they?"

"There is one on the inside of each of the lion's front paws. They're barely visible, Dempsey. I wouldn't have noticed at all if you had not set me to studying the thing. On the three other lions that Berinwick has, is there something between the lions' paws."

"Just so," acknowledged Dempsey. "A crown with a griffin rising from it. Devil it! How am I going to show the thing to Berinwick? He'll imagine that some remnant of the Pole family still exists. He'll think the fellow killed Meg simply because she worked for the Thornes. He'll go off in a huff and challenge to a duel any man who even intimates that he has seen such a lion as this. Or worse yet, shoot someone in cold blood just for looking as though he has ever seen such a lion as this. He has not as much patience now as he had when he was younger, our duke. And Veronica and Hannah—Well, needless to say, their teeth will be set on edge. Which is why, if I can discover to whom the thing belongs before Berinwick comes to know of it, I will save us all a good many anxious days and nights. I doubt there can be anyone else bent on sacking Blackcastle and having revenge on the Thornes. It is more likely that whoever the fellow is, he bought the lion—already altered—from some jeweler. And yet, and yet, there *might* be another relative of the Poles."

Mallory closed his fist around the trinket. "May I suggest, Dempsey, that you leave this lion in Gazenby's and my charge for a day or two?" he queried.

"Why?"

"Well—"

"Mal and I," Gazenby interrupted quietly, "could nose about among the gentlemen who have come to bid on the squire's horses, Dempsey. We could show it around and ask if anyone is missing such a fob as this. The fellow who lost it would not acknowledge that he had done so, if you were doing the asking. He would guess, you know, that since you were the one who found the girl's body at the cottage, that you might have discovered his missing fob there as well. But do Mal and I ask and say that we found it near the squire's stables, why there is no telling but that the man will think it perfectly safe to step up and own the thing. He will not have the least suspicion that he is naming himself a murderer by doing so. And then, of course, there will be no reason for Berinwick to run off half-cocked, for we'll give the fellow over to Constable Lewis on the spot."

Dempsey thought about it most seriously. It seemed a reasonable plan. And he would keep his own eyes and ears open during that time and see to it that Veronica and Hannah and even Berinwick were watched over, wherever they went, just in case another Pole *was* on the horizon. He need only request assistance from the Blackcastle grooms to achieve that—at least for Lady Hannah. It would be near impossible to keep someone always beside Berinwick, but Tom Hasty would do his best to keep the duke in sight. And he and Langton could see to Veronica. She was already carrying the small pistol he had given her. To convince her not to ride out without himself or Langton at her side should not prove an impossible task.

"All right," Dempsey agreed with a nod. "For a day or two. But no longer. If you cannot discover its owner in that time, then I will have it back."

Mallory and Gazenby both nodded solemnly. "My word on it," Mallory said. "Now, if you will excuse us,

Dempsey, we had best get back to the squire's and begin our inquiries, eh?"

"No time like the present," added Gazenby, and both gentlemen turned and with long strides hurried around to the front of the cottage and their horses. Neither of them spoke a word until they were down the drive, into the lane, and well on the way to the Tofars'.

"It's Silverdale's lion," Gazenby said then. "He came asking if I had seen the thing."

Mallory nodded.

"Then why did you not say as much to Dempsey, Mal? My gawd! Sly! I have always thought him a slimy toad, but a murderer of young women? I cannot believe it."

"No, neither can I," Mallory replied, fishing the lion from his waistcoat pocket and staring down at it. "I grant you that Sly is part slimy toad and part slithering snake in the grass some of the time, but he cannot have murdered a young woman, Martin. He's annoying, but he's not evil and you and I both felt the cold hand of evil on our necks at that cottage."

"We both felt something familiar, too," Gazenby pointed out soberly. "Silverdale, Mal, is familiar to both of us. And there is one other thing."

"What?"

"For all the worrying about Poles and Dights and Hurleys and revenge, Dempsey forgot one thing."

"What one thing?"

"It's you someone attempted to kill yesterday, Mal, not Berinwick or his mother or his sister. And Berinwick told me himself that he thinks someone at Brambles altered my directions in hope that the dogs would make a meal of you on the moor."

Ten

Mrs. Dearing's temporary boarder was a bit confused. From all he had been able to learn, he had expected to discover merely sheep in the Blackcastle park and perhaps a semisomnolent shepherd or two. The idea of a lad and a halfling fencing there had never occurred to him and so their appearance had thrown his thoughts into turmoil.

Berinwick has no sons, he thought, as he moved lithely through the wood. He has a sister. Lady Hannah Thorne. But no wife and therefore, no sons. Were the lads his brothers, then? No, Meg said that he had no brothers, none that lived. Deucedly lucky for him, too, that none of them lived. All that money. All that power. And he the eldest son. And who was that lady? Berinwick's mother? Yes, that's likely. She married the rector, Berinwick's mother did. I remember that. She lives in the rectory by the church and might easily ride to visit him at Blackcastle. I should like it if my mother married a rector. Only I would wish her to marry one far away from home. So far away that she must take a sailing ship across the ocean and three separate carriages to come and visit me.

Mrs. Dearing's temporary boarder knew well the path he was on. He had been here before, any number of times, and he flowed along this deer track like a river flowing along a perfect bed. His long strides carried him confidently in the direction of the high road.

Ought not to have left the blasted horse in that shambles of a barn, he thought. Ought to have tied him here in the wood somewhere. "Somewhere close," he mumbled, gazing back over his shoulder, sensing that the lady and the two boys were attempting to follow him. One of them had hailed him. He had heard that clearly enough. But why would they set off after him into the wood? They ought not, and yet—

No, he told himself silently. They ought not to follow me. Not one old lady, a skinny halfling and a child. It is pure foolishness to follow some stranger into the wood when everyone knows there is a murderer running about. Why, they might be killed. He smiled at the thought. They might all be killed. What a shame that would be, would it not? Innocent young lads. Innocent old lady.

He frowned, remembering his last glimpse of Meg. He had not intended to kill Meg. It had been her own fault that their night at the cottage had ended as it had. A tragedy was what it was. He had been perfectly satisfied with Meg for years, and he had intended to go on being perfectly satisfied with her for the rest of his life.

Never could have married her, of course, he thought sadly. Would never do for a titled gentleman to be married to a mere serving girl. But I'd have kept her nonetheless. If only she had not proved so damnably obdurate. After all the years, after all I've given her, you'd think she would have done exactly as I asked. It is not as though she owed anything at all to this Lady Hannah. She was her servant, not her sister, for glory's sake! But no, Meggy must make such a great fuss about my wishing to do the lady in that she drove me quite mad.

He sighed, a sound like the soughing of the wind itself. "Nothing goes precisely as I plan," he whispered to the trees as they gathered close around him. "The gods have set themselves against me. But I'll succeed in spite of that. I am destined for greatness and the gods must admit of it soon. What care I if Mallory did not get lost on the moor and throw his hands into the air and ride directly back to Brambles? Had he done so, I should not have grown so furious with him and tossed that rock at his head. But had I not tossed that rock, I should not have come to recognize the futility of my first plan or conceived of the correct answer, the everlasting answer, to my problem. He was born under a lucky star, Mallory. But his luck will run out shortly. My eyes have been opened. I know, now, that I have been going about the thing all wrong."

A smile creased his face and he began to hum a little tune as he hurried along his way. Boys or no boys, he thought. Lady or no lady, Meg spoke true about the barn and the Blackcastle maze when first she told me of the place. And there is a door in the residence that leads straight out into the park. I saw that much before I was forced to retreat. But I should like to have had a closer look at that maze. I surely should like to have had an opportunity to discover the way to the middle of it in the daylight. Now, I expect, I shall have to unravel its puzzle by the light of the moon.

The puppy ran, paused and sniffed, ran again, stopped, leaped into the air and then scrambled about in a circle after his tail. Once he caught the tail, he chomped on it enthusiastically, then rolled on his back, waved all four feet playfully in the air, righted himself, sniffed again, and scuttled away with his nose to the deer path, tugging on his makeshift lead, pulling an excited George behind him.

"What do you think, Davey?" Hannah queried as they followed behind the two rascals.

"I be thinking that dab of a dog will be a wonder once he be trained," Lancaster confessed in amazement.

"Do you mean to say that the puppy is still on the correct scent, David?" Veronica asked.

"Aye, your grace. There were the print of a bootheel just behind us. I reckon it be a fresh one. Just barely visible, it were, but there to see if one be on the lookout for it."

"What are you thinking, Mama?" Hannah asked, noting the smile that spread slowly across Veronica's face.

"Only how much Richard would love to have a hound again. He misses Theophilus to this very day."

"And yet, he never did purchase another hound, Mama."

"No. He never did. He thinks that there can never be another Theophilus and so he fears he will not love another hound as much or be as patient and attentive with it as he always was with Theo. Which, of course, is balderdash, and so I have told him over and over again. George," she called abruptly. "Stop right there. Do not go out onto the road alone."

"It be most curious," Lancaster observed as the three adults hurried to catch up with George and the puppy. "Fellow did not bring his horse into the wood at all. Walked the entire path from the high road. Puppy will lose the scent now," he added.

"I should think so," agreed Hannah. "Whoever our unannounced visitor was, he has gotten away free and clear."

They came up with George and the puppy and stood, the lot of them, gazing up and down the road for a glimpse of a horse and rider galloping off in one direction or another, but there was not so much as a puff of kicked up dust to be seen.

"I did not think that we were so very far behind the man," Veronica murmured.

"Neither did I, but likely he was running, Mama, and

covered the ground with a good deal more speed than we achieved. And we did wait for Lancaster and George to return, you know."

"Yes. I wish we had not waited. I cannot think it was a mistake on the gentleman's part any longer, Hannah— that he simply became lost in the wood. He left his horse behind him on the road and came prowling the entire way afoot. So as not to be seen, I should think. He knew perfectly well that that deer path would take him to Blackcastle's park. He was spying on you."

"No," Hannah protested. "What reason could any gentleman have to spy on me, Mama?"

"You are a young woman. That is reason enough."

"But no one could know that George and I would be out in the park, Mama. It's more likely, I think, that he was a gentleman from London wishing to return home and boast of having seen more of Blackcastle than any of the others."

It was just then that the little hound bayed. He bayed so loudly that he frightened himself and scampered around in a circle to be certain that there was no other dog present. Then he put his nose to the ground, sniffed, bayed again, and tugged on his lead so hard that George was pulled, stumbling to keep his balance, right across the road, up the small berm on the other side and into the wood once again.

The three adults looked questioningly at each other and then followed. "He be chasing a hare or a fox now," Lancaster declared, rushing to catch up with George, take the lead from the boy and bring the puppy's mad little dash to a halt.

"I expect you're correct. The best thing to do is to take the fob to Silverdale and ask him directly how he came to be in that cottage and why." Gazenby sighed as he and

Mallory rode slowly along the lane at the bottom of Hatter's field which would eventually carry them to the high road.

"I can't think what else to do," Mallory said. "Perhaps Sly simply happened upon the place and, finding it deserted, went in to poke around. I mean to say, Gazenby, Silverdale might well have assumed it was the cottage in which the servant girl was murdered and thought to be of some assistance in finding the villain who did the thing."

"Sly? Think to be of some assistance in solving the murder of a serving girl? When he has never given thought to anyone's welfare but his own in thirty-some years? Surely you jest, Mal."

"Well, but perhaps he has changed."

"When would that have happened? And how, Mal? Did the hand of God come down and tap Silverdale on the shoulder and God whisper in his ear, 'Best change your ways, old fellow'? That's what it would take, I should think, for Sly to so much as offer his assistance to anyone else when he does not see some profit in it for himself."

Mallory frowned. "Perhaps he does see a profit in it this time. He knows how Lady Hannah feels about the girl's death. And Sly is determined to have her—Lady Hannah, I mean, not the dead girl—and if he were to be the one to discover the perpetrator of this heinous crime—"

"I say, what's that?" Gazenby interrupted.

"What?"

"Dismount, Mal," Gazenby ordered, drawing his own horse to a halt and swinging down from the saddle. "Do as I say. I hear someone in the wood. Climb down at once before you are hit with a ball from a long gun this time instead of a rock from a sling!"

Mallory drew tight on his reins and sat listening.

"Climb down, Mal. Hurry."

"No, no, it's not anyone about to shoot me," Mallory replied. "I daresay it's a family party headed for Hatter's field with a luncheon in a basket."

"What?"

"Be still, Martin, and listen with your ears, not your fears. A single man cannot possibly make that much noise going through the wood unless he is afoot, weighs sixty stone and limps badly. And talks to himself," Mallory added as he detected voices. "And believes himself to be a hound," he added again as a dog bayed. "Hello!" he called in the direction of the sounds. "Are you in need of any assistance in there?"

"I should think so," replied a sweetly familiar voice. "Lord Mallory, is that you?"

"And Gazenby."

"Remain where you are. I am coming to get you."

"We do not require you to come get us, my lady," Mallory said loudly with a hint of laughter in his voice. "Gazenby and I are safe here on the road. It's you and your friends who are lost in the wood."

"We are not lost," Hannah replied, chuckling, as she stomped up to the top of the berm and looked down at them in the lane. "Some of us are a bit tied up, is all."

Mallory's jaw dropped as he saw her in breeches and morning coat, foil at her side, hands on her hips and her short, dark curls playing free in the soft breeze.

"Close your mouth, Mal," Gazenby hissed.

Mallory did that and discovered that he could not gather in enough air through his nostrils. His jaw dropped again. His heartbeat increased considerably. His face flushed. He felt lightheaded and bewildered and very, very fine.

Mrs. Dearing's temporary boarder stopped at the verimost edge of the wood. He gazed carefully around and seeing no one, stepped from the cover of the trees into Hatter's field and strode purposefully through greening grass and wildflowers toward the old barn that stood amidst the unplowed, unplanted land. He had been correct about the lads and the puppy from Blackcastle giving him chase. Not too long ago, he had heard voices behind him. Once, he had heard a hound bay. But, apparently, they had ceased their hunt for him now, because there was not a hint of anyone behind him at the moment.

He had found the idea of such a rascally scamp of a puppy and two lads trailing him most amusing. He had, in fact, slowed along the way and planted his bootheels firmly in the moldering leaves from time to time, merely to give them something to follow. They would have lost his trail sooner, else. He smiled. Ought to have waited and popped out and surprised them, he thought. But no, that would not have done at all. Ask me who I was and what I wanted at Blackcastle. Wouldn't have had an answer for them. Not as if I could say I had been riding to Squire Tofar's and gotten lost, not without a horse anywhere about. His smile widened into a most beguiling grin. He pictured himself riding brazenly up to Tofar House, knocking at the front door and asking, in a perfectly polite manner, to speak to the Marquis of Kearney and Mallory. And then he pictured himself stepping out from behind the butler or the maid, or the man of all work—he was not in the least certain what servants a squire kept—stepping out from behind whomever had escorted him into Mallory's presence, bowing elegantly to the lucky marquis and with finesse, genuine urbanity, and a deal of elegance, shooting Mal dead on the spot.

His eyes glowed a deep emerald green as he approached the barn. His smile widened. He laughed. He felt more the thing at this moment than he had felt in years. In fact, he had been in the most extraordinarily good humor since first he had landed in London and begun this decidedly fine adventure—well, except for that night in the cottage when Meggy had chosen to defy him—he had not been in very good humor then. But that had been Meg's doing, and he'd recovered very nicely once she had ceased to scream like a banshee.

Yes, he thought. I have suffered needlessly for years and years and all the while the path to true happiness lay directly at my feet, merely waiting for me to choose correctly and stroll down it with courage and fortitude. Had I not been so blinded by all that went on around me, I would have come to the correct answer a good deal sooner. It is not this Lady Hannah, or any other lady who must die. It's Mallory. It's the only way. Once he is dead and buried, I shall never have cause to worry over anything again.

"How on earth did such a thing come to be?" Mallory asked, hands on his hips, a sparkle in his eyes, as he studied George, Veronica, and the puppy.

"It came to be most unexpectedly, Lord Mallory," offered George, his dark eyes luminescent in the bits of sunlight filtering through the trees above him. "The puppy was following this fellow's scent and I was holding to the other end of the puppy's lead. And he was running straight along the path, but then he went off the path and around this tree. And so I went around the tree as well, but I tripped on that wretched root there. And her grace came to help me up."

"And instead of helping you up, she tied you up?" Gazenby queried, his eyes alive with laughter. "And she tied herself up as well?"

"No, sir, Mr. Gazenby. The puppy did all of that. He thought we were playing, you know, and so he ran around and around us and jumped in and out of the bushes and—"

"—And he wove the two of you into a scarlet web," Mallory finished for the boy. "And a considerably good job of weaving it is, too. Hand me your blade, Lancaster, and I will cut the ties that bind them."

"Oh, no! You may not cut them free, my lord," Hannah declared with a determined effort to keep from chuckling. "If that were the answer, Davey and I would have done so the moment it happened."

"I may not cut them free? And why is that?"

"Because our scarlet web is woven from the sash to my riding dress, Lord Mallory," Veronica explained, a dimple flashing in her cheek as she attempted to shake part of the ensnaring sash from around her ankle. "My *new* riding dress. A riding dress most unsuited for the wife of a rector, a riding dress that cost a veritable fortune considering his income, and a riding dress that was sewn from a pattern that the rector picked out himself."

"I cannot believe it," Mallory replied.

"That the dress cost a veritable fortune? Or that it is most unsuited for a rector's wife? Or that my husband picked out the pattern himself?"

"That so long a sash is needed to fit around as slim a waist as yours, madam," Mallory responded.

"It winds five times around her waist," Hannah offered gleefully, taking the utmost delight in the way her mother's cheeks flushed with pleasure at Mallory's compliment. "And then both ends dangle nearly to the ground when she is in the saddle. It is the loveliest thing to see—Mama upon horseback in her new riding dress."

"I imagine it is a most charming vision. We must unwind the sash, then, Lady Hannah, if we dare not cut it."

"I expect unwinding it will seem a bit like dancing around a Maypole in reverse."

"Shall we dance, then?" Mallory asked, winking at her most outrageously.

"I should love to, my lord. You take the end with the puppy."

"No, no, untie the puppy and give it to me," Gazenby suggested at once. "You'll make the rascal dizzy else, and then most likely it will—all over you, Mal—and I am not riding beside you the rest of the way to the Tofars if that happens."

Lancaster, who was keeping a keen eye on the woods around them, could maintain his composure no longer. He slapped a hand over his mouth and turned his back on the lot of them. But even so, they could all see his shoulders shaking with laughter.

"So," Mallory began as he untied the lead from the little hound and set the dog in Gazenby's arms, "you were schooling such a young pup to hold a particular scent? Did he do well? Who was the fellow you set him after? One of your stableboys?"

"Not precisely," Hannah replied, the opposite end of the scarlet sash in her hands as she crawled—quite gracefully, Mallory thought—beneath a holly bush and emerged on the other side of it with a number of shining green leaves in her hair. "We only thought to try and see if the pup could hold to a scent. A spur of the moment thing, actually. We do not know whom we were following."

"You were trailing a stranger?" Mallory asked, twisting in and out, up and down among the branches of a small pine.

"We think he was a stranger. We did not see more of him than the tail of his morning coat and the glint of his buttons." Hannah turned in several circles, unwinding the sash from a series of saplings. "Apparently he was spying out the park at Blackcastle. When he noticed that we saw him, he ran off."

"What?" Mallory exclaimed, moving backward, very near the ground, unweaving the sash from between a number of tree roots at George's feet. "Are you mad? To go chasing off into a wood after a man you don't know, when there is a murderer running about? The lot of you might have been killed."

"I think not," Hannah replied, also low to the ground, unwinding the sash from around her mother's ankles. "I am not carrying this foil at my side for decoration, Lord Mallory. I am most proficient in the use of it. And Davey Lancaster is a perfect master with that knife."

"I s-see," Mallory stammered as they touched, back to back. He sprang to his feet at once and Hannah did likewise. They turned to face each other, a length of sash gathered in Mallory's hands, another length gathered in Hannah's, and less than an inch of it between them.

"And—and—if the man had not come f-forward to meet his fate at the tip of a foil or the sharp end of a b-blade?" Mallory asked around the lump that was rising in his throat as he stared down into those most remarkable eyes of hers.

Oh, but the sight of her and the feel of her so very near makes a fellow's blood rush through his body at twice the rate it ought, he thought. How beautiful she is and how thoroughly beguiling with those holly leaves caught in her curls and the scarlet sash dangling from her hands. Gads, but when did it grow so very warm out here? And we are standing in the shade, too. Say something, you peabrain. Finish the thought you began. And don't stutter either. She will think you a perfect nodcock if you stutter. "What if the fellow had turned and pointed a gun at you, Lady Hannah? What then?"

"Then Mama would have shot him d-dead with her little silver p-pistol," Hannah replied unsteadily, looking up at him, unable to look away, noticing abruptly how warm the day had grown and how unnerved she felt, wishing—and why, she could not think—that her hands were holding him and not her mama's sash at all. "Have you s-seen my mama's little silver pistol, my lord?"

"He *will* see it if he does not hand you the part of my sash he holds and take two steps back from you at once," Veronica announced with considerable authority from directly behind her daughter. "Not that I do not trust you, Lord Mallory," she added, "but I am Hannah's mother and as such there are certain proprieties I am forced to uphold—when they apply to her—when she is in the wood—when she is wearing—breeches."

"Of all things," George declared, freed at last and gazing up at the three adults, a thoroughly puzzled look on his face. "What have breeches to do with anything?"

"Do you recognize the man?" Dempsey asked in a whisper as he stood beside Berinwick in the late Widow Thistledown's flower garden and gazed at the man just then leading a horse from the old barn in Hatter's field across the way. "Or the horse?"

"Neither. Barn is too far away, Dempsey. We'll get our own horses and see can we bring him to a halt, eh?"

"Indeed, if he comes this way. Does he cross to the lane at the foot of the field and ride in the opposite direction, we'll have a devil of a time to catch him, though."

"Still, we'll make the attempt," Berinwick declared as they hurried back through the flower garden to the front of the cottage where their horses waited. They mounted and proceeded slowly, with as little noise as possible, down the drive, halting in the shade of a low-hanging sycamore, where they hoped they could watch the man without being noticed themselves.

"Damnation," Berinwick murmured, as the man mounted and turned his horse's head toward the far end of Hatter's field. "Appears that we shall be forced to chase him down, Dempsey."

Dempsey nodded. "We had best hail him, first, though. Do we not call out, he will have every right to claim that he is simply an innocent gentleman and attempted to escape us because he thought us villains in pursuit of his purse."

"That's so," Berinwick agreed, giving Darling's neck a pat. "Tell you what, Dempsey. You ride into the field after him. Call out to him that you are the parson and wish a word with him, and Darling and I will take the lane around to the foot of the field. Does he flee from you, hopefully we'll have enough of a start to abort his escape or at least catch up with him somewhere along his flight."

"You think he may be the murderer?"

"I do. And even if I am wrong in the matter, no one has reason to be in the Hatter's field barn. We may conclude, I believe, that he is not simply admiring that decrepit building. Hiding there, more likely."

"Indeed. You don't think, Berinwick, that he knows about the cave entrance?"

"We sealed it up."

"We put a new floor in the barn and that floor covers the entrance, but wooden floors can be got through."

Berinwick scowled and nudged Darling with his knee, sending her forward at a trot. "True. But how would he know to look for it? Any number of people from beyond Barren Wycche know of the Blackcastle maze, but the entrance to the cave through the Hatter's field barn—"

"Perhaps," Dempsey interrupted, urging his horse into a trot as well, "Meg told him of it."

As they reached the bottom of the drive, Dempsey crossed the lane and rode up the berm and into the field. "I say," he called to the fellow who had turned in the saddle at the sound of horses. "A word with you, sir, if I may.

I am the Reverend Mr. Dempsey of St. Milburga's of the Wood and—"

Berinwick did not hear the rest nor see the man's reaction to being thus addressed. He had reached the first turning in the lane and he set Darling to a run.

Hannah halted at the very bottom of the berm and turned almost in a circle as the sound of galloping hooves grew louder. She was unable to distinguish, at first, from which direction they came. But then, like a streak of red lightning slashing across the edge of her vision behind the thunder of their approach, the bay horse and its rider topped the rise in the lane. "George!" she shouted. "George!"

The boy who had just followed the puppy from the wood out into the middle of the roadbed looked up at her shout, saw the horse and rider bearing down on him and stooped hurriedly to gather the little hound up into his arms and carry it to the safety of the opposite berm. But the puppy was terrified by the ever-increasing pounding and fought to escape George's arms and George would not drop the hound and run.

Certainly the rider can see the lad, Hannah thought. Surely he will steer his mount to the left or the right of the child. But he came straight on, down the middle of the lane, and she saw, then, that he looked back over his shoulder and so took note of nothing before him. With grim determination, Hannah launched herself into the lane, hoping by the sheer power of her momentum to sweep both George and the puppy before her, out of danger, to the opposite side of the roadbed. Her knees pumped furiously. Her legs moved as fast as ever they had done. She reached them, grasped George's shoulder, stumbled and fell to one knee. The lane trembled beneath her. The pounding surrounded her on all sides.

The sun glinted off slashing hooves as the animal thundered toward them. And then an enormous shadow blocked Hannah's vision, a tremendous weight knocked the air from her lungs and she was flying, then falling, then rolling, entangled in a confusing ball of arms and legs, heavy muscles and delicate bones, yelps and shouts and shudders.

Berinwick, looking more demon than man, astride Darling, gained the top of the rise, saw the jumble of humanity at the side of the lane and his prey disappearing around the next bend, heard his mother's voice shouting, and brought Darling to an abrupt halt. He swung down from the saddle even as the mare reared, slashing at the sky. In an instant he was bending down beside his sister, George, the puppy, and Mallory who still held them all securely in his arms. In the next instant, Veronica, Gazenby, and Lancaster were there beside him.

"They are safe now, Lord Mallory," Veronica said. "Turn loose of them. William, help Hannah to her feet. I have George. Can you stand, George? Yes, of course you can. Goodness, what a close call that was. You came near to being trampled to death, the lot of you."

"Y-yes," George acknowledged from the security of Veronica's arms. Tears streaked the dust on the boy's cheeks and he shuddered as he breathed. The puppy shuddered as well and whimpered and burrowed beneath George's arm.

"He c-came straight at us," Hannah said with a gulp as Berinwick tugged her to her feet. "I meant to push George and the hound to safety but I t-tripped. He never swerved aside, Will. The dastard never made one attempt to miss us."

"Never mind," Berinwick murmured as his arms closed around her. "You're safe now, my girl. Are you hurt? Any bones broken? I vow I'll flog the blasted villain to within an inch of his life for this before I watch him hang. Mallory, are you in one piece?" he asked over Hannah's shoulder as that gentleman stood and brushed at the dirt on his breeches. "You saved their lives. I am in your debt for it."

"Who the devil was that madman?" Mallory grumbled.

"Don't know. Saw him leaving the Hatter's field barn. Broke and ran from Dempsey. Might be Meg's murderer."

"Then go after him. It's Hannah's Darling standing there in the lane, is it not? She's the fastest horse in all of England, I've heard. You may still be able to catch the fellow."

Berinwick stared at Mallory thoughtfully. "Here," he said after a moment. "Take my sister. Look after her and the lot of them," and giving Hannah a quick kiss on the cheek, he freed her from his arms, dashed back into the lane, stepped up into Darling's saddle and set off in pursuit of the nameless rider.

No sooner did Darling break into a run than another horse and rider appeared before the stunned little group at the side of the road and drew abruptly to a halt.

"Richard!" Veronica exclaimed as Dempsey dismounted and hurried in her direction. "George and Hannah were nearly trampled to death a moment ago."

"But they were not, eh?"

"No. Lord Mallory saved them."

"Thank goodness for Lord Mallory then. You are safe as well, eh, Vernie?"

"Yes, I am fine. But a rider came neck-or-nothing up the rise without a thought for anyone and George and Hannah were in the middle of the lane and—"

"Was that Berinwick just now departed?"

"Yes," Veronica replied. "He has ridden off after—"

"I know who he is chasing, Vernie. The stranger from Hatter's field. Norville is not as fast as he once was, or I should have been closer behind that villain myself. Thank goodness for Hannah's Darling. Berinwick still stands a chance of catching the man astride Darling." As he spoke, he took Veronica into his arms, closing George and the puppy cozily between himself and Veronica as he did so. He placed a warm kiss on the duchess's lips. Then, keeping one hand on her arm, he knelt and, seeing the boy's tearstained cheeks, gave the child a hug. "Are you all right, George?" he asked in the kindest tone. "Of course, you are," he smiled. "What a silly question to ask. You're a fine, brave young gentleman and not like to die from a skinned knee or a bit of roughing up. Anyone can see that."

"Just s-so," George sniffed, raising his chin. "We were frightened is all, but we have got pluck, Gulliver and I."

"I should think so," Dempsey replied. "And is this Gulliver in your arms? What a fine looking hound he is."

"I thought he had no name as yet, George," Veronica said. "Did you not tell me you were going to wait to name him until Sunday?"

"Yes," George nodded, "but one has to call him something in the meantime. So I am calling him Gulliver, because he is bound to have enormous adventures, just like Gulliver in the book. He has already had one."

"Gulliver," Hannah whispered, turning in the circle of Mallory's arms to gaze up at him.

"Enormous adventures in the offing," Mallory whispered back. "They ought not to be parted, that boy and that dog."

"Precisely what I was thinking. I shall speak to Will about it. Did Clare Simmons have other puppies?"

"Indeed. Six or seven."

Hannah nodded. "I shall speak to Will first thing this evening about purchasing a different puppy for Richard."

"And what will he say to that, your brother?"

"Oh, he will grumble that no dog is worth the price that Mr. Simmons demands for his blooded hounds and he'll suggest that I go out on the moor and snare one of the wild dogs for Richard. And then tomorrow he will ride over to the Simmonses and purchase a pup with his own money to replace Gulliver."

It was the oddest thing, but the more this young woman spoke, the more Mallory wished her to go on speaking. Even if it was in whispers. Especially because it was in whispers.

"I do thank you, Lord Mallory, for saving our lives," Hannah said, her eyes alive with light and shadow. "I thought George and I would both be killed."

"You're quite welcome, I'm sure. Pleased to be of service." Did that sound as inane as I think it did? Mallory wondered. Yes, and ludicrous and insipid to boot. "Had I seen George there in the middle of the road, you need not have imperiled yourself so, but I was so busy discussing horses with your groom that I did not look up until you shouted."

"Shouted? You heard me shout? You are mistaken, Lord Mallory. My heart was in my throat and left no room for words to reach my lips. Perhaps it was my mama you heard?"

Mallory's arms tightened around her, drawing her closer. Her face was grimy, her clothing grass-stained, dirty, and disheveled, her hair tumbled about her face like an unruly string mop, all of which, quite unaccountably, made her the most alluring young woman he had ever encountered.

She smells of sunshine and shade, of tree bark and moldering leaves, he thought as his pulses pounded in his ears and his head bowed unwittingly toward her. How can such a scent be more alluring to me than all the perfumes and sachets and soaps concocted by all of the scent makers in all of England, in all of Europe? And yet, it is so. It is maddeningly seductive. *She* is maddeningly seductive. His lips brushed hers, slowly, tenderly, and his tongue flicked out, tasting the dust from the lane that lingered on her lips.

"I dare say when Berinwick told you to *take* his sister he did not intend for you to *take* her in quite that manner, Mal," Gazenby said loudly, giving Mallory a sharp slap on the shoulder in the midst of the kiss.

Mallory drew back on the instant, his face flushed, his eyes filled with wonder. "I—I beg your pardon, Lady Hannah," he stuttered uneasily, noting over her shoulder that both her mother and stepfather were now staring silently in his direction. "I don't know what came over me."

"You don't?" Hannah asked, suddenly released from the circle of his arms, but not taking one step backward.

"N-no. I—I am not generally so—so—forward."

"Is Mama glaring at you?"

"No, not precisely glaring, but she and the parson are—are—studying me as though I am some bug on the end of a pin."

"Oh, poor man," Hannah replied, smiling softly up at him. She raised her hand and pressed it to his flaming cheek. "It's because of the breeches," she whispered. "Mama cannot be at all opposed to my being kissed by a gentleman, not when he has just saved my life. But she cannot be complaisant about my being in your arms and in breeches at one and the same time, I think."

"And your stepfather?"

"Oh, there is no knowing what goes on in Richard's mind. He met Mama secretly in our gatehouse once and William caught them there kissing each other soundly. He's an odd duck for a parson, our Richard."

"Hannah, come along. Richard and I will accompany you back to Blackcastle," the duchess announced. "Lancaster, lead the way. Mr. Gazenby, I would request that you and Lord Mallory chase after William, but there is not the least chance that you will catch him up, so I have another request to make of you instead."

"Yes, your grace?"

"Do mount up, Mr. Gazenby, and take your cousin directly to your favorite fishing place. I know you have one."

"Indeed, I have."

"Just so. And he has not yet seen it?"

"No, your grace."

"Excellent. Take him there at once—and toss him in."

"Mama!" Hannah exclaimed on a giggle.

"It will do him good," Veronica declared. "The poor man is burning up."

Berinwick slowed Darling to a trot, then to a walk. It was pointless to go on riding neck-or-nothing after a mere shadow of a man. Somewhere along the way the fellow had left the lane and taken a path through the wood. He must have done so, for there could be no one ahead of Darling and Berinwick at this point, not as hard and as fast as they had been traveling. The Byerly Turk himself could not have escaped them, had he kept to the road.

There are far too many paths through Grydwynn Wood, Berinwick thought angrily. By the time I determine which of them he took—if I can determine which of them he took—he will be wherever it is he's hiding. Which is most likely somewhere in Barren Wycche. "We'll go into the village, eh, Darling?" he murmured, giving the horse's neck a pat. "Inquire at the inn's stable if any bay has just arrived looking as though it has had a hard run. Inquire the rider's name and direction as well."

At least I know our man is a gentleman, Berinwick thought. Saw enough of him at Hatter's field to deduce that. Burgundy morning coat, buckskin breeches, owns a blooded bay who runs like the wind. Most definitely a gentleman. Rode like a gentleman, too, one who has spent a good many years in the saddle.

"Perhaps Silverdale was correct," he said aloud, causing Darling to prick her ears in his direction. "Perhaps Meg did run off with a gentleman, believing that he would marry her and that they would live happily ever after just as happens in faery tales." A gentleman, he thought, considering the option seriously. Or even a lord. "Silverdale," he hissed then on an exhalation of breath. "Silverdale rides a bay. And he's a lord. And he first appeared at Tofar's the day following the murder."

And yet, it was Mallory who began to tremble at the first mention of Meg that evening after dinner, he reminded himself. Now how the devil does that fit into the puzzle? It was certainly *not* Mallory I was chasing just now. No, he, in fact, dove into the road to save Hannah and George from being trampled to death. He must be above suspicion on that count alone. And yet, what was it that Elliot said that evening in the drawing room? That perhaps Mallory had ordered one of his minions to do away with Meg while he, himself, sat innocently in the squire's parlor?

"Could the man be a servant of Mallory's?" Berinwick whispered, amazed at the thought. "Mallory has a gentleman who works for him. Gazenby said as much. A gentleman secretary. Might Mallory have been planning to meet that secretary at the Widow Thistledown's cottage? To pay him for his successful effort, perhaps?" Berinwick scowled at the idea. He had no wish to believe it, but it seemed plausible.

This secretary fellow might have heard Dempsey and me coming up the lane from the opposite direction Mallory would take and so hid in the barn, just to be careful, he thought. And when Mallory arrived and discovered us there and not the man he expected, he decided to perform that little drama of listening for ghosts to cover his true reason for being at the place.

"No," Berinwick protested. "Mallory had Gazenby with him. And Gazenby would never allow himself to be used in such a way. No matter what Elliot said about the difference between appearances and what is actually in someone's heart, Gazenby is a veritable saint inside and out."

But perhaps, he thought, running his fingers through his hair in frustration. Perhaps, Gazenby had no idea that he *was* being used.

"No, never," he protested again. "I am all about in my head. Mallory cannot have any part in it. Hannah is growing fond of him. I can tell she is growing fond of him. And she would never grow fond of a murderer. Not Hannah. She knows better than anyone how to read what is in a man's heart. Did she not read what was in mine when she was a mere child? Even before Mother ever did?"

And yet, Berinwick could not be at all easy in his mind. He would have sworn last Season in London that Hannah had grown terribly fond of Silverdale, just as she was now growing fond of Mallory. Silverdale had already had a reputation as a gambler, a drinker, a rake and a rogue—a gentleman walking a thin line between good and evil, sometimes leaning one way and sometimes the other. But Berinwick had told himself then that Hannah had seen something in the man, something worthy of her love, and he had ascribed Silverdale's reputation to rumor and gossip and nothing more. Had she truly read that gentleman's heart? Or had she been deceived? She certainly treated Silverdale now as if she had been deceived. Was Mallory in the process of deceiving Hannah as well? Was Mallory deceiving them all?

Eleven

In his room at the Three-Legged Inn, Silverdale held the silver lion lovingly on his palm and sank down into the wingback chair beside the bed. "I cannot thank you enough, Mal," he said in a voice husky with emotion, a voice most unlike his own. "I thought it was gone for good. I intended to sell it soon, you know, to provide me money to influence Berinwick in considering my suit of Lady Hannah. But—but—since it has been gone, I have begun to realize how I should feel not to have it with me. I have always had it with me, ever since Father's death. It is the only truly personal thing I have of father's. He always wore it, you know, on his watch chain. And when it disappeared—when it disappeared and I thought that I should never have it with me again—" Silverdale's voice cracked and he ceased to speak on the instant.

Mallory's gaze met Gazenby's. True sympathy shone in both pairs of eyes. Their communication, though silent, left neither of them with the least doubt what the other was thinking—that Silverdale was in the midst of a drastic alteration of his character and that the alteration would make him a much better man. He was coming to see the true value of things, not in monetary terms, but in terms of life, love, and humanity. But they would not say as much to him. A fellow didn't speak of such things as that. A fellow merely knew. And there was, as well, a most serious matter to be confronted at once.

"You have never been to the Widow Thistledown's cottage, have you, Sly?" Mallory murmured, sitting down on the bed across from Silverdale. "Never in your life."

"Where? Whose cottage?"

"The Widow Thistledown's cottage," Gazenby repeated softly, stuffing his hands into his breeches pockets, leaning back to rest his shoulders against the mantelpiece of the narrow, tile-ornamented fireplace.

"No," Silverdale replied, stroking the silver lion with his thumb. "I can't think that I have. I don't know any Widow Thistledown. Does she live here in Barren Wycche? Is there some reason that I *should* know her?"

"None," Mallory replied. "No reason at all."

"Then why do you ask? Why are you and Gazenby looking at me like that? What the devil is wrong, Mal?"

It was the first time since the death of Silverdale's father all those years ago that Mallory could remember his heart stirring on Silverdale's behalf. "I wish I had no need to tell you," he said. "But I can't think of a way to discover what's happening without telling you. Your lion was discovered inside the Widow Thistledown's cottage yesterday."

"Then it was some elderly woman who found it first? A widow? Did she find it along one of the lanes and take it home with her? Oh. Likely she wishes a reward, eh? Well, that's all right. Is twenty pounds enough, do you think? Twenty pounds is a great deal for a widow. I thought at first to offer as much to anyone who returned it."

"The Widow Thistledown did not find it, Sly," Mallory replied quietly. "She's dead. Has been for a number of years. It was Berinwick's stepfather found it where someone left it to be found—in the widow's cottage where one of Berinwick's servant girls was murdered but days ago."

"Oh, m'gawd! That Meg girl whom Tofar and Berinwick were discussing after dinner that evening at Black-castle! Oh, m'gawd, Mal! They will think that I was there, that I had something to do with it!" Silverdale's remark-able eyes widened in genuine fear. "He will kill me straightaway, Berinwick will. What am I going to do? What ought I to do?"

"First of all," Mallory said, "Berinwick will not kill you, Sly. We have laws in England."

"Yes, but when has that ever stopped Berinwick from doing whatever he pleases?"

"Many times, I should think. He is not as black as peo-ple paint him."

"No, he is much blacker. I vow I have never been to the place, Mal. No, and I have never set eyes upon the girl ei-ther. Not that I know of. I haven't the least idea what she looks—looked—like. How could my lion have come to be there, in the place where she was murdered?"

"That's what we've come to find out," Mallory replied. "Someone—the murderer, I should think—either found it where you lost it, Sly, or stole it from you and placed it in the cottage so you would be blamed for his crime. Per-haps he is someone who pretends to be a friend of yours but actually wishes you ill."

"Or perhaps he had no idea to whom the lion be-longed and merely wished to send Berinwick and the constable after anyone but himself," Gazenby added.

"Can you think of anyone who might wish you harm, Sly? Anyone who might wish to see you blamed for the girl's murder?" Mallory asked. "Anyone at all?"

"I am quite aware that Lord Silverdale generally rides a bay, Will," Hannah replied to her brother's suggestion, "but the entire village is overrun with gentlemen and I should think a number of them ride bays as well."

"Eighteen of them," Berinwick replied. "That is to say,

there are eighteen bays stabled at the inn. I checked. And perhaps this particular animal is not stabled there, but hidden away somewhere."

"Well, there you are. You cannot go around thinking that Lord Silverdale is a murderer simply because the fellow you were chasing yesterday rode a bay." Hannah folded her napkin and set it down beside her plate. "Besides, he would never murder anyone, not Lord Silverdale. I know him well enough to tell you *that* with certainty. He is brazen and audacious and a bit of a rake, but a murderer? Never!"

Berinwick nodded and raised his cup of coffee to his lips.

"Will you ride to the Simmonses' place this afternoon?" Hannah asked just as he swallowed.

The coffee caught in Berinwick's throat, seemed to boil there a moment and then dropped straight to his stomach. He coughed until his eye watered and then he had to stand up and cough some more.

"Good heavens!" Hannah exclaimed, standing herself and rushing around the table to pat him soundly between the shoulder blades. "I had no intention of making you choke to death, Will."

"N-no," Berinwick managed. "I w-won't. I f-forgot."

"About the puppy?"

Berinwick nodded, gasping for breath.

"Better now?" Hannah asked.

Berinwick nodded. "Went down all in a clump," he muttered, waving his sister back to her seat and sitting back down himself. "It was the thought of having Gulliver underfoot for years to come, I expect," Hannah grinned.

"No, not that. Elf."

"George? What about George?"

"I like having that elf around. You will not tell him that, by the way, or I'll knock you severely about the head with a milking stool, Hannah. But I cannot keep him here at Blackcastle if I am to raise him properly as his father expected me to do. He must go off to school. A lad cannot succeed in this world without an education. Especially not a commoner."

"No. But he need not go to school until the next term begins, Will. He need not even go until next year. He has never been, you know, so—"

"That is just the thing," Berinwick interrupted. "He has never been and I should like to keep it that way, but I cannot think how. There is no one in Barren Wycche to tutor him and do I place an advertisement in the London papers—Well, I don't like to do that, you know. Once people took note who wished to hire them, they would never answer it. And there's no telling but I'd become a jest in Lords for the longest time because of it—so great a jest that I'd be forced to call someone out to end it."

"You would hire a tutor for George?"

"Yes, if I could. I have been to school. I would not wish it on my worst enemy."

"Oh, William, school cannot be as terrible as that."

"Not if you are a large, confident, elder boy. But for one as delicate and young as George it is like being dumped down into Hades. I should not like to be responsible for dipping even one of the elf's toes into Hades."

"Then I have an idea," Hannah said.

"No, I will not send him off to board with some clergyman in Ludlow. I thought of that at first, but it won't do."

"Not just any clergyman, Will. And not in Ludlow. Right here in Barren Wycche. Richard."

"Dempsey? Dempsey is not a tutor."

"Merely because he has never thought to be one. He is a brilliant gentleman, our Richard. He is a Fellow of the Royal Society of London. And did Richard agree to do it, George need not leave Blackcastle at all except to ride over to the rectory for his lessons."

Berinwick frowned and took a sip of his cooling coffee. "Dempsey," he murmured. "I wonder. Does George know he is to keep the hound? Gulliver, is it?"

"Yes, Gulliver. And no, I said nothing at all to him. But you cannot separate them, Will. Not now."

"No. But there is something I have just thought to do today that precludes a trip to the Simmonses' farm. And tomorrow is already Friday and the ball is Saturday. Do you think, if I give you the money, Hannah, that you can tell George we have decided that he is to keep Gulliver for his own, then take him with you to the Simmonses and the two of you pick out another pup—one eccentric enough to appeal to Dempsey? But you must convince the elf not to become attached to that one as well. We must have one to bestow on Richard."

Hannah grinned. "I think I can do both things."

"And you ought to take one of the carriages. I have had a go at carrying a wriggling hound on horseback. A carriage would be better. And let John Coachman drive with one of the grooms up beside him."

"One of the grooms up beside him?"

"With a long gun in his hands," Berinwick said decisively. "I cannot think why anyone would murder Meg, or knock Mallory in the head with a rock, or peer into our park from the wood and then run off, or hide a horse in the Hatter's field barn. I cannot even be certain if there is one man did all these things, or four separate men did one apiece. But until I discover just what is going on, I don't wish for you to travel about without an armed guard, Hannah. Neither you, nor Elf."

"Cumberton?" Mallory's eyebrows rose. "I cannot imagine young Cumberton involved in anything the least bit nefarious."

"No, neither can I," Silverdale admitted with a sigh, "but

he is the only one who has actually paid me the least attention here. Everyone else is primed for the auction and they speak of nothing else. Cumberton says he came merely to have a look at the horses and bid on one or another of them on his brother's behalf. He is not interested in any of them for himself. Perhaps his brother is not interested in the horses either. Perhaps it is just an excuse to—to—"

"Yes, I get stuck there as well. Every time," Mallory muttered. "With every gentleman who comes to mind. To do what? Why bring the girl back to Barren Wycche to murder her when one might accomplish the same thing far away from Berinwick's view. And why attack me? And why go nosing about the Blackcastle grounds? Why not depart this place as quickly as possible after the girl's death?"

"Meg was ladies' maid to Lady Hannah and Anne," Gazenby mused aloud. "Perhaps that has something to do with it. Perhaps we are considering the wrong things altogether."

"Do you mean to say that this villain may be after Lady Hannah?" Silverdale asked.

"Lady Hannah?" Mallory rose abruptly from the edge of the bed and began to pace the chamber. "But then why attempt to place the blame for the girl's murder on Sly? Oh, devil it! Because Sly courted her in London and came here to continue to court her and the man wished to eliminate him from the competition! And he threw a rock at my head, thinking that I wished to court her and to eliminate me as well. He has his mind set on having Lady Hannah for himself and is not adverse to killing people in order to achieve that end!"

"That's it!" Silverdale exclaimed. "The fiend learned all that he could about Lady Hannah and Berinwick and Blackcastle from the maid and then cruelly disposed of her!"

"And there is something about your silver lion, Sly," Gazenby added, growing excited at the possibility of having come at last to the correct conclusion. "By George, but I think we are on to something. What was it the parson said about the lion? That it resembled a number of trinkets belonging to sworn enemies of the Thornes of Barren Wycche, the Poles or some such."

"What?" Silverdale stood abruptly at the words. "An emblem of sworn enemies of the Thornes? My lion? Well, that's rubbish, Gazenby! My father had not the least enmity toward Berinwick's father. Why, they barely knew each other. And I have nothing against Berinwick. By gawd, I am in love with his sister!"

"And she is in love with you?" Mallory queried softly.

"No. She was coming to be in love with me," Silverdale sighed, "but then I—I—lost my mind and did something unforgiveable and she will never have me now—not were I the last gentleman left upon the earth."

"Oh. What did you do, precisely?"

"It is none of your business, Mallory."

"No, no, none of my business," Mallory replied, remembering the secret Hannah had shared with him and wondering if he ought to inform Silverdale that he already knew what had occurred. But he could think of no good that would come from it and so he kept his peace.

"I shall never have her," Silverdale declared with a scowl, "but I'm damned if I will see her happiness threatened by marriage to some dastardly villain. I'm damned if I will stand by and do nothing to save her!"

"Then we must go and speak with the Reverend Mr. Dempsey and let him study that lion of yours, Sly," Mallory replied. "It was he who discovered the thing in the cottage, and he who told us of its likely meaning to Berinwick. Perhaps this fiend we seek took your lion because he, too, knew of its significance to the Thornes and wished to damage your reputation even further in their eyes by associating you with Berinwick's sworn enemies."

"Not satisfied merely to get me killed, eh?" Silverdale asked, crossing to take his hat from the top of the chest of drawers and placing it on his head. "Fellow wishes to get me killed *and* make Hannah believe that I was her secret sworn enemy to boot! Well, that's not going to happen. Come, Mallory, Gazenby, we're off to St. Milburga's of the Wood, the lot of us. We'll see what Dempsey has to say. With four of us thinking it through, we are bound to discover the answer to this puzzle and capture this dastard before he can do any more harm. But it ain't Cumberton involved in it. Cumberton is not intelligent enough."

Berinwick stopped first at the Hatter's field barn and gave a sigh of relief as he walked inside to discover that the floor had not been broached and that the cave— which ran from beneath Hatter's field all the way to below the maze in Blackcastle's park—had not been discovered by the stranger.

Ought to have sealed the thing off more fully, he thought as he strolled from the outbuilding and remounted Darling. Ought to have used gunpowder and brought the rocks down and closed it tight. If Dempsey had not been so eloquent in his defense of it, I would have done so. But no, I must listen to his prosing on and on about the possiblities of antiquities being strewn about in there somewhere. I must believe that Owain Glyndwr lies in his burial shroud beneath the maze and that artifacts of his days of power litter the place. Has anyone ever found his body? No. Has anyone ever discovered any artifacts? No. Has Dempsey, who spent so much of his life digging about all over England for antiquities ever so much as gone back down into the place to look for anything of importance? No.

Of course, that is not his fault, Berinwick conceded. Every time he thinks to go down there, he remembers what happened to m'mother and cannot bring himself to do it. I expect if the woman I loved had been abducted and threatened with a cruel death beneath my very feet, I would not feel much like going back down to the place she might have died either.

"If there were a woman I loved," Berinwick murmured. "If there were a woman who loved me in return. Ha! As if that could ever be!" He turned Darling back toward the lane and once he reached it, he set the mare in the direction of St. Milburga's of the Wood.

Please, God, he prayed silently, whatever is going forward at the moment, don't let Mallory have a part in it. Don't let him have ordered Meg's murder. Don't let Mallory have ordered some fellow to hit him in the head with a rock to distract everyone from the truth of his guilt. Because—because Hannah's eyes glowed like coals in December when she told me how he kissed her in front of Mother and Richard. And ever since, her smile has been as bright and hopeful as ever I've seen it. She is falling in love with the man and if I must send him to his death, she will never be able to look at me again without her eyes brimming with pain. She may never be able to look at me again at all.

Berinwick knew that he was not an exemplary sort of gentleman. Not at all. He was hotheaded and brusque and most unappealing to the eye and some of the stories that the gossips told about him were true. But he loved his sister dearly and he did not think he could bear to see her eyes fill with pain at the sight of him. In fact, he knew he could not. Anyone else in the world might look upon him and see a veritable beast. That, he did not mind one bit. But for Hannah's heart to fill with pain each time she looked upon him, that he would not be able to bear, not for a single moment. That would crush him entirely.

* * *

John Coachman slowed the Berline, then brought it to a halt almost beside the gentleman. On the box beside him, Tom Hasty held his long gun at the ready, the business end pointed unapologetically at the gentleman's heart.

"I do beg your pardon," the gentleman said, gazing up at them. "I would not have waved you to a stop, but I have had a spot of trouble and—I say, must you point that thing at me?"

"Yes," Hasty replied succinctly.

"Oh. Well, I am not a highwayman or anything of that sort. I assure you of it. I have merely had a spot of trouble," the gentleman continued, brushing at the considerable dust on his breeches. "Something frightened my horse and—I'm embarrassed to say it—I was not paying the least attention and he threw me off and dashed away up the road. I doubt he has gone far, but apparently I turned my ankle in the fall and cannot give chase. Do you know, there is barely any traffic along this road. Yours is the first carriage I have seen and I have been limping along for nearly a quarter hour."

"Who be ye?" Tom Hasty asked gruffly.

"Lord Harry Denham," the gentleman replied. "You may know m'elder brother. He is the Marquis of Kearney and Mallory and has come to this place to bid on a horse."

"You are Lord Mallory's brother?" Hannah asked, poking her head out through the carriage window to study the dusty gentleman more closely. He was a tall, lean young man with broad shoulders, a straight back, curls the very color of Lord Mallory's and eyes a shade greener than Oriental jade.

"Good morning, ma'am," Lord Harry replied with a courteous bow. "Do you know Mal?"

"Indeed. He is visiting with Squire Tofar at Tofar House."

"Tofar? Yes, that sounds like the name. Married m'cousin Martin—a Miss Anne Tofar. Well, she will be Mrs. Gazenby now, of course."

"Tom, do set aside that gun, let down the steps and help Lord Harry into the carriage," Hannah requested. "Certainly we have nothing to fear from Lord Mallory's brother. We are not going to the Tofars' at present," she continued, her gaze returning to the gentleman. "We are on a special errand for my own brother at the moment. He is the Duke of Berinwick, and I am Lady Hannah. Do we not find your horse, Lord Harry, and do you not mind waiting on us, we will be pleased to deliver you to Tofar House once we have accomplished our task. Is Lord Mallory expecting you?"

"No. Not at all," the gentleman replied as he stepped up into the Berline and took a seat beside George and opposite Hannah. "I'm to be a surprise."

"Like Mr. Dempsey's puppy?" George queried.

"This is Master George Ethan Warren," Hannah said with a bright smile. "Master Warren, Lord Harry Denham."

"Pleased to meet you," George said with a curt nod. "*Are* you to be a surprise like Mr. Dempsey's puppy?"

"Well, I don't know," Lord Harry replied. "Is this Mr. Dempsey at all expecting to have a puppy come to him?"

"No. Not at all."

"Then, yes. I am precisely the same sort of surprise. M'brother is not expecting to have me appear either. I have been in India, you see, with the Nineteenth, and Mal believes I am still there."

"You're a soldier!" George exclaimed as the coach once again began to roll toward Clare Simmons's farm.

"A cavalryman, actually, though I don't care to admit *that* at present, my horse and I having so ignominiously parted company. I am generally an expert horseman, but I rather think I dozed off."

"On horseback?" Hannah queried.

"Unfortunately, yes. And look at the result," Lord Harry chuckled. "I have embarrassed myself beyond belief and must beg aid from complete strangers. I cannot thank you enough for taking me up, Lady Hannah. You are as kind as I knew you would be."

"As you knew I would be?" Hannah tilted her head a bit to the right, studying the gentleman.

"When I saw you," Lord Harry explained at once. "The very moment you looked out at me from this carriage, I recognized the kindness in your eyes, in your expression. Your face was a portrait of kindness."

"Why are you not wearing a uniform?" George asked, abruptly. "There was a cavalryman at Blackcastle when I came and he wore the most impressive uniform."

"Did he? Well, I have a most impressive uniform, but I did not wish to go riding about England in it. Much too ostentatious, I think. Do you know what that means, my little fellow? Ostentatious?"

"Of course I do," George scowled. "I'm not stupid."

"George!" Hannah exclaimed.

"Well, I'm not. And I am not a 'little fellow' either. I am as large a fellow as I can be at present and I am going to grow larger, too. His grace says I shall and he is always right."

"Is he?" asked Hannah, smiling.

"Yes."

"How do you know that, George?"

"He told me so."

Berinwick noted, somewhat amazed, the number of horses tethered in the rectory yard. What the deuce is going on? he wondered as he dismounted and tethered

Darling beside the others. He strolled to the door and pounded decisively upon it. When it did not open immediately, he pounded again.

"That'll be Berinwick," Dempsey announced and rose from his chair in the front parlor. "No, Veronica, remain seated. I'll let him in."

"How does he know it is Berinwick at the door?" Silverdale asked nervously, running his fingers through his curls.

Veronica chuckled. "No one knocks on our door quite as determinedly as William. Perhaps you did not take note, but he tends to rattle the windows with every knock."

"I noticed," offered Gazenby. "He does the same thing when he comes to call at the squire's. Anne says he always has."

"Just so," Veronica replied. "I cannot think why, but so it is. When William knocks, he will be heard in the farthest reaches of any and all establishments."

"What the deuce is going on?" Berinwick's voice reached from the entryway into the parlor without the least impediment. "If I didn't know you better, Dempsey, I should think it a church meeting. But I do know you better. G'morning, Mother," he added as he preceded the rector into the parlor. "Mallory? Gazenby? Silverdale? What the devil are you doing here?"

"At the moment, William, we are discussing the possibility that one or more of us may actually know Meg's murderer," Veronica replied. "Do join us. I thought to send for you, but Richard was certain you'd appear on our doorstep sometime today—after you'd gone to check the Hatter's field barn. Did you go to check the barn, Will?"

Berinwick lowered himself into the chair that Dempsey had recently abandoned while Dempsey seated himself on the sofa beside the duchess. "I just came from

Hatter's field," he admitted. "No one has disturbed the barn floor."

"We know, darling. Richard checked it as well."

"He never told me that he did."

"No, because you went chasing after the man before he could do so, and we have not seen you since. Lord Silverdale has something you should see, William."

Silverdale's face grew a shade more pale at her words. "I d-don't think—" he stuttered.

"Yes, yes, he must see it sometime, Lord Silverdale," Veronica insisted. "And the sooner the better. Do not bellow at Lord Silverdale when he shows it to you, William. It is not his fault that he has it. It belonged to his father and came to him as part of his inheritance."

"Bellow? Why would I bellow at Silverdale?"

"Because of th-this," Silverdale said, standing and crossing to Berinwick, holding out the silver lion in the palm of his hand for Berinwick's scrutiny.

The duke took it from him and stared in disbelief at the trinket. "Well, by gawd!" he bellowed, coming close to shattering several sets of eardrums and sending Silverdale two steps backward. "But there's no crown or griffin," he added more softly. "Is it merely a coincidence that the lion itself looks so much like the others? Or did someone make a copy of the lions?" he asked, his gaze directed at Dempsey.

"Look more closely, Berinwick," Dempsey replied. "Bring it here to the window where the light is better."

Berinwick did just that, stepping around Silverdale to do so. "It's been altered. Here, between the paws where the crown ought to rise. It *is* another one of them. Father was correct about the number then. Where did your father get it, Silverdale?"

"I have no idea, I'm afraid. If I did know, I would tell you. Dempsey has explained about the Poles and the Thornes and all, but I'm certain I never knew any Poles, nor do I wish you and your family any ill. And how it came to be in the Widow Thistledown's cottage, I cannot think."

"It was in the Widow Thistledown's cottage? Who found it there? Why the devil didn't—"

"I discovered it," Dempsey inserted before Berinwick could ask the question. "Yesterday. Entangled in the curtains. And I did not bring it to your attention because I thought to bring it here with me and determine if it was one of the original set of lions before I added it to the host of worries already upon your shoulders. I did not want you thinking Meg's death to be the work of one of the Poles' descendents if it was not."

"But before he could do so," Mallory said, speaking for the first time since Berinwick had entered. "Before he could do so, he showed it to me and I convinced him to give it to me for a time. I lied to him. I said I would ask around to see if any of the London gentlemen might claim it when I already knew to whom it belonged. I am sorry for the lie, but I could not bring myself to believe either that Silverdale held an enmity toward your family or that he had anything to do with the murder of a poor servant girl. And I was correct. Sly did lose the trinket, but he has never been in the Widow Thistledown's cottage. Someone placed it there after the girl's body was discovered, I think, to point everyone in Silverdale's direction."

Berinwick looked from Mallory to Silverdale to Gazenby and back again. "How do you know that Silverdale was never in the cottage? Simply because he said as much?"

"I am not a fool, Berinwick," Mallory replied, standing and strolling toward the duke. "I know how to ask questions and read what lies behind the answers. In the matter of the girl's murder, Silverdale is as innocent as a newborn babe. But whoever is guilty of the thing lingers about Barren Wycche yet. The lion was not there when your sister and I searched the cottage but it was there when you and Dempsey did so. There was the space of a day between. Someone took the lion and entangled it in those curtains on purpose, to make us look in the direction of an innocent man."

"And how am I to be certain that you did not entangle the thing in the curtains yourself to draw suspicion away from some hireling of yours? Someone you paid to do away with Meg?" Berinwick asked quietly as Mallory halted beside him.

"William!" Veronica gasped.

"Well, he is Silverdale's cousin, Mother. He might not have done the deed himself, but he could easily have found the lion when Silverdale lost it, or stolen the lion from Silverdale for that matter. And he had every opportunity to place the thing in the cottage when he went there with Hannah, to make us look in a direction completely away from himself."

"Hannah would have noticed did he do such a thing," Veronica declared. "Your sister is not blind and she is not a dunce!"

"No, but she was most distracted at the time. He had already convinced her that he had heard Meg's sobs and screams and she feared for his well-being when they reentered the place."

"And she went so far as to crawl on her hands and knees under the sofa to look for clues," Mallory added calmly. "I might well have taken that opportunity to entangle the lion in the curtains. But I did not. There was no lion present when we entered the cottage or when we departed, Berinwick. I give you my word on it."

"What good is the word of a murderer or, at least, a man who pays someone to murder for him?"

"None. But *my* word is as good as gold."

The two gentlemen studied each other intently as the others in the room fell silent. For the second time in his

life, Mallory felt the full strength of the glare of Berinwick's one good eye upon him, and for the first time,
he felt the cold stab of it in his heart.

It held no grave threat for me in Lords, he thought,
that icy glare. No threat at all. But now, now that his
thoughts and what he concludes from them could end
the joy of my relationship with Lady Hannah—

"Why did you tremble that evening, after dinner, when
we began to speak of Meg?" Berinwick asked, interrupting Mallory's thoughts. "No one else did so. Silverdale
did not."

Mallory remembered it. He remembered it clearly. "I
don't know," he said after a moment. "It was the oddest
thing—as though someone had touched the back of my
neck with a handful of snow. I could not control it. Perhaps it was because the girl's screams and sobs were
attempting to reach me even then. Perhaps it was simply
the presence of ancient ghosts around your dining table.
I felt the most raw, savage emotions rampaging around
Blackcastle when first we turned into your drive that
night. Perhaps they had an effect on me even though I
attempted to shunt them aside. But whatever it was, my
hand did not tremble because I had murdered or ordered the murder of an innocent young woman and
feared to have my crime discovered. And if you do not
believe me, then you may call me out here and now."

"And when you and Gazenby came to the cottage, you
did not come because you—No, why would you?" Berinwick muttered.

"What? Why would I what? What were you going to
ask?"

"Only if you came that day, expecting the cottage to be
empty, to retrieve something that you had lost there. It did
occur to me that all that nonsense about feeling the emotions that lingered there was designed on the spot to
distract Dempsey and me. But retrieving this lion wouldn't

make a bit of sense if you had put it there in the first place
to send us in the wrong direction."

"But you did not know that anything had been found in
the cottage until moments ago, William," Veronica inserted with a bit of astonishment. "How could you possibly
have suspected Lord Mallory of hoping to retrieve—"

"There was a fight of some sort between Meg and her
murderer, Mama. Something might well have been lost
and the guilty party might well have returned to find it,
even though the rest of us could not. Well, Dempsey did
find it, but he might not have done. I cannot help that I
am suspicious of everyone and everything. I was born to
be suspicious of everyone and everything. I have learned
through the years that almost nothing is as it seems, not
even in my own life. And Hannah is falling in love with
this—this—Mallory. I need to know for a certainty that
he is not a—a—"

"She is falling in love with me?" Mallory asked, not caring at the moment what else Berinwick had to say. "Are
you certain? How can you tell? I know that she allowed
me to kiss her, but she is so—so—Well, she's an unusual
young lady. Not one to shrink away from a kiss or two."

"Like her mother," Berinwick responded, cocking an
eyebrow in Dempsey's direction.

"Has she said something about me?" Mallory queried,
his hands suddenly leaping into his breeches pockets to
hide themselves away. "Something that leads you to believe—"

"Her eyes glow with a secret light whenever she speaks
of you now," Berinwick replied. "Her smile is filled with a
certain hopefulness that I never thought to see again after
her—disagreement—with Silverdale here. She has not
said she is falling in love with you, but I can see that she is.
And if you are not willing to accept her love, then you had
best tell her so straightaway, because if you lead her on and
then break her heart, I *will* call you out. I give you notice

of that. Would have called Silverdale out, but Hannah would not have it. Would not so much as tell me what happened between them. Won't be influenced by her a second time. Thank gawd," he added, under his breath.

"Thank gawd what, Berinwick?" Dempsey asked.

"Thank gawd that Mallory's not a murderer. That he did not set someone to doing away with Meg."

"You accept his explanations for everything?"

"No. But were he the villain I suspected he might be, my mentioning Hannah's falling in love with him would not have interrupted his defense of himself. Not at all. At least, I don't believe it would have, do you?"

"No," Dempsey grinned. "No, I think he might have given it a nod of acknowledgment and then gone right on with more explanations of how he could not possibly be involved."

"Just so. I believe you, as well, Silverdale," Berinwick added. "If Mallory is the honorable gentleman I believe him to be, then I must accept his certainty of your innocence. Here, take your lion. I don't want it. I hope never to see any more of the things ever again. There is always death around them. Always."

They discovered Lord Harry's horse munching grass along the berm several miles up the lane. Tom Hasty leaped down from the box at once, gathered up the animal's reins and led the horse to the carriage door.

"Well, I'd best be on my way," Lord Harry said with the most infectious grin.

"Can you ride with the pain in your ankle?" Hannah queried.

"I had best be able to do so," Lord Harry replied. "From the look on your groom's face, I ought not to have entered your carriage in the first place, but trod along beside it until we found the animal."

Hannah laughed. It was certainly true. Tom Hasty had not been at all happy to have the gentleman climb inside the carriage and his impatient scowl as he stood beside the halted vehicle now, with the horse behind him, made it most obvious that he expected the gentleman to depart on the instant.

"I thank you again for your kindness," Lord Harry said as he reached for the door handle while Hasty lowered the steps. "You will not tell Mal that you have seen me, eh? I wish to see the expression on his face when I suddenly appear before him. It's a grand idea, you know. To wait until the ball at Blackcastle on Saturday. I cannot thank you enough for suggesting it."

"It will be the grandest surprise," Hannah acknowledged. "And I am certain if you stop at Mrs. Dearing's—you remember her direction—"

Lord Harry nodded.

"—I am certain she will rent you a room. She has already rented out one of the bedchambers, I hear, so she will not think it odd that you ask her to rent another. You must simply say that Lady Hannah suggested it and she will be pleased to take you in."

Lord Harry nodded again, stepped down from the carriage and then reached back in to take Hannah's hand. He bowed and kissed the back of it. "Until Saturday, then, my lady," he said. "And the very best of luck in selecting a suitable hound. A hound for a parson," he added, and with a grin and a shake of his head, he took his horse's reins from Tom Hasty and climbed up into the saddle. "Fare thee well," he called with a sweeping bow and, giving his horse's sides a nudge with his knees, he rode off up the lane in the direction of the fork which would eventually carry him into the village of Barren Wycche.

Tom Hasty closed the carriage door and folded back the steps, then once again took his seat beside John

Coachman and took the long gun into his hands. "Wouldn't trust that fellow as far as I could throw him," he muttered as the coachman gave the team the office to proceed.

"Seemed an elegant sort to me, Tom," John Coachman replied.

"Oh, he were elegant enough," Hasty mumbled, "but elegance don't make a gentleman honest."

"You be too accustomed to our duke, Tom. Not all gentlemen be as down to earth as our duke. Some of them be dandified and elegant. You can't hold that against them."

"No. But I'm pleased he's gone," Hasty replied. "I be pleased he did not accompany us all the way to the Simmonses and that Lady Hannah did not propose that we drive the fellow all the way into the village. I should have gone inside and sat next to Lady Hannah with this gun across my knees had he ridden with us much farther. I can't be putting my finger on it, John, but there were something about the fellow I could not trust."

Inside the carriage, George raised very serious eyes to meet Hannah's gaze. "It was not your idea at all," he said.

"What was not my idea, George?"

"That he should wait to surprise Lord Mallory until the night of our ball. It was he proposed it."

"Did he? I thought that I—"

"You merely said we were going to give a ball for everyone. It was he who said what a surprise it would be did he wait and present himself to Lord Mallory then."

"Well, but it is a grand idea, George, no matter who thought of it. Only think how surprised Lord Mallory will be to see his younger brother stroll into our ballroom."

"I hope it's a *welcome* surprise," George mumbled, staring out at the passing landscape.

"Well, of course it will be a welcome surprise. If you had a brother you had not seen in years, you would think it the finest thing in all the world to see him again at last."

"I expect so. It's going to be a forest glade," George added, returning his attention to Hannah.

"A forest glade? The ballroom do you mean?"

"Uh-huh. And there are going to be trees and birds and deer and everything!"

"In our ballroom?" Hannah stared at the boy aghast.

"Not real birds and deer," George giggled.

"Thank goodness," Hannah sighed, waving her hand melodramatically before her face. "I was about to have a fainting spell right here in this carriage imagining our guests attempting to dance across the ballroom floor with deer skittering about and birds flying overhead."

"And what if the deer were to—all over the floor," George giggled. "And the birds, too. Everyone would be hopping about attempting to avoid stepping in it or being hit by it. But we thought of that, his grace and I, and so we are just going to make deer and birds."

"Make them? Draw pictures of them, do you mean?"

"No," George replied. "We're going to make them. Tonight. After everyone has gone to sleep."

Twelve

Mallory felt the smile growing inside of him before it ever reached his lips. The last remnants of chagrin at the realization that Berinwick had—if only for a short time—suspected him of ordering Meg's murder vanished.

She is the most remarkable young woman, he thought. Only look at her crouching there beside the boy, peering through a knot hole in a fence. Would any one of my sisters do that? Would any one of the ladies who have cast their nets for me do such a thing—crouch in the dust without the least heed for her gown or for who might see her do such a thing? Why the devil is she doing such a thing? he wondered abruptly. Well, I expect she will have a credible answer. Hannah has a credible answer for everything—even for things that appear to be most outrageous, like wearing breeches. It's one of the reasons I love her.

The smile on Mallory's face widened. "I do love her," he said in a whisper. "Some day I must thank Berinwick for forcing me to admit that to myself. If he had not said that she was falling in love with me and challenged me to tell her straightaway that I did not return her feelings, I should have gone on debating and attempting to deny it to myself for a goodly long time, I expect."

Well, but what have I ever known about falling in love? he wondered as he dismounted, tied Simon to a tree branch and advanced as quietly as possible in Hannah's direction. I have always thought falling in love to be a game of sorts—some female-concocted diversion that involves painted faces, artfully reconstructed bodies, batting eyelashes, and pouting lips—something quite different, that game, from the feelings of devotion, passion, and respect that linger in some rare places and reach out to touch my mind across centuries. Somehow, I did not think that one had anything at all to do with the other.

As Mallory drew nearer the fence, George spied him. Mallory signaled the boy to silence. Whatever Hannah was looking at through the knot hole, it held her attention completely. She did not so much as turn when he knelt down beside her. "What do you see?" he whispered.

Startled, Hannah pulled back abruptly. The top of her head connected solidly with Mallory's jaw. "Oh!" she exclaimed.

"Ouch!" Mallory replied, his eyes filled with laughter as he rubbed at his chin. "You must have the hardest head in all of Shropshire."

"No. That particular honor belongs to my brother," Hannah chuckled. "What are you doing here, Lord Mallory?"

"Your brother told me that this is where you would be found. He did not, however, tell me you would be spying on someone through a knot hole. What in the world are you about?"

"I am to keep Gulliver for my very own," George replied in an excited whisper before Hannah could answer. "His grace said so. And he sent us here to pick out a different puppy for the Reverend Mr. Dempsey."

"I see. And you are hiding behind a fence, peeking through a knot hole because . . . ?"

"Because Clare Simmons says it is the best way to know which of the little hounds has the best nose." Hannah grinned.

"No, is it? How can that be?"

"Well, it is quite reasonable when one stops to consider it. None of the puppies can see us here, and yet, they ought to be able to catch our scent. The first one to do so, quite likely has the best nose."

"You have a predilection for noses, I think," Mallory said, his eyes twinkling.

"I do?"

"Indeed. First it was my cunning nose, and now it is the puppy with the best nose."

"Well. But one has nothing to do with the other, your lordship. Blooded hounds are prized especially for their noses, you see, and people are not."

"Not most people."

"No." Hannah was having the hardest time not to laugh. "You, of course, Lord Mallory, are the exception."

"I *am* prized for my nose then?"

"Just so," Hannah replied, giving that particular appendage of Mallory's a gentle pat.

"May we come back again tomorrow?" George asked, his eye now pinned to the knot hole that Hannah had abandoned.

"No, George," Hannah responded.

"But Mr. Simmons said it is best to try this for two or three days in a row."

"Yes, but his grace said we are to choose a puppy and bring it home with us today."

"But the one that noticed us first and has come back again and again to find us is a girl dog."

"And you have something against girls, George?" Hannah queried with a significant cock of an eyebrow.

"Well, no. But it was you who said that the Reverend Mr. Dempsey is most intrepid and that his old dog used to lead him into the most wonderful adventures. And his old dog was a boy."

"Does not matter in the least, George," Mallory said.

"It does not?"

"Not at all. A sense of adventure has nothing to do with whether a hound is a girl or a boy. It has merely to do with the individual hound itself."

"Just the same as with people," Hannah added. "I will lay you odds, George, that my sense of adventure, for instance, is quite equal to Lord Mallory's."

"Is that so?" Mallory queried.

"Yes, indeed. Equal to and perhaps even superior."

Berinwick looked from his mother to Dempsey and back again. Silverdale, Gazenby, and Mallory had departed a considerable time before, but Berinwick had chosen to remain. "I expect the answer is no," he murmured after a considerable silence.

"I did not say that," Dempsey replied.

"No, you have not said a word. If the answer were yes, you would have said as much by now."

"That's not true, William," the duchess declared. "There are things to be considered."

"Like what?" Berinwick queried, sitting forward in his chair, his arms resting on his knees. "What sort of things?"

"Whether I can do a good job of it," Dempsey replied quietly. "I have never done such a thing before, Berinwick."

"You have been personal assistant to the Bishop of Hereford. You have squirted through caves, climbed mountains, gone down into wells to rescue and identify and prove the truth of the existence of innumerable antiquities. You are a Fellow of the Royal Society and have published an enormous number of papers—important papers, too. And you doubt for a moment that you can teach one small boy his lessons?"

"Yes," Dempsey replied with a grin. "That's precisely

what I doubt. I have never attempted such a thing before, Berinwick. No. I take that back. I have, through the years, attempted to teach you a thing or two and—"

"And every Sunday you attempt to teach your entire congregation things," Berinwick interrupted. "And you do. We are all better Christians and more intelligent ones than we were before you arrived, are we not, Mother? And there are any number of people who can read and write and cypher in Barren Wycche who never could before. And you should hear the words that come out my grooms' mouths these days, Dempsey. Quote books you have taught them to read and understand, they do. Even Tom Hasty," he added enthusiastically.

The Reverend Mr. Dempsey's cheeks colored a bit and his sky blue eyes brightened.

"You see, Richard," Veronica said. "I have told you time and again that William admires the work that you do here. He does not nod off during the services as an insult to you."

"I don't nod off during the services at all," Berinwick laughed.

"What is it you're doing then, sitting there with your head against the back of the pew and your eye closed?" Dempsey queried.

"Listening. Thinking."

"Balderdash!"

"All right. I'm pretending to be asleep in order to drive you mad, Dempsey."

"William!" Veronica exclaimed.

"No, no, do not scold him, Vernie," Dempsey chuckled. "I have always thought he did it to drive me mad. Though, you were never used to pretend to nod off when Theophilus was in attendance, Berinwick."

"Well, of course not. Did I close my eyes when Theo was in attendance, I might have missed some outrageous thing that that beast of yours thought to do."

"Just so. I taught him to do outrageous things while I preached for that precise reason—to keep everyone awake."

"You never did."

"Yes, I did. I did not preach often in those days, not having had a living of my own until your father presented me with this one and so my preaching was a good deal more dreary from lack of practice. I miss Theophilus," Dempsey added with a sigh. "I did not realize quite how much until I encountered that little hound of yours yesterday, Berinwick. Gulliver, is it? The boy has had a profound effect on you already. I never thought to see the day that you would go out and purchase a hound."

"Neither did I," Berinwick murmured.

"It's a fine pup," Dempsey continued. "It's a *blooded* hound, you know."

"Yes, I know," Berinwick replied. "I have also discovered how pricey blooded hounds are. You cannot possibly afford one."

"I can."

"You cannot. And even if you can, Simmons hasn't one pup of the litter left to sell. Gulliver was the last of them."

"Oh. Well, perhaps another time."

"Yes," Berinwick agreed, hoping the parson and Simmons would not meet before Sunday and Clare Simmons be forced to lie as well as he to keep the parson's present a surprise. "I shall tell Simmons to inform you when the next litter appears, eh? But in the meantime, if you should care to have a pup about, I could arrange to send Gulliver here with the elf when George comes for his lessons."

Veronica smiled. "Yes, do, William," she said, taking Dempsey's arm and bestowing a kiss upon his cheek. "We will be more than pleased to have them both running about the rectory. Despite all his humble hesitation, Richard truly does wish to have a go at teaching George, do you not, Richard?"

"Be forced to give lessons to them both," Dempsey grinned. "Cannot afford to have the boy grow up in your image, Berinwick. I'll not have a moment's peace does that happen. And what you know about teaching a dog will fit into my waistcoat pocket."

Mallory stood with his back to the maze, almost directly behind Hannah, as they watched George and both hounds chasing each other around and through the sprinkling of sheep. "Just look at her," Hannah laughed. "To think that George thought because she was a girl, she would not be as adventurous as Gulliver! Of all things! Oh, Mal, she has goaded that sheep into chasing her! Run, little one! Run!"

"There go George and Gulliver to her rescue," Mallory observed. "Nothing at all for an adventurous young lady to fear when she has *two* heroes to save her. Did you just call me Mal?"

Hannah took a deep breath. "Yes," she said, turning to face him. "I hope you do not mind. Titles place people at such a distance and I find that I do not like to be placed at a distance from you. I am quite spoiled, you see," she continued, her cheeks pinking a bit. "Mama and Papa did never address each other formally, nor did they ever call Will by his title. In my family there has always been the intimacy of Christian names to bind us closely together."

"Well, in that case, you must call me Mal if it pleases you," Mallory said softly, his breath stirring a wisp of a curl beside her ear. "But some day, I shall hope you will call me Ian, to share with me the particular intimacy of Christian names that your family so prizes."

Hannah studied him most seriously. He was a good, kind, generous, and insightful gentleman. This she already knew. What she did not know was whether he was, at the moment, simply being his good, kind, generous, and insightful self, or if he was implying that he wished for an increased intimacy between them—an intimacy that would suggest a relationship between them that did not yet exist.

"How perfectly kind of you," she replied, an increased huskiness to her voice. "And do I come to call you Ian, you will come to call me Hannah?"

"I have been wishing to call you Hannah since first we met."

The dimples in Hannah's cheeks flashed into view as she gave a dramatically sad shake of her head. "Well, I know that is balderdash."

"No, it is not."

"Yes, it is. Because when first we met, Lord Mallory, the only wish you had, sir, was to be led off of Little Mynd moor. You would have called me Your Majesty, did I stipulate that as part of my terms for rescuing you."

Mallory chuckled.

"I am correct, am I not?" Hannah prodded, her eyes meeting his, sparkling with laughter in the sunlight.

"I'm ashamed to admit it," Mallory murmured, his smoothly shaved cheeks flushing just a bit, "but yes, Your Majesty, I'm afraid I would have done or said anything to be led off the moor. It was not merely the dogs, you know, that frightened me. I am—I grow—a bit nervous—when I am alone in the dark."

"At last, an honest gentleman," Hannah observed, unable to resist touching just one of his blushing cheeks tenderly. "A gentleman courageous enough to admit that he is sometimes afraid and wishes to be rescued."

"But once I was rescued," Mallory added with a decisive tightening of his strong jaw. "Once I knew myself to be safe at last, I wished to call you Hannah straight-away. It's a pretty name, Hannah. Of course, I knew I dared not."

"Why? Because you knew that Davey Lancaster would be aghast did you presume to be as forward as that?"

"No. Because I knew that Lancaster would tell your brother that I had presumed to be as forward as that."

"But you are not afraid of Will, I thought."

"I am not terrorized by him. But a gentleman would need to be a fool not to be afraid of him a bit. And a fear of Berinwick is a good thing to have—to steer by—when a gentleman is seriously thinking to court Berinwick's sister."

"C-court?" The lights in Hannah's eyes sparked into a perfect blaze. "*Are* you thinking to court me?"

"Oh, yes. Planning on it, in fact. If you don't mind, that is. You don't mind, do you, Hannah? If I promise never to utter the phrase 'your eyes remind me of my favorite horse' ever again, at least not at any time during our courtship?"

Mallory, watching her cheeks stain with red, could restrain himself no longer. His arms went gently around her and when she did not resist, he drew her to him, leaned down the slightest bit to avoid a collision with the brim of her carriage hat, and kissed her soundly.

"I say, you ought not to do that. Her grace said as much yesterday," declared George, dashing up to them, two hounds bouncing at his heels. "She was most adamant, her grace was. Don't you remember, Lord Mallory? Her grace ordered you tossed into a stream."

Mallory's and Hannah's lips parted on instant laughter.

"It is not humorous," George insisted. "She is not here at the moment, but—"

"It's all right, George," Hannah said, turning in the

tight circle of Mallory's arms and smiling down at the boy. "Ian has just declared that he wishes to court me."

"Ian? Who the deuce is Ian?"

"I am, George," Mallory replied, his heart grown warmer with the sound of his Christian name on Hannah's lips, his arms grown stronger for the feel of Hannah within them. "It's my name—Ian Michael Denham—though you may not use it unless I give you permission to do so."

"And you just gave Lady Hannah permission to do so?"

"Indeed. I am in love with her, it seems."

"Oh. Love," George said. "I expect that's what all the kissing is about then."

"Precisely," Mallory replied. "That is precisely what all the kissing is about and her grace would not be so adamantly against it at the moment, I think. Not at the moment, because—"

"I know!" exclaimed George. "It is because at the moment Lady Hannah is not wearing her breeches!"

Mrs. Dearing was most amazed at the condition of her temporary boarder's clothing when he entered her establishment through the side door until he explained to her in the simplest of terms that he and his horse had abruptly parted company on his way to contemplate Squire Tofar's horses one more time.

"Such happens," she said with a curt nod. "T'aint nothing to be ashamed of. I can remember times when our duke himself flew like a bird from the saddle. A splendid rider he be, our duke, and as capable astride as any man, but he has flown once or twice, he has. Ye be not harmed, lordship?"

"No, not harmed. Thank you very much for asking, Mrs. Dearing. My pride has merely taken a bit of a bruising, nothing more. And that I shall survive, I think."

"Aye. One survives bruised pride most of the time."

"Most of the time?"

"Well, be it bruised too badly, it do set a man back apace," Mrs. Dearing observed. "I be knowing a man or two never got over such a thing. But they be old men. Old men. There be a missive arrived for you, lordship. Where did I . . . ? Aye, here it be. Here in my apron pocket." Like magic, a finely lettered square of parchment appeared in Mrs. Dearing's hand and she held it out to him. "'Tis yours," she said when he did not reach out to take it from her.

"I don't think it can be," her temporary boarder responded with narrowed eyes. "No one knows I am here."

"Well, as to that, it come from our duke and our Lady Hannah, though it was our Mrs. Gazenby and our Mrs. Tofar wrote them out and the squire's men delivered them. Every gentleman come to take part in the squire's auction be receiving one. They know, of course, a gentleman be boarding with me, so this one be yours."

Her boarder took the parchment into his hands, stared down at it, looked up, stared down at it again. "An invitation to a ball," he said as if such a thing were most unexpected.

"Aye. Will not be an uppity sort of ball like in London," Mrs. Dearing advised him. "A bit of dancing, good fellowship, an opportunity for young ladies and gentlemen to come to know each other is all it will be. A bit of fun."

"Yes, I should enjoy a bit of fun, Mrs. Dearing. And I should certainly like to see the inside of Blackcastle."

"Aye, most everyone what sees its outsides wishes to be seeing its insides," Mrs. Dearing agreed. "It be mystifying inside, it be."

"You have been inside Blackcastle?"

"Any number of times," Mrs. Dearing replied, her

nose rising slightly into the air. "For the harvest ball, on Boxing Day, at Easter. Everyone in Barren Wycche and its environs has been invited to Blackcastle at one time or another. He do not be ashamed to be associated with any of us, our duke," she added with an accusing glare at her boarder. "Not high in the instep, our duke. Not above himself like some people."

Mrs. Dearing's temporary boarder took instant note of her tone and the position of her nose and the inherent meaning of her words and he apologized quickly for the impression he had obviously given her. "I should not like to have you believe, Mrs. Dearing, that I find it amazing that you have visited Blackcastle because you are not—not—a titled lady. That is not the case at all. It is merely that I know little of Berinwick and some titled gentlemen, you know, would never think to invite common people into their residences."

"Is that so?"

"Yes, indeed. Generally they see common people as existing merely for their own convenience—to serve their own needs, you know. Not that I agree with that, of course, but I could not believe the same of Berinwick. He has a fierce reputation in London, and one would not imagine that he would—"

"Bah! London!" Mrs. Dearing exclaimed. "Simpletons, Londoners are. Don't know their heads from a hole in the ground. Not a one of them. Comes from drinking the water of the Thames."

That evening after dinner, for the first time since George had arrived, Berinwick sat down at the pianoforte in the smallest of the Blackcastle parlors and began to play. Why he chose to do so, he could not say. Perhaps it was because he was pleased to think that Hannah had at last discovered a gentleman she could love without reservation and that she had said as much to him that very afternoon. Perhaps it was because the elf need not be sent away to school as Berinwick had dreaded, but instead would become a welcomed student at Dempsey's knee. He treasured Dempsey, Berinwick did, though he would never say as much. He need not say as much. Dempsey knew. Or perhaps it was because, for this small period of time, Berinwick felt himself to be no longer a fiercesome beast, ugly and intimidating, but a fine and noble gentleman at last. Whatever the reason, the music that flowed from his soul into his fingertips and thence to the keys of the pianoforte contained a solemn, hesitant, but delightful joy that floated through the ancient building in the most mystical manner, causing everyone within those cold stone walls to pause at their tasks and listen and smile.

Gaines set aside the silver and sat down on his stool in the butler's pantry as soon as the music reached his ears. His eyes glowed with pleasure. There is a new tone in his playing, he thought. A magical sort of tone. A joyful tone. Something glorious dances tonight in our duke's soul.

Cook ceased her work, the kitchen maids hushed, even the smallest boy who scrubbed the pots and pans grew quiet and held his breath as he listened. The footmen paused at their dinner and grinned at the parlor maids who smiled back with laughing eyes. And the upstairs maids set their forks aside and wiggled a bit in their chairs to the rhythm of the music. Even the duke's farm manager paused and set aside his books to smile at nothing in particular and wonder what on earth had wormed its way into the Duke of Berinwick's soul.

George, his eyes wide, set aside the book he had chosen to read and stared at Berinwick's broad shoulders and proud, straight back. Hannah stood and went to sit beside the boy on the arm of his chair. She ruffled his hair and placed an arm around his thin shoulders.

"He hasn't any music laid out before him," George whispered. "Where is his music?"

"It is in his heart," Hannah replied. "And in his soul, too. He has no need to borrow someone else's notes, George. His grace was born with all the musical notes anyone could ever need right inside of him."

Mallory stood quietly at the outside door to Snoop's stall, gazing up at the ever-widening moon and the winking spikes of silver that were the stars just beginning to appear in the descending darkness. Liddy wound herself around his ankles, purring seductively and Snoop poked at his shoulder insistently, but he ignored them both for a moment longer. Somewhere, off in the distance, he thought he heard music, but that, of course, was impossible. No, the music was not off in the distance at all, but somewhere inside his head.

"I am going completely mad," he murmured to himself. "But I don't care a bit. Not a bit. Though how the very thought of her can make me hear music that is not there, I cannot imagine. Perhaps there is music. Perhaps Hannah is hearing it even now and I am hearing it through her."

He knew that could not be true. But for a moment, just for a moment, he enjoyed thinking that it was—that his soul and hers were so closely united that whatever Hannah heard or saw or felt, he could hear or see or feel himself. "Now that would be a true gift," he whispered. "That would be a gift worth having."

"Mrrrrr," Liddy replied, continuing to weave in and out between his feet, striving to divert his attention from his thoughts to herself. She hoped for a bit of a stroking and a kind word or two—and perhaps, a bit of pheasant or a chicken bone or a tidbit of fish. He had brought her things often in the past few days, this odd sort of gentleman from the big house, as if he wished to gain her good will, and she was more than willing to grant it to him if he continued in his generous ways.

"All right, you little beast," Mallory laughed, reaching down to the cat and lifting her in one large hand up to the wide top of the bottom stall door. He reached into his coat pocket and took out a tiny package wrapped in brown paper. This he opened and placed before her a boiled chicken liver. He stroked her as she ate it, his smile almost as wide as the circumference of the moon. "And no, I haven't forgotten you, you villain," he said as Snoop nudged him once again. "I've brought you sugar and a carrot and an apple because we are celebrating, you great hulk of an undisciplined horse. We are celebrating because I came here merely to please Martin and perhaps to purchase you and instead of any of that—though Martin is pleased and I may still outbid the other gentlemen and take you and Liddy both home with me—I have discovered the most wonderful, the most remarkable, the most alluring woman in all of England, and she loves me."

"Does she?" asked a quiet voice, thoroughly startling Mallory so that he stepped away from the stall door and produced a blade from his coat pocket in an instant.

"Are you certain that she does? Do you love her in return? Because if you do not and you lead her on, I will have your guts for garters, Mal."

"Silverdale? What the deuce are you doing here?"

"Nothing. I should put that blade away if I were you. It doesn't look good, Mal, to be holding your cousin at bay with the point of a knife. Besides, I have a pistol right here in my hand, do you see?"

Mallory was nonplussed. He sputtered something completely unintelligible. His smile quickly became a scowl. "Put that thing away, Sly," he said at last.

"Yes, all right," Silverdale agreed, easing the small pistol into his coat pocket. "It's French-made," he informed his cousin. "Shoots seven times without reloading if it is working properly."

"What the devil are you doing lurking about the squire's stables with a thing like that?" Mallory sputtered. "Should anyone see you, they might well believe that it was you murdered that poor girl and that you are the fellow bent on murdering me."

"But you don't believe it."

"No," Mallory said decisively. "No, I do not. You made me doubt for an instant, a moment ago, but I'm not so muddled in my mind as to believe you would kill anyone."

"You are wrong there. I believe I could kill someone if I were forced to do it. If they threatened harm to someone for whom I cared greatly, for instance. Which is why I asked, Mal, if you truly care for Hannah or if you merely intend to enjoy her while you are here and then forget about her once you depart. Because she has been disappointed enough in me. I will not allow you to disappoint her as well."

"You'd shoot me for it?"

"No. I'd tell Hannah straightaway that you don't truly love her—except that I think you do."

"With all my heart as near as I can tell," Mallory admitted. "But if you don't intend to shoot me whether I love her or whether I don't, why the devil are you lurking about the squire's stables with a pistol?"

"I'm attempting to assure Hannah's happiness," Silverdale said quietly, "by keeping watch. Gazenby and I spent the afternoon discussing all that has gone forward and—and we decided to take turns at keeping watch."

"What? Over this yearling?"

"No, you peabrain. Over you."

* * *

Mrs. Dearing's temporary boarder led his bay inside the old Hatter's field barn. This time he had kept his eyes wide open. This time he had made certain that no one lingered across the lane at the cottage or in the wood surrounding the field, or in the field itself. This time, he had left his overconfidence back in Barren Wycche and had come to the barn with caution and cunning—and a diminutive hatchet from the widow's abandoned chicken coop.

Likely as not they have checked the barn two or three times by now, he thought. Certainly, they have. Did they not see me depart from it? Did they not give chase? Certainly, they will have checked this barn thoroughly and will not return. Still, I shall have to be most cautious, most cautious indeed.

He fumbled about a bit searching in the darkness for the peg that held the lantern. For a moment he feared that one of the men from yesterday had moved it from its peg. If that were so—but it was not so. His gloved hand touched the lantern and he lifted it down and set it alight.

"Better," he murmured, closing the shutters on all but one side, giving himself only enough light by which to work. He doffed his riding coat which tonight was fashioned of black velvet, rolled up the sleeves of the black silk shirt he wore beneath it, took the hatchet in hand and went, as quietly as possible, about his business.

Good Meggy, he thought as he worked. Sweet Meggy. I will not kill your mistress now. Do you see? Do you see how it all works out? I have come to my senses at last, just as you longed for me to do. I see quite clearly now precisely what must be done and slaying Lady Hannah is not the answer as I thought it was at first. Not at all. There will only be some other lady, Meggy. You ought to have told me that. If you had told me that and made me believe it, you would be beside me even now. I did not so much as give a thought to it, you know, until I saw Mallory riding and tossed that rock at his head. I only did it because I was most upset and could not help myself. But that's when it all became perfectly clear, Meg, that I cannot go on forever chasing after Mallory and doing away with every young woman he might find attractive. No. No, I cannot. I was wrong to think that Lady Hannah would be the only one. There will be others, you know. If Gazenby does not provide them, then some other of Mallory's friends will. It cannot be helped. Matchmakers are everywhere in England. The oddest people turn out to be matchmakers. Whoever would have guessed Gazenby would be one, for heaven's sake? He giggled to himself. For heaven's sake? he thought. I doubt heaven has anything at all to do with it.

He wiped his brow with his forearm. The night was chill, but he was growing warm with energy and anticipation and perspiration insisted on popping out on his brow.

Perhaps I will marry Lady Hannah myself, he thought as he set the hatchet aside. She has a lovely face and figure and she is kind and well-spoken besides. And she is apparently fond of children. We will have a house full of children, she and I. All boys. Only boys. Does she bear me a girl I will take the puling infant out and drown it. But she will not do that—bear me a girl. Not if I make it clear from the first that I will not have one about. Yes, I will marry her, he decided. "There, you see, Meggy," he whispered into the shadows that surrounded him. "You can be at peace now, eh? Not only shall I not wring your precious Lady Hannah's neck, I shall marry the woman. What more could you ask of me than that?"

* * *

It was very near eleven o'clock when Hannah left a grumbling Berinwick and a giggling George to their work and took herself off to her own chambers. Making deer, she thought, a smile playing about her lips. I can see how Will intends to make the birds, but making the deer, that must prove almost impossible. Especially so with the assistance of a boy who is overflowing with excitement. The puppies are much too tired to cause Will any aggravation, but George is so—so—enthusiastic and filled with ideas—

Hannah stepped into her sitting room and discovered her abigail busily engaged in repairing the hem of a silver ball gown. "Oh, Martha, I must beg your pardon once again," she said, crossing the floor and taking the gown from the abigail's lap. "I have once more changed my mind. I have been thinking about it all evening and I do not like this gown particularly."

"But it is so very beautiful, my lady," the abigail replied.

"Indeed, but much too—too—elaborate. I think he is a gentleman who prefers simplicity. Well, not simplicity, precisely, but a definite lack of ostentation."

Martha Alderman, her sewing box open beside her, her needle and thread dangling from the hem of the gown Hannah held, scrutinized her mistress thoroughly through wide brown eyes. There had been speculation belowstairs that her ladyship had discovered in Mrs. Gazenby's cousin-in-law a gentleman worth considering, but only her ladyship's favorite groom, Davey Lancaster, was willing to say it was so. And when Lancaster said it was so, he said it with such a decided nonchalance that no one could tell if he were being serious in his answer or not.

"He, my lady?" Martha's fingers crossed hopefully as she set her sewing box aside and rose to follow Hannah into the dressing room to help her prepare for the night.

Hannah grinned to herself. "The Marquis of Kearney

and Mallory," she said. "Has anyone placed a wager on it yet, belowstairs? That I have at last found a gentleman whom I can love? Because if they have not, you ought to suggest it, Martha, at once, and bet on Lord Mallory, not Lord Silverdale."

"Oh, my lady, I would never—"

"Yes, you would. Do not pretend with me, Martha Alderman, I have known you since first you came to work at Blackcastle when you were barely thirteen years old."

"And you were barely ten," Martha responded.

"Just so. And you are as likely to take part in a wager today as you were then—and you were very likely to do it then."

"I did do it then," Martha admitted, unfastening Hannah's gown. "But I have not wagered since I lost an entire pound betting against the Reverend Mr. Dempsey's remaining in Barren Wycche long enough to read himself in as rector of St. Milburga's."

"You bet *against* Mr. Dempsey?" Hannah's smile widened as she stepped out of her gown. "Oh, Martha, a most unfortunate wager."

"And don't I know it. Cured me, it did, of wagering."

"Still, you would do well to place a wager on Lord Mallory. Two pounds. That will make up for your earlier loss."

"Oh, my lady," Martha said softly, slipping Hannah's nightgown neatly over her head, "do you truly love him?"

"I do," Hannah replied in the most winsome tone. "I love him more every day. He is a fine, honest gentleman, Martha, and sweet and funny."

"And odd, they say."

"Yes, he is that, in a very interesting way. But what care I if a gentleman is a bit odd? I am odd myself."

"You are not," Martha protested, hanging both the

ball gown and the gown Hannah had just discarded away in the armoire.

Hannah settled on the stool before the dressing table and took a silver-backed brush to her curls. "Yes, I am odd. Among the young ladies who gather in London each Season, I am considered excessively odd. I expect it is because I never did learn the language of the fan or bat my eyelashes at a gentleman or simper at one either. And as for pretending to be some sort of a peagoose with nothing but air between my ears—Well, if I were such a woman, I would not dare to show my face beyond the Blackcastle walls, much less in a ballroom in London. Although, I was a bit of a peagoose when it came to Lord Silverdale."

"Never," Martha said, taking the brush from Hannah and stroking it through her mistress's hair herself. "He made himself seem a fine gentleman, Lord Silverdale did. And he has the most beautiful eyes. And he vowed that he truly loved you. How could you help but be misled by him?"

"I am not misled by Lord Mallory. He came here looking for a horse, not a wife. He had not the least intention of falling in love with any woman. And yet—and yet—"

"He has fallen in love with you," Martha said in a whisper.

"He says he has. He says that he plans to ask permission of Will to pay me court. Can you imagine, Martha? To ask formal permission of William to pay me court as though Will were just an ordinary man?"

"And do you love him, my lady?" the abigail asked quietly, her brushstrokes coming to a halt.

"With all my heart," Hannah replied, amazed to see in the looking glass her own cheeks blush at her words. "Oh, Martha, I ought not to love him. I have known him merely a few days. I suspect that Annie and her mama invited him here expressly so that I would fall in love with him. And I will be utterly devastated if he is leading me on. And yet, I find that I do not care why he came to Barren Wycche. I do not care if his presence is the result of one of Mrs. Tofar's matchmaking schemes. And I cannot believe that he is playing any sort of a game with me or with my heart. But it is so very sudden, so unexpected, and just when I thought myself destined to become a spinster. It is a good deal like a faery tale floating about in my mind and I fear that when I wake in the morning, I will discover him to have been nothing but a pleasant dream."

"When you wake in the morning, my lady," Martha said softly, "you will discover the house in an uproar preparing for the ball on Saturday, and his grace and Master George no doubt making a muddle of the decorations in the ballroom, and a plethora of perfectly irresistible smells rising from the kitchens. And you will know on the instant that all that has gone forward to this point, including your love for Lord Mallory and his for you, is not a faery tale or a dream, but as real as the stones of Blackcastle itself."

Hannah bid her abigail good night and wandered into her bedchamber, her heart filled with happiness. It had been a perfectly glorious day and a truly lovely night and she could think only the most exhilarating thoughts as she wandered to the window seat to settle herself among the pillows and gaze out at the moon and the stars. She must quiet the beating of her heart and the dancing of her thoughts soon, or she would not get a wink of sleep this night. The moon and the stars must work their magic upon her and calm her rejoicing soul or she would begin to sing and waltz around her bedchamber like a young woman in love.

I am a young woman in love, she thought then. A young woman truly in love with a gentleman who is truly in love with me. Why should I not dance and sing? Anyone would dance and sing at such luck as I have had this day. To hear the man I love say that he wishes to court me. And what does it mean, to court me, but that he wishes to marry me at the end of it?

"He wishes to marry me," she whispered as the moon and the stars began to weave their mystical web around her. She closed her eyes and once again she was in Ian's arms. She rejoiced in the strength of them as they wrapped around her. A woman might face any burden, any threat, any tragedy and survive as long as those particular arms were around her, as long as that particular gentleman supported her. Once again she tasted the passion of Mallory's kiss, felt the sunshine of his smile, heard the honesty of his laughter and she sighed.

Then she remembered the surprise that awaited Mallory on Saturday night—the arrival of his younger brother returned to England after years of soldiering abroad—and she imagined the joy Mallory would feel at the first sight of Lord Harry. What would Ian do? Would he cry out at sight of the gentleman? Would he cross the ballroom on his long legs, his feet barely touching the gleaming floor? Would he take young Harry into his arms? Would he place an enthusiastic kiss on one of Lord Harry's tanned cheeks? Would he ruffle the young gentleman's hair? She could not guess. But whatever Mallory did—whatever *Ian* did—it would be a straightforward, honest, and loving reaction—a reaction unadulterated by any social posturing, any play-acting—a reaction born on the instant in Ian's heart, and she would treasure the memory of it forever.

With a tired smile and a slow wink, Hannah bid the moon and the stars good night, departed the window seat and made her way to her bed. She doffed her slippers and her robe and slipped between the sheets. As she blew out the lamp on her bedside table, she wondered how it would feel to slip between the sheets and into the arms of the gentleman she loved, and she thought she could imagine it. She made the attempt to do so, and as sleep overcame her, she floated into a dream where Ian Michael Denham, Marquis of Kearney and Mallory, lay beside her, his arms snugly around her as he whispered words of love into her ear. She kissed him passionately, thoroughly, soundly. And then—and then—he took her breath away.

Thirteen

"I have come a-begging," Hannah admitted, her eyes twinkling with suppressed laughter.

"Begging for what?" Anne queried as she welcomed her best friend into the Tofars's parlor.

"For you to come riding with me, Annie. Will has expelled me from Blackcastle and ordered me not to return until I have learned to comport myself with dignity. That, I warn you, is not likely to occur until dinner, because I shall not be able to cease giggling in Will's presence until then, so I asked Cook to pack a bit of a nuncheon and I am off in search of adventure. Well, not adventure, actually, just off in search of something to do that will keep me out of Will's way until he is ready to beg for my assistance."

"Your assistance in what?" Anne asked as the two settled comfortably down upon the sofa together.

"In decorating the ballroom. He promised me that I should not be required to do the least thing for the ball tomorrow, you know, but he is in such a muddle already this morning, Annie. By dinner time, I expect he will swallow his pride and allow me to take a hand in it."

"Oh," Anne said, one hand going to cover her lips. "Oh, Hannah, I ought to go to Blackcastle at once. Martin and I both. It was our idea to have the ball but I did not think for a moment about any decorations for the ballroom. It is splendid enough without the least thing added. If there is any decorating to be done, Martin and I ought to be the ones to do it."

"No, no, no," Hannah protested. "Will does not want anyone's help. Well, no one's but George's. They were awake most of the night laughing and arguing and making deer and birds."

"Making what?" Anne's lips parted on a chuckle.

"Deer and birds. Yes, I promise you. I saw one—a deer—I think it was meant to be a deer. Will had it under his arm when he ordered me out of the house. Oh, Annie, it was the most frightful looking thing! All bits of wire and scraps of damp paper. I dared not so much as comment on it lest Will beat me soundly about the head with the thing. But he was laughing beneath the scowl he bestowed on me. I could see that he was. And George stood beside him, giggling. They are making such a muck of it that I shall be forced to step in and do something. But they are having such fun at the same time, that I shall not deprive them of it until the evening is near and there is no more time to be wasted."

"Martin and I and Mal will come visit you this evening after dinner and help," Anne decided with a curt nod of her head. "That much and more we owe you for being so kind as to let us hold our ball at Blackcastle. Perhaps we ought to pick some wildflowers while we are out so we can set them about in vases."

"Then you will join me?"

"Of course. Why would I not?"

"Well, I did have my doubts, Annie. Because of Lord Mallory, you know."

"Because of Mal?"

"Yes, indeed. I rather thought that you would invent some silly reason why you could not come and urge me to ask Lord Mallory to accompany me instead. Or perhaps, plead with him to take your place—so that I need not ride out unprotected—completely ignoring the fact that Davey Lancaster will be up beside me."

"Why would I do that?"

"Because you are attempting to make a match between Lord Mallory and me."

"Make a match? Me?"

"You and Martin and your mama and papa as well, I think. A conspiracy. Confess it, Annie. Confession is good for your soul."

Anne laughed, her hands going to cheeks grown warm with embarrassment. "Who told you such a thing?" she asked.

"No one. I deduced it for myself. Lord Mallory has not suffered any tremendous tragedy, has he? He is not melancholy and does not require my presence to soothe his soul. In fact, he does not require my presence at all."

"Oh, yes, he does. You cannot imagine how much he requires it. He has no conversation of late except that it concerns you, Hannah. You are always in his words and on his mind. Do not tell me that you are still uneasy whenever he is near you. I could not bear to hear it when he is so enamored of you. Can you not bring yourself to like him just a bit?" Anne asked.

"No," Hannah replied.

"Oh."

Hannah was startled to see tears spring to Anne's eyes.

"What have I done?" Anne murmured. "I have acted like a perfect peabrain, have I not? I ought not to have insisted that Papa include Snoop in the auction just so that Mal would be certain to come here. I ought not have thrown the two of you together with such bouncers as I told. But I knew you would never go to London for the Season again, Hannah, and—and—he is such a fine man. Truly he is. And I thought if you but came to know him as I have done—and if he came to know you as I know you—Well, but he has done that. He sees you as I have always seen you and loves you for who you are, just as you are. And yet—and yet—Oh, Hannah, I have ruined Mal's life. He *loves* you and yet you cannot bear the sight of him!"

"I never said that, you peagoose," Hannah declared.

"You did. You said you could not bring yourself to like him just a bit."

"That's true. It's because I like him a great deal more than just a bit, Annie. I like him a tremendous lot. And on top of that, I love him."

"You do? Oh, Hannah!" Anne's arms went around her best friend in the most enthusiastic of hugs. "Oh, Hannah! Nothing could be more wonderful than that! You are both so deserving of happiness—of the kind of happiness that Martin and I have discovered! Martin! I must tell Martin! He will be so excited! It is his first attempt at matchmaking, you know, and for it to come out so well—"

"Annie, cease and desist at once," Hannah ordered, working her way out of Anne's grasp and straightening her riding dress. She lifted her chin in a vague attempt at dignity, but the laughter glittering in her eyes betrayed her. "You will not say a word to Martin or he will try his wiles again on some other poor, unsuspecting souls. You know how gentlemen can be once they get a taste of true power."

"Oh, they can be dreadful," Anne agreed, laughing. "Just so."

"Trees, your grace?" Gaines asked, one eyebrow lifting in skepticism despite his effort to appear bland at the request.

"Well, not full grown trees, Gaines. Saplings, merely. How difficult can it be for the men to dig up a few saplings, slap them in a pot and bring them inside?"

Gaines had no answer.

"Difficult beyond belief, I should think," offered a voice from behind Berinwick. "Likely they'll die from the shock of it—the trees, I mean, not the men."

"Mallory? What the devil are you doing here?" Berinwick dismissed the footman who had escorted Mallory through the maze of stairways and corridors with a wave of his hand and then stood, one hip cocked, his hands in his breeches pockets, studying the marquis. "If you have come to see Hannah, you are much too late. I drove her away hours ago."

"Is that so? Took a whip to her, did you?"

Berinwick grinned. Mallory was thoroughly surprised to discover that grin infectious. It cannot be, he thought as he felt a grin rising to his own countenance. And yet, he is making me smile just by looking at me. Am I seeing the real Berinwick at last? Well, by gawd, if that is not auspicious, nothing is.

"Don't stand there staring, Mallory," Berinwick said. "Say what you have come to say and then go away. We are exceptionally busy here today."

"Yes, so I see. Busy destroying your ballroom."

"Decorating our ballroom," Berinwick corrected.

"We are making a forest glade of it," George piped up, poking his head out from behind a marble column. "It is going to be the most amazing thing!"

"Yes, indeed," Berinwick agreed. "Amazing. Like a picture from a volume of faery tales."

"This particular picture from this particular volume," George offered, walking carefully across the polished ballroom floor with an opened leather-bound book in hand, which he presented to Mallory once he reached the gentleman.

"Good gawd," Mallory gasped. "You'll never be able to do it. Not that. Not in one day. Not in a thousand days."

"Yes, we will," George replied blithely. "We have already

got the deer and the birds and the rabbits and the fountain and those tiny mice."

"It's the trees that have us stumped," Berinwick added.

Mallory's eyes lit at the pun, but he refrained from pointing it out. "What made you pick such a difficult theme, Berinwick? You might simply have ordered up some plants and flowers and set them about."

"We've got plants and flowers," Berinwick replied. "But it will not be the same without the trees. And I want it to be very much the same. As alike as I can manage. It's Hannah's favorite faery tale. She has dreamed over that picture since she was three. And, well, I have hopes that this particular ball will be equally as precious to her as that picture has always been."

"You do?"

"Yes. And you are distracting me from that goal, so get on with it, Mallory. What is it you want?"

"I—ah—I would like to speak to you alone, Berinwick, if you don't mind."

"Why?"

"Well, because"—Mallory gave the book back into George's keeping—"because it's a rather private matter and . . ."

"Gaines knows everything that ever goes on in Blackcastle. Don't you, Gaines?"

"Yes, your grace."

"And this elf, here, is quickly learning how to know everything. Are you not, George?"

"Yes, your grace."

"And the footmen and the maids are not listening. They are far too busy. So spit it out, Mallory. I haven't the time to go traipsing off to some deserted drawing room to hear you out."

Mallory stuffed his hands into his breeches pockets and attempted to glare at Berinwick, but he found he couldn't do it. That odd, infectious grin once again dominated Berinwick's face and he was helpless to resist it. "Well, damnation, Berinwick," he protested with a shake of his head. "You don't make it easy for a fellow. Not at all. I've come to ask your permission to pay court to your sister and—"

"I told you so, Gaines," Berinwick interrupted. "Did I not say it would come to this between them?"

"Yes, your grace," Gaines replied, his eyes sparkling.

"You told your butler it would come to this? When? Only yesterday, Berinwick, you suspected me of being a murderer," Mallory protested.

"To tell the truth, I suspected you before that. But then, I did not see how it could be you. And then I could see it. And then I thought that you would never do such a thing. And then I thought that possibly you would. But none of it kept me from hoping that you might, in the end, turn out to be a gentleman worthy of Hannah. I have endless hope for my sister's happiness, you know, despite the obstacles an obstinate fate chooses to place in her way."

"Himself, our duke means by obstacles," Gaines asserted bluntly. Then, realizing that he had spoken aloud, his elderly cheeks blushed and one hand went to cover his mouth.

"You see, Mallory," Berinwick continued without batting an eyelash in his butler's direction. "Gaines knows everything. If I give you my permission to court Hannah, what are your intentions?"

"My intentions? Why, I should think my intentions ought to be perfectly clear to any man."

"No, not actually."

Mallory stared at Berinwick, his eyes wide. One hand abandoned his pocket to allow him to run his index finger around the inside of his collar. His chin tilted upward and the toe of one boot began to tap against the hardwood floor.

"Well, spit it out, Mallory. Haven't time to listen to you sputtering about. Let me help you, eh? Do you intend, after all is said and done, to marry the girl?"

"Yes, if she will have me."

"She will have you. I assure you of it. Unless you misstep in some way. Don't misstep, eh, Mallory? In fact, ask the girl to marry you first and then court her. Much less opportunity for anything to go wrong that way. I know it's not the way it's generally done," Berinwick declared holding up his hand to stop the words of protest about to drop from Mallory's lips, "but if you are certain—"

"She'll think me an arrogant fool."

"Arrogant? Never. She thinks you're odd, Mallory. Asking her to marry you before you actually court her will only make her think you odder. Nothing wrong with that. Fond of odd things, Hannah is. Fond of me, isn't she?"

Mrs. Dearing's temporary boarder had spent most of the morning preparing. He had discovered a ladder at the back of one of the cottage's outbuildings and transported it to the Hatter's field barn. He had cleaned and filled and carried four lanterns and an oil lamp into the barn as well. Carefully, he had taken all of them down the ladder, into the cave beneath the barn's floorboards and now he was preparing to distribute them along the path that stretched into the darkness ahead of him.

He was not fond of the dark, and could he think of a better plan, he would avoid the use of the path through the cave altogether. But he could not think of a better plan. This one was as perfect as a plan could be. A gift from the gods who had thwarted his every ambition until now.

It's because I have finally come to the correct conclu-

sion, he thought, a smile playing across his face. They are smiling upon me now, the gods, because I have gathered my courage about me and am prepared to do what must be done at last. And I shall not face a bit of danger either. With all those people milling about at Blackcastle for the ball, no one will so much as miss Mallory for hours. And when they do miss him, they will never stumble across his body accidentally. Certainly not. I will be gone and half way to London before anyone thinks to look for him in the Blackcastle maze.

I could force him down into the cave before I do it, he thought then. No, no, I don't want to do that. I want his body to be discovered, just not quickly. I shall not attempt to improve upon a plan that is already perfection.

The perfection, however, required that Mrs. Dearing's temporary boarder gather up the lanterns and lamp and distribute them along the underground path that stretched from Hatter's field to Blackcastle. He could not make good his escape through a blackness darker than night, after all. He must have some light. He had not as yet walked the path. He had no idea if it were hospitable or treacherous. Taking a deep, steadying breath, he knelt on the cold clay of the cave floor, lit the oil lamp, took the lanterns by their handles and made his way into the main portion of the cave.

"I am not afraid," he whispered. "I am not a poltroon like Mallory. There is nothing to fear in darkness. Darkness is a natural thing."

"He is afraid of the dark," Anne said, settling on the blanket Lancaster had put down for them, her back against the trunk of an elm. "He turns down the lamp beside his bed at night, but he never puts it out completely, Martin says. You will not hold that against Mal, will you, Hannah? Because it is not his fault. Martin leaves his lamp aglow as well and it is no bother, really. I have grown quite accustomed to it."

Hannah looked up from the cold pheasant she was just then unwrapping, handed half of the bird to Anne, kept the other for herself and then reached down into the basket again for the loaf of bread and the bottle of wine that rested within. "I cannot imagine a gentleman of Lord Mallory's years being afraid of the dark," she said, handing the bottle to Lancaster to open, and breaking the bread herself. "Pour yourself a glass as well, Davey," she said as she heard the wine come open. "And here is some bread and cheese and another pheasant if you want some."

"Thank you, my lady," Lancaster replied, presenting both Hannah and Anne with a glass of wine and, with his own portion of the nuncheon in hand, departing to take up watch on a rock nearer the stream from which he could easily keep an eye on the two young women without being privy to their conversation.

"Why are Ian and Martin afraid of the dark?" Hannah asked, settling herself beside Anne. "Tell me."

"Ian? You call him Ian?" Anne asked excitedly.

"He said that I may."

"Oh, Hannah, there is no one who calls him Ian. Not even his mama! How much he loves you!"

"Yes, so he has said," Hannah smiled. "But you are going to tell me why he and your Martin fear the darkness."

"Well, it has taken me forever to get Martin to speak of it. He told me only last night. When they were children, Martin and Mal went down into one of the coalpits near Brambles to see how the coal was got out. And there was a tremendous explosion and they were trapped there, under the ground, for hours and hours. It was so black, Martin said, that he could not see his fingers wiggling before his eyes. There were a goodly number of men and women and boys and girls trapped there with them and they were all certain they would die. Some of them did. It grew very hot and difficult to breathe, Martin said, and the least movement caused more rocks to fall in upon them. Voices cried out and sobbed and cursed all around them, but they could not see to whom the voices belonged. It was what Hades must be like, Martin said. Surrounded by unseen agony and death and no hope to help anyone, or that help would come from above either. It was Mal who saved them in the end."

"How? How did he save them?" Hannah asked.

"'Hush,' Mal said after a long time had passed. 'Be still, all of you. Can you not hear? It's Grandfather calling out to us.' And then Mal scrambled about and found a pick and began to chip away at some stones. They could all hear him doing it. `There is a way out through here, Grandfather says.' That's what Mal told them. 'If we can but open a space between these two rocks, we shall be saved.'"

"And they did open a space there?"

"Yes," Anne said in a hushed voice. "No one could actually see the rocks, but an older man called Peter Killigan took his pick from his belt and found where Mal was huddled. Mal put Killigan's hand on the spot where they were to dig and the two took turns at it. And then Martin found his way to them and took his turn as well and others joined in. And the rest of the ceiling did not so much as tremble where they dug, and no more rocks came sliding down, and after hours and hours they opened a crawl space into a larger cavern where the sun shone down through a venting hole. And they called up to those who had come to rescue them and were saved."

"How blessed they were," Hannah said quietly. "How blessed that Ian's grandfather should find them and tell them the way."

"More blessed than you know," Anne responded, "for

he was Martin's grandfather as well—and he had been dead, at the time, for more than five years."

Mrs. Dearing's temporary boarder took the time to be adequately amazed at the beauty that lay hidden away beneath the ground. He was so amazed, in fact, at the glory of one large pure white stalactite as it appeared in the circle of the lamplight before him that he forgot to watch where he set his feet, stumbled over an outcropping of iron ore and tilted precariously to his left. Beneath the side of his left boot, he could feel and hear gravel slipping away and down—very far down. He righted himself at once, then turned and carefully peered at the spot where his boot had been. The side of the path lay open there to a deep ravine. He swiped at his brow with the sleeve of his jacket and sighed. "Have to remember to keep to the center of the path," he said quietly. "Shouldn't like to tumble down into that pit." He held the lantern out, farther over the crevice and thought he saw something sparkling part way down. He closed his eyes, opened them again, hoping to see more clearly and when he did see more clearly, he gasped. "By gawd," he whispered, "it's a skeleton with a ring glittering on its bone of a finger." He stared at the thing, considering. Then, "No," he told himself. "Not worth the attempt to go and fetch it. Might well end up a skeleton myself. Shouldn't like that. Not at all."

He proceeded, with a deal more caution, in the direction he was bound, depositing, on an outcropping here and a smooth, flat rock there, the lanterns he carried, estimating the distance yet to be covered and the amount of time the fuel in the lanterns was likely to last. The lamp in his hand sputtered and threatened to die just as he reached what looked to be the end of his journey. He quickly lit his one remaining lantern by the wavering light and, setting the oil lamp aside, raised the lantern to gaze around. The clay at his feet was solid, no ravines waiting anywhere to swallow him up. And to his right, a rickety-looking old ladder, its rungs laden with moss, leaned against one of the cave walls. He wiped the rungs, one by one, with his handkerchief and seeing it had not the least effect, stepped gingerly up the thing, leaving the lantern at its base so that he could use both hands to hold on to the sides of the ladder. On the fifth rung, his nose came even with a wooden board. He pushed at it. It remained steadfastly in place. He tried pulling it, but that proved useless as well. And then, in frustration, he gave it a glancing blow with his fist and it popped outward.

"Simply stuck a bit," he muttered. "By Jove, I expect no one has used it for years and years. Not since the time Meggy told me about when some villain abducted the duchess." In a matter of moments, the wooden board was popped all the way out and the gentleman emerged into the afternoon sunlight. He discovered himself standing beside a small belvedere surrounded by a lush lawn and a hedgerow that towered well over his head.

I have done it, he thought. I have reached the middle of the Blackcastle maze. Now all I must figure out is the correct path through it and into the park. Ah, but first I must go back down, snuff out the lantern and bring it up here where it will be easy enough to find in the dark. Set it on the floor of the belvedere, I will. Right here above the entrance to the cave. Will not waste a moment searching about for it then. And a good thing, too, because I will not have a moment to waste. Not if I intend to be half way to London before they discover Mallory's remains.

* * *

Hannah returned to Blackcastle merely a quarter hour before the dinner bell. In a rush to wash up and change from her riding dress into a more presentable gown, she did not so much as pause to peek into the ballroom. It will most likely be a dreadful mess, she thought, as Martha assisted her into a plainly cut, long-sleeved gown of ruby red velvet. We shall likely be forced to take everything out and begin again. Well, but I think Mama has some bunting put away in the attic. I will convince Will to abandon his idea of a forest glade and settle for a fair-like atmosphere instead. After all, it is not as though it is to be a formal affair. Most of the gentlemen will be forced to appear in riding togs, I should think. Not many of them will have packed evening dress to bring with them to a horse auction.

"Have you seen the ballroom, Martha?" she asked, as she settled before the dressing table and took a brush to her curls.

"No, my lady. That I have not," responded the abigail. "But I did hear his grace bellow any number of times. And I saw the footmen and the grooms and the gardeners dashing in and out and about the entire day. And there was a great deal of laughter."

"Laughter? Truly?"

"Oh, indeed, my lady. Bellows and laughter both. And the puppies got in, you know, and everyone set to chasing them."

"The puppies? Got into the ballroom?"

"Yes, my lady. So said Mr. Gaines when I spoke to him this afternoon. Gave everyone a merry chase, they did. His lordship caught them at last and carried them out to the stables."

"His lordship?"

"Lord Mallory, my lady."

Hannah set aside her brush, studied herself in the glass for a moment, and then stood. "Lord Mallory was here, Martha?"

"Indeed, my lady. Still here, he is. Invited the gentleman to remain for dinner, our duke did." Martha's eyes glowed with good will as she gazed at her mistress. "Our duke likes your Lord Mallory, I should say," she murmured.

It was at that very moment that the dinner bell sounded, echoing through the corridors of Blackcastle and up into Hannah's chambers like some great oriental gong. Hannah glanced once more into the looking glass, arranged one errant curl and stepped out into the hallway. Ian is here? she thought as her slippers whispered along the carpeting. He caught up the puppies and carried them to the stables? How long has he been here? Has he been helping Will to decorate the ballroom, then? Oh, my goodness! William and George and Ian all loose in our ballroom with footmen and grooms and gardeners to do their bidding! Hannah grinned as she descended a short staircase, traversed a corridor to the right and began to descend a second set of steps. "Well, but Annie and Martin are coming tonight to lend me their aid. We shall have the entire evening to repair the damage," she whispered to herself. "Even William and George and Ian together cannot have utterly destroyed the ballroom. Although, I am not taking into account the help that the puppies gave them."

Silverdale had read the message from Gazenby, sent a reply in the care of the groom who had carried the message to him, and was merely stepping around from the Three-Legged Inn to the Fallen Dog when he happened to see, from the corner of his eye, a most familiar form in the stableyard. His feet altered direction at once and carried him quickly in that gentleman's direction. "Harry?" he said, coming up behind the fellow and touching his shoulder.

"Sly!"

"I knew it was you," Silverdale said. "There is no man in all of England carries himself quite as elegantly and with as much style as you do. What the deuce brings you to Barren Wycche? When did you arrive? Where are you putting up? If you're counting on engaging a room at the inn, you're out there. Place has been full to overflowing for almost a week. Although, I might be convinced to share my room with you if you promise not to keep me awake the entire night."

"No, no, I have rented a room in a small establishment," Lord Harry replied.

"Have you? You did not just arrive then."

"No. Arrived this morning. Saw the inn was full. Asked about for other lodgings and quite luckily found a room just waiting to be rented. So you see, there's no need to put yourself out on my account, Silverdale. Here to woo the Lady Hannah, are you? Just as you said you planned to do?"

Silverdale shoved his hands into his breeches pockets and stared for a moment at the toes of his boots. "It's why I came, Harry, but I have given up on it. She'll not have me."

"I'm sorry for that. Prefers my brother, eh?"

"Yes, but it's not what you think. Mallory did not set out to woo her away from me."

"No. No. It's like you told me in London, I expect— Martin and his little wife attempting to make a match. They set a trap for Mal and he stepped right into it. She did as well, eh? Your Lady Hannah? Innocents, both of them."

"I expect so. What the devil are you doing here?" Silverdale asked as Lord Harry began to stroll toward the street.

"Why, I've come to surprise Mal."

"He'll be surprised all right," Silverdale observed with the cock of an eyebrow as he fell into step with the younger gentleman. "Considerably surprised. He thought you were still in India, Harry, right up until the moment I mentioned that I had spoken with you in London."

"You mentioned to Mal that you saw me in London?"

Silverdale nodded. "Why? Ought I not to have done so?"

Lord Harry shrugged. "I can't see that it matters a great deal. Simply that it would be more of a surprise when he sees me, did he still believe me to be in India. But then, he cannot possibly expect to meet me here in Barren Wycche, can he? So my presence will still be most unexpected. Knows I've not enough money to go traipsing about the countryside bidding on horses. Probably thinks I never heard of a place called Barren Wycche."

"You've plenty of money," Silverdale replied. "You've your military pay—"

"Pittance that it is," interrupted Lord Harry.

"Yes, well, but added to that, you have the princely sum of four hundred pounds every quarter from Mal. And don't tell me that he has ceased to send it, Harry, because I know Mallory and I know you. I'm not that easily hoodwinked."

"Just so. Mal sends it and I spend it, but it isn't enough. It's never enough. This waistcoat alone cost me fifteen pounds."

Silverdale glanced at the blue silk waistcoat with stars embroidered upon it. "I say, Harry, you've a stain on the thing."

"Lamp oil," Lord Harry responded with studied nonchalance. "A bit of an accident at my rented rooms. I shall give it to Lakerby to clean when I see him."

"That will no doubt make Lakerby's day. Will you join me for dinner at the Fallen Dog?"

"I think not. My kind landlady will be holding dinner for me. I am much later than I expected to be. Out gazing about the countryside, you know. And besides, Sly, I have no wish to meet any acquaintances. Don't want word to reach Mal's ears that I'm here. Planning to be announced on the threshold of the Blackcastle ballroom. I cannot wait to see the look on Mal's face when he hears my name."

"You've received an invitation to the ball?"

"Yes, indeed. All the London gentlemen who have come to Barren Wycche have received one, have they not?"

"Just so," Silverdale murmured. "Just so. Where is it you are staying, Harry? The direction of the house, I mean."

"Do you know, I don't recall at the moment."

"But you do recall your landlady's name, eh?"

"Oh, certainly. Darling. Dearest. Something like that. An elderly widow, she is. Fussy old bird. Won't like to have you come a'calling on me, Sly. Not much for other people's company, she's not."

"And yet, she rented you a room."

"Yes, well, she saw an opportunity to gain some income beyond the ordinary, eh? Bit of an opportunist in her."

"Bit of an opportunist in all of us," Silverdale replied. "Leave you here, then, Harry. Fallen Dog is back around that corner. Promised to dine with Cumberton. He'll be waiting."

Cumberton paused with a tankard of homebrew almost to his lips. "Are you mad?" he asked. "Lord Harry Denham a murderer?"

"I expect I am mad," Silverdale conceded, leaning back in his chair, a brooding expression on his face. "But you did not see him, Cumberton. You did not speak with him. Had bits of red clay clinging to his coat and breeches and boots. Wet red clay. And lamp oil on his vest. And a holly leaf caught in his hatband, and he did not realize any of it. Not at all."

"Well, but you pointed out the stain on his vest and he had a perfectly good explanation for it," Cumberton replied. "And as for the rest, likely he took a tumble from his horse."

"Harry? He's an officer in the cavalry, Cumberton. He does not take tumbles from horses."

"Might have done."

"Never. When did you receive your invitation to the ball at Blackcastle?"

Cumberton's brow creased at the abrupt change in the direction of Silverdale's thoughts. "Yesterday. Why?"

"Mine arrived then as well, and it was addressed to me."

"Well, certainly. Went to a deal of trouble, the squire's ladies did, to obtain the names and titles of all the London gentlemen. Came asking the landlord at the inn to see his book. I was there when they came. Likely as not asked around the village for all the names of the gentlemen residing in private residences as well. Old Wycove is lodging just down the street with a Mrs. Blesser and his invitation was properly addressed as well. He was amazed by it and thoroughly pleased. Wycove delights in such little niceties. Exclaimed over it to me on the way to the squire's."

"Harry said he arrived only this morning," Silverdale murmured, reaching for his ale. "Odd there should be an invitation awaiting him upon his arrival—especially when he merely chanced upon a woman with a room to let."

"Didn't get one, I'll wager," Cumberland said. "Woman told him about the ball, most likely. Entire village knows of it. Making too much of the thing, Silverdale. Your imagination is running away with you. Lord Harry has always been a bit—odd."

* * *

Hannah stood, stunned, on the threshold of the ball-room.

"You need to say something, m'dear," Berinwick whispered behind her as his hands came to rest on her shoulders. "It's the reason I invited Mallory to remain for dinner, you know. Because he has spent the entire day helping the elf and me. Deserved to dine with you tonight after all the thought and effort he put into this."

"She is utterly speechless. I knew she would be," George crowed proudly. "It is the best forest glade ever! Better than a real one!"

"Do you like it, Hannah?" Mallory asked quietly. "There is still time to change it if you do not."

"No," Hannah murmured. "No, do not change a thing. It is—It is—a faeryland."

"Just so," Berinwick acknowledged. "A faeryland. Took us forever to build it—we two trolls and the elf here and all our minions."

Hannah smiled softly at that.

"Step inside," Berinwick urged her, and gave her a gentle push. "And take this troll here to guide you about," he added, seizing George by the collar and pulling him backward as he gave Mallory a hearty shove through the door. "The elf and I have things to discuss. Things that have nothing to do with ballrooms or forest glades."

"What things?" Hannah heard George ask as Berinwick tugged him away down the corridor. "You never said anything about things to discuss. You said—" And then George's voice ceased abruptly.

"You don't suppose he just strangled the boy, do you?" Mallory queried, smiling down at her.

"No," she grinned. "Simply put his hand over George's

mouth, I expect. Oh, Ian, however did the three of you manage? I never thought—I never imagined—"

Hannah stepped farther into the room and twirled slowly about. The ruby red velvet gown she had chosen to wear for dinner whispered about her, swished across the shining floorboards and clung to her as she turned, clung in just the places a young lady's gown ought to cling. The very sight of her so, in the muted candlelight of the two chandeliers they had left alight, caused a mystical winged creature to rise in Mallory's belly and flutter and wiggle its way up into his throat.

He coughed.

"How did you manage, Ian?" Hannah asked, ceasing to twirl and coming to take his hands in her own. "When I departed this morning, I was certain I would return home to utter disaster."

"Well." Mallory coughed again. "Well, it wasn't so very difficult once we convinced your brother to abandon the idea of digging up real trees and slapping them in pots and got him to settle for imaginary trees instead. Made them out of wire and paper and paint, George and Berinwick and I. And they looked so—so—mystical— that Berinwick sent Gaines to fetch every gemstone in the castle to set among their leaves like glittering flowers. I never imagined any house had so many jewels lying about, but Gaines kept bringing them and bringing them and we kept pasting them on. Even the deers' eyes, and the rabbits' and the birds' are bejeweled. And there is the most incredible peacock with its tail spread. It's near the fountain. Let me show you. You will not believe it until you see it." He took her hand and placed it through his arm and led her to a fanciful fountain of wire and paper where water of cerulean blue—that was not water at all, but made of ribbons—seemed to flow down over the fountain's edges and splatter onto a forest floor where the peacock had stopped to drink.

"It's the peacock from my favorite faery tale," Hannah murmured. "The whole of the ballroom is got up from my favorite faery tale." She stared up at him and her eyes blazed so in the muted light that Mallory thought they must be jewels as well. His chest ached with love for her and before he could stop himself, the love rose up in him and spilled from his lips like the water from the fountain.

"*You* are like a faery tale," he said, his arms going around her. "I never believed in love until you came into my life. I never believed that love was anything more than a bit of undigested spinach disturbing a fellow's sleep and causing him to dream things that did not, could not, truly exist. I thought Martin was mad when he raved of his love for Anne. I was certain that any number of my friends had fallen prey to too much drink and too little sense when they became enraptured with this woman or that. But I was wrong. Love does exist. It must, for I find that I love you without doubt, without reservation and I shall until the day I die. Be you faery or elf, pixie or sprite, Hannah Thorne, be aware that from this day forward you are the mistress of my heart and the guardian of my soul."

"Gracious," Hannah whispered, her hands going gently around his neck. "Has Richard been giving you books to read, too?"

"Richard? Books?"

"Never mind," she smiled, drawing him down to her, kissing his cheek. "Never mind. I will explain it to you one day." And then her lips met his and he clasped her more tightly against himself and dreamed how it would be to hold her just so for the remainder of his life.

"Will you marry me, Hannah?" he asked quietly as their lips parted and he imagined that he saw the very essence of his being melting into the starry night of her eyes. "Will you marry me and be my wife and live with me forever in a faeryland of our own making?"

Hannah's heart leaped with joy and the thrill of his words set her to shivering in the circle of his arms. Her nerves tingled at his touch and she licked her lips as she gazed up at him, tasting the sheer elixir of his kiss as it lingered, wishing to taste the full flavor of it again and again. "I gather you asked permission of Will to pay me court today," she said quietly, her dimples flashing into view.

"Indeed. And he said that I might, though his suggestion was that I ask you to marry me first and then go about courting you. I thought it a bizarre suggestion. But it does not seem so very bizarre at the moment. Will you marry me, Hannah? May I at least hope that you will?"

"You may do more than hope that I will, Ian Denham. You may depend upon it. There can be nothing in heaven or on earth will keep me from becoming your bride."

The night had grown chill and Silverdale had gone back up to his chambers to don his greatcoat before riding out to Blackcastle to meet Mal, accidentally, as Gazenby had asked him to do in his note. Though Gazenby and Anne had intended to make the trip to Blackcastle themselves, help with the ballroom and thus escort Mallory back merely as a matter of expediency, a message had come, dismissing them of any obligation to do so. It fell to Silverdale, then, to ride guard beside his cousin. But thoughts of Lord Harry rattled about in the back of Silverdale's brain. "He *did* lie to me about when he arrived in Barren Wycche," Silverdale murmured, setting his hat at a rakish angle on his golden curls. "Either that, or he lied to me about receiving an invitation to the ball. Why would he lie about either one?"

Stuffing his prized French-made pistol into his greatcoat pocket, Silverdale turned on his heel and exited the chambers. He descended the staircase slowly, intent on thoughts of Lord Harry, his uneasiness pricking at him like an itch he was unable to scratch. Silverdale paused at the bottom of the stairs, then saw the innkeeper and stepped up to him. "I say, Mr. McGowen, may I have a word with you?"

"Indeed," McGowen replied with a smile. "How may I serve your lordship?"

"I was merely wondering, Mr. McGowen, if you would perchance know of an establishment in the village belonging to a widow by the name of Darling?"

"Darling? No, no Darlings in Barren Wycche—except his grace's horse when he rides her in," the innkeeper chuckled.

"A Mrs. Dearest, then?"

"Be it a jest?" asked McGowen, a twinkle in his eyes.

"No. A friend of mine is lodging with a widow whose name I cannot quite remember and—"

"Ah! It be Mrs. Dearing you be wanting."

"Yes. That's likely. Could you give me her direction."

"There bean't no such things as numbers on houses in Barren Wycche," the innkeeper replied. "This bean't so fancy a place as London. But it be simple enough to find Mrs. Dearing's residence. Ye go past the stableyard to the end of the street, turn to your right and it be the third house ye come to. A fine house it be, too. Mr. Dearing were—"

"I thank you," Silverdale replied, cutting off McGowen in midsentence, turning away and walking quickly out into the night.

He stopped at the stable and had his horse brought out to him, mounted and rode the short distance to Mrs. Dearing's establishment. There, he remained in the saddle debating whether he ought to go up and knock on the door or not. Perhaps Harry *had* just come to surprise his brother and spend a bit of time with him. It was likely enough. They had not seen each other in years, not since Mal had paid for Harry's commission in the cavalry and Harry had gone off to India. And yet—and yet—

"What the devil," Silverdale muttered. "Nothing wrong in paying a visit to an old friend. Won't disturb Harry and it'll make my mind a good deal easier. Just step in for a moment. Fussy old woman cannot take offense at that and neither can Harry."

Silverdale dismounted, tied his horse to a hitching post, approached the door, lifted the knocker and let it fall.

Fourteen

"I cannot think what happened to him," Gazenby sighed, as the receiving line began to break up and move into the ballroom behind the guests.

"All of the guests have not yet arrived, Martin," Anne observed quietly. "There will be any number of late-comers. Likely he will be among them because he has been unavoidably detained."

"Detained by what?"

"By an attempt to tie the perfect knot in his neckcloth."

"Annie!"

"Well, you know how Lord Silverdale is, Martin. Always such a dandy. Everything about his appearance must be perfect or he will not leave his room."

Gazenby would have protested, except that it was true. Silverdale was a stickler about his appearance. Still, the knot in his neckcloth or the set of his coat across his shoulders would not have detained him last night, and yet, he had not appeared then, either. The groom had delivered the message and returned with word from Silverdale that he would do precisely as Gazenby had suggested. And yet Mallory had arrived back at the squire's alone.

"Do cease scowling, Martin. This is to be a festive occasion," Anne whispered in his ear. "Look. Hannah is positively glowing and Mal is grinning from ear to ear. Even Will is managing a smile for people now and then."

"Yes, well, that's because none of them are aware of it."

"Of what?"

"Nothing. Nothing." What was he to say? That he and Silverdale had sworn an oath to protect Mal from whomever threatened his life? No, he could not say that. He had not confided that particular bit of information in Anne when it had happened and she would be angry with him did he first mention it now. Still, they had sworn, and Silverdale ought to have been awaiting Mal outside Blackcastle last evening and he ought to be here at the ball this very moment to help Gazenby keep an eye out for any threat. It upset Gazenby no end that Silverdale was nowhere to be found.

For some reason, Mallory could not cease grinning like a simpleton. He did make the attempt as the evening progressed. Several times as he stopped to be introduced to this group or that, to join in one discussion or another, to lead this young lady or that into the dancing. He forced his lips into a straight line and narrowed his eyes slightly and once or twice cocked an eyebrow as if in cynical disbelief. But the corners of his lips kept turning back up and his eyes would not remain narrowed and his eyebrow uncocked almost immediately he cocked it.

"If you don't cease grinning, Mallory, people will begin to imagine all sorts of things about you, and I shall be forced to announce your secret to the entire ballroom just to avoid the gossip," Berinwick murmured as he came down the dance with his mother on his arm directly past Mallory.

Mallory intended to reply that he was making the attempt to wipe the foolish grin from his countenance, but Berinwick was already beyond him.

"Do not pay the least attention to Will," Hannah said as the dance brought her to a place beside the thoroughly frustrated marquis. "He is teasing you. You may grin all you like. Tonight Blackcastle is filled with happiness and no one will take special note of yours."

"Are you certain?"

"Yes," Hannah chuckled, taking his hand—which was not required by the dance at all. "I am positive. I have been smiling and laughing from the first and no one has made the least thing of it, not even Mother."

"Well, but she knows, I expect."

"That we are betrothed? How can she know? I did not say a word to her as yet."

"Berinwick will have told her."

"Will? No. He is having far too much fun teasing you about keeping it a secret."

"How long must we keep it a secret?" Mallory queried. "I only ask because I feel like shouting it from the top of the Blackcastle towers."

"Shouting what from the Blackcastle towers, Mal?" Anne asked as the figure of the dance drew Hannah away and placed Anne beside him instead.

"Oh, nothing. Just babbling on," Mallory managed, his gaze following Hannah as she danced on down the line.

Anne smiled, following his gaze with her own. "Hannah is perfectly lovely tonight, is she not?"

"Beautiful," Mallory replied in a tone so filled with admiration and longing that Anne laughed aloud.

"What? What did I say?"

"Nothing. Nothing at all," Anne answered, her eyes aglow. "May I wish you happy?"

"No. Not yet. That is, I mean to say—" and then they were parted by the dance.

It was nearing ten o'clock when Gaines, who had been entering the ballroom to announce latecomers for almost an hour, entered once again, but this time he made his way around the dancers, directly to the place where Hannah stood laughing up at Mallory, her eyes filled with stars.

"I beg your pardon, my lady," the butler said quietly. "He has come. I have asked him to await you in the corridor as you requested."

"Who has come?" Mallory asked.

"A special guest," Hannah replied. "You shall meet him in a moment." She tucked her arm through his. "Lead us back through these merrymakers, Gaines, if you please."

Gaines nodded and did so, making a comfortable path along which they strode until they paused several feet from the first set of ballroom doors.

"You will remain here, Ian," Hannah directed.

"Why?"

"Because this guest has come especially to please you and I wish the two of you to be able to come together in an instant."

Mallory could not think to whom she referred though he cudgeled his brain to do so as she and Gaines walked out into the corridor.

"What's going on, Mal?" queried Gazenby, approaching to stand just behind Mallory's right shoulder.

"I'm not certain, Martin. A special guest Hannah said. Someone come especially to please me."

"Silverdale?"

"Silverdale? I think not. Why would she think Silverdale's arrival would prove exceptionally pleasureable to me?" Mallory ceased to speak and turned quite suddenly to face Gazenby. "Do you mean to say that Sly is not already here, Martin? I had not noticed. Surely, you have merely overlooked him in this crowd."

"No. I have been expecting him with every new arrival, but there is, as yet, no sign of him. I cannot think why he should be so very late, or why he did not appear last evening to accompany you back to the Tofars. He—"

"Accompany me back to the Tofars? Last evening? Sly? What the devil are you talking about, Martin?"

"Lord Harry Denham of Yorkshire," Gaines announced in sober tones from the main doorway just as the music ceased.

Gazenby gasped and Mallory spun back around as that most elegant of young gentlemen appeared from behind the butler with Hannah on his arm, his appearance in the full dress uniform of His Majesty's Nineteenth Light Dragoons causing all the eligible young ladies to sigh and their hearts to beat at least three times faster than they were already.

"What the devil," Mallory muttered. And then, "Harry!" he said quite loudly and in five long strides he was before his younger brother. "Harry, you mongrel, what the devil are you doing here?" Mallory's arms flailed a bit as if he wished to hug the young gentleman, but then, at the last, he did not.

"Surprised, dear brother?" Lord Harry asked, a most beatific smile encompassing his angel's face. "We thought you would be, Lady Hannah and I."

"Hannah? You knew about this? You knew Harry was here in Barren Wycche?"

Hannah grinned impishly. "George and I discovered him in the lane the day we went to purchase another hound for Richard. Lord Harry will not like me to tell tales on him, but he took a tumble from his horse and there he was, limping along the lane ahead of us. What could we do but offer the poor gentleman a ride? And then, to discover that he was your younger brother! Well, we planned to surprise you that very moment in the coach."

"I am that," Mallory replied. "I am surprised. You look splendid, Harry."

"Yes, I know," drawled the young soldier, his green eyes sparkling.

Hannah laughed.

"I should like to get you alone for a moment or two, Mal, if you wouldn't mind. There are things I should like to say to you before I actually join in this wonderful entertainment. You would not mind, Lady Hannah, if Mal and I were to step into another room. Merely for a moment or two."

"Not at all," Hannah replied, releasing Lord Harry's arm. "Gaines, do escort these gentlemen to some place where they may have a comfortable coze, will you not?"

"Indeed, my lady," Gaines replied. "If you will follow me, gentlemen." He led them beyond the ballroom to a small drawing room where lamps had already been lighted and a fire burned on the hearth. "If there is anything you need, gentlemen," he said.

"No, no, nothing," Lord Harry replied at once. "This will do nicely, thank you. What an excellent idea to have a drawing room here. We shall not lose our way returning to the ballroom at least. I have never seen such a place for twists and turns and odd little staircases. Off with you, Gaines. We require nothing more." Lord Harry gave the elderly butler a wave of dismissal quite equal to any a Royal might have given, and Gaines exited the room at once.

"Grown regal on me, have you, Harry?" Mallory asked, looking his brother up and down with a slight frown. "Planning to become the next king? There's someone has already applied for that position, you know."

"So I've heard. Chubby sort of fellow with an eye for the ladies, if I recall. You're developing an eye for the ladies as well, eh, Mal?"

"Me?"

"Indeed. Could not help but notice, old boy. Charming young woman, Lady Hannah. Cares for you, I believe. Cared for Silverdale once, but now she won't have him. Will she have you, do you think?"

322 _Judith A. Lansdowne_

"How do you know she cared for Silverdale? She never told you—"

"No, no, never said a word. Sly told me, of course. Told me in London. Told me all about your plans to visit with Gazenby's in-laws and bid on some horse, too. Snip? Snap? Blast, I cannot recall the name! Told me about Gazenby's little wife and her plans to lure you into marriage, as well."

"What?"

"You didn't know, Mal? Planned the entire thing, she and Gazenby, the auction and all, just to get you here to meet the girl. Certain you would fall in love with her and ask Lady Hannah to marry you. They were certain the chit would have you, too."

Mallory watched as Harry spun down onto a chintz-covered sofa, draping his arm negligently along the back of it, stretching his long legs out before him.

"Sit down, Mal, do. It has been centuries since last we spoke. _Did_ you fall in love with her? Are you going to ask her to marry you? Will she have you, do you think?"

Mallory strolled behind the wing chair that faced his brother and stood with his hands grasping its back. "Yes," he said after a long pause. "I have already asked her to marry me, Harry. And yes, she has agreed to it. I care not if the match was planned from beginning to end. In fact, I expect I shall make a point of it to thank Anne and Martin now that I know they took a hand in our coming together."

"Just so," Lord Harry smiled up at him. "So much for your vow never to take a wife."

"I never vowed never to—"

"You didn't vow it, perhaps, but you said it over and over for years and years. Still, she is a perfectly beguiling little chit. And I expect I knew it was bound to happen. Counted on you, Mal, to hold to your bachelorhood, but a gentleman ages, I have learned, and he begins to yearn for—"

"Why the devil are we talking about this?" Mallory interrupted. "It is none of it your concern, Harry. What are you doing here? Why aren't you in India with the rest of the Nineteenth? They are still there, are they not?"

"Oh, yes. Still there as far as I know," Lord Harry replied yawning and stretching comfortably. And then his hand slid inside his uniform blouse and reappeared holding a pistol almost as small as an inkpot.

"What the devil is that?" Mallory queried, an eyebrow cocking.

"Why it's a tiny popper, Mal. Don't say you have never seen one before. Quite the thing these days. Borrowed this one from Sly, I did."

"From Silverdale?"

"Just so. He didn't wish to give it to me, actually. But in the end, I convinced him. It's no good for dueling, of course. Not dependable across long distances. But quite accurate at close quarters." Harry rose, took two quick steps forward and pointed the business end of the pistol directly at Mallory's heart. "Never misses when a fellow is as close as this."

The night was chill but not dark. Above him a full moon, plump and jolly, shone in a cloudless, star-filled sky. He shivered and swiped at his brow with the sleeve of his coat. I'm freezing and burning at one and the same time, he thought, finding the sensation intriguing. He caught the toe of one boot on the heel of the other and stumbled a bit but kept his feet, catching hold of the doorframe to maintain his balance. He closed his eyes, opened them again slowly. The world was not spinning around him at as great a rate as it had been a moment before, though it still spun. Silverdale took a deep breath and forced his feet to step forward. One step. Two. Three. He reached the hitching post before Mrs. Dearing's house and clung to it with both hands as the ground seemed to swell, then drop, beneath him.

Not dead, he thought, a shaky smile rising to his face. I'm not dead, Harry. Admirable attempt on your part to bring it about, but you failed. Where the devil is everyone? How late can it be? How long did I lie senseless in that root cellar? He squinted his eyes and stared up the street. No one. He peered in the other direction. No one there, either. And Lorna was no longer tied to the damnable hitching post. What the devil had Harry done with her? Returned her to the stable? No, he wouldn't have done that, Silverdale thought. Stablehands would recognize she wasn't Harry's bay. Harry's bay has stockings on three of her legs. Lorna has none. Silverdale held tightly to the hitching post, pursed his lips and whistled. The shrillness of it set off a thundering headache behind his eyes, but it would be worth it if Lorna were free somewhere near, because she would come to the whistle. She always had come to it since she was a filly. Perhaps someone else will come, too, Silverdale thought hopefully. Perhaps even the constable to say it is much too late to be roaming about whistling.

Constable Lewis did not appear, however, nor did any other man, woman or child. Silverdale stood, shakily, his hands gripping the hitching post, and whistled again. He attempted to remember where the constable could be found, but his mind was considerably muddled and he could not recall where that gentleman might be located. What Silverdale could recall was Harry requesting a glimpse of his French pistol the moment he had replied that it was the pistol that made the bump in his coat pocket. What he could recall was how a few words on his part had abruptly sent Harry into a raging diatribe against Mallory, how Harry had stomped about his chambers cursing Mal up and down for everything he had ever done, and how Harry had taken Sly's own pistol and pointed it directly at him.

Mad, Silverdale thought. Completely mad. Always was a bit, but now every dish in his cupboard is broken. Got to warn Mal. At Blackcastle, Gazenby's note said. Unless he has already departed. Dear God, don't let Mal have already departed because Harry will kill him does he come upon him alone in the night. That's certain. Harry will kill him.

Some time had passed. Silverdale would not have known it, except that Lorna, who had not been anywhere about, was quite suddenly standing before him, nudging at his shoulder. He reached out to the mare. She was still saddled and bridled, confirming Silverdale's impression that he had not lain senseless in Mrs. Dearing's root cellar for more than an hour or so. Painfully, his head throbbing and with a wretched ache in his side, he took hold of the mare's reins and mounted to the saddle.

Ride back to the inn, he thought. Send someone there for the constable. Send the constable out to warn Mal, then lie down on m'bed and rid myself of this headache. See what's wrong with m'side, too. Hurts like blazes. It did not occur to Silverdale that he had not, in his struggles to free himself from the root cellar and make his way out of the establishment, seen Mrs. Dearing or heard her voice. He did not notice that the moon had grown fuller since first he had entered Mrs. Dearing's establishment, or that the night sky had altered from one with numerous clouds darting about to one clear of all clouds. Silverdale had not the least idea that he had lain, senseless, in that dark, damp cellar for almost twenty-four hours with Mrs. Dearing crumpled, silent and unseen merely a few feet from him.

* * *

Hannah wandered along the corridor, the sounds of music and dancing and conversation dwindling away behind her. Where can they have gone? she wondered. Certainly, they cannot have gotten lost between the blue drawing room and the ballroom. Not even a blind man could lose his way in such a short distance. Perhaps Ian took his brother to look at some of the artifacts? No. Why would he do such a thing? Did he and Lord Harry wish to view anything, they would ask Will to show it to them. Will is master here. It would be most extraordinary for them to go wandering about Blackcastle without Will as an escort. And yet, they have wandered off somewhere, Hannah thought, for they are not where Gaines left them, nor have they returned to the ballroom. Oh, but William will have a fit does he discover them traipsing about through the collections on their own! He'll invite them to depart Blackcastle on the instant. She smiled a bit then, envisioning her brother, chin high, finger pointed, ordering Mallory and Lord Harry out into the night. Would Ian go? she wondered.

She turned a corner to her right and descended a short flight of stairs. She was quite far from the dancing now and on another level entirely. "Ian?" she called quietly. "Lord Harry?"

"Hannah, no! Run!"

"What?" Hannah spun around at the sound of Mallory's harried voice. Her eyes widened as he seemed to stumble from the muniment room out into the corridor behind her.

"I should not run if I were you, m'dear," Lord Harry said stepping out into the hallway directly behind Mallory. "If you do, you know, I shall be forced to shoot you on the spot."

"Sh-shoot me?" Hannah stammered.

"With my little pistol. The one just now resting between Mal's shoulder blades. If you wish to see it, you must come back here, because I've no intention of re-moving it. Unless, of course, I must do so for the instant it will take to shoot you."

Hannah's gaze met Mallory's and held. In the dim light of the corridor, without one word, he spoke to her and her eyes sparked with comprehension. "I should like to see your pistol, actually, Lord Harry," she said, stepping around Mallory.

"You should?"

"Indeed. You will think it most unladylike of me, but I do have a certain interest in pistols. Gracious, how small it is! I do not believe I have ever seen such a tiny pistol."

"It was made in Paris."

"You have been to Paris?"

"No. But I shall go there one day. First, however, Mal and I must find our way out of this confounded pile of stones."

"There are any number of ways out," Hannah replied.

"Yes, but we cannot seem to *find* any of them," Lord Harry complained. "You know where all of them are, do you not?"

"Indeed."

"Then you will lead the way and we will follow. There is a door that leads into the park—the park with the maze."

"That particular door is a goodly long way from here," Hannah replied. "It is at the very rear of the west wing, your lordship, and at the moment, we are standing in the east wing."

"I care not," Lord Harry replied. "That's the particular door we wish to use, Mal and I, and you will lead us to it."

Hannah nodded. "If that is what you wish, your lord-ship. May I take your arm? There are a number of uncarpeted corridors and staircases to traverse along our way, especially in this ancient part of Blackcastle, and this gown is like to prove absolutely treacherous to me."

"Gawd! Do you think I'm stupid?" Lord Harry exclaimed.

"Harry!" Mallory growled, turning to his brother so that the pistol pointed once again at his heart.

"Well, she must think I'm stupid, Mal. She plans to take my arm and then attempt to pull me away from you."

"She does not. Why would she do such a thing?"

"To keep you from getting killed, of course. You think I am stupid, too, don't you? Well, I am not."

"No one thinks you the least bit dull-witted, Lord Harry," Hannah said quietly. "It is merely that if I lead you deeper into Blackcastle and then trip on the hem of this gown and break my neck, you may not find your way out for days. Besides, what makes you think that I care a fig whether you kill Lord Mallory or not?" Hannah queried, slipping her arm gently through Harry's.

"Of course you care whether I kill him or not," Lord Harry replied, allowing her arm to remain in his. "Mal has asked you to marry him and you agreed."

Hannah smiled. "That certainly is true, but he is not the only eligible gentleman in the world, you know. There are a host of others. And I am not an undesirable young woman—especially when one takes my brother's fortune into consideration. We must go back down this corridor to the last of the staircases," she added. "Turn around, Lord Mallory, and lead on. Slowly, please. I will tell you which way to turn at the top of the stairs."

"You must come at once, your grace," Gaines murmured. "It is Constable Lewis and Mr. McGowen from the Three-Legged Inn. I put them in the blue drawing room."

"I thought Mallory and his brother were reminiscing about old times in the blue drawing room."

"No longer. We have a serious problem, your grace."

Berinwick, making not the least apology to those with whom he had been conversing, turned on his heel and strode across the width of the ballroom and out the door, Gaines following in his wake. "What serious problem?" he asked, as the butler caught up with him in the corridor.

"Lord Mallory's brother, your grace. Apparently, he attempted to murder Lord Silverdale and—"

"What?"

"He attempted to murder Lord Silverdale, your grace. He may have succeeded, from what McGowen says, for Lord Silverdale barely stammered out the tale before he collapsed in McGowen's arms. And Lord Mallory and his brother have gone missing," Gaines added as they turned into the blue drawing room. "Lady Hannah went off almost a quarter of an hour ago to search for them. I said I would go in search of them, your grace, but Lady Hannah insisted that I must look to arranging the supper room and—"

"Well, damnation!" Berinwick scowled at his two visitors. "Lewis, McGowen, what the devil is going on? Spit it out! Gaines, we three will find Hannah and Mallory and his brother. You must go to m'mother and Dempsey and tell them that Silverdale is in dire straits. Dempsey must ride to Silverdale's aid, and Mother must see to keeping our guests occupied and out of our way."

Hannah directed Mallory through dimly-lighted corridors, up some staircases, down others, to what seemed like a bridge of sorts. They crossed it and gained access to the balcony that surrounded the Great Hall. Here Hannah hesitated.

"Which way?" Lord Harry queried as Mallory and he halted.

"Hush," Hannah said.

"Do not be telling me to hush. I am not some child to be ordered about by a woman," Harry protested.

"Do not you hear it?" Hannah whispered, releasing Lord Harry's arm and taking Mallory's instead, turning him around to look at her, saying one thing to him with her eyes as her lips murmured something completely different to his brother. "It is the ghost of Owain Glyndwr. He died here, you know. He is buried beneath the belvedere in Blackcastle's maze. He knows where we are bound. We are bound to desecrate his grave."

"I never said we were bound for the maze," Lord Harry protested.

"But that is the door you seek. The door that leads out to the park and the maze," Hannah said, her hushed voice echoing eerily through the Great Hall. "And he knows it, Lord Harry. I cannot think how, but ghosts know these things."

"Death to the English," Mallory whispered. "I can feel him, Lady Hannah, somewhere near, and I can hear him, too. 'Death to the English,' he is saying." Mallory shivered visibly.

"Balderdash!" exclaimed Harry impatiently. "You are both mad as hatters. What a shame she will marry me and not you, Mal, because the two of you are just perfect for each other! You'll not get away with this rubbish when you live with me at Brambles, Lady Hannah," Harry declared, his pistol wavering between Mallory and Hannah. "I'll not put up with such nonsense."

"It is not nonsense, Harry. You must feel him and you must hear him. Cease waving that pistol about. Be still a moment and listen," Mallory insisted.

"You know I cannot feel anything, or hear anything either," Harry frowned. "It's only you have the gift in our family. You have everything worth having in our family. I might as well have never been born."

"Lord Harry, be still!" Hannah demanded.

And for a moment Harry was.

The drafts from the hall below wafted up and around them, touching them softly. In a far corner of the balcony the wick on one of the oil lamps sputtered and winked. And then from the ceiling came the sound of footsteps and scratching followed by a most abominable sound. Mallory shuddered and Hannah squeaked and pressed herself between the wall and the corner of a long, oak table on which one of her father's collections rested.

"Death to the English," moaned a deep voice that filled the entire hall. "Death. De-a-th. Deeaathth."

Lord Harry inhaled spastically. The pistol in his hand shook. "I f-feel him," he whispered in amazement. "I h-hear him."

"Enough," Hannah said loudly as she took one of her father's stilettos into her hand and hid it in the folds of her skirt. "Enough! Go away, you Welsh fiend! Hurry, Lord Harry," she cried, stepping quickly away from the table and the wall. "Hurry! We cannot remain here any longer or he will take us. Lord Mallory, follow around the balcony to your right. There is a door there and a staircase that leads down. Turn left at the bottom. Hurry!"

"They are bound for the p-park and the—the maze, your grace," Harold Belowes sputtered, out of breath. "Lord Mallory and this Lord Harry fellow both. Lady Hannah is with them and he has a pistol."

"Who has a pistol?"

"This Lord Harry fellow."

"How do you know, Belowes?" Berinwick asked. "Are you certain?"

"Y-yes, your grace. I was in the Great Hall and Lady Hannah and the gentlemen were on the balcony. I heard everything. I pretended to be Owain Glyndwr's ghost like Lady Hannah hinted for me to do and she got them to dash off in fear."

Berinwick cocked an eyebrow at that, but he abandoned his search of the east wing nevertheless and hurried off in the direction of the west wing, shouting over his left shoulder for Belowes to send the constable and anyone else he could find out to the park. "But don't disturb the company, Harold," he added as he disappeared from sight. "Hannah will never forgive me if I allow all this to disrupt the danged ball."

Above the Great Hall, in the kings' chamber, George scrambled into his breeches and boots, took a sword from the wall and with shirttail hanging and the puppies scrambling after him, lunged out into the corridor and toward the servants' staircase. He still got lost in Blackcastle. It was a tremendously huge old place. But he knew the speediest way to the door that led into the park because he had agreed to take the puppies out whenever they required it if the duke would only allow them to remain with him in his room at night. Who would ever have guessed that such a task would provide George the opportunity to rescue Lady Hannah from a gentleman with a pistol? Yes, and who would have guessed that Gulliver would let go with such a spine-chilling howl after George had pounded his boots on the floor above the Great Hall? It had been perfect. Just perfect. Almost as if Gulliver had been listening to Lady Hannah's words filtering up from the Great Hall and understood every one of them. Of course, the moaning and words of the ghost had made George's spine tingle, but then he had guessed it must be one of the footmen, listening just as he had listened, and doing his best to frighten the gentleman with the pistol, too, just as George had done.

"We have got to be very careful," George warned the puppies as they all came together behind the green baize door at the bottom of the staircase. "A sword is not the most excellent weapon against a fellow with a pistol and we cannot allow anyone to be shot, you know. Unless it is the fellow with the pistol himself," he added, patting each of the puppies on the head. "I expect his grace will not put up too much of a fuss if the villain is shot. Are you ready? All right then. Here we go." George took a deep breath, held the sword tightly in one hand and pushed the door open with the other. The lot of them tumbled out into the corridor beside the smallest of the kitchens and directly into Berinwick.

"What the devil is this?" Berinwick exclaimed in a whisper. "Elf, what the deuce?"

"Lady Hannah and Lord Mallory are captured by a gentleman with a pistol," George hissed. "We are going to rescue them."

"As am I," declared Berinwick, seizing George's sword.

"That's mine," George protested.

"But you don't yet know how to use it effectively and I do."

"Do you mean I cannot go?" George queried, ready to protest.

"Not at all. Shouldn't think of depriving you of an adventure, Elf. You take this," he added, placing a silver dueling pistol into the boy's hand. "Cock. Aim. Squeeze the trigger. Try not to shoot anybody but the villain."

"Who is the villain?"

"Fellow in a cavalry uniform with a sword at his side. And don't shoot him unless it proves necessary, Elf. He's Lord Mallory's brother."

"Jupiter," George whispered, hefting the pistol in both hands. "And to think I always wanted a brother."

* * *

Hannah slipped her arm through Lord Harry's once again as they started across the park in the direction of the maze. "Are you certain you wish to go in there, your lordship?" she asked.

"We must," Lord Harry replied.

"We ought not," Mallory warned, coming to a halt and turning to face his brother and the pistol once again. "I can feel Glyndwr's ghost all around us, Harry. He will kill us all do we step inside that place."

"He will not. Ghosts cannot kill anyone."

"Yes, they can," Hannah said quietly. "It was Glyndwr's ghost killed my father."

"Killed your father? A ghost?"

"Just so. Everyone in Barren Wycche knows of it. Mr. Harvey Langton saw it happen, too."

"Then this Mr. Langton is a madman. There are no such things as ghosts. Besides, I have already been in that maze and in the cave, too. And I emerged from both unscathed."

"You were very lucky, I expect," Hannah replied.

"I am rarely lucky. Mal has always been the lucky one in our family. But that's about to change. I will become the Marquis of Kearney and Mallory when Mal's death is discovered, you know, and that alone is like to make me more pleasing to the gods. At least, I will become a marquis if you do not snitch on me and say that it was I who did Mal in. I cannot quite decide whether to trust that you will keep silent or not."

"What must I do to help you decide, my lord?" Hannah queried.

"Well," Lord Harry paused to think. He had already thought it through on the way from the house, but he had always held that it was most prudent to think things through at least twice. "I expect that first you must allow me to shoot Mal without any fuss. No screaming or sobbing or such."

Hannah nodded.

"Because this little pistol shoots seven times, you know. It's a veritable wonder. And if you scream and sob, I expect I shall just be forced to shoot you, too."

"I shouldn't like that," Hannah said softly.

"No, I shouldn't like it either," Lord Harry sighed. "Which is precisely the reason I wish it had not been you who discovered us and led us here. I should not have minded shooting one of your footmen or one of your maids, but I am rather fond of you."

"Are you?"

"Yes, but I was fond of Meggy, too, and yet, that did not keep me from killing her."

"No."

"And I think you must run off with me to Yorkshire directly after the deed is done," he said, "and vow on the Bible to keep forever silent about all that happened. And then, I will marry you and make you a marchioness—because your brother will expect me to marry you, won't he? I mean, if we run off together? It would be the honorable thing to do, after all."

"Just so," Hannah replied. Well hidden still in the folds of her skirt, the Italian stiletto turned slowly over and over in her hand.

"They will all think that Mal blew his brains out because you preferred me to him," Lord Harry explained. "They will believe that he discovered we had run off together and could not bear the humiliation of it. And when we hear of it in Yorkshire, we will be suitably upset and penitent."

"Yes, indeed. We must be upset and penitent," Hannah agreed.

In the moonlight, Mallory's eyes caught hers, then looked to where she twirled the stiletto. Hannah nodded once.

"I think we have come quite far enough, Harry," Mallory said, his voice seeming to boom through the quiet night. "We are now well beyond sight and sound of any accidental wanderer from the ball. I believe I shall go no farther."

"You will go as far as I say," Lord Harry declared.

"No, I think not. If you are going to shoot me, you must do it here."

"That's not my plan! It must look as though you took your own own life inside the maze—so you won't be found at once—so that Lady Hannah and I will have time to escape to Brambles."

"Do you know, Harry? I do not particularly care about your plan. I am loathe to go inside that maze. I can feel the threat of it from here."

"You will care about my plan. I will make you care. I will—I will shoot Lady Hannah if you don't do as I say, Mal!" Lord Harry declared adamantly, turning the pistol on Hannah.

It was only a slight mistake on Harry's part. He knew it the moment he did it and attempted to rectify it immediately by turning the pistol back on his brother. But Mallory's right hand was already around the pistol's barrel, twisting it upward and away. And Mal's left fist was flying toward Harry's stomach. And from the corner of his eye, Harry saw something spark in the moonlight. Something in Lady Hannah's hand. A blade, he thought. She has a blade!

The pistol popped. Popped again. Popped a third time. And then it soared from Lord Harry's hand and the full force of Mallory's blow landed in Lord Harry's stomach. Harry doubled over in pain.

"I should unfold myself quite slowly if I were you," Hannah whispered in his ear, touching the tip of the stiletto delicately to the back of his neck and pricking him gently with its point.

"And if I were you, I wouldn't unfold myself at all," bellowed an angry voice as Berinwick closed on them,

George scurrying at his heels with the dueling pistol held tightly in both hands. "Because the moment you do, I am likely to send you flat to the ground and run you through, you dastard."

"Just so," George shouted. "And then I'll shoot you."

"Arrroooohhhh!!!" added the puppies in chorus, charging in at Lord Harry's knees and leaping upward with ears flapping to lick tormentingly at his face.

"Be ye safe, your grace?" called Harold Belowes at the head of a small army of footmen quickly closing on the little scene. "Be Lady Hannah and Lord Mallory rescued?"

"You brought every footman in the house with you, Will?" Hannah asked, taking the blade from Lord Harry's neck and turning to look at the approaching regiment as Mallory took hold of one of his brother's arms and Berinwick seized the other. "I expected Harold to wish to be in on it, of course, because he was on duty in the Great Hall and caught on immediately to what was happening, but—You brought every footman in Blackcastle out here with you?"

"I told Belowes to bring Constable Lewis and whomever else happened to be about," Berinwick admitted grudgingly. "Well, I didn't know precisely how difficult a situation you and Mallory were in, Hannah. This villain might have had an entire pack of fiends waiting to aid him out here."

"But Will, if all of our footmen are out here, who the devil is helping Gaines to serve our guests supper? By Jupiter, they will think all the Thornes are utter barbarians."

"Never," Mallory said, giving custody of his muttering brother over to Constable Lewis and several of the footmen. "Everyone *knows* that Berinwick is a barbarian. They will blame it on him. You, my dear, will remain in their minds the charming and elegant innocent that you are."

"I beg your pardon?" Berinwick asked cynically. "Hannah, a charming and elegant innocent? My Hannah?"

"No, Berinwick, *my* Hannah. Go away, do, and take George and the hounds and the footmen and everyone else you've invited with you. There is something I wish to say to Hannah privately."

"He is going to kiss her again, I'll wager," George declared.

"Yes, well, we don't want to see that," Berinwick replied. "Disgusting sight, two grown people kissing!"

"Just so," agreed George as one of Berinwick's arms went around his shoulders and they turned to walk away. "Disgusting!"

"Do not send Harry off with the constable yet, eh, Berinwick? I must speak with Harry and you and Constable Lewis," Mallory called after them as he took Hannah tenderly into his arms. "But first I need to kiss you, m'dear," he added softly. "And to thank God that you are courageous, intelligent and the perfectly remarkable young woman that you are. We might be dead this moment, Hannah, had you not kept your wits about you."

They gathered together in the smallest of the Blackcastle parlors once the guests had departed—Berinwick, Mallory, Hannah, Gazenby and Anne, and Veronica, with Lord Harry securely restrained between Constable Lewis and Mr. McGowen.

"Richard has sent word from the inn," Veronica said quietly, her hands clasped tightly together in her lap, her eyes focused intently on Lord Harry. "Lord Silverdale will survive, as will Mrs. Dearing."

"Mrs. Dearing? What the devil happened to Mrs. Dearing?" Berinwick asked.

"Knocked her in the head," Lord Harry muttered. "Interfering old woman. Would not go away. So impressed to have two lordships in her house that she must bring tea. I told her not to do it. I told her to go up to her bed. But would she listen? No. Women! Always find a way to upset a fellow's plans. Screamed she did, to see Silverdale lying all bloody on the floor. So I knocked her in the head to shut her up. Stuffed them both into the root cellar."

"But why harm Silverdale, Harry?" Mallory asked, one hand holding tightly to Hannah's while the other loosened his neckcloth. "You always liked Sly. And yet, you attempted to blame Meg's murder on him and then you—you—"

"Only put his lion there because I could. Found it in the street. Left it in the curtains for the constable to find. Meant to send the blasted gendarme in a direction that had nothing to do with me. But then Sly came to Mrs. Dearing's and he got me to spout off about m'plans. Swore he would defend you to the death, Mal, all for *her* benefit," he grumbled, glaring at Hannah. "Had to do something. Did. Shot Sly with his own popper."

"And Meg?" Hannah queried softly. "How did you come to know Meg? Why did you murder her?"

"Didn't wish to murder her," Harry sighed. "A good girl, Meg. Bought her from a man in London. Man name of Tillet. Don't know how he got her. Snatched her, I should think. I took her off with me to India, I did. Brought her back, too, when I escaped the Nineteenth. Would have kept her. But then Gazenby had to go arranging a stupid match between *you* and Mal, and Meggy would not help me to dispose of you. No, Meg would not. I'm pleased she would not, now," Lord Harry added, his green eyes abruptly meeting Hannah's. "Never understood until I gained your acquaintance. Like you. Very much. But you ought to have let me kill Mal. We could have escaped through the cave beneath the belvedere. I would have taken you to Brambles. You would have been a marchioness once I inherited."

"She *is* going to be a marchioness," Mallory replied, his hand squeezing Hannah's. "*I* am going to marry her, Harry."

"Yes. You have all the luck. Rest of us might as well not exist. Wrote to Gloria, I did. Had her make you a separate set of Martin's directions so you'd get lost on the moor. It was Meg told me about the moor. Thought you'd throw your hands in the air and ride home, I did."

"Gloria? Our sister, Gloria?"

"Of course, our sister, Gloria. What other Gloria do I know to write to? Told her it was a jest. Gloria loves a jest. But you didn't ride home at all. Got yourself rescued and taken straight to where you wished to be. Damnation, if I had as much luck as that, I'd be on my way to Brambles this minute. But no. You must have all the luck, all the money, all the power."

"I hope I have enough power, Harry," Mallory murmured sadly. "I pray I have enough power to save you from the gibbet."

"Never," Berinwick declared.

"He's mad, Berinwick. Can't you see? Can't you hear?"

"He killed a young woman, Mallory, and attempted to kill Silverdale and Mrs. Dearing and you, for gawd's sake! And had everything gone as he planned, he might have ridden off with Hannah, forced her to marry him and one day killed her, too!"

"I know. I realize all that," Mallory murmured, running his fingers through his hair. "But he's my brother. And he's mad. I cannot abandon him to the gibbet. There must be something—"

"There is Bedlam," Berinwick suggested grudgingly. "But I think he would rather be dead than tossed into that hell hole."

"There is Rising Star, Mal," Gazenby offered quietly,

his arm tightening around Anne's shoulders. "You might hire a staff and some keepers to stand watch over him there. You never go there anymore. None of us ever go there. It's little more than a box in the wilderness but there's no one near for him to harm."

"Is it a secure place? A place from which he cannot escape?" Hannah asked softly.

Gazenby and Mallory both nodded.

"Then you shall confine him there, Ian, with a competent staff to look after him. And physicians to see to him. And—"

"Hannah!" Berinwick exclaimed.

"Lord Harry is unsound of mind, Will. Even you cannot deny that. What if he were your brother? Would you see your brother hanged because he was unsound of mind? I know I would not wish to see you hanged because of it, not if I could be certain to keep you safe from the world and the world safe from you."

Berinwick glowered at her, then at Mallory, then at Gazenby and Anne and Veronica. "What the devil," he said at last. "Mallory and Gazenby and I will look to this villain, Lewis. I'll lock him up in the south tower until Mallory is ready to leave, and then pack him off under guard to this Rising Star. You and McGowen will put some story about in Barren Wycche concerning his capture and ultimate death, eh? Sometime soon. Tomorrow after services, perhaps."

"His ultimate death, your grace?" Constable Lewis asked.

"Just so. We will be obliged to kill the scoundrel off, Lewis. We cannot say that he escaped us or Mrs. Dearing will never have another peaceful day in her life. Be waiting the rest of her years for the blasted assassin to come back and put a period to her. We wouldn't want that, eh?"

"No, your grace."

"And we cannot say that we have given him over to his brother's care, because the law won't stand for it, not without a good deal of wrangling and ranting, and even then we cannot be certain he'll not be condemned to the gibbet. No, best to put it about that he came to a fitting end."

"We'll say you caught him attempting to attack Lady Hannah," McGowen offered, his eyes alight with anticipation at the effect such a tale would have on his mates. "Speak of it in whispers in the church yard tomorrow, Lewis and I will. Say that you caught the poltroon attempting to attack Lady Hannah and that you ran him through on the spot. We'll say that you were so aggravated that, even though Lewis and I attempted to stop you, we could not and you cut off the villain's ears to feed them to the dogs on Little Mynd moor and then dumped his body down into the cave beneath the belvedere in the maze."

Fifteen

Mallory did not accompany the Squire and Mrs. Tofar, Anne and Martin to church the following day as he had planned, to see the Reverend Mr. Dempsey presented with the little hound to celebrate the ninth anniversary of his reading-in. He could not. He could not because of the ache in his heart and the constantly increasing size of the lead ball in his stomach. His heartache over Harry pulsed like an open wound, and his fear—his fear was palpable.

How could I have been so presumptuous, so lacking in common sense, he wondered, gazing from the Tofars' parlor window out across the lawn, yet seeing none of it. How dare I say that Hannah would be a marchioness— my marchioness—that I was going to marry her? After my own brother killed her serving girl, planned to kill Hannah, attempted to kill me, how could I be so audacious as to imagine that Hannah would still wish to be my wife?

"But she allowed me to hold her, to kiss her," he whispered, stuffing his hands into his breeches pockets. "After Berinwick and the others departed, after Harry was taken away, she—she—allowed me to—Oh, gawd, but I thought I should die, did I not hold her in my arms that very moment. And yet—I ought not to have done so. Why did she allow me to do so?"

Pity. The word burned through him like scalding oil.

She pitied me and therefore would not deny my immediate need for her, he thought. She is noble and kind, my Hannah. Noble and kind and compassionate in all she does. She would not take the hand of a drowning man and use it to push him farther under the waters. But she said nothing to me. Not a word.

"Well, and what the devil did I expect her to say?" Mallory muttered angrily. "I am sorry, Ian, that your brother is a madman and that you must lock him away for the remainder of his life? I do beg your pardon, Ian, but the thought of spending the rest of my life with you, the brother of a madman—wondering if you might run mad one day yourself, wondering if madness is in the blood, wondering if our children will be mad—is not precisely my idea of an ideal marriage? No, of course she would not say any such thing to me just then. She could not have said it. And yet—and yet—how could she not have helped but think it? How can she not be thinking it even now?"

He turned from the window, from the view of the lawn that he had not truly seen and, head lowered, began to pace the room. He had not been as frightened as this since the day the coal mine had collapsed around him. He had believed that he would die that day. He thought he would die now—die from the grief of what he had suddenly become—the brother of a madman. No longer fit to be a husband or a father, because the taint might well be there. In him. In his blood. A single tear slipped from the corner of Mallory's eye and seared its way down his cheek. He wiped it away, angrily. He had not cried since he was an infant. He would not cry now. Gentlemen did not. They did not.

"But why did he not come to the church?" Hannah asked, sitting across from her brother and George in the coach. "He knew we were going to present the puppy to

Richard. He wished to see us do it. He said as much to me when first we fetched her home."

"But he did not know then that his brother was truly mad and a murderer," Berinwick replied, "and now he does know."

"Yes, but what has that to do with—"

"I expect he's humiliated beyond belief," George said. "I would be."

"Worse than humiliated," Berinwick murmured. "Much worse. I expect that he sees the bright new world he wished to seize crashing down around his ears by now, Hannah."

"What bright new world?"

"You," Berinwick said quietly, fixing her with his one, startlingly expressive eye. "You, Hannah. Marriage. Children. All things I'll wager he once declared that he could well do without, but that he has come to long for now. And now, even the hope of them is forbidden him."

"That's purely stupid," George observed as Hannah's lips parted with sudden understanding. "Why should anything his brother does keep Lord Mallory from marrying Lady Hannah?"

"Would you wish to be the sister-in-law of a madman, Elf?" Berinwick queried.

"I shouldn't wish to be anyone's sister or sister-in-law," George declared. "Of all the things to say! Oh! You mean Lady Hannah—"

"Just so. And who knows but that such madness flows through Mallory's veins as well."

"Take me to the Tofars, Will," Hannah said. "Tell John to take the fork to Widowen Lane. I must speak with Ian at once."

Berinwick nodded and called up to the coachman through the hatch. "Are you certain, Hannah?" he asked when he had finished. "There is no shame in it should you wish to—"

"What would you do, William?" Hannah asked, the very tone of her voice challenging him.

Mallory heard the Squire and Mrs. Tofar, Gazenby and Anne enter the residence and steeled himself to face them, attempting to assume an air of nonchalance, hoping to seem unaffected by all that had happened and to appear interested in the events at St. Milburga's of the Wood. He turned his back to the doorway as he strove to compose himself. Footsteps came to him along the corridor, and voices. He felt someone pause on the parlor threshold behind him. His countenance as stoic as he could make it, Mallory turned to welcome Anne or Martin or whichever member of the family it was and to feign interest in how the Reverend Mr. Dempsey had reacted to the presentation. His lips parted to speak something totally inane, and then his heart hitched upward in his breast and he gasped. "Hannah!"

She said nothing. She crossed the room to him, slipped her arms through his and rested her head against his breast. She listened to the beating of his heart, felt his arms come hesitantly up around her, heard the words he could not say and shivered at the very thought of them.

"Hannah," he said again, on a stertorous breath.

"I do not care that your brother is mad," Hannah said softly. "Will intimated that you would think such a thing, that you likely think I will cry off from our betrothal because of it. I will not cry off, Ian. I will have you to be my husband and the father of my children. I will have you beside me for the remainder of my life. I will not be driven away by the mere threat of what might be, or by anything that the future does bring. I love you, and love is not so simple a thing as people make of it. It is not an irrational emotion, but a knowledge deep in one's heart and mind and soul that whatever one suffers, whatever glories come, whatever happiness or sorrow awaits, it will be shared equally between two people who honor and respect one another and are committed to facing all of life's surprises, good and bad, side by side."

Mallory's arms closed more tightly around her and he leaned down to rest his cheek against the feathery softness of her curls. "You are as brave as always, and loyal," he whispered. "But you must think clearly, Hannah. What if I should run mad someday? Or, heaven forbid, Harry's madness travel through my blood to one or all of our children? You cannot wish to tie yourself to such a life as that will be."

She pulled back then and stared up into his eyes, her own eyes flashing golden stars that could only have come from the heavens. "Balderdash," she said. "I dare to couple my life with yours whatever comes, Ian Michael Denham. Madness! Pshaw! Is the mere threat of madness to hold sway over us? Life is always uncertain. Life is always threatening. But life is intended to be lived. The joy of it is in the living of it. The Thornes know that. We have always known it. We are not mere wisps of glistening dust to be blown from place to place by frivolous, unfeeling winds. We are like the Stiperstones, those great rocks—solid, dependable, determined, and very, very obdurate."

"Yes, you are," Mallory replied, his lips twitching upward into a smile. "Gawd, Hannah, how lucky I am to have discovered you. How much I love you."

"Yes, and she loves you, too, Mallory," Berinwick said from beyond the parlor doorway, "so cease your nonsense and get on with it. Kiss the girl and promise to marry her before the autumn, and promise as well that, no matter how much it costs, you will outbid everyone for the squire's Snoop and take the wretched beast off with you to Yorkshire. If you take Hannah, you must take Snoop as well. And Liddy, too. The cat will wither away without Snoop's company. And if Liddy withers away, I'll slip my little dagger ever so slowly up between your ribs."

"What the devil is he doing here?" Mallory exclaimed.

"And you were worried about Lord Harry," Hannah grinned. "Only think, Ian, when we are married, Will will be your brother-in-law. Our family will have one madman locked away and a second running loose and coming to play with our children."

"Ye gods," Mallory laughed. "I hadn't thought of that—Berinwick coming to play with our children. He'll teach the girls to fence, no doubt. And wear breeches. And think themselves able to walk stride for stride beside any man."

"Just so," Hannah acknowledged. "And I will teach them the same. Will it be so devastating, Ian, to have daughters quite as educated and adventurous and capable as your sons?"

"Not devastating," Mallory replied as his lips touched hers, softly, tenderly, a mere whisper of breath passing between them. "It will be perfect. Just perfect."

Historical Romance from
Jo Ann Ferguson